CONTENTS

Timeline of the Endless Frontier	V
Copyrights	VI
Acknowledgements	VII
I	1
II	17
III	25
IV	39
V	53
VI	68
VII	79
VIII	94
IX	106
X	126
XI	143
XII	154
XIII	170
XIV	183
XV	195

XVI 213

XVII 238

XVIII 249

XIX 268

XX 284

XXI 297

XXII 310

XXIII 335

XXIV 355

Endless Frontier Book 2 Preview 359

Author's Note 373

About the author 377

ENDLESS FRONTIER

BOOK 1

THE HUNTER AND THE KNIGHT

Brett Lurie

TIMELINE OF THE ENDLESS FRONTIER

ALL TITLES AVAILABLE NOW!

04/19, 3766 *Sky Guard*

05/15, 3788 *The Rider in Black*

14/14, 3790 *The Case of the Gill Ripper*

07/22, 3799 *The Cold Brook Job*

09/17, 3799 *Of Duels and Debts*

11/01, 3800 *The Hunter and the Knight*

12/27, 3802 *Blood and Soul*

Cover Art by Sutthiwat Dechakamphu

Cover Layout by Mushfiq A.K.

Interior Illustrations by Violet Bast

Edited by Tammy Salyer - Inspired Ink Editing

1st edition 2024

ISBN: 979-8-9897742-0-3 (Hardcover)

ISBN: 979-8-9897742-2-7 (Paperback)

ISBN: 979-8-9897742-1-0 (e-Book)

ACKNOWLEDGEMENTS

For Rhyan, who never once refused to listen when I had ideas to bounce off him. For Kai, who grew up alongside the maturation of this work. For Violet, my nymph of the woods. For mom and dad, who believed in me even when I did not. For Eric and Elora for offering the thorough, heartfelt and honest feedback that the manuscript needed in its early stages. For Tammy, for strengthening my ideas and giving me the courage to publish this work myself. And for readers who have decided to go on this adventure with me. This world and this tale are for you.

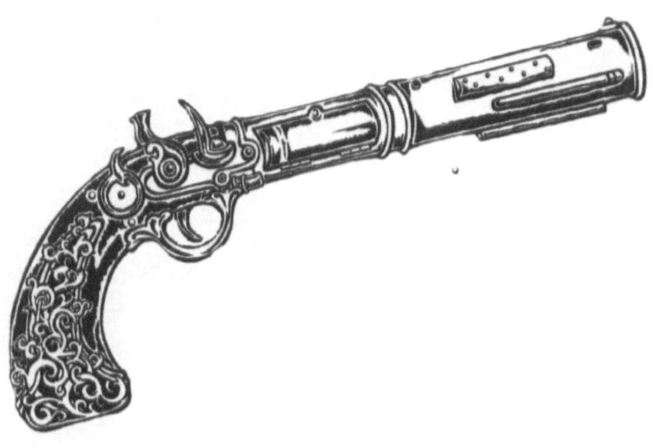

INTERIOR ILLUSTRATIONS BY VIOLET BAST

DIVINITY
CRESCENT HEATH
FROZEN FALLS
KARREDILE SOUND
GRAND SUMMIT
HAELOVAN FOREST
ANGELWOOD
GUARDIAN'S GLACIER
THE RYT
GREY VALLEY
WILLOW WIND
WHITE STONE
BLACK ST
THE SALT RAPIDS
SEA HAVEN
PINE FALL
CARMINE
THE PILLAR
THE IMPER
ARC
HAVEN WHISPER
EDGE CLIFF
DEADSET RI
THE GORGE M
MOSSWOOD PORT
BLACK LAKE
MOSSLAND SUMMITS
OX WELL
MI
STORMGATE
VAND
PRAIRIELAND
BLOOD BOULDER BASIN
RIDGES
THE ELDRITCH FOREST
THE TEMPLE OF JELLINOK
THE BLACK SAND HILLS
COPPER DESERT PASS
INDIGO COVE
PLATINUM
BARREN ROCK
MIRAGE CANYON PASS
MIDWAY L
OLD SKULL VALLEY
RIVER POINT
DUNELAND
SOUTHERN F
BENDING GROV
SHELLBORN
DEAD MOON
TO ROGUE HAVEN
COVE OF THE SOUTHERN SERPENT

WYRM ISLE
DISCIPLE'S RAPTURE
EN SONG ISLE
WATCHER'S SHORE
LIOS MMIT
Mount Morvius
RAVEN FORT
SANCTUARY
THE HOLY HARBOR
S OF ICATION
SILVERKEEP
LAKE SHAL
ANDRO COAST
THE HIGH IMPERIUM
H VALLEY
EEL'S MOUTH
HOLLOW MESA
COLD BROOK
EN CREEK
ONYX CANYON
GATE HARBOR
ADBANK
DRAELEKAR
L FLATS
VAELIZ ESTATE
CACTUSTOWN
ULTURE
THE VALLEY OF TOMBS
OM MESA

I

The Hunter and the Knight

The hunter dug her boots into her stirrups. She unleashed a firm kick into the midsection of her mount. Circuits hummed beneath the beast's scales with its acceleration, its claws leaving a fading trail of amber dust behind its gallop. On the wide brim of the hunter's hat rested an optical tracking system. With a touch of the finger, the device lowered over her right eye. A smirk slid up the side of her face as the tracking display confirmed that she was closing in on her target. Her name was Kasta Krane. And this hunter would have her prey.

"Hold!"

The sound of her companion's voice disrupted Kasta's focus. The noble knight's words were almost indecipherable, muffled by his helmet. But he was also speaking from afar, much farther behind than she had believed he was following. "Don't fall behind, Dresco. I ain't waiting for you," she shouted with a shake of her head.

"Charming," he replied. "I shall be left behind in this forsaken wasteland because I do not know how to convince this overgrown lizard to obey my commands."

Kasta turned to Sir Dresco Norte and let out a grating chuckle. "It's because you're trying to get him to *obey* you, Norte. He'll ride with you, not for you."

Kasta turned forward and grabbed a tight hold of her reins. She leaned low, placing her head between one of her mount's indented ears and its curved black horn. "And maybe you can go just a bit faster for me, girl?"

The draconic beast cocked her head to the right; the pupil of her ashen eye narrowed to a thin slit. A hiss crept between the beast's lips as she extended her long forked tongue.

"I know, I know. You're moving damn fast already, girl. But if you take it up another notch for me, I'll double your meat portion tonight. How's that sound, Kai?"

The beast's tongue flickered again, but this time, a roar followed.

Kai's emerald scales tightened as she quickened her pace. Her gallop turned aside the desert plains with authority, crushing deep-rooted indigo cacti and casting crimson shrubs to great heights. The cybernetic implants that lay under her skin were functioning at their full capacity. This allowed her to move at a pace that was far from natural for a trugan, or any other known beast. Vertigo came over Kasta as the world around blurred. However, there was no time to worry about such things.

"Good girl." Kasta gave her mount a pat on the head.

Dresco again yelled from the distance, but he was now too far behind to decipher at all, left in the dust by Kai's sprint. The hunter sighed. She tapped the transmission icon of her optical display with her index finger. After a few moments, Dresco answered the transmission. "What are you yammering about? I can't hear you way back there," Kasta said, her eyes locked on the tracking display.

Dresco's voice came through the small speaker attached to the device over Kasta's right ear. "He's heading for those hills," he said. "He's going to try to lose us in the hills!"

She examined the path ahead. Dresco was right! The target was diverging toward the Black Sand Hills, several miles away. "Good eyes, Sir Norte. Let's go get him!" she said, pointing toward the summit.

"Wait!" A light crackle accompanied Dresco's voice as it came through the speaker. "What if it's a trap?"

"Oh, it is," she was quick to reply. "But remember that we're the ones chasing him, and there's no way out of the Black Sand Hills that's out of my range. Not that he can get to tonight, anyway." The hunter smiled, her finger hovering over the disconnect toggle of her optical display.

"Now come on, Dresco, let's move!" Kasta disconnected the transmission. Her focus narrowed on the pursuit. Athenis crawled behind the northwestern corner of the Black Sand Hills, where the last rays of its blue light receded from the slopes. The skies darkened from the bright violet of day, shifting to a cool purple. 'Darkness is not going to save you,' Kasta thought. 'Not tonight.'

Kasta tugged on Kai's reins, commanding the beast to slow her pace. "Ease up, girl. Ease up." It was not wise to bring a trugan to a complete stop when riding at near-maximal speed. It created too much stress on both their biological and bionic organs. The circuitry under Kai's skin decelerated; the droning of mechanical gears and electrical currents shifted from a high-pitched howl to a soft hum. Vibrations in the beast's body came to a halt, and before too long, Kai did as well.

Kasta gave Kai a pat on the head and stepped off the saddle. Her knees trembled as her boots sank into the dirt. She shook her head back and forth, her cyan eyes widening. The stars above and the plains around appeared to spin. Nausea struck her stomach. 'Water,' the hunter thought, reaching for her canteen. Kai grunted from behind. Kasta poured a stream of water into the trugan's mouth before allowing herself a drop.

She caught her breath and looked to the darkened hillside. Dusk claimed the sky. Shades of amethyst and sapphire circled the atmosphere in a battle for supremacy. Vibrant stars looked down on the world from the distant reaches of space. Entaega, the large moon, coated the Black Sand Hills with its glowing aura, proving their title was no misnomer.

The hunter took one last deep breath and pulled her rifle from the pannier that lay on top of Kai's back. The barrel squeaked against her leather jacket as she rested the weapon on her shoulder and edged toward the summits in the distance.

"Stay, girl." She cast Kai a glance. "Rest up, I got this for now."

The large reptile yawned and tumbled to the ground with such velocity that the hunter felt the vibration beneath her feet. As her mount panted, Kasta carried on, her black leather boots crunching the dirt and gravel.

She placed her rifle over a flat rock and lay in a prone position. The rifle appeared grey in the darkness, but the moonlight revealed a slight shimmer. Dents and tarnishes lay scattered on the weapon's charcoal-silver body, alongside engravings of a trugan, a treasure chest and a wolf. Kasta heard the healthy flow of the rifle's electrical current as her cheek rested on its stock, the metal like coarse ice on her blue-grey skin. Her index finger slid over the trigger.

Kasta looked through the gold scope, ensuring that the rifle synchronized with her optical targeting system. She kept the weapon pointed at the hills, scanning for signs of life or movement. "Come on, you little cretin," she whispered. She probed the hillside, zooming in closer. "Show yourself."

A graceless gallop approached. The nervous dismay in the voice of the rider revealed that this was no adversary. The galloping stopped about twelve paces from Kasta's vantage point.

"Hey, look who finally made it," she said without turning around.

"Yes, after a battle with this cold-blooded monster." Dresco's voice trembled as he stumbled off his mount, though he managed to land on his feet. "He actually sought to thrust me from his back!"

Kasta let a crooked smirk grow on her face as she adjusted her sights. "Now that's funny."

Dresco's armor clanked with his approaching steps. "I am fine, by the way. Thank you for asking."

"I didn't."

Dresco grunted before whispering a few words to himself at the end of a deep breath. "Any sign of our friend out there?" he asked, leaning on the sheathed sword that rested at his waist.

"No," Kasta answered with a shake of her head. She took her left eye away from the scope and looked to the soaring hills through her tracking system. "He ain't showing up."

"Do you think he got away?" the knight asked.

"Not a chance." Kasta placed her rifle down. She stood. "It means he's hiding somewhere up there." She laid one finger on her targeting system. The device beeped and returned to its skyward-facing position.

"Just as I initially thought, then. A trap. He is going to try to lure us into the hills and pick us off."

Kasta brushed the dirt from her slacks and her dark-grey leather jacket before picking her rifle up. Her eyebrows rose. "That's right," she said. "But we're too smart for that, aren't we?" She laid the rifle over her shoulder and strode toward Kai.

"Let us hope so," Dresco said, stepping toward his own mount. His voice fell faint under the soft, whistling breeze.

After returning the rifle to the pannier on Kai's back, Kasta climbed atop the saddle. "To the hills, girl, let's go."

The hunter and the knight rode for the Black Sand Hills; they were not far off. 'No need to force the trugan to move too fast,' Kasta thought. 'They've ridden hard enough already.' As they approached the summit, Vharris, the smaller companion moon of Entaega, emerged overhead and illuminated the hillside in streams of white and silver. Kasta slowed down as they reached the base of the Black Sand Hills. She noted the tracks in the sand. "He moved up the summit on foot. So will we."

"I am troubled by this situation, Miss Krane," Dresco said, not far behind. "He has an advantageous position, strategically speaking."

Kasta choked up on the reins, slowing Kai to a walking pace. "First of all, call me Kasta. Second, you worry too much." She pulled the reins harder. "Whoa, girl, you can stop us here."

Kai responded to her rider and came to a full stop. Kasta stepped off her saddle. "Third, look to the sky. We got a hunter's moon. We can't lose, my good knight."

"A hunter's moon?" Dresco's loud, metallic steps approached. "What might that be?"

Kasta smiled and pointed toward the binary moons above. Each celestial body looked down on them with glowing wonder. "The ancient river clans used to only hunt on land when both moons were full; brightest nights you'll ever see." Kasta crossed her arms and pivoted toward the moons, Dresco in her peripherals. "Hence, the hunter's moon." She turned to the hills and reached for her left hip, pulling her long-barreled pistol from its holster.

Dresco stood near, his eyes aimed skyward. "Yes, but since the moons so intensely illuminate the world, does that not mean he could see us as—?"

"And fourth," the hunter interrupted as she opened her pistol's chamber. The electrical current was stable. The charge crystal was secure.

"I'm Kasta Krane, best treasure hunter in Vanda. Hell, best to have ever walked the lands of Eramaa. And this time, my armor-clad friend, our treasure is a bounty." Kasta sealed the chamber and gave the weapon a twirl before sliding it back into her holster. "Let's go get this guy," she said, turning toward the slopes of the Black Sand Hills.

"I only hope that I am not here to witness the hunter become the hunted," Dresco uttered, loud enough for Kasta to hear. But a smile crawled up one side of her face when the sound of his clanking armor trailed behind.

"We'd have a better chance if you didn't ring a bell for our target with every step you take."

"Why would I ring a bell?" Dresco asked hesitantly.

Kasta stopped in her tracks and rolled her eyes. "Your footsteps, genius. You sound like a sledgehammer that grew legs."

Dresco grunted as he continued to walk on. "Oh please, I am capable of silencing my movements, Miss Krane. And I shall do so when we approach the enemy."

"It's Kasta," she corrected him, moving forward as well. "And I don't see any way that you'll be able to shut that tin bucket up. Not while you're walking on rock."

Dresco tried to find an appropriate rebuttal but could barely spit out the beginnings of a syllable. The knight instead opted to remain silent.

The companions continued to ascend the slopes of the hills. The hill chain's namesake grew truer with every step; amber sands of the desert plains hid beneath blackened grains. Even the rocks changed. Thick stones of obsidian surrounded the path, shimmering in the light of the dual full moons. Indigo cacti, shrubs, tumbleweeds and other plant life became a rare sight, replaced by black sands and black ore.

Anytime they rounded a curve, Kasta would signal for Dresco to halt. She activated her targeting system and lowered it over her eye, glancing around the corner to make sure that the coast was clear. Much to her surprise, Dresco managed to maintain a quiet pace despite his heavy armor, though the scenery stole his attention; his gaze shifted up and down the moonlit, blackened slopes.

'Mind your surroundings,' Kasta was about to say. Instead, her steps stopped, along with her breath. She extended her arm sideways and made a fist. A sharp corner lay ahead. "Hold up," she whispered. "My sensor is picking up a reading from right there!" She pointed around the corner. A red light flashed on her optical system. The device let out a soft tone.

Dresco inched forward. "What kind of reading are you getting? Is it a mine?" he whispered.

"No, don't think so," Kasta said, shaking her head. She studied the calculations appearing on the screen over her right eye. "I'm not picking up anything that powerful. It's probably a trip wire."

Dresco's voice lowered and his tone turned troubled. "Is it explosive? Or is our *friend* just trying to slow us down?"

"Hmm." Kasta peeked around the corner. She zoomed in on the wire. "It doesn't seem to be explosive—at least, not based on my optical system's readings. But I'm going to disable it just in case." The hunter began to step toward the mysterious device.

"Wait!" Dresco attempted to whisper and yell at the same time. "There is no need, Miss Krane. Let's just go around."

Kasta turned back toward Dresco with widened eyes and a slight grin. "You just don't get it, do you? I'm Kasta Krane. Stuff like this might scare chivalrous knights such as you, but I can do it in my sleep with two bottles of whisky in my belly." She took another step toward the device.

In a moment of instinct, Kasta dropped to the ground. A bolt of electrical energy surged over her prone body.

"Get down!" Dresco warned with as much haste as he could. But by the time the words left his lips, the weaponized bolt of lightning had already struck the path and combusted into a roar of thunder.

Kasta rolled back down the slope and around the corner, evading a second electrical blast. Dresco placed a hand on her arm and helped her to her feet. The companions took cover.

"Are you alright?" he asked as he leaned toward her, looking for injuries. "You did not get hit, did you?"

Kasta drew heavy breaths with a wide smile on her face. She shook off Dresco's touch, resting her hands on her knees. "No, I didn't get zapped," she said. "Close though, huh?" As she let out a grating laugh, another bolt of electricity burst across the ground. Dresco flinched at the following echo of thunder. "Take it easy. Just a warning shot," she said.

Dresco nodded. He removed his helmet and wiped the sweat off his brow. "He did not give us much of a warning when he first fired," he said with a sigh.

"True," Kasta said. Her voice went up in pitch. "Did you see where the shot came from?"

Dresco's right hand brushed his long brown hair away from his eyes. "From the cave, up at the top of the ridge."

"Just as I thought," Kasta said, placing her thumb and pointer finger on her chin. "He was watching the wire, waiting for us to check it out. But now the idiot's given his position away." She turned away from Dresco and peeked around the corner, catching a glimpse of the cave in the distance. "Let's go get him."

"How are we going to get over there?" asked Dresco. "That trip wire will—"

The click of Kasta's bronze pistol leaving her holster interrupted his statement. She turned and fired two shots, one at each end of the trip wire. The blasts struck the trap, and it overloaded in a blinding burst of electrical energy.

"What wire?" She twirled her pistol as she turned back toward the knight. Three more shots rained from the slopes above, striking the hillside around the corner.

"That is one less problem, I suppose." Dresco rested his helmet under his arm. "But are we not still under fire from a long-range shock-cannon?"

"Yep, which is why I am going to go around."

"You are going to do what?" His grey eyes reflected the bright light of the moons. "What are you going to do? Climb straight up the slope?" He pointed to the ridge above.

Kasta removed her jacket and tossed it on the ground. "Of course not. That'd take too long." She started unbuttoning her black leather vest as she continued. "He'd run away by the time I got to him."

Dresco looked toward the drop-off beyond the corner. "Oh no, you are not going to try to climb *around* the pathway, are you? Have you seen how steep that is? One misstep and you will assuredly fall to your doom."

"Thanks for the words of encouragement," she said with a sneer. "But I'll be fine. Comes with the job." She leaned over the edge of the path. The blackened hillside declined in a series of steep slopes and long drops, nothing along the way save for the occasional boulder or cactus. "It'll be fun," she added with a smirk and a shrug.

"Fun." Dresco leaned against the hillside, his brow furrowing. "She says it will be fun. That. Is not. Fun."

Kasta loosened the buttons on her grey shirt at the collar and shook her head. "No, no, you're not going that way. With that hunk of metal on, you'd fall to your death in a matter of seconds. The fact that you're gigantic by nature only brings your odds of survival even closer to zero." She looked his tall frame up and down. "You're going to run right up the pathway and take our friend head-on."

Dresco's eyes grew heavy as storm clouds. "Oh, that sounds exponentially less hazardous. Thank you, Miss Krane. I've always wanted to play the role of the cannon fodder."

"Well, if you would be willing to use a shock-cannon just this one time, you'd probably be fine."

"I will do no such thing." He brushed aside her suggestion with a brazen strike of his hand. "I will not sacrifice my honor so that—"

"I know. Please stop. I know," Kasta interrupted with a cringe and shake of her head. "Which is why you're going to take off that ridiculous suit of armor and use your Imperial skin to our advantage. Camouflage and sneak up on our friend with the sniper rifle up there."

Dresco perked up, and a slight grin found its way onto his face. "An excellent idea, Miss Krane. But removal of my armor shall not be necessary." As the knight spoke, the circuitry within his armor vibrated with an electric hiss. The lustrous chrome suit began to shift to the same black as the hillside and adopted hints of the underlaying amber shades.

"Your armor matches the pigmentation of your skin?" Kasta nodded, pursing her purple lips. "Impressive."

Dresco placed his helmet on his head. He flashed a smug grin before the visor had a chance to hide it. The silver helm shifted to a glossy black, ever-present in their surroundings.

A dusk wolf unleashed a breathless howl in the distance, though Kasta remained focused. "Alright, let's do this. You get the drop on our friend in his cave. Keep him busy for a few minutes, and I'll come in there and back you up."

"What if he runs higher off, into the hills?" Dresco asked.

"Oh, I'm counting on it," Kasta said as she stepped off the path and set foot on the ledge.

There was enough room for the hunter to walk, though she had to mind her balance. The moonlit horizon distracted Kasta from the danger of her task. She surveyed the wide plains of Vanda, an open offer of prosperity, freedom and risk.

The notion of scenic observation ended when she rounded the corner. The rock ledge narrowed; it was just wide enough to balance on with only the balls of her feet. She took a deep breath. A strong gust of wind came over the hillside, pushing her long black hair over her shoulder as it whispered 'turn back' in the ancient language of the natural world. 'I can do this,' she thought. "I can do this," she repeated, this time aloud.

She hugged the rock wall as she sidestepped across the ledge. It stretched to level ground on the opposite side, met by a rising slope. The end looked miles away. 'It's not as far as it looks. Just don't look down,' she reminded herself. The glossy black stones may have been unique and beautiful, but they did not feel durable. She was close—only a few steps from stable ground.

A stone loosened beneath her feet, crumbling away. A jolt raced up Kasta's spine. "Not good!" she shouted. The ledge split on both sides as the stones lost their foundation. She jumped across the gap toward the slope on the opposite side. With an extension of her hand, she managed to grip the ledge, though her body slammed into the hillside.

The hunter pulled herself over the cliff and rose to her feet. She brushed off her vest and placed some pressure on her rib cage to check for bone damage. She was not sure if there was any, though she did feel a sharp, tender pain. It would have to be dealt with later. She drew her pistol and hiked up the summit pass. 'This bounty better be worth it,' she thought.

Kasta had to crawl on her hands and knees to ascend the steep incline, though it was preferable to shimmying on along the ledge of the cliff.

The cave lay around an upcoming bend. Atop the slope, a sudden burst of unnatural thunder ended the summit's silence. The target had fired his weapon again. 'Oh, Dresco you better not be dead,' Kasta thought with a grimace. 'Don't you dare screw this up for me.'

She ran up the slopes, stumbling as she battled the hill. Moments later, Kasta heard a horrified scream; it was too high in pitch to have come from Dresco. As she rounded the corner and caught a view of the cave entrance, she heard the hiss of electro-blades igniting. The clashing weapons left a glow of white and blue in the shadows.

The two men emerged from the cave. Dresco released an onslaught of strikes with his massive sword. His opponent backed away, blocking the knight's attacks.

Kasta thought about intervening but opted to hide behind a large boulder and watch the conflict unfold. Her target's eyes widened as he shrank back from the knight. Dresco's physique was imposing enough, but his thick plated armor made him appear not only daunting but ethereal—a wrathful angel. The target's lightweight electro-blade was no match for the colossal longsword of Dresco Norte. The knight pulled his sword high above his head, both hands wrapped around the black grip.

He swung the blade with the ferocity of an executioner, but Kasta knew he was holding back. The target closed his eyes and raised his small electro-blade over his head, attempting to stay Dresco's strike. The small blade shattered. Its electric current remained outlined around the point of impact before it vanished. Dresco's opponent stumbled to the ground. A gasp escaped from his lungs. Standing over his defeated foe, the knight relaxed his grip on the hilt of the electro-blade.

"Wow," Kasta said to herself.

The target hesitated for a moment before bringing himself to his feet. He raced away from the cave in the direction of Kasta, who still hid behind the rock. Dresco made little effort to stop the assailant's escape attempt. Kasta lowered her left hand to her hip and drew her shock-cannon. When the target ran by, she stuck a leg out from behind the boulder and sent him to the ground. She kept her pistol pointed on the man as he lay in the dirt, his lavish white tunic sullied to an olive-green. His hat fell from his head; the black sand submersed the brim beneath it.

"Well, well," Kasta boasted with a grin. "If it isn't Quintis Saveer. Long time."

Quintis turned over, backing away on all fours. "Krane, come on. You're a good businesswoman, let's make a deal!" he said with a nervous cackle.

"Already made a deal, Saveer." The hunter's cyan eyes sparkled as she kept aim on her prey. "And you are the concession."

"No, no, no!" Saveer cried, covering his face in panic.

Kasta fired a single shot from her shock-cannon. The bolt of weaponized lightning struck Saveer in the throat. Electrical streams traveled from head to toe. His body convulsed and squirmed before his nerves stilled.

Kasta gave her pistol a single twirl before she placed it back in its holster. She slouched and crossed her arms. "Concessions don't get to negotiate."

Dresco dashed from the cave entrance, his armor slapping against the rocks with each step. He came to a halt and stood next to Kasta. "By

Athenis' starlight, you did not kill him, did you?" he asked, looking at Saveer's motionless body.

Kasta laughed and shifted to face Dresco. "Of course I didn't kill him. I set my cannon to incapacitation."

"Oh, thank the Guardians," the knight said with a sigh of relief.

Kasta gave Dresco a soft slap on the forearm. "He ain't worth nothin' dead."

II

Belief

Later in the night, Dresco and Kasta set up camp. The Black Sand Hills, which they had climbed so high, looked down on the companions, casting shadows in the moonlight. Dresco sat over the fire, armor removed except for his chainmail. Kasta placed blankets at each end of the campfire and a large pan over the flame. Sapphire shades of the night sky overpowered the bursting tones of amethyst, creating a mirage of a royal city flooded by the ocean. Despite the drowning purple above, there was no sign of rain. 'No need to put up any overhead shelter,' Kasta thought.

She picked up the pan and brought it to the two trugan standing at the camp's perimeter. Their forked tongues dripped with saliva at the sight and smell of sizzling meat. Kasta dropped a generous portion of rare oxen meat in front of Kai, with a small serving of beans on the side. She reversed the proportions of meat and beans for Dresco's trugan, though he did not seem to notice. Both beasts stabbed their dagger-sharp fangs into their meals with a series of victorious snarls and growls.

"Is that how you get the beast to heed your commands?" Dresco asked, taking a sip from his metal canteen. "You spoil it rotten?"

Kasta thrust the spatula in Dresco's direction. "No, she and I have a respect for one another." She turned toward Kai and ran the back of her hand down the beast's snout. "Don't we, girl?"

Kai grunted as she tore a piece of fat from her slab of meat.

With a smile, Kasta looked toward Dresco's trugan. He was not as large as Kai, but what he lacked in stature, he recouped in beauty. His cobalt-blue scaled skin bore three turquoise stripes on each side; it would have been the envy of any hide collector. "And don't you worry, Crevallus, you'll learn to get along with your rider over there."

"Learn to get along with me?" Dresco stretched his legs and sank backward against a rolled-up blanket. "That is just fantastic. I have to *learn* to get along with my steed." The knight rested his hands behind his head. "I like loyalty in my beasts. The titan wolves, the snow tigers, they are *loyal* creatures. You can ride them without having to break them in with friendly chats and cute nicknames."

Kasta returned to the center of the encampment and placed the titanium pan over the fire. She poured a new batch of beans and meat atop the sizzling skillet. "And they're also dumb as dirt."

Dresco shook his head as a grin unfurled on his face, his white teeth gleaming in the flame. "Oh, not Maigavara. She is brilliant. I have climbed my country's highest summits and crossed our widest valleys. I can tell you for certain that she is the most beautiful creature that the Imperium has ever conceived. Have I ever told you of her before?"

Kasta rolled her eyes and let out a groan. She stirred the meat and beans as they crackled over the hot flame. "Yeah, a few times." Her eyebrows arched. "But would you trust her with your life?"

Dresco sighed, reflecting on the question. "I should not have to," he answered with a stiff glare.

Kasta turned toward Kai with a slight smile. "Well I trust Kaiar with mine." She dipped the spatula into the stew. With a nibble, she pondered the meal. "Not bad," she said with a shrug. She poured a portion of the pan's greasy, sloshing contents into a bowl and handed the steaming dish to Dresco along with a small wooden spoon.

Dresco blew cold breath on the meat-and-bean stew. Kasta filled up a bowl for herself.

"Looks like our friend is waking up," Dresco said, looking toward Quintis Saveer. He sat wilted at the back of the campsite, restrained by an electromagnetic chain. For further security, Kasta had bolted the chain to the ground. He squirmed, and his upper lip began to twitch.

"Yeah, figured he wouldn't be out much longer." Kasta dipped her spoon into the stew and took a large bite. She looked at Dresco, leaning back as she gnawed. "You know, for a minute there, I thought you killed him when I heard him screaming like he was."

Dresco's hair changed to a lighter shade of brown. Kasta was not sure whether it was the reflection of the flame or if his hair had changed color with his mood. "There was no reason to kill him," Dresco said with a solemn expression. "But I actually thought *you* had killed him when you discharged your weapon."

Kasta shook her head and looked down at her bowl. "Nope."

"She doesn't kill anyone," a croaking voice said from behind. Saveer had awoken. "The Merciful Hunter, that's what they call her." The smile spreading across the lower part of Saveer's face rested in contradiction with his glazed-over eyes. He struggled to keep them open.

"Look who's awake," Kasta said, one arm over her knee. She let out a subtle laugh, observing Saveer's weakened condition.

"I have heard that title attributed to you before," Dresco said. "There is more to your line of work than meets the eye. It's not just the money, is it?"

Kasta turned toward Dresco and tossed her empty bowl to the ground. She reached behind for an unmarked bottle of whisky. The cork plopped out and fell into the sand. "You ever hear of a target being worth more dead than alive?"

"I suppose not," the knight answered with a long blink. "But you really do not ever kill an assailant? That is quite a burden to bear considering the danger of your occupation. There *must* be more to that than money."

Kasta halted a response with a raised finger. With her other hand, she introduced the whisky to her lips, tongue and throat. "Of course, there is." She spoke at a soft murmur to avoid burning her vocal cords with her own breath. "Where's the challenge in killing a target? I'd be bored into early retirement." With a gravelly laugh, she brought the bottle back to her mouth.

"Well, regardless of your reasoning, I suppose that is an admirable code," Dresco said, looking at the stars above, then to the sterling light of the full moons opposing one another over the plains.

"Excuse me," Saveer said, squirming in his chains. "Any chance there's something in your code that allows your captive some of that stew?"

"No, there is not," Kasta replied, one leg shifting atop the other. She leaned back onto her supply bag. "They'll have food for you in jail." Her attention returned to the tingling numbness of her whisky.

Dresco shook his head. He stood and slogged across the campsite. The knight knelt and placed a spoonful of oxen stew in front of the captive's face. Saveer sat up, taking a bite of meat and beans.

Kasta turned, resting her weight on her arm. "Whoa, whoa, what are you doing?" she asked in a sharp tone.

Dresco's chainmail rattled as he turned toward the hunter. "He is hungry. I am feeding him."

"He's a job. We don't feed him." She hung the bottle of whisky over her knee. "Our goal is to make money off him, not dump our resources down his throat."

Dresco's face remained blank as he fed another spoonful to Saveer. "I am feeding him from my bowl."

Kasta sank into the supply bag, laying her head back. "Damn straight you are."

Dresco finished feeding Saveer, then sat by the fire and crossed his legs. "We would not have to be as concerned about our supplies if you did not take us off course from our mission to go on this little manhunt of yours."

"I made you fully aware that when you ride with me, you ride by my rules. No questions asked." Kasta grunted as her back straightened.

"I am aware, I remember," Dresco stated, raising both hands. "But we have a task at hand, Miss Krane. A more important—"

"I haven't forgotten about the other job. Quit worrying, Norte," Kasta interrupted. She picked up a handful of twigs that she had placed in a pile and tossed them into the flames. "But I'm a busy woman. I got lots of jobs. If I see something along the way that looks good and doesn't disrupt another job, I take it. If you don't like it, you can ride with someone else."

Dresco sighed. His gaze fell to the dry terrain. "Let's just get back on the road as soon as we turn the culprit over to the authorities."

"Agreed," Kasta said with a nod.

Saveer cleared his throat. "Or..." He spoke with a slight stammer. "You could take me up on renegotiations? I'm prepared to pay you double what the marshal in Barren Rock is offering for my bounty." A nervous cackle slipped between his buck teeth. "Perhaps we can find some honor among thieves?"

Kasta shot up. Her fist clenched as her eyes narrowed on her captive. However, her anger passed like a swift wind. "I am not a thief. I'm a treasure hunter. *You* are a thief, and that's why *you* are going to jail. Nothing to negotiate. So, you may as well just give it a rest."

Dresco chuckled at the exchange. Kasta removed her leather jacket and vest and sat down. Her whisky found its way back to her purple lips.

Saveer stammered, searching for the right words once more. "Then, Madame Treasure Hunter, perhaps I could negotiate a sip of your whisky?"

"Quiet, Saveer!" Kasta demanded, pointing toward him without turning her head. "Or I'll tell the lawmen in Barren Rock that you attempted to murder a bounty hunter and a civilian. That'd be a bit more serious of a charge than bank robbery, wouldn't it?"

"Fine."

"And quit squirming. The more you do, the more those chains will tighten."

"Did I hear you properly?" Dresco intervened. "Did you just refer to me as a civilian?"

'Oh, he did not like that,' Kasta thought. "You are a civilian out here, my good sire," she said with a smirk, unfolding her blanket.

"That is not the case, Miss Krane." The knight pushed his hair behind his ears.

"Kasta." She was quick to correct him once more. "Please, for all that is good, just call me Kasta." She leaned forward and crossed her hands. "And it actually is the case. You ain't a member of the Imperium anymore. Therefore, you ain't a knight. Hate to break it to you, bud, but that is how it works."

"My knighthood is not based around servitude to the Imperium." Dresco's voice grew prideful. The glow of the fire danced on his grey skin. "Even when I was a member of their ranks, they were not the highest power that I served."

"Oh great, here we go." Kasta buried her face in her hand. "You're a grunt in shining armor, Norte. I don't need to hear any delusions of grandeur right now. I just want to sleep. We have a busy day tomorrow." She placed her black hat over her rolling eyes, laying her head back.

Dresco's voice rang with anxious excitement. "The Imperium was once an order which represented the will of the Guardians, but it has fallen from grace. I and my brothers and sisters, whom the Order now refers to as 'fallen knights,' represent the true and noble doctrine that the Guardians originally intended."

"Please stop," Kasta attempted to interject.

However, Dresco continued, "We are Knights of the Order, the *true* Knights of the Order. We vowed to fulfill and protect the Guardians' original intent. We seek to spread their gospels and teach others of their holy message."

Kasta took another swig of whisky before dropping the bottle to the ground. "Can I make it any clearer how much I do not care?"

Peeking under the brim of her hat, she saw Dresco stand up. He gazed into the distance, chest out and head high. "So, you see, Miss Kra—um, Kasta. I am not a civilian, nor is my legitimacy as a knight based on the laws of the High Imperium. I am a divine warrior, sent to carry out the will of the Seven Guardians, the keepers of order and serenity on Eramaa."

Kasta lifted her head, inching her hat upward. "Just one problem with that, my good sire." She slapped a hand on her lap. "Your Guardians aren't real. Seven deities watching over us and protecting the planet? It's all children's stories."

Dresco bit his lip, trying to hold his anger. He failed. "Oh, and I suppose you have found something more rational to believe in? Perhaps you believe in the *absurd* and primitive Draelek mythologies of a Great Serpent which holds the entire world together? Is that a more rational narrative for you?"

Kasta laughed at his angry query. Her hat fell to her lap. "Of course not. But don't you understand that the tales of the Guardians are just as ridiculous?"

Dresco gawked at her for a silent moment. "Then what do you believe in?" He held his chin high.

"Say again?" Kasta glanced upward, shaking the dust from her hat.

Dresco once more asked, "What do you believe in?" He sat down with an arrogant smile etched across his face, still inching wider. "If you are so above the teachings and scripture of the Guardians, if you have it all figured out, then tell me, what does Kasta Krane believe in?"

Kasta needed no more than a couple of seconds to mull it over. "Me."

The arrogant smile that had been overtaking Dresco's face receded in an instant. "I beg your pardon?"

"I believe in me," Kasta asserted. "I have the advantage of actually being real. So, there's that. Oh, and I can answer all my own prayers." The hunter was satisfied to see Dresco's jaw drop before she tilted her hat back over her eyelids. "And I haven't let me down yet," she said with a slight grin as her eyes closed.

III

THE BOON OF LABOR

The light of Athenis crawled over the eastern horizon. Blue daybreak shined on desert plains and warmed the wind. Kasta and Dresco awoke and dismantled the campsite. They extinguished the last embers of the fire, folded the blankets and strapped the cooking supplies to the panniers, which sat on the trugans' backs, over the beast's saddles. Both Saveer and Kasta would ride Kai. Kasta felt sympathy for her mount, as carrying two riders would be a great burden. But she did not trust Dresco to manage more weight. Not with his poor riding skills.

Though they left just after dawn, they would not arrive in Barren Rock until late in the afternoon. It was a long ride through the plains of western Vanda. Violet overtook the atmosphere, unshrouded by the dispersion of thin clouds. Athenis' beams reigned over the desert and danced across the sands. The blue star above scorched the cacti, the dead trees of Vanda and the riders who dared to venture across its plains.

'I hope Dresco has a cooling system in that fancy suit of armor or he's gunna get a stroke,' Kasta thought. 'They don't see heat like this in the Imperial mountains.'

The travelers passed over a cracked surface that had once been a lake. Small tendrils of green and carmine peeked through crevices, reaching for the pale, dead trees, which stood as crooked companions to the cacti. There was little sand in this area. Hardened, splintered soil covered most of the terrain.

Kasta granted Saveer intermittent drops of water, enough to ensure his survival. She did the same for herself. Though her gills craved the sensation of submergence, thirst was an instinct that she had learned to subdue.

"Is this some kind of hellish mirage, or are we truly nearing a realm of *relative* civilization?" Dresco's voice crackled through the communication system.

Kasta tapped a small panel on the optical device, which sat on the right side of her hat. "We're back, Dresco. Back in good old Barren Rock, Vanda."

Athenis grew tired of staring on the travelers. The blue star fell below the horizon, its heat still intense enough to burn, its light still bright enough to blind. The thin clouds did little to distract from its command over the remains of day. Barren Rock itself shone in streams of cerulean-blue as the riders approached its arched gateway.

Contrary to what its name suggested, Barren Rock was quite cultivated. Long green fields lay outside the city. Overhanging and intersecting irrigation pipes covered the crops with a steady spray of mist. Two pearl trees, their petals sprouting a deep maroon, stood on each side of the gateway. Their delicate grey leaves absorbed the blue starlight as diamonds in a clear river.

"I've been meaning to ask. What is the purpose of the gate if there is no wall?" Dresco asked as they approached the archway.

Saveer answered with a strained voice, "They can't afford nothin' like that in this one-trugan town." The captured suspect coughed, losing control of his own cackle.

"Shut up," Kasta ordered, thrusting a finger toward Saveer. He slumped like a chastised pet. Her attention turned to Dresco. "That gate was the first thing they ever built in this town, so it's a landmark of sorts."

The hunter reached into her jacket pocket and pulled out a cigarillo. It dangled from her mouth, unlit. "Also, not every protective barrier takes the form of a wall. Just about everyone in this little town owns a shock-cannon, from the farmers to the store clerks."

Dresco turned toward Kasta. The blue daylight outlined the three ravens engraved on the knight's chestplate. "Well, it seems their wall of militia did not catch our friend here," he said, motioning toward Saveer.

"Nope." Kasta grinned behind the unlit cigarillo. Her eyebrows climbed up her forehead. "We did."

The black metal bars of the arched gateway opened. The smell of burning wood, cooking meats and flowing dust combined to welcome the hunter and the knight as they entered the town. Coarse, thick stone composed much of the architecture. Most of the structures bore a similar beige color, though each varied in style and design. While some were small boxlike rectangles with straight edges, others were taller, exhibiting curved corners and circular rooftops.

Among the first buildings they passed was the Barren Rock Munitions Shop. On display in the window lay a handcrafted semiautomatic carbine. Its golden barrel and pristine brass grip glimmered with the radiance of an unfired weapon.

Next to the munitions shop stood an apartment building that climbed three stories high. The windows were translucent and blurry. A woman opened one and leaned over the edge to smoke her pipe. The front doors of the apartment building opened with a rolling, metallic sound as a young couple stepped out. With smiles on their faces, the man and woman locked arms and strolled down the creaking wooden sidewalk toward the munitions shop. The automatic door closed behind them.

Parallel glass cylinders hovered over each side of the road, supported by the streetlamps. These tubes contained luminous electrical currents, which fed themselves into coiling power supplies atop the buildings. The encapsulated electrical streams circulated through the blue lamps, brightening the streets below.

A group of three riders on truganback approached from the opposite direction. Tall hats and olive-green masks covered their faces. The glowing streetlights shined past the shadows under the brims of their hats, revealing their light-blue-grey skin. The man in the middle tipped his hat to Kasta as she passed the trio of riders by. Kasta veered his way, returning the gesture with a smile and a slight nod.

As the companions rounded the corner, Kasta felt tension coming from her saddle. Chains rattled behind. "Can we not just stop for one drink?" Saveer said with a groan.

Kasta looked across the street. Saveer referred to the saloon on the corner. "We can," she said. Her peripherals caught Saveer's watering mouth and longing eyes. "But we won't."

The music of the saloon traveled across the street. Fiddles presented a discordant melody, somehow both dragging and uplifting. A small section of electric stringed instruments provided a rhythmic tempo akin to a gallop. The percussionist hit amplified pieces of metal and wood with deliberate delicacy. The words of the vocalists were not decipherable, though it was obvious that mind-altering substances affected their performances. The patrons did not disapprove. They sang along, cheering with disoriented enthusiasm.

Dresco spoke sharply. "And besides, we have no time for such things, am I correct, Kasta?"

"Yes, Dresco. You are correct," she said, a shameless irritation in her voice. "As soon as we get this clown to jail, we'll get right back on our little vision quest."

Saveer sighed. The chains dangled at his feet as he deflated.

They rounded the street corner. The saloon music faded into a clattering rumble. The encased streams of electrical energy that powered the town converged at the three-way intersection. Athenis escaped down the western crest of the planet, leaving a green and yellow glow in its wake. The luminosity of the tubes and lamps intensified as the blue star descended and the sky darkened.

Many Vandeni made their way down the wooden sidewalks, heading in the opposite direction. It looked as though most were on their way to the saloon or some banquet. Several pedestrians had donned silken suits and ruffled gowns. Most chose not to show such ostentatiousness but still wore their fanciest hats and shiniest belt buckles.

Kasta and Dresco brought their trugan to a halt in front of a wide one-story building marked "Barren Rock Marshal's Agency." Kasta was first to dismount. Her boots dug into the dirt road. She firmly grasped Quintis Saveer's forearm. "Nice and easy, Saveer," she instructed. "This is the last place you want to try anything foolish."

"Oh, come on," Saveer said, his shoulders sagging. "We both know you ain't gonna kill me. We've been through this."

"That's true," Kasta said, inputting a code on the electromagnetic chain's digital screen. "But you see those two law officials over there?" She aimed her gaze toward two Vandeni sitting under a blue lamp. The man and woman wore blue dress shirts and brown leather vests. Their silver badges shimmered with fresh polish.

Kasta continued, "If they see you try anything, they will shoot. And I can guarantee that *they* won't have their cannons set on incapacitate." Two low-pitched beeps confirmed that the chain had detached from the saddle. "Justice can be an unforgiving lady, Saveer. Better not to do her wrong."

Dresco flung himself from Crevallus' back with another awkward landing and struggled to gain his footing. He removed his helmet and tucked it under his arm. "Why do they all look at me with such bewilderment?" The grey streak in the Imperial's hair spangled in the electric glow that coursed over the town.

"Who, the people?" asked Kasta. She grabbed Saveer's arm and dragged him up the staircase leading to the marshal's office.

"Yes." Dresco tied Crevallus to a post near the trough. "Half of them look at me with suspicion, and the other half with mocking laughter."

Kasta chuckled. "Maybe it's because you're in a full suit of armor. Literally. A full. Suit. Of armor."

Dresco's clanking footsteps followed behind, stomping up the staircase. "Well, in the High Imperium, a knight is greeted with honor and respect. Not with vile banter."

Kasta reached the top of the stairs and turned around with widened eyes and an especially crooked grin fixed to her face. "In case you haven't noticed, there aren't any knights here. They probably think you're going to a costume party."

Saveer laughed with Kasta before she shook his arm, rattling the chain that held his hands together. "What are you laughing about? You're going to jail, remember?"

She hauled Saveer toward the slate-grey metal double doors at the top of the stairs. But her attention careened to a monitor mounted on the wall of the building. The rectangular screen left a blue glow on the faces of the two law officials sitting at the nearby table.

"Wait," Kasta said. "Hold this for me for a second." She grabbed a handful of Saveer's shirt and thrust him toward Dresco, never looking his way. The law officials shared a cigarillo as they played a game of cards.

"Deputies," Kasta said with a nod, sidestepping the back of the woman's chair.

"Krane," the woman said. She tipped her hat and placed her cards facedown on the table. "Looking for your next job already?"

Kasta tapped the icon on the screen marked "Bounties." A new digital page opened on the blue screen. It flashed, giving a high-pitched crackle. "You know how this line of work is. Take 'em when they come. We all gotta eat, right?"

Two rows of faces manifested on the screen, with the word "WANT-ED" centered at the top. The hunter scrolled through different pages of bounties, swiping her index finger to the left on the glass.

The female law official spoke again. "With as much as you work, I'm sure you can eat just fine."

Kasta looked behind with a grin. "I like fine dining."

The female law official laughed, her large stomach trembling with her mirth. The deputy on the other side of the table, however, did not display any amusement. His glare was unwavering, though his face remained concealed by the thick smoke arising from his cigarillo.

Kasta directed her attention back to the screen. She continued to swipe before her hand came to a sudden halt. "There you are," she whispered. She tapped on an icon marked with the words "Breylu Dast and the Moon Shadow Riders." The screen displayed seven faces, each with names and monetary values underneath.

The first picture was of the masked Vandeni man named Breylu Dast, wanted for eighteen thousand platinum. The Draekalagon male pictured to the right of Dast was named Nellik of Grathank. His vertical eye slits and elongated snout were distinguishable, despite the pixelated quality of the image. He was wanted for six thousand five hundred platinum. The other five members of the gang were two thousand platinum each.

Kasta's eyes sparkled in the bright light of the screen. "Up another three thousand," she said to herself, biting her lip. "Been up to no good, haven't you?"

"Miss Krane, please. We must make haste. We've spent enough time on this escapade," Dresco said with Saveer's arms tight in his grasp.

"Oh, shut up." She reached into her jacket pocket and removed her own mobile data system. She synced the small square device with the bounty database. After a short download, the Moon Shadow Riders' wanted poster appeared on the screen in the palm of her hand.

"Okay, I'm ready. Let's go." Kasta put her mobile data system back in her pocket, then walked toward Dresco. She flashed the deputies a glance and a casual wave. Two beeps came in rapid succession before a green light turned on over the doors. They rolled open with a slow, dragging pound.

Kasta and Dresco entered the marshal's office, and the doors closed behind them. The inside of the building was plain but well kept. The walls were not of the same stone as the outer casing of the building. They were brown in color and smoother in texture. A woman in a blue shirt with short brown hair sat toward the back of the room. She scrolled through a large electronic data system embedded into her desk. "Oh, you're back already," she said in a high-pitched voice as Kasta and Dresco approached. "And in good company!" She took her hands off the screen. Her fingers overlapped atop her desk as she leaned forward.

"Yes, ma'am!" Kasta rested her right elbow on the law official's dark wooden desk. "The perp wasn't my most challenging hunt, that's for sure."

The hunter stole a glimpse of Saveer's trembling face. The chains that held him rattled as his fists tightened. She knew how much he wanted to recite the full story of his last stand on the Black Sand Hills. But doing so would further add to his list of offenses.

'Oh, to be caught in the conundrum of pride versus prison,' Kasta thought with joy. "Would you do us a favor and let the marshal know we're here?"

"Oh, why yes, of course," the woman at the desk said. She placed her communication device over her ear and tapped it. "Marshal Bovien. Yes, Kasta Krane is here to see you." The woman paused, looking toward the ligneous, cascading ceiling. "Yes, she has the suspect in custody. Okay. I'm sending her in." The woman tapped her device again. "The marshal will see you now," she said with a smile, exposing her jagged yellowed teeth.

"Much obliged," Kasta said with a tip of her hat as she started down the hallway. Dresco also expressed his gratitude and followed behind with Saveer's arms in his grasp.

The marshal's station was quiet and nigh vacant. A few law officials made their way up and down the halls. One lawman, who was in his elder years, had fallen asleep at his desk with his whisky bottle still in hand. His office door stood wide open as he sat in his slumber. Dresco followed Kasta to the back of the hallway to an unfinished wooden door marked "Marshal Raelyn Bovien."

Kasta twisted the brass doorknob and entered the office. At the back corner of the room stood a sturdy wooden desk, which bore a dark, roseate gloss. In the cushioned chair sat a Vandeni woman with short red hair draping from the sides of her hat. Her smoky beige eyes crawled up from the light of the electronic screen embedded into her desk. "Kasta

Krane," the woman said, standing from her seat. "You're back earlier than I expected."

"Marshal Bovien," Kasta said with a nod. The hunter entered the office and crossed her arms, peering at the marshal; she had smooth skin and a narrow button nose. "Don't you know better by now than to underestimate me?"

Marshal Bovien raised an eyebrow. Her impassive glare otherwise remained. "Apparently not." She stood up straight with her chin elevated. "And I see you even have the suspect in one piece."

"Actually," Saveer said, squirming in Dresco's grip. "They have mistreated me since the point of my arrest, and I believe it is the law's duty to set me free. Or at least to review the situation?"

Kasta tilted her head back in laughter. "Okay, Saveer. Now that was pathetic. Are you even trying anymore?" She snapped her gloved finger and pointed toward Marshal Bovien. "Marshal, would you do me the honor and pleasure of getting this snake out of my sight?"

With a nod and a chuckle, Bovien pressed an icon on her monitor.

A voice came through the small speaker on her desk. "What is it, boss?"

"We have Quintis Saveer in custody." Bovien leaned over the speaker. "Please retrieve him from my office and escort him to his cell."

"Right away," the voice said before a low-pitched beep signaled the end of the conversation.

The marshal looked up. "Did the perp give you any trouble? He was marked 'armed and dangerous.' "

Kasta faced the suspect. She could double the list of charges against Saveer by mere mention of his attack. "No," she said with a sigh. "One of the most boring catches I've ever netted. Honestly, I can't believe you were offering so much for him, Marshal." She turned back to Bovien and leaned over, placing her hands on the edge of the desk. The sound of Saveer mumbling indignant words brought a sparkle to her eyes.

Two law officials entered the marshal's office and began to take custody of Saveer. "Thank you, sir," one of them said to Dresco. "We'll take it from here."

"Don't let 'em take my chains." Kasta reached into her jacket pocket for her still-unlit cigarillo.

The marshal grinned and shook her head. "Switch him to our chains," she said with a wave of the back of her hand.

"Lend me a light?" Kasta asked, her cigarillo clenched between her teeth.

Marshal Bovien pressed an icon on her screen, which raised a silver utility tool from the inside of her desk. The marshal grabbed the tool and pressed one of its circular buttons, igniting a blue flame, which lit the tip of the cigarillo.

The lawmen escorted Saveer out of the office. The suspect was now bound by taxpayer-funded electromagnetic chains. "I could have paid you better, Krane," he hollered as they led him out the door. "I'm a very rich man!"

"No one cares, Saveer," Kasta said through a cloud of smoke, her eyes rolling toward the closing door.

Bovien stepped from behind the desk, her heavy boots pounding against the wooden floor with every stride. "I'm glad you were riding through, Krane," she said, leaning her rear against the desk. "Quintis has hit two general stores and a bank in just the last couple of weeks. None of our local hunters have been able to track him down."

Kasta took a long pull from her cigarillo. "Well, if everyone was as good as me, the world would be a lot safer and I'd be a lot poorer," she said, squinting through the smoke.

Dresco groaned as he shook his head, his eyes falling to the floor.

The marshal chuckled once. She pulled down on her vest. The gold badge pinned to her chest reflected the dim light above. "If it's more work you want, Krane, I got another job for you. Bandits along the Mirage Canyon Pass. They've been giving travelers trouble from time to time." The marshal turned her head, though her beige eyes did not break contact with Kasta's. "I'll give you eight hundred platinum. Per suspect." She flashed the hunter a wink. "And that's an exclusive offer."

Kasta's heart accelerated with beats of bliss. 'Eight hundred per suspect?' she thought. They were only two hundred per on the official bounty board—not worth her time. But eight hundred? There had to be at least five bandits. Maybe more considering all the reported damage that they had done.

With a roguish raise of her eyebrows, Kasta turned toward Dresco, who stood with his arms crossed. His jaw clenched as he swallowed. She smiled and looked back to the marshal. "I think we'll pass on that. We have another contract to fulfill." She heard her companion's chainmail slide against his armor and a quiet exhalation of relief.

"Too bad." Bovien stood straight. "Then I assume that you will be taking your pay now?"

Kasta tapped the back of her cigarillo, raining ash on the office floor. "Three thousand platinum."

"And I trust a direct deposit into your account is okay?" Marshal Bovien tapped an icon on the desk's flat screen.

"Half into my account, the other half in coin for the noble knight back here." Kasta pointed in her companion's general direction.

The marshal looked up at Dresco with a sideways glance. "Okay," she said, her voice sour. "If you are going to take coin, I trust you don't mind a mix of metals? How's two hundred platinum and the rest in electrum?"

The knight paused, his mouth stretching open. "That—that should suffice."

Bovien ordered one of her deputies to bring in Dresco's coin reward. Kasta looked at her mobile data system to see that fifteen hundred platinum was already within her account. The gills on her neck widened with her grin.

"So, who's this other target?" Bovien asked, slumping back in her chair. "High-profile gangster? Corrupt banking solicitor?"

"The question is not who, but rather, what." Kasta's eyes remained fixed on her data system.

"Oh yeah." The marshal's gapped teeth showed with her wide smile. "I always forget that you're also a grave robber."

Kasta's eyes shot up from the small screen. "Treasure hunter."

"Right, right. Of course."

A law official entered the office and handed Dresco a large satchel. The coins in the bag rattled as he placed the strap over his shoulder.

"Well, I guess we'll be on our way then," Kasta said as she tipped her hat. "Been a pleasure, Marshal. I'll buy you a drink next time I'm passing through."

Dresco opened the door to the office and Kasta followed behind.

"Oh, Krane, one more thing." Bovien leaned forward.

Kasta had seen that acute glare on Marshal Bovien's face many times; she wanted to speak to her alone. The hunter pulled her cigarillo from her mouth and looked to Dresco. "Get the trugan ready. I'll be right out." Dresco nodded and proceeded down the hallway. "What is it, Marshal?" she asked.

Bovien's voice fell quiet. "There was a strange character here at the station this morning. He was asking questions about you."

Kasta blew a pair of smoke rings. "Potential employer looking for my services?"

Marshal Bovien shook her head. "I don't think so." There was an atypical sense of unrest in her words. "He was asking about where we last saw you and your hunting tactics." She motioned toward the door. "Now I don't know what you're doing riding with that Imperial, but I *do* know you only like to work alone."

"An employer suggested we work together," Kasta said, an arch of smoke following the motion of her hand. "Temporary partnership."

"I figured as much. Just watch your back, Kasta."

Kasta's face grew coy as a shrug rode up her shoulders. "I always do, Marshal."

IV

THE TEMPLE OF JELLINOK

"So, what is Jellinok anyway?" Dresco asked. They rode across a bridge that stretched over a river. The wood of the overpass was rough and aged to a dim brown; it answered the trugan's heavy steps with a stout resonance, devoid of vibration. "I do not believe that Imperial scholars deemed the region to be worthy of study."

Kasta shook her head. "Well I am *completely* shocked, Sir Dresco, that somehow in the vast libraries of knowledge beheld by you and the *great* scholars of the *High* Imperium, you managed to overlook the history of Jellinok the Resolute."

Dresco's shoulders sagged. Her mockery cut his pride like a rusted blade. "So, he was a, um..." The knight tried to find the words, unable to look past Kasta's derisive glare.

"It's okay, you can say it." A long blink shrouded Kasta's widened eyes. "Don't be afraid."

Dresco's voice fell faint and acute, as though he were asking a question rather than giving an answer. "A person."

"A king," Kasta was swift to specify. "Or at least, as close to a king as the ancient Vandeni ever got. He amassed giant armies, united almost all the houses of Vanda and built grand temples that still stand to this day." She faced forward, both hands on the reins. "But none of the ancient lords thought any of his children were worthy leaders. So, Jellinok's dynasty ended with his death."

"We speak of this legend in the Imperium as well, though its hero is referred to by a different name."

"You mean the wrong name?" Kasta said.

"He was initially an infantryman, yes?" Dresco asked, ignoring her jab. "After several years of devout loyalty, he became a diplomat on behalf of the House of Vellon?"

Kasta's head tilted. "Not as inaccurate of a summary as I would have expected," she said through twisted lips. "Though he did an awful lot of killing for a diplomat."

"He *was* a diplomat." Dresco took a short breath. "However, the important thing is that we get to the temple and obtain the map. We can allow no further delay."

The end of the bridge drew near. "I hate to break it to you, Norte, but there is almost no chance we find that map in there. In fact, it's nearly impossible."

Dresco banged his hand against his armored thigh. "Impossible?" he asked. "The sources that we have collected with the help of Madame Vaeliz—"

"Yes, I know our employer believes the map is there," Kasta interrupted. "That's why she's paying us just to investigate, after all. But that temple has been raided thousands of times. There ain't nothing left worth more than a single platinum. And you'd have to dig pretty deep for that."

"And how do you know this?"

"Because I've been there, Norte. I've raided that whole pile of rubble. There's nothing there no more but writing on the wall."

Dresco remained silent. Kasta turned forward. Though he did not speak, she could sense disapproval seeping from her companion. "Hey,

I hope we find it too." She flicked her reins, directing Kai to accelerate. "We get paid more if we find the damn thing."

Kaiar staggered off the bridge. Circuits within the beast hummed in steady elevation of volume and pitch. Small lights of blue and green embedded in her reptilian skin flashed. The hunter and her steed took off, leaving the bridge behind. The stars and mountains blurred together across the sky.

They traveled northwest from Barren Rock along the tall, steep and rocky Narrow Mountains. Dresco pleaded for a rest, citing Crevallus' struggle in dealing with the harsh terrain.

"Don't blame your trugan for your own weariness," Kasta barked. "Crev will do just fine so long as you stay focused." She turned to the knight as he rounded a corner, trailing behind. "And correct me if I'm wrong, but were you not the one who was panicked about 'making haste' and 'returning to our mission'? So, let us *make haste*."

"Must you always be so cross?" Dresco brought his reins down on Crevallus' back with a hard slap. The beast answered with a soft snarl. "I went with you on your self-fulfilling little escapade to capture that foul man. All I requested was an hour or two of rest. It is not an unreasonable request—"

"Oh wait, wait, what's that?" Kasta held her communication device over her right ear as if she were receiving a signal. "Oh really?" She looked skyward. "Oh my, I'll be sure to let him know. Thank you." She looked to Dresco with a sullen scowl. "That was the Guardians. They told me not to allow you any rest until after the mission." She broke into laughter, holding on to the top of her hat.

"I do not find that humorous," Dresco said, sitting stiffly in his saddle.

"It's not," she said, still fighting off her own laughter. "It's not, I agree. It's serious stuff. Let's go!" Kasta and Kai took off again, sending dust and stone sliding down the mountain. The knight followed behind.

After several hours of traveling around the mountainside, the Temple of Jellinok appeared in the distance. It stood as a tall, lonely structure in the middle of a large valley. Layers of thick stones climbed inward, receding from the base of the structure to the top. A statue of an ophidian hawk standing on a crescent moon lurked on the tip of the pyramid.

Dresco's body froze. His eyes climbed the pyramid's stair-like structure. "It is as if they were steps built for the Guardians themselves. A path from our world to the cosmos."

The temple appeared to grow as they approached, reaching for the stars in the cloudless sapphire skies. Stone pillars slanted upward from one step to the next. Though they were jagged and chafed, they could hold strong for centuries more.

"This temple's design..." Dresco paused. The gallop of the two trugan slowed. "While it is an impressive monument, it is so... artistically banal considering its importance."

"It didn't used to be. It was once ornamented with gold and gems. But like I already told you, everything of value, it's gone."

Dresco groaned. "That is horrible. How could the Vandeni be so disrespectful of their own history?"

Kasta bit her lip. "Business is business," she said with a shrug.

The hunter and the knight dismounted from their saddles. Standing rigid, the ancient temple cast a dark shadow over them. The crescent statue on top of the pyramid rested in the moonlight of Vharris, waning gibbous in the night sky. And the ophidian hawk gargoyle guarded its prize, with no intention of allowing the small moon to shine full again.

Dresco tied Crevallus to a nearby tree. Kasta pulled out a dried piece of meat from her pannier and fed it to Kaiar. She reached for her pistol and began a routine functionality inspection.

"Norte, you watch your step in there," Kasta instructed, looking up the stairs that led to the entrance. "There may be traps that haven't yet been sprung."

Dresco lifted the visor on his helmet to take a drink of water. "I thought you said this structure had been excavated in its entirety."

"It has. The traps have probably all been discovered already, whether by someone clever enough to find them or stupid enough to fall into them." Kasta chuckled. She checked her pistol's sights and twirled the weapon around the tip of her fingers. "But you never know in a place like this. If the ancient Vandeni didn't want you to be somewhere, they made sure to add plenty of security measures." She reholstered her pistol.

Dresco followed up the stairway. The stairs led the companions to the second level of foundation and a doorless entrance to the shadows of the inner temple. Shapes lay carved into the outside of the entryway, outlined by empty etchings that once held gold.

"Watch your step," Kasta said once more.

They set foot through the entrance. Kasta moved her optical system over her eye. She touched a sensor on the device, activating a small light.

"That little headlamp is not exactly going to illuminate our way," the knight said. Moonlight and starlight brushed the entryway. But the hall ahead lay shrouded in blackness.

"Hold on." Kasta sidestepped the wall. She brushed her hand across its surface in a circular motion.

"What are you doing? Have you completely gone mad?"

"Hold on!" She continued to move along the wall. At last, Kasta found a loose piece of stone. She pushed the slab inward. On its own, it rotated.

"There we go." A yellow light blossomed from narrow tubes fixed on each side of the ceiling, casting a faint glow on the hallway.

"Unbelievable." Dresco's hands gripped the hilt of his sword. He looked up to the lucent tubes. "The power is still functional."

Kasta nodded. "Well, kind of. Archeologists and excavators had to repair some of the lines, but it still pulls that geothermal power. Just like in the ancient days."

The two companions came to a crossing at the end of the hallway. "Okay... so left leads down to the lowest sanctum of the temple. That's where all the gold and platinum is." Kasta sighed as her tone fell dismal. "Or where it used to be." She shook her head and crossed her arms. Her gaze fell to the floor. "The right leads to the higher sanctums. Mostly shrines and tributes to Jellinok himself."

Dresco looked down each hallway. "So—which way do we go?"

Kasta's brow arched high, yet her eyelids narrowed. "I don't know."

"What do you mean you don't know?" Dresco turned toward his companion. "Are you not supposed to be some sort of expert on ancient temples?"

She let out a soft chuckle and responded, "Well yes, but you're the one who thinks there's a legendary ancient map here, remember? So, you'll have to tell me where you want to look. And I'll get you there."

Dresco took a long, slow breath and relaxed his stance. "Let us go to the higher sanctums," he said. "I have no need for material trinkets."

"Thank you for reminding me how altruistic you are," Kasta said through her teeth with a tight-lipped smile. "Seriously, I was starting to forget. But I appreciate that you made me aware again." She led him to the right. "I wouldn't want to offend the noble knight I ride with by overlooking his great benevolence." She kept a hand on her pistol—in case Dresco would consider drawing his blade.

They continued down the hallway. Pebbles rattled, and dirt crunched with every step. Kasta's leather boots left a hollow echo. Dresco's armor clanked against the stone. The sounds of the travelers' strides collaborated to create a steady rhythm, as if ancient drums welcomed them to this sacred structure.

The hallway led to another stairwell. Torches accompanied the rising flight, burning in hot blue flame, courtesy of the temple's geothermal power. Though less than half of the torches burned, the way was lit. The stairs climbed high, but the companions traversed them well. Dresco carried on as if his heavy armor were an extra layer of skin.

The stairwell ended, leading to a great hall. The ceiling recessed in a shallow cylindrical shape. Yellow lights opposed one another on each side. One did not need to be an archeologist or treasure hunter to recognize the evidence of excavation. There was no art on the walls. Fissures that once were mounted with precious stones sat dark and empty. The statues rested on the floor as unrepairable piles of rubble, their majestic gems long removed. A glass vase lay broken and discarded in the middle of the walkway. 'Too bad,' Kasta thought. 'That thing actually could have been worth some coin.'

At the end of the hallway stood two large corridors. One led to another staircase, and the other into a rectangular room. Kasta stepped inside the room and stood slouched, crossing her arms. "Well, this is it. This was the chamber of Jellinok. Not much left, as you can see." The floor was scattered with broken glass shards and shattered pottery, the aftermath of a tornado of greed.

Dresco looked up to the ceiling. A stenciled portrait of a man bearing a flag with a triangular crest loomed over the room. "It's really him," he said. "Seravinen himself."

Kasta released a loud fake laugh. The chamber joined her in the form of an echo. "His name is Jellinok. I've already educated you on this."

"That is not his kingly name." Dresco waved his hand, shooing her away. "Not in the eyes of the Guardians."

Kasta's eyes slanted. Her upper lip rose. "Well in real life, Jellinok was his name. So, I'm glad we've settled that." She turned from the knight and stepped toward the center of the room. The treasure hunter analyzed the walls, looking for imprints or signs of undiscovered artifacts. Her optical system showed nothing resembling cartography of any kind. "As you can see, there is no map here."

Dresco dug through a pile of broken acrylic glass. "It has to be here somewhere."

The sanctum held several objects of interest, though nothing of monetary value. "There's only one place left to look," Kasta said. "The third sanctum. The sanctum of the Guardians."

"That must be where the map is. Why did you neglect to inform me that the third sanctum was attributed to the Guardians?"

"Don't get excited, Norte. There ain't nothing up there but religious hieroglyphics. Nothing of value."

Dresco marched toward the exit of the second sanctum. "Not to others, but perhaps to us."

Kasta shrugged. Her eyes rolled to the cracked floor. "We're already here. Might as well try it," she uttered.

They returned to the great hallway and entered the nearby corridor, which led to a stairway. As the stairway spiraled upward, the walls narrowed.

"Stop!" Kasta shouted, halting Dresco with her arm over his breastplate.

"What? What is it?"

"Never, ever walk on a stone that is a distinct color from the others in an ancient structure." She pointed toward the stone in the middle of the stair on which Dresco was about to step. It was an odd mahogany color compared to the dull-yellow stone that made up most of the temple's foundation.

Kasta leaned forward. There was a small hole in the wall above the off-colored step. "This trap has already been sprung," she said, tapping Dresco on the shoulder. "Some unfortunate fool probably got a poison dart in his neck."

"That's horrible." Dresco shuddered and shook his head.

"Well," Kasta said, stepping on the off-colored stair. "If you're too stupid to go up these stairs without using caution, then the ancient Vandeni believed you weren't worthy to walk though their temple."

Dresco followed behind. "A rather harsh punishment, is it not?"

"I don't know. Build your own temple if you don't like it."

The travelers reached the third sanctum. It was a single circular room. Four pillars traveled up the walls. The stone in this sanctum was different. It was orange in color and smoothed down to a glossy finish. Four torches stretched from the pillars, illuminating sections of the room.

Dresco slid the back of his hand down one of the pillars with a delicate caress. "So, this is where Seravinen himself prayed to the Guardians."

Kasta sighed and pressed her palm to her forehead. "Yes, this is where *Jellinok* engaged in prayer."

"Magnificent," Dresco declared, placing his hands on his hips and pivoting in circles.

The hunter and the knight searched the room. Dresco sank to his hands and knees, quarrying through the rubble. Kasta lowered her optical system. She cycled through various visual scan settings. But she was unable to locate any hidden images or peculiar markings. The data scans found no heat traces besides that of her knightly companion and the dim torches. Worse yet, she found no signs of gems or precious metals to compensate for the predictable lack of an ancient map.

She kicked aside some of the rocks that Dresco had rummaged through, then leaned over to pick up a decoration made of a rare green marble. It was a simple cubical shape with no intricate designs. But it was in fair condition considering its age. "I know I said nothing in here was worth more than a platinum, but this one may be worth three!"

Dresco did not notice that she was speaking. An arbitrary stone in the center of the room had stolen his attention. It looked to have fallen from the ceiling, no different from any other piece of debris within the temple, though the knight found it intriguing. He stood over the rock with his hand over his chin. Motionless and silent.

'How helpful,' Kasta thought as she turned away. 'I'm the only one actually looking for this map. This map he has deemed *so* important. And he's staring at a rock. Damn fool.' She tucked the marble piece under her arm and circled the room.

After treading halfway around, she paused. She rested the decorative piece on the floor, then slid her optical system back to its upward position. Kasta squinted as her eyes followed a series of fine grooves on the wall, concealed by a thick layer of dirt. She wiped her hand over the surface, revealing an ancient carving. A cloud of dust flurried from her gloves as she smacked her palms together. "Dresco, you're going to want to see this."

Dresco's footsteps clacked against the stone floor, reverberating around the small room. The knight's silhouette emerged from the shadows as he stood in the light of the nearest torch. "What is it?" He stood stiffly, with his hands interlocked behind his back.

"It's just what I told you we'd find." Kasta presented the artwork with a flaccid stretch of her arm. "Writing on the wall."

Dresco's head tilted forward. "Is this? Is it really—?"

"Your blessed Seven Relics. All in glyphic glory."

With a tremor in his voice, Dresco said, "Seven Relics for Seven Guardians." He was lost in his own reverence, breathless before the artwork. "I have never seen this early a depiction."

"This is one of the earliest I have seen as well," Kasta said. "Notice how the other six Relics are in a circle, surrounding the sword in the middle."

"Vellon's Blade." Dresco pointed toward the largest image of the seven: a longsword, clutched by a pair of armored hands.

"Exactly," Kasta said with a nod and a smile. "The Defender of Liberty." She lowered her optical system and captured a digital image of the engravings, then continued, "In ancient times, legend said that the power of the other six Relics was drawn from Vellon's sword. Thus, it is typically depicted in the center."

She stepped away from the engravings and toward the middle of the room. "In most of the temples constructed later in history, the Relics are depicted equally in size. And adjacent to each other, rather than in a circle."

Dresco glanced at her. "For a nonbeliever, you are quite educated in theological history."

Her head tilted toward her shoulder. "I'm quite educated in *treasure hunting*, my good knight." Her arms stretched out. "But as you can see, there is no treasure here. I've scanned everything. There's no maps or anything of any value, really." She held the marble decoration at eye level, her upper lip bent in a snarl. "At least I got my little cube." She studied it for a moment more before she let it roll off her fingers and onto the ground, realizing she did not want it.

Dresco marched back to the center of the room. He pointed toward the orange boulder that he was inspecting before. "What is this stone?"

Kasta leaned over the boulder with a blank countenance. "Looks an awful lot like a stone." Her eyes shifted to her companion. "Dresco, there ain't no map here. We tried, but we just ain't gunna find it. Let's go get paid—"

The sharp tone of Dresco's blade drawing from its sheath interrupted Kasta. "Whoa, whoa," the Vandeni woman yelled as she leapt back and drew her pistol, under the impression that the knight's frustration with her had boiled to the point of a violent reaction.

Instead, Dresco thrust his blade into the stone at the center of the room. The sharp tip found a seam in the rudimentary object that he had found so curious. The small hole swallowed Dresco's weapon, leaving a sliver of blade between the stone and the cross guard.

The floor trembled. A yellow glow matching the temple's geothermal lighting effloresced beneath Dresco's embedded sword. Heavy chains tingled and rattled as they crawled through the walls. The companions followed the sound with their eyes. The crawling chains halted with a sudden clunk. After an adjustment from what sounded to be a large metal object, the floor shook again. This time, with greater force.

The sounds morphed into a heavy gallop: massive gears working together. With substantial resistance, a section of the wall between two pillars began to climb toward the rounded ceiling. The ascending barrier gave view to a small room, still hidden by shadow.

"Dresco, you're a genius," Kasta said, her eyes fixed on the secret doorway.

Dresco's arm protruded toward her pistol. "Did you really believe I was going to kill you?"

She still grasped her weapon, though with a relaxed grip and at her side. "You never know," she said, holstering the pistol. Her attention turned to the sword Dresco had plunged through the stone. "So, tell me, Norte." She crossed her arms. "What in the name of Athenis gave you the inspiration to stick your sword in this rock?" She knelt toward the yellow light which bled from the small slit. "And what are the odds that it would happen to fit so nicely?"

Dresco marched away, half stepping toward the secret doorway. "It was the will of the Guardians. When you are on the side of the divine, no odds are too great."

Kasta raised her eyebrows and chased after the knight. She grabbed ahold of his armor-clad biceps. "Or maybe it was your own brute strength. I'm surprised you didn't *break* the mechanism."

Dresco remained silent. They set foot inside the hidden chamber. Kasta turned on the night-vision setting of her optical system. She could see nothing in the round room, which was no larger than ten feet in diameter. Nothing but a rectangular-cut stone on the floor.

She began to conduct a digital analysis of the odd stone. But before she could even run basic tests, Dresco stepped toward it. As he approached, an orange light beamed from the stone's corner, emitting a radiant line from the crevices. Kasta's eyes widened—her jaw dropped. Night vision would not be necessary.

The orange gleam expanded from the rectangular rock and projected a three-dimensional image into the center of the hidden chamber with the radiance of a star. The room became brighter than any in the temple. Falling into place, the light created replicas of flowing oceans in shades of vermillion. Detailed landmasses floated overhead—mountains, valleys and whitewater falls, roaring from high summits.

"It's really here," Dresco said at the edge of his breath. "We found it. The map to Vellon's Blade."

"I'll be damned," Kasta said. She admired the floating neon projections above. "It's a map alright. But let's not get ahead of ourselves. We have no idea what it's trying to point us to." The hunter lowered her optical system to her eye, recording images of the map. "We'll need to conduct further analysis. The continents, they're in a completely different formation. This thing is ancient."

Her optical system detected no electric pulses or wavelengths. She leaned close to the map, her mouth gaping and her eyes narrow. "Dresco, I'm not even getting any digital readings. How could this complex of an image not run on any form of computation?"

"It is protected by divine magic." The knight sounded choked up. Was his helm hiding tears?

She looked to him with a roguish grin. "Whatever it is, it's going to make us some good coin." Dresco stepped back. Her attention returned to the levitating map.

A click came from the direction of the entrance, followed by the halt of Dresco's footsteps. The large stone door that the knight had unlocked slammed shut. Kasta removed her optical system and turned to Dresco. His right foot rested on a panel indented into the floor.

The orange light dimmed. The projection of the map faded away. Four holes opened on the ceiling. Sand spilled from the openings and fell to the floor.

Kasta looked to Dresco with a clenched fist as her lips trembled. "Dresco, you're an idiot."

V

WATCH YOUR STEP

"I ... I do not know how it happened. I was just trying to get a better view of the map." Dresco looked to the sunken floor panel that he had stepped on. The falling sand had already covered it.

Kasta buried her face in the palm of her hand and caressed her temples. "Watch your step. Just watch your step. It was simple, straightforward advice. Easy to comprehend. Easy to follow." Her eyes flared like opaline pearls cut from a clam as she stomped her foot on the floor. "But somehow you managed to screw it up!"

"I'm sorry. I truly am," Dresco said with his arms raised as if to offer his surrender. "I was—I was captivated by the map. I lost my senses." His arms extended outward, his palms facing Kasta as their eyes met. "And it seemed like every trap had already been activated. Even you said—"

"No, no, no." Kasta shook her head and wagged her finger. "Think about this for one minute, will you?" She stepped toward Dresco. The knight stepped backward. "Most of the traps are sprung *out there*." She pointed toward the closed doorway. "We are in a secret chamber. One that no one has stepped foot in for, oh I don't know, probably about five thousand years. The ancient Vandeni viewed overcoming obstacles as a measure of worth for walking in their sacred structures. This building was designed with a defense mechanism to arm all the traps as soon as an artifact was removed from its grounds. Did you really think that the ancient Vandeni would neglect to put a trap in a secret chamber? Did you really think that it was somehow already sprung?"

Dresco stammered. "I do not know—"

"Evidently not!" Kasta pointed toward the sand falling from the ceiling. "This is why I work alone." She stomped away, halting before the rectangular stone at the center of the room. The object that had projected a vibrant map moments ago had dimmed to a faint amber glow.

Dresco let out a heavy sigh. "I really am sorry. I am no treasure hunter. That is your expertise." The room was silent, save for the pelting whisper of falling sand. "How much of the map did you capture, anyway?" he asked hesitantly.

The corner of Kasta's eye rolled toward the knight. "I think all of it," she answered.

"I guess it will not matter if we are going to be killed."

"Don't worry about that." Kasta lifted her head toward the ceiling, resting her thumb and index finger on her chin.

Dresco stepped forward. He ran his hand through one of the sand streams. "It is somewhat hard not to worry when we are in the process of being buried alive."

She looked to him with eyebrows raised and a close-lipped smile. "I'm Kasta Krane. I can get out of anything." She lifted her foot from the floor and shook off the sand that had started to arch over her boot. "However, I'm currently open to suggestions."

The knight stepped to the entryway. "We can open it! The Guardians will give us the strength!" he said at the edge of his breath, pulling on the bottom of the door. "Come on, help me!" He buried his shoulder into the door, trying to push it outward. The gears would allow only vertical movement.

Kasta's eyes narrowed as her chin tucked in. "Norte, please stop wasting your energy." She lowered her optical system and began an analysis of the room's architecture. "From the look of it, we will be drowning in sand within an hour. So please, save your strength and let's figure out a way out of here."

Dresco panted. He lowered his head and rested his arm on the door. "If only I had my sword," he groaned at the edge of his breath.

Kasta shook her head as she scanned the room. "Your sword got us in here. I don't think it would be any help getting us out."

"We would have better luck cutting our way through the door, at least." He turned to face her. "There is no other exit."

Kasta's head swayed from shoulder to shoulder. She raised her optical system to its upright position. "It does seem that this chamber's only entrance is the doorway. That and the..." She became distracted by her own thoughts. Her line of sight crawled to the ceiling.

"What?" Dresco said, his gaze tilting upward as well.

"The holes where the sand is flowing from."

Dresco's eyes remained fixed on the ceiling. He spluttered, searching for the proper words. "What? Are you—are you *completely* mad?" He took a heavy step through the ankle-high sand. "The sand is flowing too vigorously. It will thrust you right back down. Not to mention, it is far too high. What are you going to do? Stand on my shoulders?"

"Maybe," Kasta said with a slight shrug.

"Miss Krane, I was obviously using hyperbole—"

"I know, I know. We're just brainstorming, remember?" She looked to the circular clefts above. "And call me Kasta."

"Miss Krane!" Dresco said with a thrust of his fist. "This is no time for that sort of behavior."

"Relax, relax. Your attitude isn't helping." Kasta refused to look at Dresco. She chuckled, thinking of the scowl hidden behind his face shield. An idea came over her. "Nah, it's too crazy," she whispered.

Dresco overheard. "What? What is it?"

"I don't even know how I come up with these things," she said with a shake of her head.

Dresco stumbled as he went to lean on his sword, forgetting that his weapon was not in its sheath. "You have my attention."

The hunter let out an elongated sigh. "You ever see what happens when sand gets struck by lightning?"

Dresco spent a moment in silent thought. "No."

A smirk slid up the side of Kasta's face. She drew her pistol from its holster and fired a shot. The knight leapt back. The stream of electricity flowed from the shock-cannon's barrel, striking the ground in front of Dresco's feet.

Dresco stumbled in the rising mound of sand. "By Athenis' starlight! Was it really necessary to aim so close to me?"

Kasta ignored him. Clearing his throat, Dresco knelt. He reached forward, plucking a fingerful of smoking sand. The translucent material crunched and shattered as he opened his palm. He made a declaration: "Glass!"

Kasta looked to her pistol. She raised the power setting to a high output. "That's right."

Dresco shuffled the glass shards in his hand. "But how does that help us?"

Kasta walked in circles around the room, staring at the four holes depositing sand from the ceiling. "We're gunna climb right on out."

"Oh. Um, oh my goodness." Dresco coughed and cleared his throat. "You were correct. That is, as you put it, 'crazy.' Shall we consider the next potential plan?"

Kasta pointed her weapon at the weakest of the four sand streams and fired. A stalk of frosted glass burgeoned from the piling mound. Dresco's armor flashed in a reflection of white light as Kasta released another blast from her pistol. She discharged her weapon several more times, each shot a deafening roar of thunder.

The Vandeni hunter stepped closer to the stream. The sprouting stem of electrically manufactured glass was growing into a high, branching, prismatic tree. Kasta could feel her pistol overheating as she raised it over her head, continuing to pull the trigger. The lightning, frozen in fulgurite form, had grown through the hole and forged an escape path.

Dresco gasped, standing stiffly. Kasta holstered her sweltering pistol. "Hold my hat." She tossed her black desert topper to the knight.

"You are not—we are not seriously going to climb this... thing, are we?" Dresco asked, looking up and down the glass structure.

Kasta took a deep breath and swung her arms out, wading toward her crystalline creation. "I am. You're not."

"Excuse me?"

She pointed in his face. "Listen to me. And listen to me good, damn it. I am about to try to climb a glass tower through a hole that's spitting sand at me. If you want to try to climb up after, be my guest. But don't you *dare* even touch the damn thing while I'm on it."

Dresco elevated his foot and kicked the surface of the rising sand. "So, what do you expect me to do? Just stand here and wait to die?"

"No," she said with a sharp tone. "Your massive body and heavy armor will bring that thing down right away. Wait till I get to the top, then you can give it a shot." Her hand wrapped around a branching arm of the glass tower. Grains sprinkled into her hair. She pulled herself up and drew a deep breath, easing her foot onto a stem of petrified lightning. "And don't worry." Though her voice shook, she held a wide smile. "If you fall on your clumsy face, I'll find a way to get you out of here."

"Oh, that is reassuring," Dresco said with a groan.

She laughed, tasting the sand. Though cautious of her footing, she could not linger. 'The more time I'm on this thing, the more likely it is to shatter into thousands of tiny pieces,' she thought. 'Gotta keep my head tucked in. I'm swallowing sand.' The rough grains irritated her gills. A cough erupted from her throat.

The opening in the ceiling was near. She raised her right hand, pulling herself up on a stalk of glass.

It splintered from the tower. The sharpened fragment cut through Kasta's glove and into her skin. Footing lost and legs flailing, she clung to the glass tower with her opposite hand, releasing a bellow of pain.

"Oh no!" Dresco scurried toward Kasta. He raised his arms in a panicked state, as if he were going to try to catch her. "Just—just hold on!"

Kasta used her own momentum to swing her body around and plant all four of her limbs on solid glass. "Thanks for that tip. Never thought of that." She blinked several times to flush the sand from her eyes.

"By the grace of the Guardians' compassion, please let her make it safely," Dresco beseeched.

"Yeah, stand down there and pray some more. That's really useful," she whispered loudly enough for him to hear.

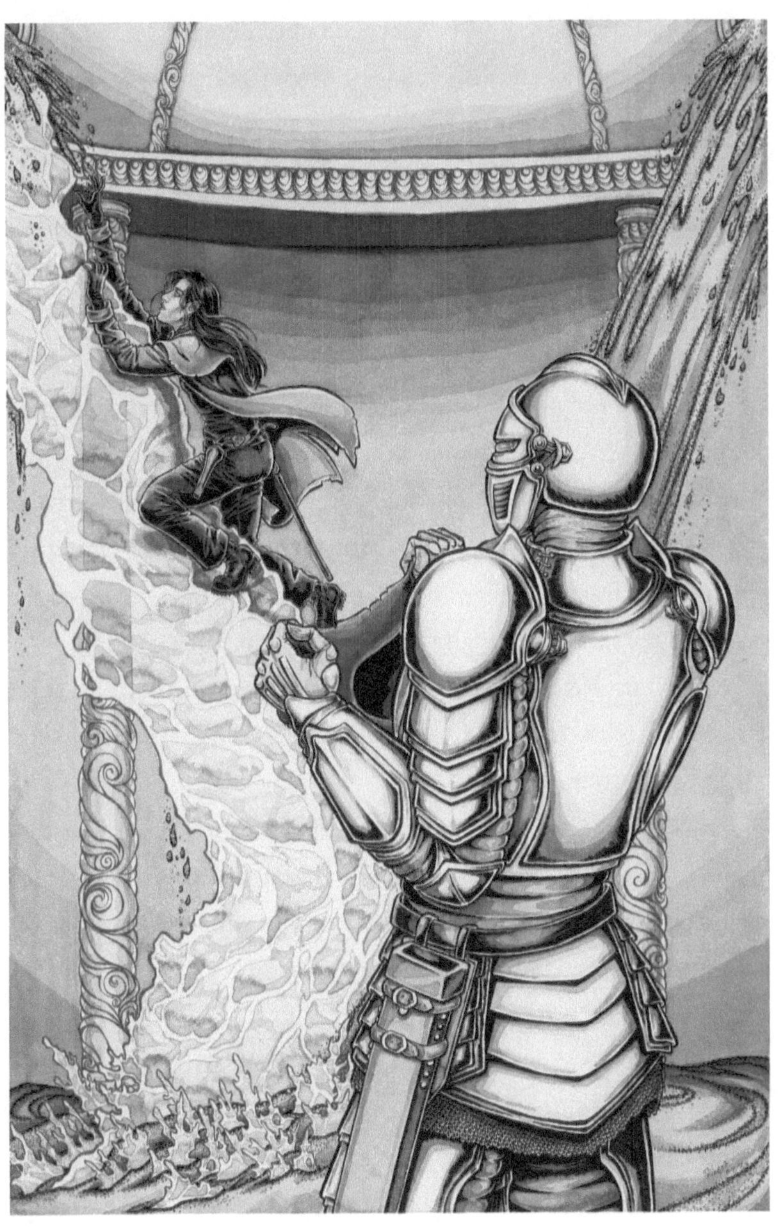

She continued to ascend, her right hand smearing an imprint of blood wherever it grasped. The gash had gone deep. Her head was starting to poke through the hole in the ceiling. The current of falling sand was heavier in the small tunnel. She had to hold her breath to avoid inhaling it. As she squinted and peeked up, she could see where the pipe changed direction. 'Just got to climb a few more steps. Then I can leap up there and work my way out.'

When Kasta took a step, she heard a tingling crack below her foot. 'Oh, come on, not now. I'm so close, baby. Just hold up a little longer.' She held still. Perhaps it was only weakening—not breaking.

Such fortune would not be found. Another pair of tingling cracks splintered up the structure. The cracks transformed into shattering bursts. "Well. Damn it," she said with an exasperated sigh. She scaled the glass with the speed of the lightning that had forged it.

Dresco must have heard the glass breaking or seen pieces falling from the opening in the ceiling. He yelled from below, "Kasta, it is breaking! The glass is shattering!"

Two steps from the horizontal section of the tunnel, the delicate glass below fragmentized and collapsed. Kasta braced her arms and knees against the shaft. Her muscles stiffened as they supported her weight, preventing her from plummeting with the tower.

The tower smashed against the ground, followed by a series of worried queries from Dresco. "Oh my, Miss Krane, are you alive? Did you make it out? What is your status? Please, answer me!"

She did not answer. She used every bit of her vitality to remain braced against the vertical cylinder, battling both gravity and sand. She was slipping. Kasta tucked in her elbows and knees. With a long, deep breath, she leapt upward with all her might. Through a bombardment of sand, she managed to clutch the ledge with her left hand. The hunter pulled herself up. Her body touched the horizontal part of the tunnel, opposite from where the sand flowed. Fear and adrenaline turned to pride. Heaving with laughter, she rested her head against the wall.

Dresco still yelled in a state of unchecked panic.

Kasta leaned over the hole she had climbed out of. "I'm alright, Norte."

"Oh, that is a relief," he said enthusiastically. "But I do have one request. Can you maybe help me... not die?"

Kasta laughed as she reached for her pistol and aimed down the hole, her sights on the remnants of the glass tower. "Stay back," she ordered. She fired her weapon into the flowing stream of sand. The tower of glass began to regrow. The first electric blasts struck with force and fury. But the thunder waned. The streams of voltage thinned. The glass stems sprang weaker from one shot to the next. "Oh, what the hell? Come on," she said.

"That does not sound like a statement I want to hear right now, Miss Krane."

"My shock-cannon is overheated, Norte." She leaned over. How tall had the tower grown? It was not enough. It was too short and too thin. Even if he took his armor off, the glass would not support his weight. And even with his long frame, he would not reach the top. "Just hang tight. I'll get you out of there."

"Oh, charming." Dresco stepped into view. "I will not hold my breath."

Kasta chuckled as she shook her head; hundreds of sandy grains drizzled from her long black hair. "You may have to." The hunter turned around, crawling through the tunnel on her hands and knees.

"Kasta, this is not the time for such comments." His baritone voice was hesitant and uneasy.

"Oh, lighten up!"

His voice faded to a shrill mumble.

She shimmied through the dark ventilation shaft. It was so small that Dresco would not have fit inside. She reached to the back of her utility belt and grabbed her hunting knife. The darkness would call for her optical system's night vision.

While she swung her knife to cut the cobwebs blocking her path, she thought of the doubtful inflection in Dresco's words. 'Does he actually think I'm going to leave him there?' she thought. 'What an idiot.' The vent turned to the right, and Kasta followed its path. The sound of sand flowing into the secret chamber echoed from behind. From this distance, it sounded like a whitewater brook. 'On the other hand, maybe he has a point. I have everything I need, and he knows how bad he screwed up.'

The vent forked in two different directions. 'What part of the temple am I in? I don't know where to go!' Her gut told her to go right. She listened. The hunter smiled as another thought came to her. 'Maybe he thinks I'm gunna try to get his half of the reward money from Madame Vaeliz?'

A cracking rumble palpitated beneath the surface. She stopped her crawl and looked down. The vibration surged up her hands. The floor was giving way. "Oh, holy hell," she said with a roll of her eyes. The old foundation crumbled and collapsed.

Kasta fell to the ground, landing atop a gob of debris. Reaching for her back, she groaned in pain; there was nothing to break her fall but rubble and rocks. "Must everything break while I'm on it?" She rolled onto the floor. "Seriously. Everything?"

She looked up with a moan, analyzing her surroundings. 'It looks like the area around the second sanctum,' she thought, releasing a violent cough. 'Not far away from Jellinok's chamber.' She removed her right glove and grabbed a strip of bandage wrap from her utility belt. She winced as she wrapped the adhesive material around the gash on her hand and forearm.

'Maybe I'll help the noble knight out on this one. He did find the chamber that holds the map. I was convinced the map didn't even exist, after all.' Kasta stretched out each of her fingers, then tightened them into a fist. The wound would require treatment from a medical professional, but she had at least stopped the bleeding. 'Not to mention, he owes me. No one is permitted to die when they owe Kasta Krane a debt.'

She patted her jacket and pants down. Clouds of dust scattered from her clothing, then dissipated. She ran up the stairs toward the third sanctum.

The hunter reached the chamber. Dresco's sword stood plumb in the boulder. Kasta rushed to the secret door that separated her and the knight. "Hey, Norte, can you hear me?"

His voice came muffled from the other side. "Miss Krane! I have never been more pleased to hear your voice. Get me out of here! Almost half the room is filled with sand and I'm starting to sink beneath. I do not have much longer."

"Okay. Okay." Kasta looked around the room. Her eyes landed on Dresco's blade. "If I take your sword out and put it back in, it should open the door again."

"Are you sure?"

"Oh, yeah. Definitely!" She turned away from the door with a raised brow. "I think," she uttered, biting her lip.

She approached the stone and placed a single hand on Dresco's longsword. "Here goes nothing." She locked a second hand on the hilt. She tried to pull the blade from the stone, but it would not move an inch. The hunter removed her jacket and tossed it aside. Her grip tightened on the sword's hilt. Though she pulled with all her might, it would not move. She placed her left foot on the stone and pulled again, screaming. "Ahhhh!"

The sword answered with a scraping, metallic growl and arose from the stone. Kasta stumbled back. The tip of the blade fell to the floor. The hilt remained in her grasp.

The hunter caught her breath, then hoisted the knightly weapon. She ground her teeth and grunted. 'It's even heavier than it looks.' As she raised the monstrous blade over her shoulder, sweat dripped from her brow. Veins bulged across her blue face. But Kasta was able to guide the sword back through the boulder. Her biceps tremored. Blood seeped through the bandage on her hand. With a clangorous slam, the gears began to turn.

'Got it,' she thought. Dresco let out a loud cheer. The door rolled open. Sand avalanched from the secret chamber.

After opening a quarter of the way, the door came to a chafing halt. The gears behind the walls ground. The room shook. Chains screamed and overstretched. Kasta sighed, running fingers through her hair. "Or not."

"Oh dear. So, would you care to explain why the door was opening a moment ago, and now it has ceased to continue to do so?" Dresco asked, his voice much clearer through the opening.

"Well," Kasta said, stepping toward the map room. "I think it got messed up when it was reopening. The door closed so suddenly when the trap went down. Probably screwed up the gears."

"Splendid."

She looked around the sanctum, attempting to conjure another way to free him. "It is an entrance to a secret chamber in an ancient temple.

It's not like it has been receiving routine maintenance. Amazing it still functions at all."

"Amazing? Less so when it is trying to kill you."

She rested her hand on the wall and leaned over. 'I could maybe get the trugan up here to break the door down,' she thought. A moment later, she shook her head at her own idea. 'No, no. They'll never fit up that stairway. It's way too narrow.' She pressed her head to the door. Sand flowed from the gap below. "Did the sand at least stop flowing in?"

"It did not. I believe it is flowing in at an *accelerated* rate, in fact."

"Great." Kasta rolled her eyes. 'Maybe I could get him out through the vent,' she thought. But she refuted her own idea once more. 'Nah. By the time I made enough rope, Dresco would probably be buried past his neck.'

"I guess there's only one option." She bit her bottom lip. The knight would not like the next words to come from her mouth. "You have to dig your way out."

Dresco stammered as he replied, "Could you repeat that? I thought you said something about digging my way out."

"No, no. You heard correctly." Kasta got on her knees, looking under the doorway. "From the sound of your voice, you're about two feet from the bottom of the door. If you hurry, you'll be able to dig deep enough to slide under it."

"It is confirmed, then. You are indeed completely mad." Dresco sounded short of breath. "I told you, the sand is still pouring down. I will never be able to dig faster than it falls!"

Kasta smirked and shook her head. "Not if you keep talking instead of digging."

"I've already started digging!"

She nodded. She used her arms to scoop piles of desert dirt from the sanctum. "Good. I've started to help you on my side."

After several minutes of burrowing, she caught sight of Dresco's armored hand under the door. "There ya are!" she said. "Just a little further."

"My progress keeps getting impeded by new sand," Dresco said, his voice strained. "Will the door not go up any higher?"

Kasta wiped her hands together, shaking the coarse grains from her wound. "I doubt it, but I'll give it a shot." She scurried to the boulder and twisted the embedded sword. After she jiggled the monstrous weapon, the chains and gears rumbled through the walls. The door rose only a few inches. "It's no use, Norte. That door is more jammed than—"

"Do it again!" Dresco interrupted.

"Do what?"

"Whatever you just did."

"Um, okay," Kasta whispered, shaking the sword once more. She heard Dresco screaming in intense agony. She looked to the opening. His armored hands attempted to lift the door. 'He's wasting his time,' she thought. 'Wait. Is the door—? It's actually budging.'

"It's moving up!" she shouted.

The throttling of the sword loosened the chains. Combined with the coercion of Dresco's strength, the gears turned. Kasta's jaw clenched. She forced the sword deeper—the door climbed higher. Dresco's helmet stemmed through the opening. "Okay..." she said, her hands wringing the hilt. "I'm gunna tell you when to go, and when I do, you let go of that door and get the hell out of there."

Kasta did not expect a response from Dresco. His concentration remained fixed on holding the door. If he let go, or his strength failed, he would be crushed.

"Ahhhhhh!" the knight screamed, sand spilling from the secret chamber as he forced the door higher.

"Now!" Kasta ordered.

Dresco let go of the door before she finished the word. In a backward summersault, the knight rolled down the pile of sand and landed outside the flooding secret chamber. The door slammed shut, cutting off both companions from the other room. The knight lay on the mound, drawing whistling breaths deep into his lungs.

Kasta stepped away from the sword and over to Dresco's deflated body. "Thank goodness," she said, bent over and extending her hand. "I thought I'd lost you." She reached past Dresco and grabbed her black hat, which lay on the sand-covered floor. With a purse of her lips, she patted the top of the crown. Grains hailed from the brim. She placed the desert topper on her head and looked down at Dresco with a sneer. "Get up. We got a long way to go." She turned and strutted toward the sanctum's exit.

The knight lay motionless on his back. He answered only with a pair of hacking coughs.

VI
MISSION ACCOMPLISHED

Athenis shined brightly in the sky when the travelers exited the temple. It was late afternoon, but they were in desperate need of sleep. After riding for an hour, they set up camp on the cliffs of the Narrow Mountains. The Temple of Jellinok stood lonely in the distance. A pack of wild trugan chased a vyaliss through the canyon below. The band of reptiles exhausted the large hoofed beast as they circled around. The jagged antlers of the vyaliss would not save it from the trugan once they moved in for the kill.

"Ah yes, the raisin spices, how could I forget the raisin spices?" Dresco said, searching through the satchel in front of him. "There we are." He pulled out a small bag and held it before his eyes. He sprinkled a black powder into the sizzling pan.

Kasta had just finished rewrapping her gashed hand. She leaned over the pan and took a long look at the thin-cut layers of sliced plants. "What the hell is that?" Her nose wrinkled at the acrid smoke.

"An Imperial delicacy." Dresco tossed the fried-plant food with a wooden spoon. "Unfortunately, this will not do it justice. These royal vines are imported. This is a dish meant to be eaten fresh." The knight reached for a small bowl and filled it to the top with the royal vines. He handed it to Kasta, who still beheld the meal with a grimace.

She squinted and took a nibble. Her body shuddered and her lips curled as she swallowed. "Ugh," she said. "How the hell do you eat that?"

The brittle texture and bitter taste overtook her tongue—then twisted her stomach.

Dresco prepared his own bowl and looked to his companion with a frown. "I told you that it is supposed to be fresh!"

"That's not it. It tastes like rotten seaweed. Didn't you get any meat?"

Dresco's face grew long. He shut his eyes and took a bite of his own meal. A small smile parted his grey lips as his head tilted back. "Oh, there is nothing like tasting a little bit of home."

Kasta took her bowl over to the two trugan and offered a fingerful of the royal vines to Crevallus. Crevallus turned his long neck to the side and grunted. Kasta presented the vines to Kaiar. She took a nibble, chewed once, and spit it onto the hardpan dirt. Kasta reached into Kai's pannier and retrieved a hessian sack. She brought the bowl of royal vines to Dresco and dropped it at his feet. "You can have that." He had already devoured most of his own serving of the bitter vegetables.

From the hessian bag, Kasta pulled out a piece of dried meat. "Perfect. Nighthawk jerky!" She sank her teeth into the thick bird meat and jerked her head back and forth. A piece tore off. The hunter's eyes widened. A soft purr escaped between her teeth and the strip of meat.

Dresco eyed her smacking lips. "That is not a meal," he said with a slow shake of his head.

"I beg to differ," Kasta mumbled, her mouth full. "I just climbed a glass tower made of sand to escape an ancient death trap. I need my protein." She stood tall and swayed toward the trugan, reaching into the sack for the four largest cuts of nighthawk jerky. She dropped two in front of each trugan.

The beasts wasted no time. They buried their snarling jaws into the terrain, attacking the meat strips. Kasta looked to Dresco with a familiar half smirk. Her eyebrows arched high. "See? Even the trugan agree with me. A little nighthawk meat beats Imperial raisin grass any day."

Dresco bit his lip and looked to the summit, avoiding eye contact with his companion. He grabbed the bowl of royal vines that Kasta had surrendered and began to consume his second serving.

Kasta removed her leather jacket and unbuttoned her vest. She took a long, deep breath and sat at the edge of the cliff. Her legs dangled from the ledge as she pulled her pistol from its holster and opened the chamber.

She set her optical system to scan for damage, but her naked eye revealed the shock-cannon's deterioration on its own. The main coil had burned out, prohibiting a stable electrical current. To make matters worse, the charge crystal had cracked. Scorch marks stretching from the coil to the crystal suggested a chain reaction. 'Definitely beyond my skills to repair. Gunna need a weaponsmith for this one,' Kasta thought, her lips pursing. 'We'll find one in the next town.'

The hunter reholstered her pistol and stood. Dresco had finished dining. His armored breastplate sat on his lap. He scrubbed it with a silken cloth, attempting to remove every blemish and grain of sand. He whispered a prayer. "Morvai, give me the strength to don this armor another day, to protect the innocent and defend the righteous. Haelovar, bless me with the fortitude to keep your peace. Andralla, may this armor defend the shape of this world, perfected by your design. Vellon, allow my soul to be my own, and never fall prey to the hunger of the Etsinnae."

Kasta tossed a blanket a few paces from the low fire. A howling whimper resounded from the valley below. "You hear that, Kai?" she said as she sat on the blanket, her legs forward. "That's the sound of wild trugan catching their dinner. Lucky for you, I drop food in front of you every night. You don't have to work hard for none of it."

A wide smile came over the hunter's face as Kai responded with a soft grunt.

"Yes," Dresco said, checking his armor for his reflection. "It does not have to work for any of it. Except that it must shuttle you around for hours upon hours every day, ranging across distances far beyond the natural capabilities of such a creature. Oh, and you have essentially turned it into a machine." He dug the cloth into his breastplate, glancing up at Kasta.

Kasta looked at Kaiar and pointed to the knight. "Kai, I give you full permission to eat him in his sleep."

Dresco's shoulders sank, his eyes swiveling toward the female trugan.

Kai stared at the knight. Her long forked tongue flickered.

Kasta chuckled, picking up her jacket. She removed her mobile data system from its pocket. "Relax, Norte. She won't come near you when you smell like that Imperial grass trimming that you call food." She cycled through different icons on the purple screen of her data system until reaching a page titled "Contacts." She removed her gloves and used her fingernails to pick jerky from her teeth. "What's with your distaste for cybernetics anyway? You guys cyberize your mounts."

"Yes, but we do not advertise it. The cybernetics on our wolves and tigers are always beneath the fur, never in sight. That is one aspect of life that I have noticed the Vandeni lack: subtlety."

Kasta shook her head, writing a message on her data system. "Yes, because it makes the practice so much better if you hide it." She raised her eyebrows, looking up at Dresco. "You're not going to tell me that you don't have any enhancements. I saw you back there in that chamber. You held a two-ton door open!" She flashed a tight smile. "Now, you're a big guy, but you're not that big."

"Actually, the armor itself is designed to enhance our strength." After putting his breastplate down, Dresco reached behind for his helmet. "But yes, Knights of the Order do receive muscle-tissue augmentations."

Kasta's head tilted. "Aha, so he's not such a perfect monk, after all." She leaned toward the knight. "I guess it's okay if it's for religious purposes, right? Otherwise, it's a *horrible sin*."

Dresco's hand fell on top of his helmet with a hollow clang. "That is not what I... ugh, I mean, look at you. You must have dozens of enhancements."

Kasta shook her head as she continued to write her message. "Nope." She let the moment linger. Dresco's jaw descended. "Only basic reflex enhancements and tissue-regeneration accelerators." Her words radiated from a one-sided smile.

Dresco's hand wiped his helmet, though his eyes remained fixed on his companion. "That's impossible. The way you move, the way you react to... dangerous situations. You must have other implants—thought motivators or advanced sensory upgrades of some kind."

She crossed her legs, and her smile slanted further. "That's all me. An overabundance of enhancements would only dilute my natural skill."

"Oh my," Dresco muttered. He remained unblinking and motionless for a moment before his attention turned back to his helmet. He struggled to clean the sand from the inside. "What are you doing on that thing anyway?" he asked, glancing at Kasta's data system.

"Writing a message to our employer. I'm letting her know the mission was a success and that we'll be making contact in four days."

"Excellent." Dresco exhaled hot breath on the top of his helmet. He dug the cloth in again and made small circles until the surface of the metal helm squeaked. "The good Madame will be delighted to hear of our progress." Insects and birds sang in harmony behind the knight's words as the evening grew darker. "What we saw in there, it was miraculous, was it not?" He placed his helmet behind him. His long brown hair fell over his face as he sat up straight and crossed his legs.

"I guess."

"You guess? What do you mean 'you guess'?' We have found the map to Vellon's Blade, one of the Seven Relics, a gift given directly from the Guardians to the people of Eramaa." His hands extended sideways. "How are you, as a seeker of historical treasures and artifacts, not mesmerized by this?"

Kasta finished her message and pressed the "Send" icon. "Because, Norte, as a seeker of historical artifacts, I know that usually stuff like this is a dead end." She picked her jacket up and pulled a cigarillo from the inner pocket. "Don't get your hopes up about actually finding that sword. I've been on a lot of wild-goose chases, especially looking for those Seven Relics. If I ever found one of those, I could live ten lifetimes off the coin it'd bring me." She leaned over the fire to light her cigarillo. She had given up on finding her utility tool. "But the problem is it's very unlikely that they even exist."

"Ah, but you said the same thing about the map itself." As Dresco spoke, Kasta buried her face in her palms. He continued, "You were ready to give up until I discovered the secret chamber."

Her eyes rolled. "A treasure map. How often do you hear about a treasure map that doesn't lead to any treasure?"

"Um—"

"Most of the time!" she said with mocking laughter, cigarillo dangling from the side of her mouth. "Most of the time, a treasure map leads you to something that used to hold an object of value, but that someone else has gotten to first. Or worse yet, sometimes it just leads you to a piece of nothing that was never anything other than just that: nothing."

Dresco cleared his throat. "May I see the digital images that you captured?" he asked, changing the subject again.

Kasta reached for her data system. "Yeah sure. What's the identification number on your mobile system?"

The knight's hair fell over his face as he stared at the fire. "Oh, um, I do not have one."

Kasta removed the cigarillo from her mouth. Her arms swung outward. "Dresco, I told you to buy one in Barren Rock!"

He nodded. "I know. I know. I did not manage to accomplish that task."

The hunter released a soft groan and shook her head. "No data system, no meat. That's the last time you go on a supply run." She tossed her system over the fire to Dresco. He struggled to catch it but managed to cradle the device against his chest after a series of juggles.

After taking a deep pull of her cigarillo, Kasta fell back with her head resting against the blanket. A feeling of comfort came over her. She looked past the summits of the rugged cliffs toward the sapphire skies. The arms of the galaxy stretched across, painting the heavens with spirals of white light. She placed her cigarillo in her mouth and unbuttoned her grey shirt, allowing the cool air to graze her skin.

"You captured some fantastic images," Dresco said from across the fire. "It will be exhilarating to see them on a three-dimensional scale once again."

She ashed her cigarillo, ignoring the knight. A peace came over Kasta Krane. The moons climbed toward the center of the sky, reaching for each other like lovers across the stars. Sleep would come easy to the hunter this night.

"Oh, magnificent! You captured an image of Relic engravings! The art on the wall."

"Mhmm," was all she vocalized as her inner arm covered her eyes.

Dresco carried on, "So the sword in the middle is Vellon's Blade, obviously. Let's see, at the top here—oh my! It is definitely Haelovar's Shield. The Protector of Peace!" He leaned toward Kasta, his voice falling to a whisper. "The scriptures regarding Haelovar have always been my favorite."

Kasta groaned and turned on her shoulder, leaving her back to the knight. He paid her no mind. "What else do we have here? Andralla's Staff of Forms! And, oh of course, a Syrenia riding a large sea creature, and there it is. The Syrenia is holding the Spear of Rytekos, the Spear of the Sea." He let out an eager laugh. "Have you ever met a Syrenia, Miss Krane?"

She squinted and sighed. "Norte, I get that you are excited, but can you please keep your choirboy rant to yourself? And no, I've never met a Syrenia. Almost no one ever does. Those fish people like to keep to themselves." She murmured at the edge of her breath, "And they have the right idea."

"Oh, I am almost done!" Dresco said. "We have a hand bearing Shal's Ring of Will. Then a crown, which of course must be the Circlet of Balance. And that last figure must be... Morvai's chainmail, the Armor of Strength..."

"Congratulations, you know the names of all the mythological deities you have dedicated your life to. Now will you please be silent?"

For several moments, Dresco *was* silent. Suspiciously so. "Is that...?" The knight took a short breath. "Is that a Draekalagon draped in the Armor of Morvai?"

"Yeah. What of it? The House of Morvai was a Draelek household."

A quivering gasp harbingered his response. "That is both blasphemous and vile!" He was not yelling but came close.

Kasta shot up, eyes wide and brow furrowed. "Wait, what the hell did you just say?"

Crevallus looked to Dresco with his neck cocked sideways.

The knight's light-grey eyes met Kasta's. "Those lizard vermin have no place in the halls of the Guardians. The House of Morvai was not a Draelek house. It could not have been."

"Listen, Norte, I don't know what they taught you in the Imperium, but here, the Draekalagons are treated just like anyone else. As with any group of people, some are alright, most are horrible." Kasta was now wide awake and reached for her cigarillo, its ember still flickering. "Also, Morvai *was* a Draelek house. Read some history."

Dresco fidgeted and swallowed twice. "But... but Imperial records show—"

"Imperial records are wrong!" Kasta interrupted. "And I'm beginning to pick up a theme of that here."

"The Houses of the Guardians were built by those who bear their blood—their descendants. Those Drake savages cannot... they *do* not bear the blood of the divine."

Kasta took a pull from her cigarillo and shrugged. "No one does. But if I were you, I wouldn't base my view of a whole species off what they tell you in the Imperium. They probably tell you that the ancient houses were all Imperial."

Dresco grasped his knees. "Why, they were Imperial, Miss Krane."

Kasta's eyes narrowed. Though she attempted to maintain a straight face, a tremoring smile besieged her lips—and she erupted with an outbreak of laughter. "Norte, no!" She laughed so hard that she coughed. Her wide grin made her face ache. "Norte," she repeated, her blue-grey cheeks reddening. "You do know that Imperials did not exist when the ancient houses were formed?"

"Maybe not as a society or a species." Dresco spoke in a placid yet firm tone. "But we were always the chosen people of the Guardians. That is why we were given the Promised Land of the Imperium."

Kasta leaned forward. "The Promised Land of an endless blizzard?"

Dresco raised his voice. "And why we were given superior natural abilities. We are stronger, more resilient life-forms." His eyes turned from grey to cyan and his hair from brown to black. "And why we were given the ability to hide in plain sight."

Kasta's spine froze at the sight of Dresco mimicking her eye and hair color, though she did well to not show her dismay. "Listen here, my good sire." She blew a smoke ring. "The Imperials are not a chosen people. You were a bunch of religious freaks who decided you didn't want to live with all the *sinners* in Vanda. So, your kind moved. To the blizzard. Lo and behold, your ancestors evolved differently. But you're still a Vandeni, like it or not. Not Posaedian Vandeni anymore, but Vandeni nonetheless." She took another long drag. "Not to mention, I know for a fact that there is something y'all wish you still had in the Imperium that you lost up in those mountains..."

Dresco fidgeted, anticipating a conclusion to the statement. But Kasta sat in silence, allowing a thick cloud of smoke to filter through the gills on her neck. "Feel like going for a swim, Norte?" she asked through a tight-lipped smile.

Dresco looked away and crossed his hands. "Sacrifices must be made."

Kasta flicked the remaining inch of her cigarillo into the fire. She broke into grating laughter. "What are you talking about? No, they don't."

Dresco stood and grabbed his own blanket from the pannier that sat on the ground next to Crevallus. "Oh, I know deep down that you believe that as well. At least to a certain extent. Otherwise, you would have left me to be buried to death by that malicious mound of sand."

Kasta waved a limp finger and lifted her chin. "Don't fool yourself. I had a damn good reason for getting you out of there."

The knight shook a mantis spider out of his blanket. The long, thin creature scurried away. "Of course, you did. You do not believe in killing anyone. To have left me in that chamber would have been equal to murder." He laid the blanket flat on the ground, maintaining eye contact.

She rested her palms behind her and leaned back. "Sure, I had no reason to see you dead. But more importantly, Madame Vaeliz promised us eighty-five hundred platinum each—*each*—for bringing that map back to her." Kasta twisted her neck until she heard a crack and flipped her hair back. "For you stepping on that trap, and for me saving your skin, I'm taking twenty-five percent out of your reward." She bit her lower lip, awaiting a response.

"Fair enough." His face remained neutral. He lay on his back and released a loud yawn.

Kasta unbuckled her belt and tossed it by her leather jacket. She sprawled over her blanket. "Act more like me, Sir Norte, and you may survive Vanda yet."

Dresco crossed his arms, staring skyward. "You and I, we are nothing alike."

"I sure hope not."

VII
The Employer

Kasta and Dresco arose at a dragging, dreary pace. Their sleep was deep, though short. The duo collected themselves as well as their belongings before climbing atop their saddles and riding down the slopes.

They stopped in Barren Rock that afternoon. A doctor examined Kasta's ribs and hand. One of her ribs had a small crack that would heal in less than a week, thanks to her implants, so long as she avoided further impact to the injury. Her hand needed stitches but would also heal swiftly.

Following a protracted argument between Kasta and the doctor regarding the price of her treatments, Dresco suggested that they stay the night at one of the Barren Rock inns. The hunter refused, citing the need for a head start on the long journey ahead. Kasta visited the weaponsmith to have her pistol repaired. When nightfall came, she and Dresco made camp in the desert plains three hundred miles east of Barren Rock.

They rode out the next day when Athenis touched the sky. The star's light peeked through grey clouds. Soft rain dripped on the companions and their trugan. Kasta welcomed the sudden shift in weather. Athenis' heat and the desert's aridity were tiresome regularities. Dresco appeared unaffected by the elements. A chill breeze and grey clouds were a taste of home to an Imperial. The hunter pulled an old pair of goggles from her pannier. Though she preferred not to don eyewear, the raindrops struck like hale when riding at high speeds.

Dresco and Kasta rode over a narrow bridge; the water roared white below. They stayed the night in the small fishing town of Midway Lake. The town rested quiet and dim on the lakeside coast. The upper level featured dozens of wooden structures. The buildings sat on stilts, high above the lake. The rest of the village was underwater. Vandeni locals of Midway preferred spearfishing, opposed to modern techniques.

As daylight receded, the rainfall subsided, though grey clouds continued to wreathe overhead. Kasta sat on the deck of the shanty inn, lighting a cigarillo and pouring a shallow glass of whisky. Smoke and spirits masked the scent of the marshy freshwater.

Dresco complained that he was weary of riding cross-country. He nagged Kasta to instead arrange for passage on an airship.

"If you're too weak to travel, by all means, buy us passage on an airship," Kasta said. "I can ride across this whole continent without sleep. We're only stopping at night because you're an Imperial: big as a tower, fragile as glass." She laughed at her own quip.

Dresco dropped the subject.

The travelers again set out at daybreak, continuing east. The world of Eramaa unrolled the curtain of grey clouds. Clear, violet skies returned to view. The terrain flattened and the soil hardened; Dresco could better keep up.

The hunter spotted a wild desert hen while riding past a quarry. She grabbed her rifle and shot the bird mid gallop. 'One shot, one meal,' she thought.

They rode well into the night, deep into the Crystal Flats. The moonlight provided an explanation for their namesake. Small crystals sparkled across the vast plains, opposing the night sky as fallen stars.

The hunter and the knight made camp for the final night of their return journey. Their campsite rested in the center of the flats. Crystals of bright green and blue flickered in every direction. Purple and red minerals glinted between them. The soft breeze, the bright light of the moons and the gleaming crystals eased Kasta's mind. She drifted to sleep.

Athenis crested the summits in the far east. The sparkling crystals waned with the rise of dawn. A sheet of blue starlight disguised the terrain as a common Vanden flatland: dry, brown, and budding with succulent life.

They rode through a narrow valley, alongside a flowing creek. Kai's claws crunched the gravel with her stride. Crevallus forced his way to the stream, stricken with unquenchable thirst. Dresco's trugan was exhausted. But there was no use in stopping for an extended period. Their destination was near.

The travelers reached the end of the valley. After circumnavigating a sharp bend, the Vaeliz estate came into view. While not the tallest residential structure in the land, the building was long, stretching across the flats. Towers stood atop the uneven roof. The bronze-red walls protruded as semicylinders in successive rows. There were windows throughout, every set of five accompanied by a balcony. A half-mile-long garden stretched across the front of the property. Several guards patrolled the vegetation on truganback.

Two small structures stood next to the manor. The first was a stable, where Kaiar and Crevallus would find their accommodations for the evening. The second was a mushroom-shaped power generator.

A pair of glass cylinders connected the manor to the generator, feeding electricity to the estate and the rest of the property. Vines wrapped around the cylinders, outlined in an electric glow. Though the foliage looked to have grown by natural means, celestial blue flowers accented the spiraling plants in a neat pattern—a pattern that followed the vines until they came to a whittled end, draping over the oval doorway.

"It is so good to finally have reached our point of arrival." Dresco grabbed the bronze knocker and tapped it against the door three times in perfect rhythm. "One more day of riding and I think I would have lost both my body and mind."

Kasta crossed her arms and slouched sideways, her eyes straining on the door.

Dresco went on, "I could go for a hot bath. What about you?"

Her lips pursed.

"Oh, and how *lovely* does a nice bed sound? Silk sheets, a soft mattress."

With a deep breath and groan, she banged the circular knocker against the door five times, each rap harder than the last.

Dresco put his hand on Kasta's shoulder. "Oh, show some patience, Miss Krane. I am sure the Madame and her staff will get to us in due time. I personally am just looking forward to a night without having to sleep in the dirt, surrounded by invasive bugs. How about yourself?"

'I'm looking forward to a night without having to hear your impudent whimpering,' she thought with a roll of her eyes, though the words were on the edge of her tongue. The hunter shook Dresco's hand from her shoulder and wrapped her fingers around the doorknob. She swung the door open. A grunt vibrated through her teeth as she entered the manor.

"Wait!" Dresco said. "We cannot just barge in. We are guests in the Madame's home! We have to wait to be greeted."

She sniped him with the corner of her eye. "After all the hell you've given me about getting here as fast as possible because of our *ever* so *urgent* quest, you want to wait at the door all afternoon until a servant boy lets us in?"

Dresco's shoulders sank as he shook his head. "Well no, but we cannot be rude—"

"Oh, shut your damn mouth and get in here. I don't even want to hear it."

"But—"

"Don't want to hear it." Kasta turned around and continued into the lobby. Dresco's clanking footsteps followed behind, dragging on the black marble floors.

The front door closed behind the companions. A man came through one of the wooden doors on the other side of the room. "My good travelers," he said as he stumbled in, his white-gloved hands held limply in front of him. "Welcome, welcome."

"Hello, Juxel," Kasta said with a short lift of her head. "We're here to see the Madame."

"Of course, of course," Juxel said, bowing his head. "The Madame has been expecting your arrival, just not this early in the day. She will be with you very, very soon! I promise. I apologize greatly for the delay."

Dresco stepped in front of Kasta and removed his helmet. "Please forgive *our* intrusion, Master Servant. We should have waited for you to allow us entry."

"No, the fault is mine," Juxel said with a downward swipe of his arm. "I saw you approaching on our security monitors. I should have prepared the household more adequately."

Kasta looked up at Dresco, shaking her head with a measured blink. She stepped in front of the knight and unleashed a discreet yet vicious elbow to his forearm. This caused herself pain—not the armored knight—though she refused to show any sign of distress. "How long is Vaeliz gunna be, Jux?" she said with a sharp breath.

"Not long, Kasta. Not long. She is just finishing up a business meeting via transmission." The man's bowtie stuck out with his chest as he crossed his arms behind his back. "Can I get you anything while you wait?"

"No," Kasta said. She stepped toward the spiraling staircase.

Dresco leaned toward Juxel and muttered, "I would actually adore a glass of cold water."

"Right away," Juxel said. "And may I take your helmet, sire?"

"Oh, yes please. Thank you so very much." Dresco's voice turned to a higher pitch, which sent a sneer to Kasta's face. She leaned on the railing at the bottom of the staircase and let out a long sigh.

Moments later, Juxel hurried back through the door. "My good travelers, I just received word that the Madame will see you now. Please allow me to escort you to her."

" 'Bout time," Kasta said, pulling up her jacket by the lapels.

A younger servant followed Juxel into the lobby and placed a glass of liquid in Dresco's hand. "Your iced water, sire," he said.

The knight gulped the water down and let out a loud "Ahhhhhh."

The hunter and the knight followed Juxel up the spiral stairs to the third floor. The steps led to a long hallway decorated by a maroon carpet. Elegant paintings and rare artifacts rested under bright lamps.

"You see that one?" Kasta pointed to a miniature electrum tree engraved with ruby vines atop a display pedestal. "I found that for Vaeliz a while back. Buried at sea with the ancient pirate lord, Gorvak."

"Hm," Dresco said, turning toward the sculpture. "Very interesting. The good Madame is a fine collector indeed. A true preserver and conservator of history."

Kasta was quick to add, "And of money."

"No, no," Dresco insisted. "She has accumulated wealth, but she is an ally of the Guardians. A true representative of their will."

"Mhmm," Kasta said. "And what about when she herself was a pirate? Was that the Guardians' will she was acting out then?"

"Well." The knight squeezed his opposite wrist. "Our past is not all that defines us. Transfiguration is a virtue. She has put that life behind her. She has awoken—reborn."

Kasta's eyebrows rose high. She pointed toward a painting on the wall. "I guess not that far behind her." The painting featured a young blue-skinned woman. She held a pistol over her shoulder, aimed skyward. The rendered figure stood at the stern of a rugged ship, dressed in leather slacks and a tight blue corset.

Dresco gazed at the painting. "Hmm." He stopped in his tracks. "I suppose we must keep reminders of our sins, so we do not repeat them."

Kasta chuckled. "Sure, let's go with that."

The travelers came to a chrome door at the hallway's end. "The Madame is waiting for you inside," Juxel said.

Dresco thanked the servant. Kasta cracked her neck and stepped forward. A low-pitched sound hummed from the automatic door before it opened, receding inside the crevice above.

The circular room was dim, an intentional effect; the crystal chandelier overhead was half lit. A grand round table sat in the center of the room. On the opposite side stood a raven-haired woman in a black dress accented by azure stripes along the bodice. The dress had large shoulder pads and left an open space along her collar bone, revealing the blue tone of her skin. While Kasta was tall for a female Vandeni, the woman at the opposite side of the table stood over her by at least four inches.

As the hunter and the knight approached the table, the woman in black's angular face glowed with a wide smile. "Kasta Krane and Dresco Norte." She took a quick breath, though her smile did not break. "It is a pleasure to see you, my friends."

"Madame," Kasta said with a long blink and tip of her hat.

"Madame Vaeliz." Dresco bowed low. "Thank you for gracing us with the honor of your presence."

Vaeliz put her hand out and shook her head. "The best treasure hunter in Vanda and the greatest knight of the Imperium are in my service. The honor is mine."

Kasta's head tilted. "Just out of curiosity, does your criteria for the greatest knight in the Imperium include stepping on obvious traps?" She angled her thumb toward Dresco. " 'Cause that's what this one did. Must be a low bar."

Vaeliz looked to Dresco with a skeptical glare. "This sounds like an entertaining tale."

Dresco had trouble maintaining eye contact with the Madame. "It really is not."

"Oh, but it is," Kasta said. "I had to save him from certain death. Don't worry, I'm docking his pay. A life that brings profit is a life worth saving, am I right?"

Vaeliz crossed her hands in front of her waist. "However, the important thing is that ye managed to obtain the map, if I am to properly understand."

"I got it all right here," Kasta said with a chuckle. She reached into her jacket pocket for her mobile data system. "Managed to capture enough digital images before Dresco set off the trap."

"Let's have a look," the Madame said with her hand extended.

Kasta approached Vaeliz and placed the data system in her hand. The Madame connected the device to a larger data system embedded into the surface of the desk. The room dimmed, and a beam of light emitted from the center of the table.

The viridian-green of Vaeliz's eyes glistered in the darkness. Amber light outlined crude shapes. These shapes transformed into geographical landmarks, bringing a wide smile to her face. The room brightened in the light of a three-dimensional projection of the map from the Temple of Jellinok. "My good mates, you may have actually found it. The map to Vellon's Blade. It is simply…"

"Magnificent." Dresco finished the sentence for her. The Madame was at a loss for words.

"Yes, exactly. Thank you, Sir Norte." Vaeliz appeared to choke up as she placed her index finger and thumb over her pointed chin. "Thank you, my friends. Thank you for bringing me this great treasure."

"Thank me with your platinum." Kasta strode along the table's perimeter, her boots thumping against the marble floor.

Vaeliz leaned closer to the map. A slight smile slid up her cheek. "Do I not always, lassie?"

The hunter flashed a single nod.

"So." Dresco leaned over the table, his finger tapping against the edge. "Can the Relic's location be determined?"

"We shall find out, mate," Vaeliz said. She looked to a small digital chart, projected beneath the map. "The continents have greatly shifted since the ancient Vandeni crafted this map. The data system is attempting to calculate where it leads."

"Ain't no one I've ever seen better at reading a treasure map than the Madame here." Kasta crossed her arms. "Honest question. Is that a pirate skill or a rich-girl skill?"

The Madame let out a soft chuckle.

Dresco's head dipped. "Must you *always* be so disrespectful?" He flashed Kasta an impotent glare.

"Must you always be so dull?" Kasta fired back.

Dresco fidgeted. "This is a woman of honor. To suggest that she learned how to locate holy objects by means of piracy is blas—"

"I learned how to read treasure maps at sea, Sir Dresco."

Kasta slapped her hands together. "Ha! I knew it."

A smile fell on the Madame's face again.

Dresco cleared his throat and released a deep sigh. "Then I stand corrected."

"Yeah, ya do," Kasta said. Her attention turned to Madame Vaeliz. "Anyway, back to important issues. What's the verdict on that old map?"

"Well, Kasta." Vaeliz's green eyes beamed upward. "This is like no treasure map I have ever beheld. It is enhanced by some unknown technology—possibly even by a lost magic. The charting and diagrams are unscathed by time; there are no signs of decay or aging. The markings are of ancient religious text, referring to the most powerful of the Guardians' Relics. This map leads to treasures far beyond platinum or precious gems. It leads to Vellon's Blade."

Kasta's jaw descended. "Magic? Madame, I know you like the ancient Guardian myths, but you can't possibly believe them. You are *far* too smart to point to some unexplained tech from an old temple and conclude that it's magic."

Dresco approached Kasta, his chin elevated. "Ah, but that is what you fail to understand, Miss Krane. There is science in the magic, particularly in the magic of the Relics. They are gifts from the Guardians. Elixirs of our essence."

Kasta's eyes rolled as she spoke through clenched teeth. "If this is about to become another religious rant, I can just go ahead and leave now—"

The Madame intervened. "Ten thousand years ago, the Guardians crafted the Seven Relics. They descended from the cosmos, presenting them to their offspring. The Guardians left their descendants with the onus of upholding balance and peace on Eramaa."

"Yep, it's a religious rant." Kasta sighed, looking to the floor. "And it's coming from the both of ya. Do you two ever think about how difficult it is to consistently be the only sensible one in the room?"

The Madame's long neck stretched toward Kasta. "Each of the Seven Relics has its own unique role and abilities, but the sword, that is the most important."

Kasta's eyelids stretched apart as she dragged her fingers down her cheeks. "Really, I've never heard this story before. It's super interesting. Please continue..."

Dresco, not fluent in the ancient language of sarcasm, was delighted to grant her request. "Well, Vellon's Blade binds the other six Relics together! It maximizes and centralizes their power."

Kasta attempted to interrupt, but Vaeliz spoke first. "All those thousands of years ago, the Seven Houses of the Guardians defeated the Etsinnae using the Seven Relics. Those hellions attempted to take our world, but the descendants of the Guardians sent those creatures back to the darkest part of the cosmos from which they came."

"But the Etsinnae promised to one day return," Dresco said, crossing his arms. "The Imperium pledged itself to protect the will of the Guardians and defend against forces such as the Etsinnae, but the Order are no longer pure. They are seeking the Relics. And they are not doing so for divine reasons."

The map zoomed in around a mountainside. "We must find the ancient Relics, find them before the Imperium does, Kasta. The Order has already opened excavation sites throughout the continent." Vaeliz's eyes moved between the map and the hunter. "The ancient Relics are essential to the defense of this world. And—"

"And they can only be properly used by descendants of the Seven Houses of the Guardians!" Kasta yelled over the Madame. "So, unless you have found a descendant of the House of Vellon, none of this really matters, does it?" After releasing a deep breath, she carried on with a tamed voice. "Yes, I know all about your fairy tales. I just don't believe them. Because I'm an adult. The Seven Houses made up stories about being descendants of deities to scare the common folk away from challenging their authority." She flashed Vaeliz a sideways glance. "Madame, how can you, a woman of candor and reason, believe any of this?"

Dresco flinched and turned away.

Vaeliz graced the hunter with a slight smile. The white gem on her ring sparkled in the glow of the map. "Kasta," she said, using the control panel to zoom in on the display. "This appears to *indeed* be the map to Vellon's Blade. It points to what is now known as the Tomb of Saigus."

"Best news I have heard all day." Kasta snapped her fingers, though her glove muted the sound. "Seventeen thousand platinum, I believe we agreed upon."

"Yes," Vaeliz said. She cycled through the data system on her desk. "And, if ye would please remind me, how am I dividing this up?"

"Ten thousand six hundred twenty-five to me," Kasta said, pointing to herself. "The rest to the sand-trap magnet over here." She motioned toward Dresco.

Vaeliz goggled at the knight.

"Yes, that is fine," he said, wringing his wrist.

Kasta picked up her mobile data system. Her reward was already in her account. A wide smile came over her face, and a warm feeling grew in the pit of her stomach. "Well, Madame, I guess I best be on my way. It's a big world out there. Lots of pretty treasures and ugly perps that folks will pay good coin for me to bring in."

Vaeliz glanced over her shoulder. "Kasta, I want you to bring me Vellon's Blade."

"Damn it!" Kasta looked toward the ceiling. Her hat lurched back. "I knew you were gunna say that."

The Madame stepped around the table, her dress flowing with her stride. "Kasta. Come on, lass. I'll pay ye eight thousand platinum just to look. One hundred thousand if ye find it."

Kasta shook her head. "There's no way I'm gunna find it, though. This is ridiculous. It's a magical sword for Athenis' sake. Not to mention, I could get two hundred thousand platinum from any lyceum if I could convince their so-called 'scholars' that I was handing them an ancient Relic."

Dresco stood tall, clenching the hilt of his sword. "We found the map. We could just as easily find the blade."

"I don't think so," Kasta said. "I have some other job offers that look more... fruitful. Eight thousand platinum is nice but barely enough of a security blanket to cover my potential costs. And honestly, I think Dresco and I could use a break from each other. Forever."

Dresco groaned. "Send me instead. There is no reason I cannot retrieve the blade on my own."

Vaeliz's face tightened, her eyes locking onto the knight. "Dresco, you know that is not an option."

The knight looked toward the table. His shoulders slouched low.

Kasta turned from her employer and her companion. She began to take long, slow steps toward the door. "I think I'm out, folks. Good luck saving the world and stuff. Believe it or not, I really mean it."

Vaeliz shouted with an atypical tension in her voice, "Kasta Krane, I will pay you four hundred thousand platinum if you and Sir Dresco bring me that sword."

Kasta looked over her shoulder, meeting Dresco's eyes. "My good knight, we ride out in the morning."

VIII
VULTURE

The Vaeliz estate held an array of amusements. The hunter feast-ed on generous portions of raw fish, garnished with expensive herbs and marinated dressings of delicacy. Unphased by the elegance of her surroundings, Kasta's lips smacked together with each chew. After gulping a glass of white wine, she slouched back and lit a cigarillo. The servants surrounded the table, offering a selection of decadent desserts.

Around midnight, the hunter paced to her quarters and turned in. She tossed her clothing, pistol and gear over the back of a velvet chair before she collapsed on an emperor-size bed and sprawled on pearl-white silken sheets. She had forgotten a surface could be so soft.

The hunter's eyelids twitched as morning light grazed her face. Her breath attacked her tongue, tainted with the taste of malted whisky. Kasta tossed her legs over the side of the bed and massaged her temples, though it did little to alleviate the pulsating pain within her skull.

She groaned, tramping into the water closet. Putting her lips under the sink faucet, she gulped down several mouthfuls of water. Kasta pulled her head back when her neck stiffened. A hiccup interrupted her pant-ing. As water and cold sweat dripped down her chin, she looked in the mirror. The whites surrounding her glowing cyan eyes were bloodshot.

She needed a shower. A long, cold shower. Refreshment would be necessary before the next journey. After bathing, she rested a towel over her damp hair and returned to the bedroom. Someone had folded her clothing and placed it atop the velvet chair. 'The servants must have done some dry cleaning for me,' she thought as she lifted her shirt, now smooth and soft. The staff was, however, careful not to touch her weapons or equipment.

Once dressed, she drew her pistol and gave it three twirls. The weapon clicked into its holster. With a loud yawn, she exited the room and treaded down the hall.

While her clothing felt clean and fresh, she did not. She would need to rehydrate herself throughout the morning. A servant passed on the other side of the hallway. "Hey," Kasta called out. "Where's the Madame and silver boy? In the dining room?"

"In the conference room, ma'am."

Kasta nodded and continued walking. Her head tilted sideways. 'Why are they in the conference room without me?' she wondered, squinting an eye. 'Group prayer?' The spiral staircase had a dizzying effect. She exhaled as her feet touched the carpeting of the third floor, her breath tinged with the whisky in her gut.

Kasta dragged her feet down the hall, back to the conference room. Raised voices seeped through the cracks of the chrome door. With her back to the wall, Kasta sidestepped closer, avoiding the automatic sensor. She removed her hat and pressed her ear to the doorway.

"I cannot possibly understand what you see in her, Madame." Though the metal barrier muffled his voice, it did not hide Dresco's inflection. "She is a bounty hunter. She has no business dealing in important affairs such as these."

Vaeliz responded, "She is also an exceptional archeologist, Sir Norte. You have seen that yourself."

"She is a bounty hunter first." Dresco paused. "She insisted on taking a whole two days to hunt some convict through the Vanden plains. No matter how many times I reminded her of the importance of retrieving the map, or how many times I brought it to her attention that she was stalling our quest, she *still* insisted on chasing this... this bounty."

"I know she can be stubborn." Compared to Dresco's, the Madame's voice was velvet. "And that she has her own way of doing things, but that is why I have ye with her, Sir Dresco. To keep her in line and on track."

Dresco fired back, "She does not care what I think. She has made that abundantly clear. I am reminded what a nuisance I am with no lack of frequency."

"But the two of ye got the job done." the Madame said. "I knew it would be rough at first, but I trust ye both to work out your differences. Dresco, think of what we have accomplished already. We have the map!"

"It does not change the fact that we are placing the fate of the world in the hands of someone who does not even care about it!"

"Dresco, that's not true—"

"It is true! She is an arrogant narcissist who is motivated solely by greed and material gain."

Kasta's hand wrung the handle of her pistol as the Madame said, "She saved your life, did she not?"

Dresco pretended to hold in a chuckle. "Yes, to take part of my 'cut.' As you heard, she was very proud of that." A sigh slipped between his words. "We have to find someone else. She is not an acceptable choice to bear this—"

"Dresco!" Vaeliz cut him off. "There is no one else. Trust me. Kasta Krane is our only option."

After the ensuing silence, Kasta made her entrance. "Am I interrupting anything?" she said as the door rose over her head.

Dresco gasped and took a step back. "Oh my! Good morning to you, Miss Krane."

"Cut the act, Norte. I could hear your whole conversation through the door," Kasta said. "And, Madame, you should seriously consider better soundproofing. For such a high-tech door, it doesn't shield all that much noise."

Dresco and Vaeliz locked eyes. Neither formulated a word.

Kasta rested her palms at the edge of the table. "I think I have heard enough of Dresco's true feelings about me for the morning, so if you are ready to depart, my *oh so* honorable knight, I am as well."

Dresco began to speak. "Did you—?"

"Sir Norte, did you not hear? Kasta has heard enough," the Madame interrupted with a soft, yet stern tone.

Dresco flashed the Madame a short nod. "Miss Krane, I shall have the trugan ready." The knight swallowed. "I am sorry," he whispered, walking past her.

"My name is not Miss Krane for the *final* time, Norte." She rolled her eyes, though did not turn to face him. "Just Kasta. It's short, simple and easy to remember. Kasta."

"Of course," he said before the automatic door sealed with a sliding clash.

Kasta's head lowered. "Appreciate the confidence, Madame. But to suggest I need some prudent crusader to babysit me—" She chuckled as their eyes met. "Well, Madame, that's just insulting."

The Madame stepped around the table. "I meant it," she said. "You are the best. But Kasta, you know how important this is to me. To you, this is just another job. Dresco, although he may be a thorn in your side, understands the importance of this task."

Kasta crossed her arms. "Madame, have I ever let you down?" Her eyes rolled in an indolent semicircle.

Vaeliz placed her hands over the hunter's shoulders. "Never. But neither has Dresco, and I need ye both for this."

Kasta's smile blended with a sour curl of her upper lip. "Whatever you say, Madame. You gave me a job, I'm gunna do it. Even if you are making me take along a foolish zealot with less treasure-hunting experience than a junk dealer." With a tip of her hat, she walked toward the exit of the conference room.

"Kasta," Vaeliz called out. "He can help you as you can help him. I trust you will find a way to function cohesively."

The hunter raised her eyebrows, looking back with an elongated blink. "You're the boss. If you want me to bring the knight, I'll bring the knight. Just don't forget who does the work out there."

"Good luck to ye, mate," the Madame said as the automatic door sealed shut.

Kasta's boots crunched the gravel path in front of the manor, her canteen swishing at her waist. The stable lay ahead. She stepped through the doors to find Dresco tugging on Kai's reins, his feet planted in the dirt.

"What are you doing, greenhorn?" Kasta asked. She placed a bag of supplies on the ground.

Dresco pulled on the reins. He reached for the straps on Kai's saddle with his other hand. "I am trying to—" Kai butted her head into Dresco, sending him stumbling back. "I am trying to put your beast's saddle on, but she is fighting me at every step."

Kasta's eyebrows rose. She reached into her jacket pocket for a cigarillo.

Dresco pulled harder on the reins, his teeth clenching. "Settle down. I am not going to harm you." Kaiar stood tall and roared. The knight flinched and raised his arms, shrinking back.

Crevallus prowled the stable, circling the knight. The reptilian beast's tongue flickered. A sharp hiss passed through his lips.

"Oh, you best not interfere, you disobedient mechanical lizard. I will deal with you next!" he said, pointing toward the male trugan.

"Dresco," Kasta muttered, lighting her cigarillo.

Dresco held his breath and crept toward Kaiar. He attempted to fasten one of the saddle straps around her neck.

The slit pupils of Kai's eyes narrowed. Her fangs sundered her snarling lips.

Dresco shook his head as his shoulders sank. "Why must you oppose me, foul beast?"

"Dresco," Kasta said, her eyes fixed on the smoke rings passing through her lips. "Maybe she's fighting you because you have her saddle on backward?"

Dresco stroked his chin, studying the saddle, which lay on Kaiar's back. It was lopsided. Unanatomical. "Oh, yes. Of course," he said, clearing his throat.

Kasta placed a hand over her opposite arm. "Why not just wait for me? Or better yet, have the stableboy take care of it?"

Dresco looked down. His foot tapped in the dirt. "I do not know." He sighed and shook his head. "I wanted to contribute more, I suppose."

The stableboy moved to put Kaiar's saddle on in the proper direction. Kasta smiled. She picked up her supply bag. "Dresco, if you need help with something like that, all you gotta do is ask."

"With all due respect, Kasta," Dresco said with a delicate tone. "You are not the most approachable person. I figured that if I asked you for guidance, it would lead only to insult or your own irritation."

Kasta tightened the supply bag on the pannier. She looked to Dresco with a stern glare. "You may be insulted, and I may be irritated, but I'll still show you." Her rifle and supplies were secure. After climbing atop the saddle, she faced the knight again. "And Dresco," she said, leaning toward him. "If you have a problem with me, say it to my face." She gave Kai's reins a slight tug. The beast trudged toward Dresco, who held his helmet tight to his torso. "But don't you ever badmouth me to an employer again. And definitely not to Madame Vaeliz."

Dresco stammered. His lips fell to a frown. "Kasta, no. You do not understand—"

"Never again!" Her teeth clenched. The leather of her glove tightened across her fingers as she pointed at him. "We clear on that?"

With a swallow, he slouched and whispered, "Yes, we are clear."

"Good," Kasta said. Kai turned to face the violet horizon. "Saddle up. We ride for Vulture."

"Vulture? We need to get to the tomb and find the sword. Miss Krane, why would we go to Vulture? That city is not even in the same direction!"

"Hyah!" Kasta bent forward and kicked her stirrups into Kai's midsection. Dresco's voice was out of audible range within seconds.

After passing the property line, she leaned into the canyon's turns. Kaiar roared with excitement, tearing apart the terrain. When they exited the canyon, the real thrill began. "Woohoo!" Kasta yelled into the wind as Kai accelerated through the flatlands at full gallop. The hum of circuitry underneath the trugan's skin was smooth and high pitched. All mechanizations were functional.

A crackle came over Kasta's communication system, dampening her enjoyment. "Kas—*Crrh-Excu—Crrrhhk-Crrch-Crrh*." The satellite connection indicator on her optical display flashed a red bar, meaning that the signal was weak. She slowed down, allowing a better connection.

Dresco's voice patched through. "Kasta, why are we going to Vulture? I at least deserve to know that much."

She activated the microphone. "I have a contact in Vulture: Marshal Jos. The Tomb of Saigus is in a valley that is swarming with bandits. He knows how to navigate that area without running into too much trouble. So, we're gunna ride down to the charming confines of ol' Vulture."

Dresco's voice buzzed through the speaker, muffled though decipherable. "But we have already wasted so much time! You heard the Madame. The Imperium has been attempting to excavate the sacred Relics. If they find Vellon's Blade before we do—"

"What are you getting so worked up about? That sword has been in the same place for thousands of years. Legendary treasure hunters and respected archeologists have failed to find convincing evidence that Vellon's Blade even exists. Do you really think a bunch of bureaucrats are gunna be the ones to dig it up?"

"You do not know the Imperium as I do."

"I can't argue with you there," Kasta said with a subtle smirk. "So, let's keep moving. Less talking, more riding." She slapped the reins on the back of Kai's neck. With a roar, the beast increased her gallop speed. "Catch up, Norte. If we keep a good pace, we'll be there just after nightfall."

A light drizzle began to fall. The skies did not turn to gloom or grey with the rainfall; the thin clouds combined with the violet welkin to create a warm shade of lavender. The crimson leaves and the purple blossoms of the surrounding Galaemia trees welcomed the drizzle. Drops of water seeped off the vibrant petals as tears of joy.

Kaiar came to a halt as a herd of livestock crossed their path. The group of slow-passing white oxen allowed the hunter to pause and listen to the whisper of the rain, as well as time for Dresco to catch up. As Kai drank from a puddle, Kasta took a long look at the uneven rows of Galaemia trees. Their slender branches stretched long and blossomed with a flourishing breadth. Kasta smiled as the sweet scent of their blooms danced across her mind.

Morning turned to afternoon. The travelers passed a prairie sprouting with blue grass from end to end. A group of hunters hid within the tall, blue blades, decked in camouflage. Kasta flashed the small light on Kai's saddle to alert the hunters of their passing. "Roar, girl," she yelled.

Kai's jaws widened. She released a growl that rose in pitch until it became a deafening screech.

The three hunters turned. One raised his arm in a limp wave. In the distance on top of a flat rock stood the hunters' intended prey.

"Idiots," Kasta whispered. 'They're trying to hunt a saber-tooth cougar with short-range weapons. Those cats are too fast and too sly for short range. It'll escape before they get a shot off. Or it'll kill them.'

Night fell over the travelers. Though the sky held few clouds, the stars were reluctant to reveal themselves. "May we stop for rest?" Dresco asked. "My back cannot take any more riding."

"You're in luck." Kasta looked over at the knight, who sat hunched atop his trugan's back. "We're coming up on our destination."

Less than fifteen minutes later, hundreds of neon lights flooded the sky in an untraceable and infinite rhythm—slinking, shifting, swirling.

"By divinity itself," Dresco said with a gasp. "Is there some sort of celebration this evening?"

Kasta laughed. They veered onto the wide road leading toward the city. "No, my good knight. That's just the bright lights of Vulture. Their welcoming mat, if you will."

"That is a rather flamboyant welcoming mat." Dresco pulled Crevallus hard to the right as a cluster of opposing traffic swerved into his lane. "My goodness, and of course they're riding drunk."

Kasta leaned forward in laughter, resting her head on Kai's neck. "We're not even in the city yet. Just wait until we're downtown."

"Oh, I am sure it is charming."

The lights grew more vivacious, outlining metropolitan structures. Though not tall enough to scrape the sky, the towers cast a glowing shadow around Vulture. The lights circled and streamed up the buildings in shades of purple, yellow, green, blood-red, back to purple again. The array of colors could spellbind wandering eyes and lost souls.

An ocean of chatter and galloping resounded throughout the streets as they entered Vulture. Laughter was not a scarce commodity, nor was the stumbling of pedestrians across the grated sidewalks.

"What is that trenchant smell?" Dresco asked. The trugan's steps clanked against the bronze-laden roads. "It is like burning sulfur mixed with alcohol."

Kasta looked to him. "It's a mix of the factories a couple streets over and the smoke shop right over there." She pointed to a wide building. A gathering of men and women stood outside, dragging on varying types of cigars and steamers. "Oh, and just... alcohol. You're also just smelling alcohol."

"Right," Dresco uttered. He fidgeted in his saddle, shaking his head. While his eyes studied a weapons store with a neon-blue sign, a pair of women on the sidewalk called to him.

"Look what we got here, an Imperial Knight," one of the women said. The other leaned toward the street, hand on her hip. "Can we interest you in any fun?"

Dresco mumbled to himself.

"Not tonight, ladies," Kasta said with a tip of her hat.

"Too bad," the second woman said.

The travelers rounded the corner and turned left. While narrower than the prior street, neon colors still dominated the avenue.

Overhead, a pair of tubes on each side of the road transferred bright bolts of electricity. The streams channeled downward and lit the lamps. Power-transfer cylinders also lay under the grated sidewalk, brightening the path from below. There was no shortage of businesses: general stores, weapon shops, liquor markets, banks, casinos, shipping centers; and most were open at all hours.

Kasta stopped Kai's gallop in front of a rectangular four-story building. The highest floor's outside wall was plated with gold. She climbed off her trugan and led her to a trough. Kai wasted no time burying her face into the water.

Dresco stumbled off Crevallus' back and pulled the trugan's horn to prevent a loss of balance. Crevallus groaned and headbutted the knight. Dresco tripped backward and almost fell into the trough. "Forsaken creature. You will learn to obey me, beast," Dresco barked, pointing in the trugan's face. A pair of men sitting on the deck laughed at the knight.

Kasta chuckled as well. "Not if you keep talking to him like that, he won't."

A stagecoach passed the travelers by as Dresco stretched his legs. Kasta sent a message using her mobile data system. Two grey titan wolves led the stagecoach. The driver was an Imperial, dressed in a thin jacket and dress slacks.

"Guardians' blessings upon you, sire," the driver said with an extension of her hand.

Dresco stepped forward, bowing his head to the woman in the carriage. "And may their light find you, my sister." He turned to Kasta and removed his helmet. A tight smile rested on his face. "Leave it to a wholesome Imperial merchant to know how to properly speak to a knight of the Guardians."

Kasta held a blank stare before turning away. "Yeah, whatever," she said with a cough. "Let's get going." She moved up the stairs toward the building's entrance.

"A tavern?" Dresco said from behind. "We are going to meet your marshal in a tavern?"

"No, no, no." Kasta set foot on the wooden deck and turned to face him. "We're meeting Marshal Jos tomorrow. We're going in here to have a drink."

"Tomorrow?" Dresco stomped up the stairs and cut in front of her. "We rode all the way out here in one day when we are not meeting him until tomorrow anyway?"

"That is exactly right," Kasta said with a tilt of her head. "This is the best damn saloon in Vanda. We're gunna have ourselves a blast. Then tomorrow, we'll get back to work."

Dresco shook his head, crossing his arms across his chest. "I do not understand you, Miss Kra... Kasta. We could have just spent another night in the Madame's manor if you wanted to waste more time."

After taking several long strides, she passed Dresco by, bumping his shoulder. "I didn't wanna stay in the manor another night."

The small sign above the entrance read "Vulture's Creek." Kasta pushed the swinging door open and entered the saloon.

IX

THE HUNTED

Dozens of smoky aromas burned into Kasta's nose as the doors swung closed behind her. Patrons turned their heads from their drinks and card games. The sound of clinking glasses, belligerent laughter and the crawling rhythm of the three-piece band brought a grin to Kasta's face.

"Well, well," a voice to the left said. "If it isn't the Merciful Hunter."

Kasta looked through the dim ochre lighting and thick clouds of smoke. It was the bartender who had spoken to her, outfitted in a top hat and shimmering copper-red vest.

"Top of the evening, Vera," Kasta said with a tip of her hat as she approached the bar. Her footsteps met the granite floors with a deadened rapping.

"Shall I get you a whisky?" Vera asked with a wide smile and tilt of her head.

"You know me too well for my own good." Kasta leaned over the navy-blue wooden bar. "Whisky indeed, my dear friend. Indulge me with a couple rocks and only your very finest."

Vera turned around and stood on the tips of her toes. She reached to the highest shelf behind the bar. "The quality of your whisky is, as always, determined by the shade of your coin." The bartender's voice strained as her arm stretched.

"And as always," Kasta said out of the side of her mouth, reaching into her pocket, "the shade of my coin is platinum." She tossed five platinum coins atop of the bar as if she were making a wish to a fountain. "Keep the change, partner."

"Don't mind if I do," Vera said with a wink as she popped open the whisky bottle. A steady stream of spirits flowed into a crystal glass over two spherical pieces of ice. "So, what brings you to these parts, Krane?" Vera asked, placing the bottle under the bar.

"Work, as always." Kasta's left hand wrapped around the glass and brought the first sip of whisky to her lips. 'Ah, that blissful burn,' she thought. From behind, a distinguishable stomp approached. "Hey, there you are," Kasta said, spinning her glass in a circle. "I thought for a minute that you weren't going to come in."

Dresco stood near the bar and pivoted, his arms stiff at his sides. "What kind of rabid lair of decadence and abominations have you brought me to?"

Kasta pulled up the nearby leather barstool, which matched the blue counter, and sat down. "Will you just relax for once, Norte?" She looked to the knight and shrugged a shoulder. "Sit down. Have a drink."

Dresco shook his head. "I do not drink."

She sighed and placed her palm over her forehead. "Why does that not surprise me?"

Dresco's fist clenched. "It *should* not! I am a herald of the Guardians, not some gambler or drinker." He eyed the card tables, while Kasta's attention turned to her glass of whisky. Dresco carried on, pointing to a Vandeni woman in a tight leather corset. "Or some mercenary harlot hunter who cannot control basic, primitive urges."

Kasta laughed up some of her whisky and coughed into her fist. "Did you just say harlot hunter?" Her voice cracked. "That's hilarious. I'm gunna remember that one."

Dresco groaned. He scratched his elbow, though his armor covered it.

Vera leaned over the bar. "This one with you?" Her eyes narrowed on Dresco.

Kasta looked up at Vera, biting her lip. "Yep."

The bartender continued to gawk. "Is he going to a costume party or something?"

Kasta pointed at her. "That's what I said!"

Dresco shook his head and slouched over the bar. "I am a Knight of the Order of the Guardians," he said. "Or I was."

"Really?" Vera asked.

"Really," Kasta said with a single nod.

Vera looked to Kasta, reaching for a glass below the bar. "Never pictured you to be one to ride with an Imperial."

The hunter's eyebrows rose. "Me neither."

Dresco looked to the crowds of people sitting at the card tables and in front of the band. "You may not enjoy riding with me, but at least be grateful that you are not in the company of one of these Drake savages."

Kasta turned around and smacked Dresco on the shoulder. She scanned the area to make sure that no Draekalagons overheard his remark.

Vera did overhear. "Well," she said with disdain. "That was not a very knightly thing to say."

"Yeah, he's got some... issues," Kasta said.

Dresco tapped his armored finger on the counter. "Barkeep, if you would please bring me an ice water?"

Vera offered nothing but a blank stare.

"At your leisure of course," he said with a stutter.

"Coming right up," Vera said, inching toward the other end of the bar.

Dresco let out a soft groan. "Gosh, she is rude, is she not?"

"Mm, not really." Kasta nodded her head to the music, once per beat in each five-count measure. "She probably just doesn't like pretentious bigots."

"It is not bigotry if it is true."

"It's only true if you believe it." She let a mouthful of whisky rest on her tongue.

Vera stomped across from the other end of the bar and dropped a full glass in front of Dresco. "Your ice water, *sire*." The water overflowed onto the blue wood.

"Um, thank you so much," Dresco said.

"Mhmm, sure," Vera replied. She stepped to the side and began to clean a glass.

Kasta broke into laughter, her whisky hovering beneath her nose. She turned to examine the crowds. "I'm gunna go play some cards," she said with a shine in her eyes.

The knight removed his helmet and grabbed hold of his ice water. "Or you could just throw your money down a drain."

Kasta slammed her whisky on the counter and leaned his way. "Oh, come on. Play a game with me! Have some fun for once."

Dresco shook his head and brought the ice water to his chapped grey lips. After several sloshing gulps, he let out a loud "Ahhhhhhh." He smacked his lips together and looked to his companion. "I understand that you enjoy engaging in this... excessive behavior. However, I am not prone to such immaturities. If we are truly putting our divine quest on hold, I will just sit down and grab a bite to eat."

'Immaturities? Immature is pouting in the corner while you drown in a cesspit of your own intolerance,' were the words that sat at the tip of Kasta's tongue, though she resisted with all her willpower the urge to say them. "Try the elk melt," she said, her lips twisted. "It's the best in the region."

"I just might do that." Dresco snatched his water and stepped away.

Kasta kicked her stool back, letting her weight rest on the bar. "Vera," she said in a raspy voice. "Send another one of these to my table when you get a chance." She held up her half-empty whisky glass.

"You got it, Krane," Vera said with a wide grin.

"I'll pay you now." Kasta reached into her pocket.

"Nah," Vera said with a tap on Kasta's forearm. "On the house."

The hunter shrugged. "No argument from me." She spun around and kicked her chair out of the way. Vera giggled as Kasta scanned the card tables. 'Who can I steal money from tonight?'

A band of drunken mercenaries screamed at one another. "Easy targets, yes," she whispered through a sip of whisky. "But they'll want to duel me if I beat them." One table over, a group of four elderly Vandeni sat with a modest amount of chips before them. 'Too small time,' she thought. Then, Kasta spotted a group of three sitting in silence as the dealer passed cards around. Each player had at least two stacks of high-value chips. 'That's my table.'

The band's lyrics flowed through the crowd like a leaden wind:
Do you remember when the old town went down in flames of sin?
They were bathing in the fury of the feeling of the end
Then the rider came a ridin' through the town to find a friend
Instead he found a broken soul that time will never mend
Kasta's finger tapped to the beat on the handle of her pistol. The vocalist's low, hollow voice synced well with the miring tone of his bass

lute. The treble string player rocked back and forth with his eyes closed, possessed by his own distorted melodies. The percussionist's vicious treatment of his drums did not match his soft, wrinkled skin nor his skeletal shape.

Kasta reached the card table. "Mind if I join you, gentlemen?" she asked, leaning over the ebony wooden top of an empty chair.

"Anyone's welcome who can pay, ma'am," the dealer said, motioning toward the vacant seat. "Three hundred platinum buy-in."

Kasta reached into her pocket and grasped a pinch of coins. "Put me in for seven hundred." She tossed the coins toward the center of the table as she sat on the thin blue-velvet cushion of the chair.

A Draekalagon in a tan leather jacket sat to the right. He extended his clawed hand. "Allagog of Kohar." His voice bore a hissing tremor. "At your service."

"Kasta Krane." She offered a firm handshake and tip of her hat. The man and woman to her left did not introduce themselves, but Kasta was quick to strike up a conversation with them, nonetheless. "Let me guess, you two are married and on a vacation?"

The woman smiled and nodded, not saying a word. But her husband's limp, nervous posture provided Kasta with more information than their lips ever could. His nub-bitten fingernails scratched the surface of the table. Sweat had flattened his slicked-back hair. His bow tie sat crooked, tight as a noose around his collar.

'Too easy.'

The dealer dropped a stack of chips in front of Kasta and passed the cards around the table.

"You're the Merciful Hunter," Allagog said, adjusting his hat.

Kasta shrugged as she finished the last sip of her drink. "That's the name they gave me," she said with an ice sphere sitting on her tongue.

"I hope you live up to that name tonight." A grunting cackle seeped from Allagog's throat.

She peeked at her cards and grabbed the black and purple dice before her. "In cards, I am never merciful."

Luck was in favor. Kasta matched her cards to the board hand after hand. When the cards failed her, the dice did not. She was excellent in the double-down dice challenges. The chips built up in front of her and drifted away from her opponents. The waitress brought her second whisky. She ordered a couple of cigarillos, knowing that the saloon would feed the card players' vices to keep them playing.

She looked to Dresco, who sat alone in the corner with his hands clasped, one atop the other. Kasta had played the couple who sat to her left out of the game. She bested Allagog several times as well, but the Draekalagon kept reaching into his snakeskin satchel for more platinum.

A woman stepped into Kasta's peripherals. She wore a long, ruffled, sleeveless dress that carried patterns of black and burgundy. A thin cigarillo dangled from her fingertips as she placed her hand on Kasta's shoulder. "Hey, beautiful. Doing well tonight, I see."

Kasta looked up to see the woman's gleaming smile, magnified by her deep-red lipstick. Her eyes sparkled like emeralds. "That's the only way I know how to do it, kid," Kasta said.

Looming to the left was a man in a green suit. "We'll give you two for the price of one," he said, reaching into his double-button vest for a utility tool. "If you are looking for someone to celebrate your winnings with." His stone-faced glare did not shift while he lit Kasta's cigarillo.

As Kasta rotated the dice in her hand, the woman began to stroke her shoulder. "I've always wanted to spend an evening with a tomb raider," the woman said.

Kasta shook her head and blew out a stream of smoke. "Treasure hunter." Her arm wrapped around the slender waist of the woman. "Listen, kid, you guys are lovely. But I'm not really in the market for your services." She glanced at Dresco, who was beginning his meal. A smirk fell over Kasta's face as she pointed to her knightly companion. "Now, my friend over there..."

The man in green cleared his throat. "You mean the one in the tin garb?"

"Yeah," Kasta said with a single nod. "I'm sure he'd be *more* than thrilled to entertain your services."

The woman in black's hand slid off Kasta's shoulder. She watched Dresco like an avian scavenger. "He's enchanting." She swayed toward the knight. The man in green followed. The woman glanced back at Kasta through the corner of her eye. "Thanks for the suggestion, beautiful."

Kasta leaned back in her chair and offered a single wave. "Keep up the good work." A fresh hand was being dealt. She tapped the dealer and Allagog on the shoulder. "Hold the cards for a moment. You guys are gunna want to see this."

Kasta and the two men at the table looked on as the man in green and woman in black approached Dresco. The woman sat on Dresco's lap, and the man leaned over him. Dresco said nothing. He sat stiffly, dropping his elk-melt onto his plate.

"Oh, by the light of Vharris, he's horrified!" Kasta swirled her whisky around.

Dresco shook his head and swallowed hard. The woman's fingers danced up his chest and onto his neck. The man whispered something in Dresco's ear and played with his hair. Dresco shuddered and slid back, causing the woman to stumble. The knight shot up from his seat and caught the woman before she fell. He released her, shook his head and threw his hands up, pleading with them.

Kasta erupted into laughter, burying her face in her forearms atop the table. Allagog and the dealer let out a slight chuckle but did not find the situation as amusing. Across the establishment, Dresco wrung his hands together and sat down in front of his meal.

"Hey," Kasta said. "I'm gunna sit a few hands out."

Allagog's nostrils flared. He released a deep grunt. "But you're on a roll here," he said with a wide, fang-filled grin.

"Don't worry." She stood from her chair. "I'll go back to taking your money in a little while."

Kasta walked around a crowd of patrons watching the band, entranced by the music. The current song was still a five count, but it was faster, with a more aggressive bassline. Some onlookers danced to the rapid rhythm. Others drank and sang along to the best of their abilities.

Kasta came to the long wooden table where Dresco dined. She sat beside him on the bench with one leg on each side. "Hey," she said with a tap on his upper arm. "Did you strike out or what?"

Dresco pulled a napkin from his lap and wiped his mouth. "I suppose you think that was terribly funny." He ran his tongue through his teeth.

Kasta shrugged, causing her cigarillo to ash and a drop of her drink to spill onto the floor. "Come on, it was pretty funny. For a minute there, I thought you might actually take them up on their offer. Even just to be polite." She chuckled and reached to Dresco's plate for a baked sprout.

The knight shook his head. A slight frown rolled down his lips. The expression of displeasure faded when he took a large bite of his melt. "I am not one to spend evenings with harlots."

"Well, that's hardly surprising," Kasta said. "But I even found an Imperial for you." Her voice shook with amusement.

"He was no Imperial."

Kasta squinted and pursed her lips. "But his accent—"

"Was fake," Dresco proclaimed.

"But his grey skin—"

"Makeup."

Kasta's head bobbed from side to side. "I guess he was kind of short for an Imperial."

"Far too short," Dresco said, his mouth full.

"Well, even if you don't want a *harlot*, pick someone out. Anyone in here. I'll shepherd you in."

"No."

"And why not?"

Dresco sighed. "Because women are a territory that I do not have the time or energy for."

Kasta leaned back on the table with a crooked smirk. "You are not going to tell me that Dresco Norte, the charming and noble knight of the Guardians, is..." Dresco's eyelids shifted from wide open to a long blink before she finished her sentence. "Romantically challenged." She put a period on her statement with a forward thrust of her cigarillo.

"No." Dresco's voice climbed higher in pitch. "I reserve my love for universal compassion. And for the Guardians."

'Oh hell, I do not want to talk about religion right now,' Kasta thought. "How's the elk-melt?" she asked, pointing to Dresco's plate.

"Mmmm," he said, chewing a large bite. He brought the napkin to his face to wipe his lips. "It is fantastic. You were right."

Kasta stood with a grunt and cracked her neck. "Order me one of those, will ya? Rare with those baked sprouts. And a coral juice." Her eyes slanted toward the ceiling. "No! A coral juice with a splash of white rum." Dresco's lips parted. He ogled the half-full glass of whisky Kasta held in her hand. "Just a splash."

"I will order," he said with a bow of his head.

"That's what I like to hear. Now give me a few minutes." Kasta turned around and began to walk away. "I have some more coin to win."

"Krane," Dresco called out.

"Hmm?" She half turned to face him.

"Watch the lizard," he said, glancing at the card table. His lips tightened. "He is probably trying to cheat you."

Kasta's gaze froze on Dresco as she stood tall, her drink and cigarillo in the same hand. "He's an old businessman! He's the least of my concerns."

He leaned closer. "You can never trust a Drake."

"You can never trust anyone."

As Kasta walked across the establishment, she felt eyes on her. Not Dresco's. No, the eyes of someone in the crowd. She returned to her table. "Okay," she said. "Let's play some cards." With a swig of whisky, she smiled widely, though the feeling of being watched did not fade.

Kasta and Allagog continued to play their game. One more gambler joined in on the action. Kasta still did well, but she could not immerse herself, for someone approached.

The dealer cleared his throat. "Would you like to roll or play your hand, Kasta?" he asked.

Kasta's gaze orbited the frolicking crowd, passing the dealer as she took a deep breath. "I'll play my hand," she said. All cards were on the table. Kasta did not win the hand. Allagog jeered her, though the hunter's attention was not in front, but behind.

Footsteps. Footsteps drew near. Not the footsteps of a drunken rancher or an aggravated waiter, but slow, skulking footsteps. Footsteps that were not meant to be heard.

A new hand was dealt. Kasta did not look at her cards. No. Instead she grabbed hold of her whisky glass. A tight hold. Her turn came again. As the other gamblers tapped their fingers, awaiting her play, she heard a click. A type of click that only occurs when a holster unfastens.

"Kasta, will you please decide whether you want to play your cards or your dice?" the dealer pleaded.

She did not respond. The only sound that mattered was the footsteps, or lack thereof. The shot was coming.

The hunter spun around and used the momentum of the turn to throw her whisky glass. The glass rocketed across the saloon and struck a woman in the throat. She fell to the ground, grasping the area of impact.

The music stopped. Chatter turned to gasps and profanity. Kasta sprinted across the room. The woman she had struck lay face-first on the ground, a silver object in her right hand: a pistol. Kasta reached across her waist and drew her sword. She ignited its electrical current.

The woman croaked and coughed as her eyes peeled open. She saw Kasta standing over her. The attacker flipped over, aiming her pistol upward. Kasta swung her sword downward, launching the shock-cannon from her hand and cutting the barrel in two.

Three Vandeni raced across the floor, their own weapons drawn. "What's going on here?" one of them yelled.

Kasta was not sure whether they were guards or concerned onlookers. "This one tried to kill me," she said, stepping toward the assailant. The woman backed away on all fours, but Kasta unleashed a powerful punch into her cranium. Her gloves protected her hands from bruising, but not the woman from unconsciousness.

Dresco dashed through the crowd. He barreled his way to the front of the circle that had formed around Kasta, his hand on his sword. "What is going on? *Who* is trying to kill you?"

The hunter shook her head and sheathed her own blade. "A little late, Norte."

Vera stood atop the bar and yelled, "Damn it! Now I have to be the one to deal with this mess." Patrons lost interest in the situation. The guards encouraged them to return to their chosen recreations. Vera looked to Kasta with a furrowed brow. "I guess I'll contact the marshal's office." The band picked up the song where they had left off.

"Yes, but not yet," Kasta said. "I have some questions for her first."

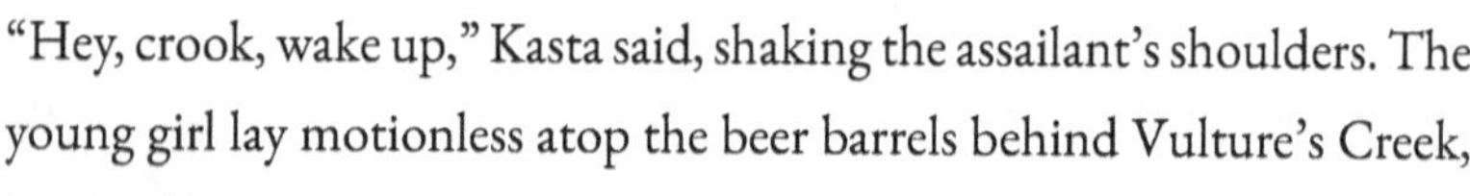

"Hey, crook, wake up," Kasta said, shaking the assailant's shoulders. The young girl lay motionless atop the beer barrels behind Vulture's Creek, her jaw hanging open.

"You pummeled her pretty good there, Krane," Vera said. The bartender stood with a limp grip on a long copper-toned rifle. "I don't think she's getting up."

Kasta grabbed a handful of the unconscious girl's pale-blonde hair. "Wake up, kid. I gotta talk to you. And I ain't got all night." After thrusting the woman's head back and forth, she pulled her eyelids apart with her pointer finger and thumb. "Come on, learn to take a punch."

"Ummm." Dresco approached from behind and cleared his throat. "Might I suggest that we take a moment to discuss the fact that someone just tried to murder you?"

Kasta rolled her eyes and turned around, her right hand clasping the unconscious woman's jaw. "Dresco, if you haven't noticed, I am attempting to discuss it right now—with the woman who tried to murder me."

He put his fingers to his forehead, massaging his brow. "Yes but, I mean... are you alright?"

"Fine, Dresco. Thanks." Kasta released her attacker. The young woman's chin thumped against hard oak. On the opposite side of the storage area, another stack of barrels leaned against the fence. "Vera, could you get me a cup?"

"Of course." Vera swanned into the saloon.

Kasta sat atop one of the barrels and looked to Dresco. A faint vibration pulsed through the wood: the bass lute rumbling from the saloon. "What is not fine is that you didn't see her coming."

The knight shook his head and stepped toward her; his boots chafed the gravel. "How would I have seen her coming? On that note, how in the name of Athenis' starlight did *you* see her coming?"

"Because I mind my surroundings, Norte." Kasta's palm clouted the barrel, swishing the beer within. "*You* were busy antagonizing all the Drakes in the room. Meanwhile, someone sneaks up and tries to take me out." She hopped to the tips of her toes, bringing herself face-to-face with the knight. "And you were completely unaware." She spoke through her teeth.

"I!" Dresco trembled and closed his eyes. Lowering his head, he whispered, "I am sorry."

"I don't want you to be sorry." Kasta flashed a tight-lipped smile. "I've watched your back since you started riding with me. Either do the same for me or go your own way."

The knight nodded.

Vera returned with a pint glass. Kasta swayed from Dresco's personal space, and he released a deep sigh. "Thanks," Kasta said, taking the mug.

"I will pay you for this." She stuck the mug under one of the barrels, filling it with beer.

Vera waved off Kasta's offer. "Nah, don't sweat it, Krane. I can't be having a reckless canonslinger coming through here, aiming for my best customers."

Kasta topped off the glass. After taking a sip, she trudged toward the incapacitated woman. "That's why I keep coming back. Pristine service." She slung the contents of the glass onto her attacker's face. The girl's eyes shot open. With a sharp gasp, she flew into a sitting position.

"Morning, kid," Kasta said. She drew her pistol and pointed it at the girl. "Nice of you to join us."

Dresco stepped closer. The attacker took long, deep breaths. Her hand crept toward her beltline.

"No, no, no," Kasta said with a thin smirk. "I cut your shock-cannon in half, remember? You have no weapons of any kind anywhere on ya. Not even that little knife you had in your boot. Very cute." Kasta's pistol hand extended farther. "So, you and I, we're gunna have a little chat."

The attacker shook her head and fidgeted. "You... you're the Merciful Hunter. You ain't gunna kill me." She crossed her legs, shaking her head once more. "I ain't tellin' you nothin'."

Kasta shrugged, pursing her lips. "Well, kid. You ain't wrong on that. I'm not known for killing my targets. *But* you see Vera back there?" The aim of the bartender's rifle rested over the young woman's slender torso. "This is her saloon that you tried to discharge your weapon in. Vera, what do you do when someone fires a shock-cannon in your saloon?"

"Kill them," Vera said with a cold tremor in her voice. "On sight."

The back of Kasta's hand covered the side of her mouth. "I've seen her do it. She's a pretty damn good shot."

The attacker's eyes turned misty. Cold beer dripped from her bandana, down her elongated cheekbones. "What do you wanna know?" she said with a loud, trembling swallow.

"Your name, why you tried to kill me and who is making you do it." Kasta did not blink while making her demands.

The assailant leaned forward. Her voice turned shrill. "And if I tell you, will you let me go?" The blue-grey skin on her face was of similar tone to Kasta's, though smoother in texture. But that smooth skin tightened with dither, as if she held back tears.

Kasta shook her head. "I think you're confused as to how this works, kid." She leaned against a barrel. With one leg resting on the wooden beer container, she turned her head to the attacker. "If you talk, you don't die. If you don't talk, you die. All other details will be resolved later." Her hands stretched outward. "Your name."

"Artia Bellikan," she said with a sigh and drop of her head.

Kasta clapped once. "Hey! Look at that, it has a name." Her gaze shifted to Vera, then back to the young girl. "Now, *Artia*, you're gunna give Vera five hundred platinum for her trouble tonight."

The attacker flung her arms. "Wait, what?!" Her contorting face shielded a stream of tears. "I don't even have that kind of money."

"Yes, you do," Kasta said with a slow nod and single blink. "I already took it out of your coin case and gave it to our friend back there." The attacker gasped, patting down her lap and torso. "Yes," Kasta said. "The little one that was in your jacket pocket. That's the price of disrupting this good woman's business."

The girl grunted, biting the side of her lip. A youthful smile erased her whimpering sorrow. "What else would you like to know, Miss Krane?"

"Kasta, kid. Just call me Kasta." She grinned at Dresco's quiet snickering. With a twirl of her pistol, she asked, "Why'd you try to take a shot at me?"

The would-be assassin swallowed and crossed her legs. "Who wouldn't want to take a shot at Kasta Krane? I'd be hailed a hero in the criminal underworld."

"You better stop trying to pass these lies off on me, hotshot. My patience is running thin."

"I was hired to," the girl uttered, her shoulders sinking. "You were a job."

"Now we're getting somewhere." Kasta gave Vera an upward nod. "If she lies again, and I'll know when she does, take the shot."

The attacker's eyes widened. Her hands froze atop her brown leather slacks.

Dresco placed his hand on Kasta's shoulder. "Kasta, are you being perhaps a bit too aggressive with the young girl?"

Thrusting her shoulder upward, Kasta knocked off Dresco's hand. "Shut up, choirboy." She took a long stride toward the attacker and crossed her arms. "Who sent you?"

The girl shook her head. "They said they'd kill me if I talked." Her wide blue eyes sparkled as they rolled up. She fidgeted, adjusting the belt angled across her torso.

Kasta gestured to Vera's rifle.

The attacker licked her lips. She spoke at the edge of a breath. "I don't know his name, and I didn't see his face. But he contacted me via encrypted message. I met him in a tavern up north." She looked to Dresco, pointing a limp finger his way. "And he wore armor just like that."

Dresco stepped forward, apprehension stamped on his face. An unfamiliar apprehension. "Exactly like mine?" His voice cracked.

"Yes," she uttered. "Only it was black."

Dresco trembled. The grey skin on his forehead tightened with goosebumps. He took a jittering breath. "An Imperial Black Knight," he said with a solemn shake of his head.

Kasta squinted at him. "A Black Knight? What the hell is a Black Knight?"

"There are not very many." Dresco cleared his throat and crossed his hands in front of his waist. "But they are the elite, secret templars of the High Imperium. The special ops if you will."

Kasta looked to the ground with a sharp sigh. "Oh well this sounds just great, doesn't it?" She let out a second sigh. Her attention returned to the attacker. "I don't suppose you know why?"

The assailant shook her head. While her eyes were full of fear, they were devoid of deceit.

The hunter placed her pistol back in its holster. "How much was the bounty?"

The girl pulled her short-sleeve jacket over her shirt. "Two hundred thousand platinum," she said with a sniffle. Kasta backed away and placed her hands over her knees. Dresco gasped. Vera swore. "And I'm not the only one they offered it to," the attacker added.

Kasta stood up straight, tapping her pistol's handle. "Okay then!" she exclaimed. "This kind of sounds like the type of situation we deal with in the morning!"

Dresco scratched his chin and raised a finger. "Wait, but she just told us..."

Kasta waved him off. "Oh, I heard her. Some people are trying to kill me for money. We'll figure it out. I think I'm ready to start winding down. Maybe have another drink or two."

Vera chimed in. "Kasta, perhaps we should consider—"

"Nothin' more to consider," Kasta said. "Not tonight, anyway."

The attacker raised her hand. Her chin angled sideways. "So, am I free to go?" she asked with a whine.

Kasta's thumbs slid inside her belt. The hunter shook her head. "Essi, you're going to jail. You tried to kill me."

All three of Kasta's company looked to her, confused and silent as she spoke the name, "Essi."

The attacker stuttered. She crossed her arms over her rib cage, wrapping herself in a tight embrace. "How did you know?"

"Three things." Kasta leaned forward, her finger in the shape of a pistol. "First, the ID signature that you have sitting in your data system. Pretty obvious fake. Did you even go to a professional counterfeiter?" Her lips twisted and her head shook.

"Ouch. Caught red-handed, darling," Vera said with a mocking laugh.

"Second, Essi, you're a wanted woman." The attacker winced as Kasta spoke. "Yes. That price on your head that you probably wore as a badge of honor with your little crook friends—I've seen it posted on bounty boards all over Vanda." Kasta's eyes crept upward. "Now, six hundred fifty platinum isn't typically a big enough bounty for me to pursue. But apparently it's enough for me to remember." She tilted her hat, pushing it up by the brim. "And who could forget those shining steel-blue eyes?"

A half smirk grew on the hunter's face. "Oh, right, and that knife that you had in your boot? It has your name on it, kid." Kasta pulled the knife from her jacket pocket, pointing to the engraved script. " 'Essi Hannar' in big, fancy letters."

Essi did not reply. She sat stone-faced, twisting her wrist.

As Vera laughed at the display, Kasta turned to her. "Contact the marshal's office. I got a bounty to collect."

X

News from the Law

Kasta turned Essi Hannar over to a deputy and spent the night in the Vulture's Creek Inn. Dresco pestered Kasta, even begged her to consider the situation, to discuss the price on her head. She disregarded Dresco but did send a message to Marshal Jos asking him to investigate the situation. Kasta dedicated the rest of the evening to relaxation and whisky. Worry could wait until daylight.

Morning came. The hunter and the knight rode downtown and arrived at the marshal's office. The building was composed of brick, laid with a shimmering blue metal. The office was two stories high, and its rooftop rose inward, coming to a sharp point in the middle. "Seems a little large for a law office," Dresco said as he looked up at the building.

"Yep," Kasta said. "You need a bigger building for extra jail cells in a city. There's a lot more perps runnin' around Vulture than there are in a one-trugan town like Barren Rock." She walked up the stairway, cast in the neon-green light of the sign above. The sign read "Vulture Law Office." "Not to mention," Kasta continued, "they get a much bigger budget."

Inside the lobby, Kasta went to check the bounty board. Dresco told the desk clerk that they had arrived. "Hmm." Kasta scrolled through the rectangular blue-lit screen. The monitor occupied an entire wall.

"What is it?" Dresco asked.

She turned to him. "I'm not on here." She stepped away from the bounty board. Her boots clinked against the floor, constructed from the same blue metal that lay between the bricks outside.

"That's good news, is it not?" Dresco's enthusiasm could have etched a smile on the neutral visage of his helmet.

Kasta shook her head. "Not really. Just means that if there really is a bounty on me, it's probably an illegal one."

"I am so sorry, Kasta."

"Don't be!" She turned toward the knight with a grin. "We just have to figure out why some secret black-ops Imperial fella would have any type of quarrel with me."

Dresco raised a finger. "Um, perhaps—"

"Kasta Krane," the deputy behind the desk called out. "Marshal Jos is ready for you."

"Excellent." Kasta strolled toward the hallway on the other side of the room. Pill-shaped light fixtures hanging side by side guided the way. She spun toward Dresco, walking backward. "And what I did to deserve a two-hundred-thousand-platinum bounty. Holy hell."

Dresco cleared his throat and scampered behind. "Yes, that is quite substantial."

"Substantial indeed." The duo passed three iron doors in the brightened hallway. They came to a set of wooden stairs. "We must have really riled them up while we looked for that map. I mean, Madame Vaeliz did mention the Imperium was looking for some magical toys too. But I didn't know they took it *this* seriously."

Dresco's steps clonked against the wooden floor.

"Whatever." Kasta's fingers tapped the smooth, cool handrail. "We'll make the Madame give us some hazard pay, right?"

Dresco remained silent.

They reached the highest floor: a narrow hallway with four doors. A bronze plaque rested on the farthest door to the right, bearing text that read "Marshal Jos."

As Kasta proceeded to turn the doorknob, Dresco whispered, "Okay… what is this?"

"What is what?" Kasta asked.

"Does this man have a first and last name? Everyone seems to just call him 'Marshal Jos.' "

Kasta shook her head once. "Of course he has a first and last name!"

Dresco shrugged, his arms outstretched. "What is his first name?"

"Jos."

"Okay, what it his last name?" The knight grunted.

"Jos." A chuckle escaped with her words.

Dresco tensed up, resting his helmeted head in his palm. "What…" He took a grumbling breath. "What name *accompanies* the name Jos?"

Kasta's finger drifted over the top of the plaque. She pointed to the same word that she said aloud: "Marshal." Her gloved hand stretched over the nameplate and pushed the door open before Dresco could conjure a response. "Marshal Jos!" she said, stepping onto the office's rosewood floor.

A man with a grey-and-black mustache rose from his chair. A warm smile fell on his face. "Well, well. Look what we got here. The Merciful Hunter has stumbled into the great city of Vulture." He stepped from behind his desk and toward Kasta, his smile never fading. The marshal and the hunter exchanged a firm handshake. His opposite hand embraced her shoulder. "How you doing, Kas?" he said with a soft, scraping voice.

Kasta's head cocked sideways. A smirk fell over her face. "New day, new job. You know how it is."

Marshal Jos released her hand, letting out a grating chuckle. "Actually, I really don't."

They crowed in laughter. "Well, on the one hand, you've got a much more boring life than me. On the other, at least you don't have people trying to kill you," she said.

Jos nodded. "We'll have to talk about that."

Dresco stepped into the room, hesitation in his stride. His eyes riveted on the antique oil paintings that hung from the wall. Each depicted a different country scene: a farm cast in blue dusk, a mother ox with her calf, an oasis prairie and a rider on truganback.

Jos stepped toward the knight. "Oh, you must be Dresco Norte." He offered a firm, two-handed handshake. "A pleasure to meet ya."

Dresco removed his helmet with his other hand and looked down at the marshal. "As it is mine, Marshal Jos."

The lines on the marshal's face twined with the wrinkles on his leather hat. His skin was of a blue-grey tone, blue the predominant shade. "How's my boy treating ya?"

Dresco's head tilted. "Pardon me. Your... boy?"

Kasta smiled. Her finger stretched toward Jos. "Marshal Jos raised and trained Crevallus, Norte."

Dresco shut his eyes and nodded. "Ah, yes. He is a... wonderful steed."

The marshal's pointed boots thudded against the floor as he returned to his desk. "One of the most beautiful trugan I've ever raised." He sat down and took a deep breath. "Well," he said. His lower lip hid below his mustache. "I've gathered some information." The marshal looked to Kasta and shook his head. "It ain't good."

Kasta pulled out a chair in front of the desk and sat across from the marshal. "A few bounty hunters are on my back for a lot of coin, and the

Imperium is mad that I'm stirring up some old dust. That's not a bother, Marshal. Nothing I can't handle."

Jos rested his elbows on the desk and crossed his hands. "This ain't just a few hunters." Dresco stood by, his eyelid twitching. Jos continued, "I've talked with marshals and deputies in dozens of towns all morning. Almost all of them... almost *all* of them, Kas, said there have been heavily armed individuals passing through their towns, asking questions, investigating the area. Looking for you."

Kasta's brow rose. "Well that can't be good." She reached into her pocket for a cigarillo—but she had forgotten her last one in the hotel room. She sighed. "Is the employer Imperial?"

Dresco chimed in. "The woman who tried to kill Kasta last night said that a Black Knight assigned her the mission. Is there any truth to that?"

The marshal's eyes sliced toward Dresco. "I don't know at this time. But I spoke with Marshal Vallia of Hollow Mesa earlier. And he said he caught a couple perps looking for the two of you. They said they were given the job by an Imperial-lookin' feller up north." Jos' dark-blue eyes widened, and his mustache slanted. "But you'd probably know more about all that than me, wouldn't ya?"

Kasta laughed, leaning back with her hands behind her head. "Don't worry, Marshal. He's not in the Order anymore. He's a 'fallen knight' now."

The marshal twisted in his chair. "I don't know what you did to piss off the Imperium, Kas, but it's led to some even bigger problems in front of ya."

Kasta crossed her legs. "Bigger than two hundred thousand platinum?"

Jos cleared his throat. His voice fell soft and crackled. "Breylu Dast is on your trail."

Kasta stopped breathing. A shiver sliced across the bottom of her waist and crawled up her spine—into the deepest corner of her mind. She swallowed once. "He's always on my trail." She could not subdue the tremble in her voice.

Jos shook his head, scrolling through the data system on his desk. "Not like this." He pointed to a digital image on the screen. "Just last night, Marshal Bovien caught one of his spies in Barren Rock. She's one of the best lawmen I've ever seen inside the interrogation room. She had more information than any other marshal I talked to in the last few hours. Bovien got this sleaze to admit he was on Dast's payroll. He was armed with infantry-grade weapons and equipment." The marshal looked at Dresco for a half second before turning back to Kasta. "And according to his ID signature, he's a former Imperial covert-ops agent. Used to watch the hostile Draekalagon clans for 'em."

"The Imperium is funding Dast." Kasta shook her head, speaking through clenched teeth.

Jos leaned back, pulling down on his brown leather vest. "It would certainly seem that way."

Dresco cleared his throat three times and smacked his lips together. "Pardon," he said with a finger raised. "But who in the name of Athenis' starlight is Breylu Dast?"

Jos began to speak, but Kasta interrupted at a louder volume. "He's my competition." She looked to Dresco with a tight smirk. "My nemesis. My chief rival."

The marshal looked down at his screen with a slow shake of his head.

Kasta snarled. She leaned toward Dresco. "I've beat him to a few targets. Dug up some old treasure that he was too dumb to find himself. He takes it a little too personally. The scum has wanted me dead for years now."

Jos fiddled with the square buttons on his sleeve. "It's more than just him and his little Moon Shadow Riders now, Kasta. And it's more than just some personal vendetta that's driving him. He's been offered that bounty on ya." Jos gestured to the data system embedded in his desk. It displayed grainy footage of a man wearing a maroon poncho, riding through a small town with several wooden cabins. "He passed through Midway Lake just a couple days ago."

Dresco gasped. "My goodness, he is right behind us."

Kasta coughed and clenched the handle of her pistol. "If I see him, I'll shoot him. *His* head price has gotten high. I've been waiting to take a shot at Dast and his gang for a while." She looked to the marshal with a raise of her eyebrows. "I can be my own bait."

Marshal Jos shook his head. He leaned forward and rubbed his brow. "Kasta, don't do this."

Kasta shrugged a shoulder. "Don't do what, Marshal?"

"This! Don't let your pride get in the way here. You know how dangerous Breylu Dast is. Hell, it's not just Dast. It's probably half the bounty hunters in Vanda at this point. Not to mention, any hostile Imperials who may have crossed the border to come after you."

Kasta sighed. "Is that all? I thought I was in for some sort of challenge." She looked to the ceiling. "How disappointing."

Jos leaned forward and extended his hand. "Kasta, please. Stay here in Vulture under the protection of my department. At least until I can officially get the bounty on you declared illegal."

Kasta shook her head, stacking her legs atop the marshal's desk. "No can do, Marshal. I'm right in the middle of a job."

Dresco pulled his chair forward. The reddish-brown hardwood let out a low creak. "It truly is urgent business, Marshal Jos. Unpostponable."

"Right. This little *expedition* you are trying to take to the Valley of Tombs." Jos groaned and scratched the back of his neck. "I don't suppose that if I offered you a thousand platinum to *not* look for whatever it is you're looking for...?"

"Nope," Kasta said with a smirk. "That's not even close, Marshal."

A smile inched across Jos' face. "So, you're really looking for Vellon's Blade?" Dresco's eyes widened. The marshal continued, "And the Imperium thinks they can find it too."

Kasta tapped Dresco on the shoulder. "He's a good detective. He can always figure out what's goin' on."

Jos took a deep breath, maintaining steady eye contact with Kasta. "Kasta, please, consider what I'm about to offer you." He forced an uncomfortable grin. "I know you like to work alone, but let me send some deputies with you. Just to watch your back. You won't even have to pay 'em."

Kasta shook her head. "No."

"That is actually a sound proposal," Dresco said. "If you do not want the marshal's deputies, I know a squad of loyal knights who would be more than willing—"

"No!" Kasta interrupted the knight, thrusting a finger in his face. "One is enough, trust me." Silence overtook the room. She placed her hand in her vest pocket.

"Alright then." The marshal's voice became soft and muted. His eyes crawled to the faded hues of his rustic paintings. "If I can't convince you otherwise, can I at least offer you some advice on traveling safely through the Valley of Tombs?"

Kasta pointed toward the marshal with her fingers in the shape of a pistol. "That's why I came to see you in the first place, my old friend."

A map appeared on the desk data system. The marshal reached into his drawer. "Nighthawk jerky?" He offered an open bag of dried meat.

"Don't mind if I do." Kasta grabbed a fingerful. Dresco shook his head in polite refusal.

"As you know, Kas, that valley is always swarming with bandits," Jos mumbled through his meat-filled mouth. "Those tombs have been excavated and robbed dry for decades, but that doesn't stop those scavengers from digging."

"Mmhm," Kasta grunted as she ran her tongue across her teeth, trying to remove any stubborn remains of jerky. "And they don't like when anyone comes through their dig sites."

"Right," Jos said with a nod. "Which is why I'm gunna recommend you take the old mining route. It's a narrow path, so it may be a tough ride, but the bandits hardly ever travel by them mines. Nothin' of value to 'em there." His finger traced the map, drawing a glowing line along the path. "Once you're out of the mining route, it's a two-mile ride through the main part of the valley, and you'll find yourself at the Tomb of Saigus."

"I like it," Kasta said. "You should be charging me for that, Jos. That's some top-notch intel."

Jos leaned back and crossed his hands over his wide chrome belt buckle. "You can pay me back by staying safe."

Kasta smiled. "I don't like to make promises I can't keep."

Jos' mustache fell low with the slight frown on his face. "I know ya don't." He sat up straight, his boot tapping against the floor. "Last thing to discuss is that bounty you sent us last night."

Kasta's lips twisted. "Our young little would-be assassin?"

"Yessum," Jos said with a nod. "This Essi Hannar. Little snake she is. Wanted for all kinds of forgery and fraud and theft. That little sweet-and-innocent act she puts on won't get her far in here."

Kasta yawned as she stretched her arms. "Didn't get her very far with me either."

"It most certainly did not," Jos affirmed. "I've sent the six hundred fifty platinum to your account already. Plus, an extra fifty for… let's call it damages."

"Call it what you want," Kasta said. "I'll call it free money."

Jos' eyes narrowed. "Now we just need to formally get some documents signed and you can press attempted murder charges against her."

The hunter shook her head and wagged her finger. She looked away from Jos toward the bookshelf to her right. "No, I don't want to do that."

Jos squinted, glancing sideways. "I'm sorry?"

Kasta brushed a strand of hair behind her ear. "I don't want to press charges against Hannar."

Dresco leaned between Kasta and the bookshelf. "Kasta, she did try to murder you, did she not?"

Her eyes angled toward the knight. "Yeah. But didn't you hear? Everyone's tryin' to kill me." She looked back at Jos. "Also, I don't got time to be filling out dull legal documents and sitting in court. There's jobs to do. Treasure to hunt." Kasta jolted up from the chair, pulling her jacket inward by the lapels. She stood tall with her chest out. "And on that note, I believe it is time for me to make my exit."

Jos stood as well, hunching over his desk. "Alright. You'll just have to do whatever you feel is fit." He shook Kasta's hand again. "Stay off main travel routes. Ride cross-country and don't go into any cities. Hell, don't go into any towns if you can help it."

With a slow nod, she squeezed Jos' hand with a tight grip. "That's a good plan, Marshal."

"Take care, Kas. Remember, if you change your mind and want some backup, give me a call. I'll ride with ya."

The hunter responded with a wink. She let go of his hand and turned away from his warm, smiling face.

Kasta stepped into the hall and let out a moaning sigh. 'Breylu Dast,' she thought. 'I knew it would eventually come down to him and me. This day has been coming for a long time. But I didn't know someone was going to pay him to try to take *me* out.'

She carried on down the hall, dragging her feet along the floor. 'Like he needs any more motivation to kill me.' The door to the marshal's office closed again—Dresco stomped toward her. He had not been following. "What are you lagging so much for?" she asked.

"Just some parting words between the marshal and I," Dresco said. "He seemed a good man."

Kasta raised her eyebrows but said nothing. She was distracted.

❖

"One thing I don't understand, Norte," Kasta said, tramping down the staircase outside the law office. "If the Imperium really is pissed off that we're muddling around, looking for Vellon's Blade, why aren't they coming after us themselves? They've hired every bounty hunter in Vanda, but Jos had no intel on any Order grunts coming after us." Her peripherals caught Dresco. "How come those Black Knights aren't the ones chasing us?"

"They probably are," Dresco said. His hand slid down the railing. "They hire Vandeni hunters for Vanden jobs because they have a greater understanding of the land. The Imperial military will also pursue us by air, land and sea, though we will never hear about it. They operate only in the shadows."

A tone rang from Kasta's data system. It was a message from Madame Vaeliz. It read:

Kasta,

I just received news that the Imperium knows of your mission and that they are hunting you. I am told the news has reached you as well. If you wish to abandon your task, that is more than understandable. But should you continue, I will have my informants keep tabs on the Imperium and their hired hunters. I will divert them from your trail if I can. As always, my resources are available for your use. And I'll raise your pay as well: an extra one hundred thousand platinum. I apologize for getting you into this, Kasta. But I must do everything in my power to prevent the Imperium from finding Vellon's Blade. Let me know what you decide to do.

Madame Vaeliz

Kasta reached the bottom of the stairs and tapped the "Reply" icon. She wrote to the Madame, "I'm still in. Just have my money ready."

"Madame Vaeliz is going to keep tabs on the Imps for us." She handed her data system to Dresco. "Hopefully they ain't as covert as you say."

Dresco read Vaeliz's message and cleared his throat. "I think I will pick up a mobile data system for myself. I need to send a message of my own to the Madame."

" 'Bout time. Don't know how you've gotten by just using stationary systems." Kasta's eyelids jolted open. "Oh, that reminds me." She reached into her pocket. Clinging noises accompanied her digging hand. She pulled out a handful of shimmering, silvery coins. "Two hundred, two fifty, three hundred twenty-five platinum." The platinum pieces slid from one hand to the other as she counted.

"Wait, what is this?" Dresco asked.

She dropped the coins into his limp palm. "Your half for Essi Hannar. I know you didn't contribute much to it, but I did promise everything we do is fifty-fifty when we're working together. I'm keeping the extra fifty from Jos, though."

Dresco's thumb shuffled the coins. "Well, Thank you, Krane." He swallowed.

"Don't thank me. But try to actually earn it next time," she said with a backhanded wave.

"I thought so," Dresco said.

"Thought what?" She stepped into the trugan stable, the tight quarters that accommodated Kaiar and Crevallus.

Dresco followed. "You do not object to being referred to as 'Krane.' Only 'Miss Krane.'"

Kasta nodded, tightening the strap on Kai's saddle. "Do I really look like a *miss* to you?"

Dresco stepped forward and shook his head. "I suppose not, but why not mention this before?"

Kasta smirked. "It's fun to correct you."

Dresco let out a long sigh. He stepped toward Crevallus. His heavy armor dragged against the stable's coarse wooden flooring.

"Oh, that reminds me," Kasta said. "Please don't wear that armor as you walk around the city. They know I'm riding with a knight. I don't need a bigger target on my back than I already have."

Dresco removed his helmet. "They know my face, though."

"Yeah, but your face can't be picked out from a hundred miles away. That shiny armor can." Kasta climbed into her saddle. She ran the backside of her hand down Kai's cheek. "Pick us up some other supplies too. Food, med kits, maybe an extra charge crystal or two." She reached to her waist for the hilt of her small blade. "I'll get us some utility tools, and maybe even buy myself a new sword."

Dresco rode behind. "What is the point of buying a sword? You don't even properly know how to use one."

She looked to him with a tight squint. "Yes, I do! Did you see me cut Hannar's barrel?"

Dresco nodded. "I saw your untamed and wild swing at her weapon." His slight frown shook, morphing into a smug grin. "That would never work in a duel."

A sneer struck the side of Kasta's face. She held her chin high, riding out of the stable. "I think it would work just fine."

Kai hissed when the light of midday struck her eyes. Her slit pupils narrowed. Kasta tugged the reins right, guiding her steed into the street. Crevallus' gallop followed. "Let's stay off the main roads," Kasta said. "We'll cut through side streets and back alleys. And hopefully get out of Vulture before every hunter in Vanda knows we are here."

Kasta sat up straight on her saddle, her eye on every passing rider and pedestrian. Any one of them could take a shot at her.

A small child in ragged, torn clothing approached. "Miss, do you have any spare coin?" he asked, lifting a tin can toward the hunter. A mask of dirt and grease covered his blue-grey face.

"Get a job, kid." She increased the speed of Kai's gallop with a soft, downward thrust of her reins. A narrow alley lay to the left. She prepared to make the turn. "Oh, and Norte, don't buy any Imperial *cuisine* this time." She looked over her shoulder. "Only real foo..." Dresco was not there.

"Norte?" she called out, turning Kai around. "Oh damn it, where is he?" Someone may have gotten the drop on him. Could it be Dast? She pulled on the reins, backing Kai into the alleyway. 'Please don't tell me his obliviousness got him captured.'

Kasta peered around the corner. 'There he is!' she thought, catching a glimpse of the knight. He had stepped off his trugan. Kneeling over, he placed a handful of coins in the child beggar's hands. A large handful.

Kasta's jaw dropped. The leather on her glove wrinkled as her fingers formed a fist. The knight approached. "What in the light of the moons do you think you are doing?" She looked to him with a deliberate shake of her head.

"I was providing aid to a starving child." He walked on foot, dragging Crevallus by the reins. "Is there some sort of problem with that?"

Kasta's lower teeth rose over her upper lip. Kaiar stepped back with a soft growl. "Yeah, there is problem with that!" she said. "You just dumped a handful of coins. We need that money!"

Dresco came to a halt. "If I am not mistaken, is my share of our reward money not mine to do with what I will?"

"Not when we need supplies."

Dresco turned his palms outward. "I still have enough for the, um, what do you call it? Data system!"

Kasta rubbed her index finger and thumb between her eyes. "And how much will you have left after that, Norte?"

Dresco's breath stopped. With a clearing of his throat, he uttered, "A modest sum."

She rolled her eyes and looked skyward. "Holy hell. You are just unbelievable. Now is a time to *save* coin. Not give it away. What are you going to do if you run out of money? Do you expect me to cover the cost of supplies for the both of us?"

"Oh, please, Kasta, have some empathy. It is part of my duty to help the weak and those in peril."

She held up a finger. "We are *not* gunna turn this into a religious thing right now—"

"The Guardians demand that monastic servants such as I do their bidding on all of Eramaa. Sympathy is one of the most treasured virtues of the divine…"

"Oh, damn it. It is gunna be a religious thing. Great. Fantastic," Kasta said under her breath while he spoke. "Dresco!" she yelled. Her face turned hot. The veins in her neck throbbed. She glanced in each direction. No one was watching, but this was no place to have a public argument. "I don't give a damn about your religious rules to live by. But practice them on your own time. Remember, when you ride with me, you ride by *my* rules." She directed Kai to step toward the knight. "And what you just did, that is not a behavior that I tolerate in my company. Don't do it again!"

"No," Dresco said, his hands in front of his waist.

"Excuse me?"

"No, *Krane*. This is one of your rules that is simply reprehensible from any kind of moral standpoint." Dresco placed his hand over his sword, angling the hilt forward. "I will not disparage an underprivileged child who merely asks for aid."

Kasta pressed her lips together and let out a groan. "Dresco, that little sewer runt was just a beggar. You can't trust 'em. They're good for nothing. If no one fell for their tricks, they'd be better off for it. Force them to have some use to the world."

"He was a starving child!"

Kasta's head tilted sideways. Her brow rose high. "So was I once. I never got no charity from no one. Never asked for it." The hunter shrugged as a smirk inched up her face. "And look at me now. Best damn treasure hunter on all of Eramaa." She rotated her hat and took another peek around. "And on that note, we should get moving before someone murders us." Kai turned into the alley. "Come on, grateful giver," she called out to Dresco.

A thought came to Kasta. She brought Kai to a halt. "Dresco." She looked behind, out of her peripherals. "What did you do with your half of the Quintis Saveer bounty that we collected in Barren Rock?" Her companion was silent. "Be honest with me, my good knight. Why didn't you buy a data system in Barren Rock like I instructed you to?"

His feet dragged against the street. "I gave it to the local church," he mumbled.

Kasta looked down and shook her head. "Wow."

"Kasta, please understand. It was... it was broken down and severely in need of maintenance. I could not let a church of the old Order sit in shambles."

"Oh, you've gotta be kidding me." She slapped the reins down on Kai's neck. The beast answered by darting through the alley.

"Kasta, wait!" Dresco called out.

"Well, girl," Kasta said, patting the top of Kai's head. "Half of Vanda is hunting us, including Breylu Dast, and we are riding with an idiot." The beast gently raised her head into Kasta's palm, shutting her pale-silver eyes. They turned a corner. "Think we're ready for this one?"

Kaiar released a screeching roar as her gallop quickened.

XI

THE VALLEY OF TOMBS

The riders resupplied and left Vulture behind. Any time Kasta saw another person, or what could be another person, they changed directions or increased their speed. Bounty hunters could recognize their faces, but not a pair of passing blurs. Kasta did as Marshal Jos instructed; she kept off main travel routes and rode cross-country. It was difficult to navigate the rocky hillsides and untrimmed brush of the Vanden hinterlands. Kasta enjoyed traversing the backcountry. Dresco struggled to keep up.

The hunter and the knight made camp by a stream under a canopy of frost willow trees. The canopy sheltered them from the light drizzle overhead and unfriendly eyes of the world. Dresco began to prepare a meal, but Kasta stopped him. They had not exchanged a word with one another since they had left Vulture.

Kasta went to catch their dinner from the stream. A river squirrel stood on the shoreline. The blue-skinned creature let out a harsh squeak and pranced into the water. As the amphibious rodent slithered along the surface, the hunter dived into the river with a hunting knife. Within minutes, she captured a mirror bass.

Dresco commented that the fish looked like a sword, due to its long body and narrow snout. But its muscle tissue was edible and best served raw.

After preparing and serving the fish, Kasta ripped off a piece and stuffed her mouth. She barely chewed before swallowing. Over the crackle of the campfire, Dresco whispered to himself. Kasta paused, a fingerful of pink fish meat in front of her lips. Her gaze veered toward the knight. His hands circled over his plate. His eyes were shut.

"What are you doing?" she demanded.

Dresco's eyes crept open. "I am giving thanks to the Guardians for this meal."

"Oh, you gotta be kidding me," Kasta said. She rolled her eyes and tossed her plate to the ground. "I caught the fish, you dogmatic fool! You should be thanking me!"

"And the Guardians provided you with the fish to catch," Dresco said.

"No, they didn't! The river did. You keep letting fairy tales run your life. Have they ever actually done anything good for you? Your creeds seem to lead to nothing but manufactured stress and old-fashioned trouble."

Dresco took a deep breath. "With respect, you are the one who seems vexed. Perhaps *you* would be happier if you accepted the will of the Guardians."

Kasta pointed at him, shouting, "No! I am happy! I am happy because I accept things the way they are. I look out for myself because I am the only one who can do so adequately. So, no, I will not adhere to your ancient gospels. Ever."

Dresco cleared his throat but did not respond. Instead, he picked up his plate of fish and leaned back against a log.

Kasta grabbed her plate as well. She chomped another mouthful, listening to the crackle of the fire.

Dresco took his first bite. His eyes fluttered her way. "Thank you for catching the fish."

"You're welcome."

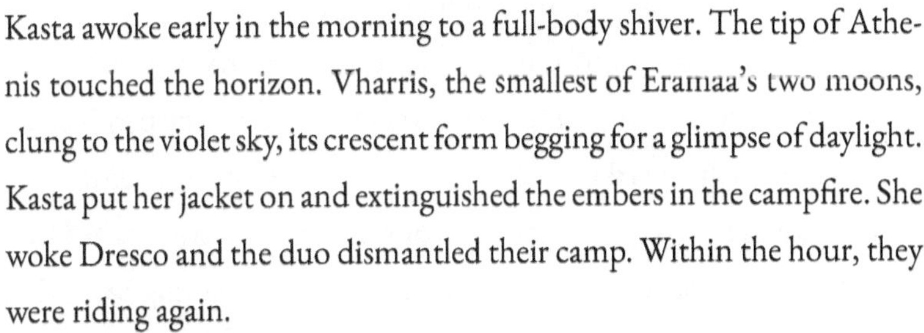

Kasta awoke early in the morning to a full-body shiver. The tip of Athenis touched the horizon. Vharris, the smallest of Eramaa's two moons, clung to the violet sky, its crescent form begging for a glimpse of daylight. Kasta put her jacket on and extinguished the embers in the campfire. She woke Dresco and the duo dismantled their camp. Within the hour, they were riding again.

They rode for several hours. After passing underneath a great arch of natural stone, Kasta opened her digital map. Jos' charted route was near. Before a ravine, the trugan halted their gallop. Two walls of smooth, golden-red stone loomed over a narrow passage. "This is it," Kasta said, pointing down the pathway. "This should lead us to the Valley of Tombs unnoticed."

Crevallus backed away. "Whoa there, lad. Relax," Dresco urged his mount, patting his head. "Kaiar seems somewhat restless too." Dresco looked toward the female trugan. Her claws dug into the rock below, leaving white scratch marks on the surface.

"They're right to be," Kasta said. Her fingers caressed the soft scales under Kai's neck. "That mining route may give us less chance of running into a bandit. But predators, those could be lurking in any corner."

Dresco chuckled. "Oh please, what could possibly be a natural predator of trugan? They're gigantic lizards!"

Kasta shrugged as her eyes grew wide. "You'd be surprised."

Dresco shook his head and held out his hand. "Do not tell me. I do not want to know."

Kasta thrust her reins down, sending Kai forward at a slow gallop. "I don't blame ya." The gravel crunched with the trugan's steps, reverberating off the canyon walls. "Mind your surroundings here, Norte."

"Yes, Kasta."

"I like the sound of that! Say that more often."

The rocks on the mining trail were jagged and sharp—not enough to damage the trugan's feet, but enough to hinder them. The path's steep incline and sharp-angled turns further steadied their pace. The travelers passed a tunnel bearing burn marks around its perimeter. A rusted cart peered from the darkness of the unnatural cave, requesting one more opportunity to traverse the mines in search of riches.

Kasta wiped the sweat off her brow with the back of her hand. While too short to grace the travelers with shade, the confining rock walls diverted any cooling breeze. The blue heat of Athenis was inescapable.

With the turn of a corner, they passed another cave bearing no remnants of civilized utility or signs of sentient creation. A whispering growl echoed from the dark: a deathly harmony, accordant in timbre but separated by three octaves. The trugan's gallop picked up. Kasta ordered that they slow down. Kai listened, though Crevallus did not. Dresco failed to decelerate his mount.

"Hey!" Kasta barked, snapping her fingers in Crevallus' face. "Settle yourself." The trugan slowed his pace, his tongue flicking to the side of his mouth.

"What on Eramaa was that horrifying sound?" Dresco whispered.

Kasta shook her head. "If that was what I think it was, you definitely don't want to know." That sound was unmistakable—the howl of a burrow serpent. And the trugan had reason to react as they did, for those snakes could swallow them whole. 'Luckily, they despise daylight,' Kasta thought.

The heat intensified as they rode down the pass. The sky shone clear overhead. Stagnant clouds and the burning blue of Athenis were all that blocked the violet atmosphere. After several hours of winding turns and harsh terrain, the travelers came to the end of the narrow pathway. Their mounts stepped onto flat ground: a thin layer of red sand atop a hard, hollow soil. The thin enclosure of the miners' pass gave way to an open canyon territory stretching toward the horizon. The whispering wind kissed her gills. Undulations of sand rippled across the plains in frail, fleeting sets. "Here it is," the hunter said. "The Valley of Tombs."

Dresco's gaze turned to a layer of rocks on the other side of the canyon. "That rock formation. The highest stone almost looks like it has a face!"

"It may have had a face at one point." She placed her optical system over her eye. The device scanned the canyon—not for rock structures, but life-forms. "This valley was a great sanctuary in Vanda's more religious times—graced with fine art and grand statues, unrivaled even by modern Imperial architecture. But that was thousands of years ago. Now most of those ancient structures are hardly distinguishable from rubble."

"How unfortunate," Dresco said. His head sank. "It was a better time for your country."

Kasta raised an eyebrow. "Yes, Dresco. I too wish we could go back to the times of religious war, famine and feudalistic rule," she said with a hoarse chuckle. "Oh, the good old days."

"I just meant that it was a more... spiritual time for Vanda."

"Alright, we're clear of hostiles," Kasta said with a shift in tone. She raised her optical system. "Let's move out before that changes. Keep at a strong gallop. We don't wanna be easy targets. But don't fire Crev's gears too hard either. We don't wanna make much noise."

Dresco nodded. "Understood."

"Good, let's go!"

Kasta and Dresco rode at a swift canter across the valley, though the world did not blur as they passed. Vultures circled and croaked above. Facial details and fine linework endured on the ancient statues, many half-buried in the crimson sand. Their carved crowns and engraved tattoos gave a taste of life to depictions of mortals and Guardians alike.

"Is it this one?" Dresco asked through his communication system as they passed a rectangular archway carved into the canyon wall.

"No," Kasta replied, cuffing the optical system's speaker with her hand. "That's the tomb of Alessia the Conqueror, I believe. Saigus' grave shouldn't be too far off."

Moments later, she veered right, directing Kaiar into a large quarry. Thick desert air flooded her lungs. In the center of the quarry wall, a staircase stood, each step carved to a curl. "There it is," Kasta said. "The Tomb of Saigus."

"This is exhilarating," Dresco said, a sharp crack in his voice. "I have never been inside the tomb of a true Relic wielder!"

Kasta looked up the high-climbing, curved steps of the staircase. "Saigus was one of the last members of the House of Vellon who is said to have wielded the Defender of Liberty. So, it would make sense if it were buried with him."

Dresco slowed down and took a sip of water from his canteen. "Kasta, do you suddenly believe we will find the sword? Why the change of heart?"

Her lips twisted. She dismounted from her trugan. "The prospect of four hundred thousand platinum... correct that—five hundred thousand platinum has made me a tad bit more... optimistic." After adjusting her jacket, she checked her pistol's sights. She stood tall, thumbs in her belt, staring at the tomb's entrance, then began to tread up the steps.

Dresco followed. "Anything in particular that we should watch out for in this tomb? Floor traps? Toxic darts from the walls?"

Kasta shrugged. "Hm. I don't know."

"What do you mean?"

"I don't know," she repeated. "I've never been in there."

The knight gasped. "You never mentioned that before! I was under the impression that there was not a tomb or temple in Vanda you had yet to set foot in."

They reached the final step: a long platform that led to the door. "It'll be unfamiliar territory for both of us," Kasta said. She looked down the long, dark hallway. "And even more of a reason to—"

"Watch our steps." Dresco finished the sentence for her. "And mind our surroundings."

"I may make a treasure hunter out of you yet, my noble knight." She flashed him a wink and a slight smile. "Let's find us a sword."

The hunter and the knight set foot inside the tomb. Darkness wasted no time shrouding the hall. Kasta lowered her optical system and activated the night-vision setting. Dresco ignited his electro-blade: a source of light of his own.

"No geothermal lighting in here," she said. She pulled a cigarillo from her jacket pocket and placed it in her mouth. "Nope. It looks like this tomb's chosen lighting is..." Kasta stopped before a torch, reaching for her utility tool. "Flame," she said, lighting the wick. The fire traveled down the hallway across an oil slick, lighting other torches in its path. Kasta removed her optical system.

"The original light," Dresco said. He deactivated and sheathed his electro-blade.

Sticking her face near one of the torches, Kasta puffed on her cigarillo.

Dresco groaned. "Oh, Miss Krane, do not smoke in here!"

"My name is Kasta, and why the hell not?"

Dresco's hand slapped his armor. "This is the tomb of... of a holy figure. A martyr!"

Kasta shrugged, blowing a cloud of smoke at the knight. "He's dead. What does he care?"

Dresco's shoulders sank. "Why do I even bother?"

"Beats me."

The hallway sloped downward. The dim light of the torches exposed small cylindrical crevices cut into the wall. Heirlooms and trinkets of long-dead lords had once rested in these clefts. But they were now empty. A bearded old man in long, flowing robes watched from the ceiling, frozen in a sequence of glyphs. In one engraving, he grasped a walking stick. In the other, a longsword.

They reached the hall's end. Kasta led Dresco to the right, following the pathway to a square room. "This is the chamber of offerings," she said. "This is where surviving relatives would leave gifts for the dead to take into the afterlife." She leaned against the doorway with her arms crossed.

"Oh, yes. A custom we still practice in the Imperium." Dresco peered inside the room.

Kasta shook her head. "You guys love the old ways." She looked to the opposite end of the chamber, scanning the walls and floors with her optical system. "Normally, this would be the best area in any tomb for a treasure hunter to search, but there ain't much left in here. Plenty of eager hands have beat us to it."

Amethyst and emerald coins lay scattered throughout the floor, covered by shards of glass. A familiar urge to stop and analyze the gemstone coins came over her, but she resisted. Time was of the essence—and a greater treasure awaited. "Come on, let's go," Kasta said. She removed her optical system and left the area.

A circular room, larger than the chamber of offerings, rested at the opposite end of the hall. Fine, intricate engravings covered the walls and ceiling. "This is it," Kasta said. "This is the resting place of Saigus of the House of Vellon." She knelt and brushed aside the dust on the floor, revealing ancient text.

Dresco removed his helmet and covered his mouth. His eyes watered as he bowed his head, whispering a prayer. A jest came to Kasta's mind, but she bit her tongue.

The knight finished his prayer. "What does it say?" He stared over her shoulder, eying the odd text.

Kasta's head tilted to the side. "I'm not completely certain. I've picked up on parts of ancient Vandeni languages from treasure hunting. Not exactly a scholarly education." Her fingers dragged along the ground, following the letterings. "Something like 'A lord of lords who needed no gold to show his status. A true defender of liberty, as the Guardians commanded.' "

"Beautiful words for a martyr," Dresco said. "Does it not make you proud of your country's history?"

Kasta stood. "Nah, not really." She strutted to the wall. Her hand traced the engraved artwork. Most of the pieces depicted Saigus and other members of the House of Vellon. All save for a large piece, which halted her fingers. "Dresco, take a look at this."

The knight stepped beside her. "Oh my," he said at the edge of his breath. "Is this really a...?"

"An artistic rendering of a battle with the Etsinnae," Kasta said. "Some considered it sin to even depict them." Her finger followed the engraving of an Etsinnae from bottom to top; inorganic heads sat atop slender, flowing tentacles. She looked to another part of the artwork. "All seven Relic wielders are represented. But of course, in the center, the Vellon twins lead the charge to defeat the foreign invaders."

Dresco's voice trembled. His armored hand clanged against his breastplate. "It is a beautiful recording of a dark time in history."

Kasta shook her head. "It's a brilliant piece of propaganda." She found her eyes locked with those of the sculpted Etsinnae—the same that her fingers had touched. The creature's eyes were lifeless, yet hungry. Her spine shivered and her muscles tensed—she could not move. Had the creature placed a hex on her? A groaning scream drowned her thoughts. She could hear nothing else. Her stomach tied in a dreadful knot as she stole a shallow breath.

"Is everything okay?" Dresco asked.

"Yeah, fine." She removed her hat and shook her head back and forth. 'Just a stupid carving,' she thought, flicking the depiction of the Etsinnae. She turned away.

Dresco stood in front of a statue at the other end of the chamber. "Ah," Kasta said. She walked toward the same sculpture. "The tomb gargoyle."

With a straightened back, Dresco crossed his arms. "Well, that is a fearsome and unsettling sight. It looks as though a Vanden wolf and a bat created some sort of infertile offspring."

Kasta laughed. "They were supposed to be fearsome. They guarded the dead on their way to the afterlife."

Dresco put his hand over his chin and flipped his hair away from his eyes. "Okay, that is not a custom I am familiar with." The knight looked the statue up and down.

Kasta chuckled and thought, 'Dresco's trying to decide whether the stone wolf is taller than him. How cute.'

She stepped behind the statue. "It was only the most... paranoid of the ancient lords and monarchs who asked for gargoyles to join them on their journeys through death." Kasta stopped in front of a circular portal made from a thick silver metal. She knocked on it three times. "This is it. This is Saigus' grave."

Dresco sidestepped from the statue and loped to Kasta. "Really?"

"Yep. It looks like his body has never been removed. This metal is too thick, and he is buried too deep. Previous treasure hunters probably decided it wasn't worth their time. Or worth the prospect of getting killed by a trap." She ran her fingers along the text inscribed on the doorway. "I think it says 'Of and liberty love.' " Kasta's head tilted to the side. "No idea what that means. That doesn't make sense."

"Kasta, could Vellon's Blade be in the sarcophagus?"

She sighed and leaned back, crossing her arms. "Only one way to find out."

"Perhaps I could be of assistance."

Kasta and Dresco spun to confront whatever voice had just spoken; both companions drew their weapons. The gargoyle had turned around and was facing them. Shuddering as it leaned back, its arms fell to its side. The stone gaze of the statue rolled to Kasta. "And, my dear, the inscription reads 'Of liberty and love.' "

Dresco backed against the wall, his sword held limply. The knight released a scream that tested the limits of his low vocal register. Kasta sprang sideways. Her cigarillo fell to the ground, leaving a trail of embers behind. She grabbed the knight's arm, though her aim never strayed from the gargoyle. "Holy hell, it talks!"

XII

AN ANCIENT AWAKENING

The statue's snout curled to the sound of grinding gravel. "Now that we have gotten over the initial shock of my living essence, shall we begin the procedure?"

"Hey, Dresco," Kasta whispered, her weapon still drawn.

Dresco hesitated to speak as he leaned toward her, his gaze fixed on the stone man. "Yes, Krane?"

She swallowed. "The statue is talking."

The statue lowered his head toward his chest and released a coarse groan. "I see we are not over this yet. That is okay, I suppose." He held out his hand. "Take your time."

Kasta's thumb slid over the small lever on the side of her weapon. For the first time in she did not even know how long, she set her pistol to kill.

Staggering forward, the statue raised his thick index finger. His sharp lower fangs slid over his lips. "My dear, the electrical currents that discharge from the barrel of weapons such as yours will have no effect on me." His eyes, absent of any pupil or iris, rolled to Dresco. "Nor will that senselessly long blade, sire."

Dresco's shoulders sagged as he lowered his sword. "What are you?"

"I believe that your companion here provided me with an adequate introduction." The statue's arm stiffened as he gestured toward Kasta. "I am the guardian of this tomb, the protector of Saigus the Benevolent as he lies in rest. You may refer to me as Veros."

Kasta took a short, deep breath. She had neglected her lungs for almost a minute. "But..." Her trigger finger quivered. "But you're a statue. You're a rock."

Veros snarled. His neck rotated with a chafing crunch. "Do you have something against rocks, Kasta? It was Kasta, right?"

"No, not at all," Kasta replied with a titter. "It's just that in my experience... they typically aren't alive!"

Dresco tapped Kasta's shoulder. "Calm down, Krane." His utterance was docile.

"Calm down? Dresco! The talking gargoyle wants to kill us."

"No, it does not," Dresco said. "You are a divine creature, are you not, Veros? Given life by the Guardians themselves?"

Veros shook his head. His gyrating torso mirrored the motion. "I was given life by clerics of old. Many of whom worshipped the deities you refer to as the Guardians."

Dresco smiled and choked up. "That is incredible." A sparkle found its way into his eye. "You are proof of the Guardians' miraculous wonders!"

Kasta's head tilted. She lowered her hat and stood tall with her arms crossed. "Okay." A sigh slipped between her words. "So, you're some sort of ancient magic trick. You say you can help us open this tomb?"

The gargoyle let out a scraping snarl. His three-toed claw tapped against the floor. "Very interesting," Veros said. "One of you jumps to a religious conclusion regarding my... sudden animation. And the other attempts to rationalize the situation." With a grumbled hum, his toes scratched the stone. "I *can* help you open this tomb, yes. But will I?"

Kasta knelt and picked up her cigarillo, which still bore a faint ember. "I don't know, will you?"

Dresco's hand gripped her shoulder. He shook his head. She took a long drag from the remnant of her cigarillo anyway.

"You seek Vellon's Blade." The statue walked toward the hunter and the knight. The weight of his own body constrained his steps. "Why?"

Dresco stood tall, chest out and chin high. "To prevent the most significant Relic from falling into the wrong hands. One day, it shall be presented to a rightful descendant of the House of Vellon—one who could protect Eramaa from the dark perils of this universe, global and cosmic."

Veros halted before Kasta and Dresco, his shadow surrounding them. "A noble cause indeed." The ridges on the statue's chest moved in and out like X-ray footage of a rib cage expanding with a breath. "You are worthy of your knighthood, it seems." Dresco grinned as the creature's pointed ears fell back. "Tell me," Veros said, "which House are you pledged to?"

Dresco cleared his throat. "Oh no," he said with a stammer. "I am a Knight of the Imperium."

"Hmm," Veros grumbled. "Never heard of the House of the Imperium before."

Dresco's lips smacked and contorted. "Oh, the Imperium is not a House—"

"And what about you, my dear Kasta? What brings you on this quest?"

Kasta took a long drag from her cigarillo, taking her time to respond. "Same reason," she said, blowing out a stream of smoke. "To save the world."

Veros' eyelids narrowed as he stared down at the hunter. "You're lying."

Kasta's legs trembled, though she forced her face to remain blank. "Fine. I'm getting paid. It's a job. Is that what you want to hear?"

"If I believed that you were only seeking Vellon's Blade for profit, we would not be having this conversation, my dear." The statue raised his hand and stepped to her side. His stone thumb fell on the silver portal that sealed Saigus' body in eternal rest.

Kasta crossed her arms. "Then why *are* we having this conversation?"

Though Veros ran his hands down the portal with finesse, his stone fingers scraped the metal surface. "Who knows?" he said, turning around. "Perhaps your knightly companion's honorable nature is what inspired me to awaken."

The gargoyle's tubular shoulder blades elevated, and his neck twisted like a stripped screw. "Perhaps there is more to your integrity than you give yourself credit for?" He trapped Kasta in the corner of his eye. "Or maybe, you are just another grave-robbing would-be body snatcher that I have to neutralize."

Kasta dropped her cigarillo to the ground. One last mushroom cloud of smoke funneled from her lips. "I'm not a grave robber. I'm a treasure hunter."

Dresco crossed his arms. "Really?" he asked, cockeyed.

"What?" She shrugged.

A hollow, grating laugh resounded over the chamber. Veros' jackal-like smile left Kasta breathless and cold. "Well, my dear treasure hunter, if you would like an opportunity to open Saigus' grave, I will give it to you. But you will first have to pass a test."

Kasta's mind was racing, but she leaned against the wall and smiled at the living gargoyle. "I can handle anything." She brought her boot over the remainder of her cigarillo.

"If you stomp that out on the floor of this tomb, you will suffer the same fate as the other *treasure hunters* who have passed through here." The statue shook his head and looked to the ceiling. "So disrespectful."

"That is what I said," Dresco said with a raise of his index finger. "Completely agreed."

Kasta eyed him with a sneer. "What? Are you best friends with the statue now?" She grunted and rolled her eyes. "Stay here with him then." She licked the fingertips of her gloves. After pinching out the ember, she dropped the cigarillo in her vest pocket.

"Oh, stop with your attitude," Dresco said.

"Attitude? You're the one—"

"The rules are simple." Veros' voice overpowered the companions. "Answer three questions correctly and I will allow you access to Saigus' grave. Answer them wrongly, and I shall end your lives. Everyone ready?"

Kasta and Dresco looked to one another, she with widened eyes and he with a sunken jaw. Dresco stammered as he said, "I beg your pardon, majestic servant of the Guardians, but I believe death is a rather harsh punishment for—"

"If you do not like it, noble knight, I believe you know where the exit is." Veros' breath rumbled. "Only those who are worthy may enter."

Kasta glanced at Dresco and nodded. The knight nodded back. With a slanted smile, she winked at the statue. "Shall we begin?"

Veros stepped into the amber glow of the fire. "Very well." His fingernails rubbed his chin with a harsh scrape—like a disdainful whisper. "We are very old, yet at times we are new. On our fair world, of us there are two. Witches have drawn us into their cults, but only at times when we are entirely full."

Dresco smiled. His head tilted back. "It's a riddle."

Kasta leaned his way. "Yeah, do you know the answer?"

He shook his head. "Is it the continents?"

"No," Kasta whispered. "When are the continents ever new?"

Veros tapped his clawed toes against the floor as he hummed an upbeat melody. "Oh, do not mind me, my dear companions. I am very patient."

Kasta's eyes darted between the gargoyle and the knight. "Is it a charge crystal?"

Dresco rested his chin on his hand. "Have you ever heard of a witch bringing a charge crystal into their cult?"

"Good point. Drawn into the cult." Her brow lowered. "But only when I am full." As she recited the rhythm of the riddle, the hunter froze. "The moons!" She looked to Veros, her eyes widening.

"Very good." The gargoyle bowed his head. "Perhaps that was too easy for you. Now let me think." Veros paused for a moment. "I got it! What words are said for a fallen monk before he or she is officially laid to rest?"

Dresco stepped forward, his chin pointed high. Kasta forced her arm across the knight's chestplate to stop him, but it was too late. "May you enter the kingdom of the Guardians as a servant of their will and know eternal peace."

As Dresco's words concluded, a dagger shot toward him. He ducked down and avoided the oncoming blade. Kasta jumped to the side.

"Oh, shame on me. I missed," Veros said, thrusting his fists downward. "I used to be such an excellent knife-thrower. I guess I am out of practice."

Kasta hunched low, peeking over her shoulder. The rock-carved knife had pierced the stone wall behind them, wedged to the hilt. With a long step, she turned to face Dresco. "You idiot!" she hissed through clenched teeth, grabbing the knight by the collar. She stood on the tips of her toes, bringing their faces into tight proximity. "You can't recite an Imperial prayer to a five-thousand-year-old murderous tomb gargoyle. He doesn't even know what the Imperium is!"

"How rude!" Veros exclaimed. "I am four thousand seven hundred forty-two! Not five thousand!"

Kasta turned around and tipped her hat. "Sorry, Veros. I didn't mean to call you old."

"Apology accepted," Veros said. He made a motion akin to adjusting his jacket, though he was not wearing one. "But do you know the answer to my question? You get another chance in light of my blade... sadly missing your companion's cranium." He looked to the floor with a solemn bow of his head.

Dresco looked down to Kasta. She shook her head, gritting her teeth. "I am sorry," the knight said. "I was too anxious to answer. I should have been more prudent."

She ignored him, pacing back and forth. "About four thousand seven hundred fifty years old," she said to herself. "What tombs have I previously explored from that era?"

Dresco's finger rose. "Did you by any chance come across any scriptures regarding fallen individuals while we were in the Temple of Serev—I mean Jellinok?"

"No," Kasta said. "And if I did, I wouldn't remember." She took off her hat and ran her fingers through her greasy hair. "Guardians be damned, what kind of a question is this?"

'Maybe I can use my data system to access the satellite network,' she thought. 'Just look up the answer.' But something told her that Veros would not allow this—and a stone dagger would end up in her skull.

She continued to pace, passing Dresco every few seconds. A memory came to her: a job she had done on behalf of a professor at a wealthy lyceum. She'd sought and recovered an ancient scripture—a scroll of the dead. She remembered skimming it. What translations did it hold?

She pressed her thumb and index finger into her forehead. 'Think, Krane, think!' Her steps stopped. 'But it couldn't be that simple.' Her cyan eyes narrowed on Dresco. "No, it couldn't be that simple, could it?" she said aloud.

"Um, what?" Dresco asked with a slight shrug.

'It has to be,' she thought, dropping her hat atop her head. "Nothing!" she called out, twirling toward Veros. "The funerals of monks were silent."

Veros stood rigid. He reached to his belt, rubbing the circular-tipped hilt of one of his daggers. Kasta swallowed as the statue began to speak. "I'll take that answer." Kasta and Dresco released a simultaneous exhalation of relief. Veros continued, "Though it was not completely silent. There was beautiful music." The statue smiled once more; this time he looked more like a tame house fox than a jackal.

"Good work," Dresco said with a slight smile, looking Kasta's way.

She responded with an upward nod.

"Okay. Our final question." Veros' fangs slid over his lips. The gargoyle stepped out of the torchlight and toward the companions. "A bloodline mixed of south and north, and the island folk's grand rogue shores. A rightful wielder of a divine device. It is to her call you will answer in the darkest of night."

"Another riddle," Dresco said with a heavy sigh.

"Yeah." Kasta leaned against the wall. She crossed her arms as her lips pursed to the side. "A rightful wielder of a divine device." The hunter eyed Veros. "A Relic wielder of some kind, I assume?"

Veros trudged toward her. "Are you truly asking me for a hint, my dear huntress?"

Kasta shook her head. "No, I am just thinking out loud." She looked to Dresco. "Any ideas? What Relic wielder could it be?"

Dresco cleared his throat. His right foot shuffled over the floor, leaving a wake of dust. "I am not sure. It could be any of them. Oh, but it must be a female. He said, 'to *her* call we will answer.' "

Kasta snapped, though her glove muted the sound. "Good thinking, Norte." She kicked herself off the wall, flashing Veros a glance. His eyes of stone followed her. "Okay," she said, aiming her finger at the knight. "Think of female Relic wielders who fit the description. Could it be Mikala Haelovar?"

Dresco shook his head as he leaned forward, his arms crossed in the same manner as Kasta's. "No. Mikala Haelovar was not a mixblood."

Kasta leered at the ceiling with a groan. "Damn, that's true. That makes this tougher. How many of the Relic wielders were said to be mixbloods in the stories of old?"

Dresco let a breath out the side of his mouth. "Very few. And even less were Islander mixbloods. In fact, I cannot think of any!"

Kasta's upper lip rose. She shook her head. "Neither can I. And he was a little more specific. He said grand *rogue* shores. He was referring to Rogue Haven."

"Nothing slips by you, does it, my dear?" Veros said with a coarse chortle.

Dresco closed his eyes. "So, we have a female with Vandeni, Islander and *possibly* Imperial blood. Though Imperial society was not yet formed when this tomb was constructed, nor were our most notable genetic traits. We think she was a Relic wielder but cannot be certain." The knight's eyes peeled open. "We have not exactly narrowed this down."

"Wait!" Kasta said. "What if it's not a Relic wielder at all? 'We will answer her call in the darkest night.' It's prophetic. Perhaps he is referring to a Guardian. Could it be Vellon?"

Veros mimicked the sound of a clearing throat. "Is that your answer?" he asked.

"No!" Kasta and Dresco answered in simultaneous panic.

Dresco's nose crinkled as he looked down. "Vellon, the Guardian of liberty, does not possess any female traits, Miss Krane!"

"Oh, how do you know Vellon's not a woman?" Kasta said with a scoff.

"Because he has never been depicted in such a way."

"He *or* she is not real anyway. What does it matter?"

"Children!" Veros said. "I believe you were answering the final question."

Kasta leaned toward Dresco. "Okay. Probably not Vellon. I'll give you that. But what other figure relates to us, Norte? You and me, right now. Or to the world? How did ancient Vandeni prophets predict that Eramaa would end up? Whose call will we answer in 'the darkest of night'? It's probably not some ancient, dead lords who swung an heirloom around."

Dresco did not respond. He stood and stared downward. Other than the slow grinding of his teeth, he made no sound or motion. His eyes shut. What was he thinking?

Dresco's eyelids sundered, revealing the entirety of his grey irises. "Madame Sariya Vaeliz," he called out, looking to Veros with a firm lift of his head.

Kasta's lower canines sank into her upper lip, almost breaking the skin. "What did you just do?" she said, a tremble in her voice. But before Kasta's anger could grow, a metallic clash grabbed her attention. The lock on the silver portal that concealed the body of Saigus unbolted.

"Huh?" Kasta's spine straightened. The coffin began to slide out from behind the aperture. "How..." She looked to Veros, her jaw dropping. "How do you know who Madame Vaeliz is? You don't even know what the Imperium is."

"I know what the Imperium is," Veros said with a slow blink. "Though my physical form may be bound to a cave, I am not fully ignorant of Eramaa's happenings."

Kasta walked to Dresco and placed her hand on his elbow. "Dresco, how did you know?"

He glanced at her with a smirk. "Deductive reasoning."

She chuckled. "Hell, that's the smartest thing you've ever said. I thought you were gunna tell me that the Guardians told you to do it or something weird like that."

The coffin continued to slide out from the tomb, made from the same silver metal as the portal. Legs grew from the bottom of the sarcophagus for weight support. "It was the Guardians who gave us the ability to reason, Krane," Dresco said.

"Quit while you're ahead, Norte." Kasta tapped the knight on the back as she stepped toward the coffin, which had emerged from the threshold in its entirety. The argent casket bore a single piece of artwork: a large engraving of Vellon's Blade. The depiction of the sword shone in an outline of gold and emerald. "Are you ready, Dresco?" she asked. Her restless foot tapped against the floor.

"Yes," Dresco said, his gaze frozen on the coffin. His body was stiff. Stiffer than usual, as if he were unable to move at all.

Kasta peered over her shoulder at the statue whose game they had won. She lifted her head his way.

Veros replied with a nod.

A grin grew on her face so crooked that it could have had its own political career. She pressed a button on the middle of the sarcophagus. The lid crawled sideways, trundling and creaking. "Gentlemen, ummm and statue." The astonishment of conversing with a gargoyle faded amid the game of riddles, hidden beneath distress and adrenaline. However, at that moment, the feeling crawled back into her mind. She shook the sensation, continuing her speech. "May we behold the greatest treasure hunter in the world, capturing the world's greatest treasure!"

The coffin top slid off. A blackened skeleton lay inside, broken jaw gaping skyward. In his left hand, he held a folded-up piece of paper.

But there was no sword. Kasta sighed and shook her head. Dresco reached inside the coffin and removed the piece of paper with delicacy. "It's a map!" he said, unfolding the document. "It points somewhere out at—out at sea. Off the western shore."

"Great." Kasta rested her hand on the coffin's edge and bowed her head. "Another map."

"Yes," Veros said, staring at the grave of Saigus. "Two men removed the sword from this tomb about eight hundred years after it was sealed. They desired its power—and passed the test, as the two of you have also done. Years later, one of the men returned and left a map. He said it led to a key that would open a sacred place. But he never returned Vellon's Blade."

Kasta stepped away from the coffin. The lid slid back on top, closing Saigus in his resting place once again. "You could have told us that before," she said, her gills flaring.

"No." Veros took slow steps around the room as the coffin slid back into the orifice. "That is not my purpose."

Kasta's head flung back. She looked to the ceiling with a fake smile. "Whatever. I'm out of here."

She stomped toward the chamber's exit. Dresco scampered behind. "Kasta, wait!"

Veros called out to the companions, "Dearest hunter, my noble knight. One word of advice." His legs stiffened and tensed. "Remember that Relics are meant for Relic wielders. If you attempt to harness a Relic's power and are unworthy, it will corrupt your soul as punishment." The gargoyle's wings spread out and his mouth froze agape. With a sound resembling a small rockslide, Veros fell still and returned to his initial state as a lifeless statue.

"Wait!" Dresco called out to the hunter. She stamped down the hallway toward the tomb's exit. "Kasta, why are you in such a hurry? We have to discuss this."

"I think I'm done, Norte," she snapped.

"Done? What do you mean done?" Dresco's steps clanked from behind like an oncoming train.

Kasta sighed and shook her head. "This is all a wild-goose chase, just like I thought. A map that leads to another map that leads to a key? We'll be doing this forever."

Dresco caught up, stumbling as he slowed his stride. "Kasta, we are close! This map will lead us to the blade. I know it!" His voice rose several steps in pitch. "Did you not notice that we just had an interaction with a statue? He was there to test us, a divine trial from the Guardians to examine if we are worthy of this quest! Kasta, this is destiny."

"What I saw was an incredibly intricate tomb trap. It was nothing but a trick, a mechanical device of ancient days."

Dresco giggled as he responded, "Kasta, even you cannot believe that. What we just witnessed, what we just took part in was mystical in nature. I will be damned. It was something significant to the course of our lives! How can you not see this objective truth?"

As Kasta stepped out of the tomb, she turned around. "Why is your skin green?" she asked, her upper lip curled.

"Pardon?"

"Your skin. It's dark-green. Why?"

Dresco removed his glove and beheld his green hand. "Oh, indeed," the knight said with a nod. "I sometimes lose track of my skin pigmentation when my mood changes rapidly. Specifically, when I'm excited."

Kasta rolled her eyes and jogged down the stairs. "Damn, you're weird."

Dresco followed. "Oh, can you stop being so crass? I am trying to have a conversation with you here."

Kasta let out a raspy chuckle, unaccompanied by a smile. "Who are you to call me crass? You just said your first swear word."

"I did no such thing!"

"You did. You said 'I will be damned.' You're becoming more Vandeni every day you spend here."

Dresco grunted and whispered to himself, his words too quiet to decipher. "Listen," he said with a shallow breath. "I think you know how important this quest is, Krane. You may not want to show it, but I believe you know, in your heart and in your soul."

Kasta's boots touched the red sand at the bottom of the stairs. "Look, Dresco, we tried to find the sword. It has been a valiant effort. But I've been down this road before. Clues and maps and artifact analysis, leading to distant excavation sites. Then you search and you dig. And you end up finding nothing but new clues and new maps." She reached for Kai, patting her on the head. "It's an endless escapade, a waste of time and a drain on my resources. A hell-bent headache."

Dresco stood next to her with his hands crossed in front of his waist. "Kasta, this time, the fate of the world may depend on investigating some dead ends. It may require some more funding. You have always stated that you are 'the best treasure hunter that Vanda has to offer.' Put those skills to use for the sake of Eramaa! Can you please find it in yourself—?"

"Dresco!" Kasta took hold of Kai's reins and leaned toward the knight. "The problem with this treasure hunt is that there are people trying to *kill* me. There's a huge price on my head. I can't be riding cross-continent right now." She reached into the pannier on Kai's back and pulled out a piece of raw meat. "We'll be dead before we reach the western shore."

Dresco lifted a finger. "We can book passage on an airship!"

Kasta fed Kai and Crevallus a piece of the meat. "Great idea, Norte." Her brow rose high. "Let's ride right into a crowded city and hop on an airship. Very discreet."

His hands extended sideways. "We'll rent our own."

"Oh, you gunna pay for that?" she asked with a vicious smile.

"But Marshal Jos would be delighted to help—"

"No airships." Kasta climbed atop her saddle. Her fingers tightened around the reins. Kai let out a soft growl. "Come on, Norte. Let's get back to the Vaeliz estate. We'll get our eight thousand platinum for our searcher's fee and lay low for a while. Then, *maybe*, once my bounty is declared illegal in every territory of Vanda, we can get back to this little errand, okay?" She ran her hand down Kai's neck. The beast's rough scales sank with her rider's touch. "But for now, let's ride. Let's try our best to get out of this valley before nightfall." She flung the reins down. Kai raced into Athenis' light, which waned behind the wall of the canyon.

"We do not have time to spare, Kasta! Every moment we waste brings the Imperium closer to possessing Vellon's Blade." She rode away from Dresco. His voice fell faint, speaking a final warning. "And if that happens, we are all doomed."

XIII

UNDER THE MOON'S SHADOW

A breeze whistled through the canyon. Kasta took a deep breath as the icy wind brushed through her hair. She was grateful to be outside, away from that tomb that bore the remains of Saigus, away from Veros. 'How could a statue come to life?' she thought. 'How could it move, converse and *reason* as well as a person?'

She exhaled through the side of her mouth. "Okay, we're coming up on the mining trail," she whispered to herself. "Moons are on the rise, and the sky is darkening. Time to get out of here and put this calamity of a quest behind me—oh no," Kasta interrupted herself as they approached the trail. The hunter rushed to activate her communication system. "Dresco, pick up speed."

Dresco's muffled voice came through her earphone. "What is it?"

She pointed up the path they had used to enter the valley earlier in the day. "There's something up on the mining trail." She lowered her targeting system. "I hear a gallop."

"Oh my," Dresco said as Crevallus groaned. "I do as well. It's getting nearer. You do not think it could be bandits, do you?"

"Could be." Kasta's digital scans came back negative. "It could also just be a couple of wild animals. But let's not ride up there to find out." She looked ahead. "We'll go forward, through the valley."

"I thought Marshal Jos said the mining trail would be devoid of bandits."

"He did," Kasta said, leaning forward. Another gust of wind passed over like a whispering wraith. "But I don't like it. We'll find another way out. Turn off all travel lights."

"If you say so," Dresco said hesitantly.

"We'll carry on, quickened pace. But quietly." Kasta patted Kai on the top of her head where the trugan's rough hide met her horn. "*Very* quietly, girl."

Kaiar responded with a soft hiss and carried on through the wide canyon. As they passed the mining route, Kasta turned and looked up the pathway. 'No one's following us. That's good.' Crevallus did his best to follow Kaiar's example of a soft gallop, but the male trugan's bulky claws crunched against the pebbles and gravel.

They rounded a corner, treading farther into the valley. Kasta felt a second urge to look back. She activated the night-vision setting of her optical system. An instinctive sensation clawed at the back of her mind; someone watched from the cliffs above the mining trail. The hunter reached down the pannier on Kai's back and brought her rifle to ready position.

She saw it. A figure in the shadows, high above. "Oh no," she muttered.

"What is it?"

Kasta did not answer the knight. Her optical system zoomed in on the silhouette. Her finger wrapped around the trigger of her rifle. The image came into focus: a Draekalagon kneeling behind a rock, armed with a rifle of her own, sights aimed in Kasta's vicinity.

'Okay, I don't think she sees our faces. If we can just keep going at a high speed, she'll think we're just a couple bandits or drifters.' The

Draekalagon's aim hovered over the hunter. 'She can't see that it's me. We're okay.'

Heavy galloping echoed behind. Kasta turned around—but saw nothing. 'That is not good.' She looked to the cliffs. The sniper's aim remained steady. The wall of galloping loomed nearer. She turned again and saw them. Four, perhaps five riders on truganback stampeding toward the hunter and the knight.

"Dresco," Kasta said over her communication system. "Ride faster." She followed her own advice and gave Kai a stern kick to the stomach.

"Kasta, there are riders behind us. Are they bandits?" Dresco asked, his voice shaking.

Her focus was on the sniper. They were nearing a corner. 'If she's going to fire, she'll do it now. Don't shoot first, Krane.' Kasta's finger twitched over the rifle's trigger. 'If you shoot first, they'll know it's you.' Or did they already know?

"Oh, hell," Kasta said with a roll of her eyes. The hunter fired three shots from her rifle, sending two streams of electricity against the rocks and one into the heavens, a bolt of lightning in retreat. The Draekalagon sniper ducked for cover. Kasta knew that the shot would not strike the Draekalagon. Not while moving at such a high speed. But it bought them time. And she hoped it would buy them enough.

Kasta turned to Dresco. "Ride hard. Full gallop! Go, go, go!" The hunter slapped her reins down on Kai's neck. The mechanisms and circuitry under the trugan's skin hummed, increasing in pitch and volume. "Ride, Norte. Ride! Ride!" Kaiar's unnatural acceleration left a cratering trail behind.

Dresco shouted back, "Who are you firing at in the hills, Krane?" His voice fell faint against the wind.

"A sniper!" Kasta screamed back to the knight. "And if it is who I think it is, you need to ride *harder* and *faster*. Now!" As they rounded the corner, an electrical stream came slashing through the valley, striking the wall behind Dresco.

They were out of the sniper's sights once they came around the bend. At least until the Draekalagon could reestablish her position. Kasta sought a way out, but she was in unfamiliar territory. The valley blurred by. Stars quaked and smeared across the sky. There was no exit path on either side of the canyon. They would have to continue straight ahead.

The encroaching gallop grew louder and heavier. She kicked Kai in the stomach, hoping that her mount had one more level of speed. She looked over her shoulder. Her companion fell farther behind. "Dresco," she said over her communication device. "Ride faster. Ride like your life depends on it. Your life *does* depend on it." She gave Kai another hard kick to the stomach.

Dresco's panting crackled through her earphone. "Who is behind us?"

"The Moon Shadow Riders, Norte! Dast found us. And if he catches us, we are dead!"

The riders continued to gain ground on them. Kasta ducked as a stream of lightning flew over her head, followed by a thunderous echo. "Head down!" She was more worried about a blast striking one of the trugan, for they were bigger targets.

Kasta turned and fired two shots from her pistol, which missed by a wide margin. She did not need to strike them. As long as the return fire cautioned the pursuers to keep their distance. "Dresco, if you ever were to decide to change your outlook on wielding a shock-cannon..."

The knight did not answer. Instead, he drew his sword, ignited its electrical current and held it high over his head. When Kasta was about to reject the *absurd* notion of Dresco using a sword in a high-speed chase, several bolts of electricity veered from their trajectory to the tip of the blade. The melee weapon had become a conductor of enemy fire.

"Different, but I'll take it." Kasta's relief was short-lived. Two more riders approached from a wide angle. "Damn it, they're trying to pincer us in. Dresco, distract the group behind us. I'm going after the two coming from the side."

"Oh yes, go right on ahead. I am doing just fine here. Thank you."

Kasta split off to the right. She rode to the opposite side of the valley, past another grave and along the jagged rock wall. She lowered her pistol, aiming for the two riders who moved to intercept Dresco. Kasta changed direction, charging toward them. They slowed down and fired several shots at her.

They missed. She used the opportunity to fire four shots back, two of which struck the riders. Though her pistol was set to incapacitate, one of the outlaws fell to the ground, unconscious. He may not have survived the fall. The other sat limply on the back of his trugan.

Sweat drizzled down the hunter's brow. She caught her breath. Her eyes widened as she turned to Dresco. The main group of Moon Shadow Riders had gained on him. They were on his tail, still firing. Kasta gasped and slapped her reins on Kaiar's hide. "Let's go!" she shouted to her mount, leaning low.

Kaiar dashed toward the Moon Shadow Riders. Electrical streams erupted from their shock-cannons. The Valley of Tombs fulminated with unrelenting thunder. As his blade absorbed enemy fire, a luminous orb of light formed around Dresco. He flashed in and out of visibility.

"Travel lights on. Brightest setting. As bright as they can be," Kasta yelled over the wind, "Yeah, that's right, you gangster bastards, take a shot at me!" Her voice cracked, for an electrical stream flashed over her head, forcing her to duck. She approached. The blasts of lightning came closer to striking her. All they needed was one lucky shot. Kaiar galloped in a zigzag formation to avoid the enemy volleys. The beast razed the crimson terrain, releasing a fearsome roar. Kasta buried her motion sickness and leaned with Kai's swerves, holding on to her hat.

She passed Dresco and screamed, "Kai, full stop!" The beast's claws dug into the terrain, launching an eruption of red sand above her rider's head. Kaiar screeched in what must have been terrible pain.

Kasta raised her pistol and aimed for the passing Moon Shadow Riders. She pulled the trigger. The blast did not strike the woman she aimed for, though she did hit her trugan. The shot was not strong enough to incapacitate the beast. However, it did slow down, dazed and weakened.

"Kai, I'm sorry, girl. But we gotta take off again; full speed if you can."

Kai shrieked and hissed. The rider on the weakened mount took aim.

"Now, Kai!"

Kaiar lunged into a gallop again, struggling to accelerate. She was exhausted. The rider fired. Kasta flinched as the blinding lightning surged over her head; the echoing thunder deafened her ears to a high-pitched ring.

The hunter's heart raced. She moved in pursuit of the group chasing Dresco. They were about a half mile ahead. Two were behind him, while one was unaccounted for. Kasta deactivated her travel lights.

The stars sailed by in a blur once more, the canyon walls like an aslant rockslide. Kai had reached her peak speed. The two riders closed in on Dresco. They had to decelerate, or they would pass him by. If there was ever an opportunity to catch up, this was it.

A shot came from behind a rock. Kaiar detected the hidden attacker before Kasta did; the beast leapt to avoid the oncoming fire. "That's my girl!" Kasta yelled. The hunter and her steed gained on Dresco's pursuers.

The outlaw hiding behind the rock fired several more shots. All off their mark.

Kasta approached the first rider: a Draekalagon male. No doubt, Nellik of Grathank. Nellik's reptilian eyes narrowed on the hunter. He yelled. While his words were indecipherable, his intention was malicious and indignant, communicated with clarity by the barrel of his scatter-cannon, staring Kasta in the face.

She screamed. A loose funnel of electrical streams spiraled toward her. Pulling the reins right, she evaded the attack, though a small bolt grazed Kaiar's skin. Kai did not slow. The pain intensified the steed's anger. She leapt to engage Nellik and his trugan with a roar.

"No," Kasta said, tugging her reins. "If you pounce on them while we're moving this fast, we'll die too!"

Kaiar grunted with displeasure.

Kasta discharged a curtain of fire from her pistol, but Nellik's motions were unpredictable. He accelerated—then slowed down, riding in a diagonal formation. There was no way she could hit him.

Kasta moved to pass the Draekalagon outlaw, mimicking his crossing pattern. She turned her head. Nellik was reaching for something: a small spherical object. He tossed it toward Kasta. Her instincts and reflex enhancers told her to stand high on her stirrups. With a wobbling struggle to keep her balance, she reached out and caught the object: a voltage grenade. She threw it back at Nellik. He brought his trugan to a full stop, his fang-filled mouth gaping wide. A flash of light erupted from the grenade and spread into a violent thicket of electric beams.

One more Moon Shadow Rider remained ahead. She did not need to see his face. She knew his shape—his riding pattern, his stance, his shadow. Breylu Dast was within reaching distance of Dresco Norte, but his attention shifted behind. Dast slowed, bringing himself parallel to

Kasta. The blue-grey skin between his leather mask and tall hat seethed in the moonlight. The darkness of night would have shrouded his eyes had it not been for their bright neon-green glow.

They reached for their weapons. Kasta fired from her pistol and Dast from his carbine. Both shots missed. Dresco turned at the sound of shock-cannon fire. Dast squinted behind the circular specs that shielded his glaring eyes. His cybernetic finger squeezed the trigger of his cannon. Kasta raised her shooting hand, and the rivals fired again. Their shots streamed high and crossed in the shape of an *X* overhead. Heavy gallops approached from the rear. Some of the other riders had caught up.

Kasta leaned low, her boots digging into her stirrups. This was not a fight that she could win. She flashed Dast a wink. He fired once more. But Kai had already accelerated past his aim.

"Dresco!" Kasta called through the communication system. "When I say, jump from Crevallus' back to Kai's!"

Dresco's voice came screeching back through her earphone, hurting Kasta's ear. "Are you bloody mad?! I'll assuredly be killed if I jump off the saddle at this speed."

"We'll be dead if you *don't* do it. We'll slow down. Just enough so you can make the jump. Either that or I leave you out here. Got it?"

After a short pause, Dresco replied, "I got it."

"Good," Kasta said. "Wait for my say so and keep that sword high above your head until you hear it."

She refused to look back. But Dast aimed for her. She was sure of it. He was waiting for Kasta to break formation, for a straight shot. Hitting a mark while moving at such speeds was almost impossible. But near-impossibilities find ways to make themselves frequent factors of life. Dast was one lucky shot away from achieving his lifelong goal: killing Kasta Krane. If his sights found her, he would not miss.

'Not today,' she thought. 'Not today.' She had a plan. She was not sure if it was a good plan, but she had one.

"Get ready, Dresco," Kasta said. They prepared to round a tight turn. The trugan slowed down as they approached the curve. When the path straightened again, Kasta yelled, "Now!"

The knight launched himself from Crevallus' saddle, reaching out. Kasta's eyes widened. He plummeted toward her. His arms wrapped around Kaiar's neck. The trugan thrust her head upward, allowing Dresco to slide to her back.

"I made it!" Dresco yelled with a cackle. "I actually made it!"

Kasta had to reach around Dresco's torso to grasp the reins. "Prepare for a hard left," she said.

Dresco looked back, his head tilted sideways. "Hard left into what?"

Kasta yanked Kai's reins, leaning in the opposite direction. She steered the beast through a narrow passage on the side of the cliff. Dresco hung tightly to the reins, his legs flailing at Kaiar's side.

Crevallus continued through the valley as Kasta hoped he would. Kaiar galloped down the path. Kasta turned her head; both to her relief and surprise, only one Moon Shadow Rider had followed them. The others had stayed on Crevallus' trail, under the impression that one or both of Kasta and Dresco were still on his back. But the trick would be worthless if the outlaw behind them called the others for backup.

Several trees, some more dead than others, grew along the sides of the path. As she passed them, Kasta fired a series of shots from her shock-cannon. Flames engulfed the trees, raining on the dry shrubs and brown leaves below. After burning several trees, she looked behind. A wall of fire blocked the pathway.

"How did—?" Dresco's voice trembled. "What just happened?"

"You're in a bit of shock, Norte. Let it pass." Kasta rode through the narrow slopes. They had to stop soon, for Kaiar's body was depleted. Bearing both Kasta and Dresco on her back increased the burden.

As they moved askew up the trail, thunder echoed across the canyon, followed by a roaring shriek. "Crevallus," Dresco uttered.

Kasta shook her head. "I'm afraid so. I was hoping they wouldn't catch him, but it sounds like their sniper just took him out." Kasta slowed down, approaching a junction in the trail. "There's one," she said.

"There's one what?" At the end of Dresco's query, Kasta turned to the right. The sight of the purple-and-blue night sky fell into a shadow of black. Kasta pulled back on Kai's reins until she was moving at a soft trot. The beast let out a hissing sigh of relief.

"A cave," Dresco whispered.

"Of sorts," Kasta said. She lowered her optical system and switched on the night-vision setting. "A tomb." The green hue of Kasta's night vision revealed a long stone hall with a doorway at the end. "A small tomb for an individual of lesser importance. They're scattered all over the side paths of the valley."

Dresco slumped down. "So, we're going to hide here?"

"Yes," Kasta said. "And I found it just in time too. Their sniper has reestablished position, and she doesn't miss much. Vinai of Oglund, they call her."

"Draekalagon scum," Dresco mumbled. "I will avenge your death, Crevallus. With the aid of the Guardians, I will avenge your death."

They turned through the doorway at the end of the hall, which led to a small room. Kasta shook her head. "Crev would still be alive if you knew how to ride worth a damn, Norte."

Dresco turned and grunted. "That is an awful thing to say, Krane."

Kasta's eyes rolled as Kaiar came to a halt. "Okay, but seriously. How are you that bad at riding? You're a knight. Didn't you ever joust or something?"

Dresco cleared his throat. "Excuse me, but no, I have never jousted. And *certainly* not on a trugan." His head sank. "Okay. I jousted once. Not all knights engage in that sort of... spectacle." He raised a finger. "But I was *excellent* on an Imperial steed."

"Dresco!"

"Fine. I was terrible," he admitted.

Kasta shook her head. She stepped from Kaiar's back and stood on her own feet. "You're not too good at lying either," she said with a groan as an assembly of aches and pains made their presence known.

After Dresco stepped off Kaiar's back, the trugan fell to the floor. Her forked tongue slopped on the ground as she panted.

Kasta reached in Kai's pannier to fetch her some water. A soft hum rang in her ear. She froze in place as goosebumps scattered across her skin.

"What is it?" Dresco asked, removing his helmet.

"Unauthorized transmission coming through my communication device." Kasta's finger trembled, pressing an icon on the device, which connected the transmission. She held her breath during the ensuing silence, a moment that felt like a full minute.

"Hello, Kasta." A crackling voice came over the speaker and slithered into her ear like an eel.

"Breylu," Kasta said. Dresco's face sank. "Sorry we couldn't catch up earlier."

"Oh, as am I." Fuzz and feedback came through the speaker. His words bled through the background noise. "But I will. Oh, Kasta, how you know I will."

Kasta leaned back and stared at the ceiling. "Let's settle it then, Dast. You and me. One on one. Just like you've always wanted, you deranged scumbag." A crooked smirk fell on her face.

A slow, ruffled laugh permeated in response. "Oh, my old friend. You know we are way past that now. There's a nice little price on your head. And you can bet I'm going to collect."

"Save your threats, Dast." Bitterness rested on her lips. "You did try to collect. And you failed like you always do."

Dresco whispered, asking if Dast could trace their position via the communication signal.

Kasta glanced at the knight, shaking her head. She continued, "You haven't got me yet. You're not gunna get me now."

Breylu Dast's voice sank low and trembled. "I am certainly glad that I have restrained myself from ending your life thus far, Kasta. Now your death will bring me gratification *and* more platinum than even you could ever dream of." Dast groaned before continuing. "Kasta, by the time I am through with you, you're going to wish that you would have killed me when you had the chance. Your merciful little code, it's going to mean your end. I'm going to kill you, your new knightly friend, your precious little Kaiar..."

Kasta's fist tightened.

"...And I'm going to find that old sword you've been trying to dig up."

Kasta gasped. Before she could conjure a response, Dast disconnected the transmission.

Dresco stepped toward her. "What did he say?"

Kasta's eyes crawled up to him. She cleared her throat. "He..." She shook her head and swallowed, unable to believe the words she was about to speak. "He knows we've been looking for Vellon's Blade."

Dresco clutched the long locks of hair on the sides of his head. "No... that can't be. How—how is that possible?"

"And he's looking for it too."

XIV

OLD FIRES

"H ow—?"

"I don't know." Kasta cut off Dresco before he could finish his question.

"Yes, but how could he even know that we—?"

"Hold on!" Kasta stuck a finger toward him. Her back thumped against the wall. "Just let me think for a minute." Her eyelids fell shut.

Dresco's feet scraped over the gravel on the floor. "Kasta, we need to consider—"

"Keep your voice down," she hissed. "There's a gang of murderers out there looking for us, remember?"

Dresco froze in his steps, shoulders sagging. "Good point," he uttered. He took a delicate stride toward Kasta. "I just want to know what our next move is."

Kasta sighed. Her back sank down the wall. "For now, we wait." She rested her hands on her knees and sat down. "And we make our exit once Dast and his gang have moved on." Her upper lip twitched. "Or until they find us. And we at least go down fighting."

"How did he find us in the first place?" the knight asked with a sideways glance.

"Could have done it a few ways. Could have been informants in Vulture; he has spies everywhere. Hell, he could have just tracked us.

It could be any combination of methods with the funding that your Imperial friends are giving him."

Dresco spoke over Kaiar's husky groaning. "There is no chance he could be tracking our data systems or communication devices?"

"Unlikely," Kasta said. "Communication devices are nearly untraceable; their signals are scrambled when they pass through the satellites. And my data system uses an encrypted code to transmit. Yours on the other hand—" Her mouth remained open as her sentence halted. "Yeah, you should probably turn that off."

"I should?" Dresco asked, panicked.

A grim smile fell on Kasta's face. "Don't worry. Even if they *could* trace your data system, it would only give them a general circumference. But just to be safe, I'd deactivate it." She reached into her vest for her utility tool and a cigarillo.

"Oh, indeed," Dresco said with a single nod. His hands fumbled about his body, patting his armor down. "I left my new data system in the pannier on Crevallus' back. At least they can't track it now." The knight frowned and bowed his head. "Oh Crevallus, poor little bugger."

Kasta nodded, lighting her cigarillo. "Rest in peace, Crev," she said, gazing upward. Her eyes examined the dark room. Empty sockets that had once held gems lay scattered across the wall, though the sarcophagus at the opposite side rested undisturbed.

"Kasta," Dresco said, a slight crack in his voice. "Why would the Imperium hire Dast to seek Vellon's Blade?" He sank to one knee, bringing himself to her level.

Kasta rubbed the nape of her neck. She rested her forearm atop her knee. "Breylu has always fancied himself a treasure hunter. And he has studied my tactics. I could see how the Imps figured he'd be the man for the job."

Dresco swallowed.

Kasta's head tilted back and forth, her lips pursed to the side. "As soon as he caught word that we were looking for the sword, I'm sure he developed an obsessive urge to find it as well. The bastard hates me." She took a short puff from her cigarillo.

"Why?"

"Why what?"

"Why does he hate you so much?"

Kasta's eyes rolled and hid behind a long blink. "I told you I've beat him to the punch on a few jobs—"

"No, no. I know this part of the story." His hand stretched forward. "I want the *whole* story."

"That is the whole story," Kasta said through a cloud of smoke.

"He seeks your demise because he is jealous that you are the 'greatest treasure hunter in the world'?"

His tone was mocking. Offensive even. However, she bit her tongue and swallowed her pride. Her anger faded. "Money makes people do crazy things," she said. Her gaze shifted toward the corner of the room. 'As does revenge,' she thought.

"His eyes," Dresco said hesitantly. "They held an unnatural glow. A bright shade of green."

"Ocular night vision," Kasta replied with a cold, monotone inflection. "He has implants in his corneas. He can do anything I can do with my optical system with his own eyes." She pointed to the device on top of her hat. "And that's just one of his many cybernetic augmentations. The scum must have hundreds by now. Thought motivators, bone metallization, regenerative tissue implants. If a biomechanical surgeon invents any type of new tech, you can bet that Breylu Dast is going to put it in his body."

The tips of Dresco's armored fingers grated against the gravel. "My goodness. Why would one defile their own anatomy to such an extent?"

Kasta looked to him with a blank expression, ashing her cigarillo with a forceful flick. "He lost his leg several years back. Once he got it replaced with a mechanical limb, it sent him on a spree of cyberizing the rest of his body. He went mad." The cold, dark chamber swallowed her whispers. "If he couldn't be fully organic, he would make it his mission to become inorganic: a machine."

Dresco squinted, his glance turning diagonal. "How do you know so much about him?"

She shrugged and inhaled a deep pull of smoke. "Know your enemy or know your death."

Kaiar's head shot up, jerking left to right. She dug her claws into the floor with a spasmodic pivot.

Kasta heard a soft gallop. "Quiet!" she said with a sharp whisper.

Dresco also must have heard the gallop, for he froze in place, leaning toward the small chamber's entrance. Kasta's fingers wrapped around her pistol. The knight did not reach for his weapon. He held still. Kai, in her weakness, did not stand or prepare to pounce. She flashed her fangs, lying on her stomach.

But a fight would not be necessary. The galloping passed.

Kaiar groaned as her head fell back to the floor. Dresco sighed. "That was close," he said at the edge of his breath. "How do we know they will not find us here, Krane? It's not the most elusive location."

"We don't," Kasta said, stomping out her cigarillo. "I'm banking on Dast thinking we'd run rather than hide."

"Reassuring," Dresco said with an intent nod, his lips tucking in.

"As always, I'm open to suggestions, my noble knight." Her eyes widened. "Please come up with a plan that gives us a better chance of survival. Because I do admit, it *is* kind of a stretch right now."

Dresco removed his gloves. "I suppose we are best off in here."

"Good, we agree." Kasta stood up and staggered to Kaiar. The hunter groaned, unstrapping her mount's saddle and pannier. After gulping down several mouthfuls of water, she poured some in a small bowl for Kai. "We'll take shifts on sleep tonight," she said. "Someone's gotta keep an eye and ear open."

Dresco fell back against the ground and grunted. "I agree," he said with a long yawn.

"Alright, you're sleeping first," Kasta said. She removed her hat. "I wanted some time to myself anyway. Some time to think."

"Think about what?" Dresco mumbled.

"What part of 'myself' don't you understand?"

Dresco's eyebrows furrowed as he removed another piece of armor. "Fair enough."

Kasta sat next to Kaiar. "But if you must know, my thoughts will probably have something to do with talking statues and vindictive psychopaths chasing me down and shooting at me." She reached into her pannier and tossed a thin blanket at Dresco. "You know, events that have somehow become frequent in my life."

She removed her leather jacket and dropped it to the ground. Dresco eyed her with a narrow gaze. "Ever since I started riding with some dogmatic fool from the Imperium," she said. A grimace fell on her face as she bit her lower lip. "Stop gawking at me and get some rest." She turned around and reached for a bottle of whisky. "I'm not allowing you much, believe me."

"Of course, Miss Kr... Kasta."

With a swift gasp, Kasta awoke. Her eyes surveyed the room. A soft blue light had crept into the hallway; Athenis was dawning. 'Been asleep about four hours,' she thought, rotating her neck. It was sore from sleeping with her back against the wall. She turned her sights to Dresco, who had fallen asleep. "Of course, he did," she whispered through a sigh. "So much for trading shifts on keeping watch."

Kasta groaned, stretching her torso and appendages. Her joints cracked and her muscles loosened, though the aches in her limbs refused to subside. As she wiped the cold sweat from her brow, a soft growl emanated from the corner of the room. Kaiar looked to Kasta from the shadows. Her eyes sank and her upper fangs slid over her lips, an expression that resembled a smile.

"Good morning, girl," Kasta said with a raspy and cracking voice, greeting Kai with a smile of her own. She pulled the thin blanket from her lap. Her legs wobbled as she stood. She buttoned the lower half of her shirt and pulled her vest over her shoulders. "You're on guard duty I see."

Kaiar grunted as Kasta strode toward her.

"Seeing as our friend there didn't succeed in staying awake." Kasta extended a hand to pet Kai, cocking her head toward the unconscious knight. "Good girl," she added, laying her fingers across Kai's rough hide.

The beast released a purring growl as the side of her head nudged Kasta's hand. The trugan shut her eyes.

"So, what do you think of him?" Kasta's fingers brushed the skin surrounding Kai's horn and glided to her snout.

Kaiar opened one eye and hissed, flickering her tongue.

Kasta chuckled. "I know," she said, looking to the ground. "But he's not so bad, right?"

The beast let out a soft grunt: hesitant, but affirmative.

The hunter patted her head. "He's useful in a fight, and at the very least, entertaining."

Kaiar tilted her head upward, signaling that she wished to be pet on the neck.

Kasta smirked and complied. Her eyes turned to the sleeping knight. "But do you trust him?" she asked.

A long, cold hiss siphoned through the beast's lips. Her vertical pupils constricted, thin and sharp as double-sided daggers. Her snout narrowed. The trugan's visage had turned serpentine.

Kasta's hands fell to her side. "You're right," she said with a nod. "You can never trust anyone." She wrapped her arms around Kai's neck, embracing the beast in a tight hug. "It's you and me, girl."

Kai rested her head on the hunter's shoulder.

"I'm sorry about Crev," Kasta said. She eased her embrace of Kai. "I know you usually don't get other trugan to ride with. He was a good kid. Didn't deserve to go down the way he did."

With a long groan, Kaiar's head drooped.

"We'll get Dast for what he did. I promise."

Kaiar hissed, this time in the affirmative.

"So, what do you think, Kai? Should we keep going with this fool's errand?"

Kai growled spiritedly.

Kasta's eyes widened. "Yes, but wouldn't you rather rest up for a while? Recover from our wounds? I'll sip on some malted whisky; you sip on some elk blood?"

Kaiar grunted, her fanged smile on display once more.

"Sit in a hot spring and just wait for all of this to blow over? It's just a stupid sword, anyway. It's not worth dying over."

Kaiar hissed again with a short hop and enthusiastic nod.

"Well come on, Kai," Kasta said. Her hair fell over her face. "We can't do both. We either find somewhere to lay low and let the world pass by, or we keep on the trail."

Kaiar brought her head low and nuzzled the bottom of Kasta's chin with her snout. Although the beast only meant to brush against her rider, she almost knocked her over.

"I guess you're with me no matter what, huh, girl?" Kasta ran the back of her blue-grey hand along Kai's cheek. "That's why we're a team." A deep voice moaned from behind. "Well, well, look who's awake," she said, turning to Dresco.

Dresco pushed himself from the ground with one arm. His bloodshot eyes swiveled toward Kasta. "I must have dozed off," he said, clearing his throat. "I apologize. Our travels have exhausted me."

"They exhausted Kai too. She endured much more punishment than you did yesterday, yet she had the sense to stay up and watch the door to make sure no one murdered us in our sleep." She reached back and patted the tip of Kaiar's snout.

Dresco sighed and rubbed his eyes. "Again, I apologize."

"Don't apologize to me, Sir Norte. Apologize to Kaiar."

He sat up and massaged his temples. "I do not speak to beasts as though they are my equal."

Kaiar's fangs showed as she yielded a soft growl.

"Easy, girl," Kasta whispered. "Dresco still doesn't understand the level of sentience that trugan possess."

He turned away. "Nor do I plan to."

"Dresco, apologize to Kaiar for forcing her to stay awake while you dozed off." Kasta's tone turned firm.

"Fine!" Dresco's brow tightened. He let his hand fall on his knee and looked to the trugan. "Kaiar, I apologize for falling asleep."

Kaiar nodded upward, stomping atop the gravel with ardor.

"See," Kasta said with a half smirk. "I told you she can understand you."

Dresco licked his grey lips and released a deep breath. "Well, I still prefer a mount who obeys rather than one who dissents, such as my dearest Maigavara, the most beautiful titan wolf—"

"In the Imperium." Kasta finished the sentence for him with a shake of her head. "I know. You've mentioned her *quite* a few times. Perhaps it's not the best time for wolf nostalgia—the morning after Crevallus was murdered?" She glanced in Kaiar's direction.

"You're right," Dresco said with a nod. "Crevallus and I were indeed beginning to get acclimated to each other, despite his untamed nature."

A canteen of water sat in the corner nearest Kaiar. Kasta picked it up and walked toward Dresco. She glanced into the hallway, its block-laid walls set aglow by the disseminated blue starlight of Athenis.

"Did you sleep okay?" she asked, standing over the knight.

"Y-yes," Dresco said, confusion in his eyes. "I needed it."

"Yeah, you did." Kasta leaned down, offering her canteen. "Today's probably not going to be any easier. We have a long way to go."

Dresco accepted the canteen and guided it to his mouth. "It is not that far to the Vaeliz estate, is it?"

"Just tell me one thing." Dresco awaited. A drop of water trickled down his chin. Kasta asked with a stiff tone, "Are you and Madame Vaeliz seeking Vellon's Blade because you think that she could be a Relic wielder?"

The knight's eyes widened as he held his breath. "I'm... I'm sorry?" was all he could muster.

"Come on," Kasta said. Her shoulders sank forward. "Veros said she was the 'rightful wielder of a divine device.' Is she, or rather, do you believe that she is a descendant of the House of Vellon?"

A long pause fell between Kasta and Dresco. Their eyes locked in a binary gaze, penetrating but enigmatic. Kaiar let out a soft hiss and leaned closer to the companions.

"We have considered the possibility," Dresco said with a strangled tone.

Kasta smiled and shook her head. "This just keeps getting better." She placed her hands on her hips. "So, you and Madame Vaeliz think she can wield the magical power of an ancient sword. That's why she wants it."

"Kasta—"

"This is what I get for working with religious fiends like the two of you," she interjected.

"Kasta..." Dresco faltered and looked away.

After pacing toward the door and back to the knight, Kasta took a long, deep breath. "Drink some more water, eat a little bit of food, then we're getting out of here. It's a long way to the western coast."

"The western coast?" Dresco leapt to his feet. "What changed your mind? Was it that the Madame may be able to wield the Defender of Liberty?"

Kasta shrugged. "In part." She kicked a few pebbles away. "I am intrigued by the idea that the Madame believes herself to be the rightful wielder of a Relic. And that an ancient living statue may agree." She paused and shook her head, realizing the absurdity of those words. "But also—" Her eyes widened, a fury rising in her voice. "The thought of Breylu Dast getting his hands on that sword and getting paid a bunch of platinum—*my* platinum—for it." Her fist clenched. "Well that just doesn't sit right with me."

Dresco smiled and pumped both fists forward. "This is grand! Regardless of your reasoning, you are back on board, Miss Krane! This is great news."

"I still doubt we'll actually find it." She raised a finger. "And I still find all this gibberish about magical Relics to be superstitious insanity. But hey, only one way to find out. Or we die trying."

With a stiffened posture and one-eyed squint, Dresco replied, "Dying is the most likely outcome within our current circumstances, is it not?"

"Oh yes, definitely," Kasta said with sarcastic enthusiasm.

"Anything we can do to alter those odds?"

"I'm Kasta Krane. I can get out of anything." She sighed, looking to her data system, which sat on the floor. "But this time, I may need some outside resources to do so."

"Really?" Dresco leaned forward. "You, Kasta Krane, asking for help?"

"Don't rub it in or I'll change my mind." She pointed toward the knight. "Maybe I'll even reconsider my decision about not calling in an airship. Flying out of this red ditch of death seems like an incredibly appealing prospect right now."

Dresco gasped in excitement. He did not reply, but he whispered to himself, "Yes, yes. Thank the Guardians. Thank the Guardians and their endless good grace."

She could not help but smile. "Get ready to move. I have to send a transmission or two—"

Kasta and Dresco stopped and turned toward the room's entrance. A soft gallop approached. She reached for her pistol. Dresco sprang for his sword. A growl purred from Kaiar's throat. Kasta looked to the beast, a finger to her lips.

She pointed her pistol toward the doorway and waited. The galloping grew louder, now accompanied by an echo. It had entered the tomb. Dresco stood by the doorway with his back against the wall, ready to strike whatever came through. As the steps drew nearer and nearer, the squeeze of Kasta's trigger finger tightened.

A blue clawed foot stepped into the room.

"Crevallus!" Dresco called out as the trugan came into view. He dropped his sword and extended a hand to pet the beast.

But Crevallus' eyes were set on Kaiar. The trugan trotted toward her, not limping but with an uneasiness in his step. The sides of their faces met, and their cheeks caressed one another. Kasta's face froze in shock. She took a step back.

Dresco smiled and stepped over to Crevallus. The trugan placed his claw atop the knight's knee. The knight laughed and looked to Kasta. "How did he live? And how did he find us?"

She stroked her chin. "He must have followed Kaiar's scent. He knows it." Peering around out the doorway and down the hall, Kasta saw no sign of adversaries. Hopefully, Dast was not following or tracking Crevallus. "The Moon Shadow Riders—" she said with a slight frown. "They must have had their weapons set on incapacitate. At least, the sniper did. If that weapon was set to kill, it would have done Crev in for sure."

"Why would they want us alive?" Dresco asked with a sideways glance.

Kasta thought for a moment, glancing down the hallway once more. "They want to interrogate us about Vellon's Blade." She smiled, twirling her pistol. "They know we're ahead of 'em."

XV
WESTWARD

"Will you please take it off?" Kasta removed a small pot from Crevallus' pannier, one of the few items that the Shadow Riders had not taken.

"Absolutely not!" Dresco said, his mouth full of mustard nuts. "My armor is the garb of the Guardians, the shimmering symbol of the true Order." He swallowed and rubbed his hands together, sending a stream of salt to the floor. "Not to mention, it protects me from harsh weather, shock-cannon fire and the sharpest of blades."

Kasta fastened the pot to Kai's pannier. "Yeah, that hunk of metal is going to protect you from a shock-cannon blast." She shook her head, chortling through her nose. "It's a big, heavy, *recognizable* metal decoration. Every bounty hunter and assassin in Vanda is looking for Kasta Krane and the fallen knight. At least don't wear a costume that screams, 'I am a knight!' "

Dresco took a large bite from a piece of dried fruit. "I wear the armor. That's final."

A tone came from Kasta's mobile data system. She turned toward the device, which lay on the top of a small pile of tools, camping equipment and a blanket. "Why are you eating so much?" She reached for her data system.

"Since Crevallus is not well enough to carry many supplies, we will likely have to leave some behind. Kaiar can only bear so much. Better to eat than let our food go to waste, I would say."

Her lips pursed, Kasta's head cocked sideways. 'He's got a point.' She glanced at the message. "It's from the Madame. She has arranged for an airship to pick us up down in the valley."

"Oh, thank the Guardians," Dresco said with a bow of his head and a long sigh.

"That is, if we can manage to make it a couple miles down the trail without getting shot first. And then survive the ride across the wide-open valley and get onto the airship." Kasta grunted and fastened her belt. "Damn airship."

"What do you have against airships anyway?"

"Nothing. But if you really insist on wearing the armor, at least take that stupid helmet off and..." She held out a finger, twisting toward the pile of supplies against the wall. She pulled a blanket from the hoard. "You're gunna wear this."

Dresco's eyes widened. His jaw dropped. "A blanket?"

Kasta dug deeper into the pile of supplies and found one of her utility tools. She activated the electro-knife setting. Her teeth ground as she cut a circle in the middle of the blanket. "No," she said, her voice straining. "A poncho." She tossed the makeshift piece of wardrobe to her companion.

After examining the large cloth, Dresco uttered, "A fair compromise I suppose." He stuck his head inside the hole with a frown on his face. The black blanket covered him, neck to wrists. His armored legs were still visible, though they did not suggest a knightly décor.

"You almost look like a true Vandeni," Kasta said with a smile. "We shall call you Vallion Tarro."

The room turned cold with Dresco's tone. "You shall do no such thing," he said.

"Fine," Kasta said. "Just trying to make you a better treasure hunter. A decent name is a good place to start."

Dresco did not respond. He was busy trying to make the hole in the blanket bigger; it hugged his neck too tightly. Kasta stepped to Crevallus and gave him a pat on the head. "I know you're still weak, Crev. But do you think you can handle the weight of Dresco, plus your saddle? And maybe a couple of camping kits?"

Crevallus responded with a purring growl, clawing the gravel like a bull preparing to charge.

"That a boy," Kasta said with a smirk. A pile of supplies lay beside Kaiar. "I guess we have to leave the rest," she said. "Some of my excavation tools, hunting gear, my electro-chains. They're all just extra weight at this point." The hunter leaned over and picked up the shackles. "I like these chains. I've sent a lot of people to jail in these chains." Her cyan eyes grew big in a playful feign of sadness.

"How tragic," Dresco said, his arm around the back of Crevallus' neck.

"I know." Kasta draped her leather jacket over her shoulder. "But I don't think we'll be putting chains on anybody during the rest of this quest. More likely that we'll be the ones in chains."

The knight climbed on top of Crevallus' saddle and said, "Or in the ground," with a nonchalant tone.

Kasta smiled wide and pointed at Dresco. "Now that's funny!"

Sweat dripped down Kasta's brow as she rode along the pathway. Not a cloud sat in the sky to interrupt the burning blue rays of Athenis. The hunter looked behind and to the top of the cliffs more than forward. Kaiar could mind the path ahead. But this narrow, linear passage would be the ideal place for an ambush. And this time, there would be no chance of escape.

Crevallus' soft gallop lumbered several paces behind. 'Just keep moving,' Kasta thought. They passed a pale, dead tree. 'A little more than a mile.' A nighthawk lingered at the tip of the mangled tree's longest branch. The bird croaked from the bottom of its throat until the sound became a squeak, like an opera singer who felt a need to warble a final note before death. "What are you gawking at?" Kasta whispered. The bird leaned forward, its deep red eyes investigating the Vandeni woman who had entered its habitat.

The red stone that surrounded the pass arched overhead, each wall curving toward the other. They made their way up a slight slope. The enveloping walls offered a bit of shade: a small taste of comfort. But that sense of ease faded when the incline flattened. Two hundred feet away, a group of three stood on the side of the small path, their trugan near.

"Damn," Kasta said with a sharp whisper.

"It is not the Moon Shadow Riders, is it?" Dresco asked, catching up to Kasta.

"No," she said. "They wouldn't just be standing around." An idea entered her mind. "Wear this." She removed her hat and saucered it to Dresco.

"You're serious?" Dresco said with a sunken face.

"Absolutely." Kasta reached behind and dug through her pannier. "Trust me." She found her goggles buried in one of the small pockets.

After fidgeting with the strap, she lifted her hair and placed the band above her ears. The goggles sat crooked over her eyes.

They approached the onlookers, who had taken notice of Kasta and Dresco. Two of them stood in front of the companions, blocking their trail. The other stood against the wall, hand on her pistol.

"Let me do the talking," Kasta whispered as she pulled back on Kai's reins, slowing her down.

"Understood," Dresco responded with an even quieter whisper. Kasta's black desert topper squeezed Dresco's forehead, compressing his skin to white wrinkles.

"Howdy, partners," Kasta called out with a gleeful inflection and a wide smile. She went to tip her hat, before recalling that Dresco was wearing it. Kasta transformed the gesture into a two-finger salute mid-motion, in a manner less awkward than she expected.

"Hello there," the man on the right side of the path said with a back-handed wave. "What brings y'all to the Valley of Tombs today?"

"Well, I was gunna ask y'all the same thing. My partner and I here were just searching for a bounty that we heard may be wanderin' in these parts," she said, motioning to Dresco.

Clearing her throat, the woman leaning against the wall tipped her short-brimmed hat upward. "Where's your manners, Darvin?" she said, stepping forward. "Please forgive us. My name's Tessile Amar. That there is my brother, Darvin." Her finger extended toward the man. "And my partner, Larria." She faced the woman who was blocking the other side of the path, presenting her with an affectionate smile. "We're on a hunt ourselves."

"Well, I'll be damned. Small world," Kasta said with an animated shake of her head. "My name is Essi Hannar." As she spoke the name,

Dresco looked at her with a tight glare. It was the first name that came to mind.

"We didn't even come down to the old valley in search of no bounty," Kasta continued. "We was just comin' on down here to get ourselves a couple of finds. Maybe catch a drifter or two—shake 'em down for a couple coins." She interrupted her own story with a raspy cackle. The lie was growing too intricate. "Anyway, next thing we hear, Kasta Krane and Dresco Norte are right here riding in the valley. And my partner and I here agreed that we just *had* to take a shot at that trashy little scavenger."

Dresco sat tall on his trugan's back and nodded.

Larria, the woman blocking the path, laughed as she spoke. "What a coincidence. We thought we might take a shot at Krane ourselves."

A slight frown found Tessile's lips. "We heard she might come through these paths here."

"Well, so did we!" Kasta said with a shrug and outstretched hands. "I see you're thinking you might be able to take a shot if she comes through on either side."

"That's the plan," Larria said.

"And you're trying to..." Tessile lingered on the word for a moment. "Pursue her?"

"Yes, indeed," Kasta said. "We just have not had ourselves any luck. But it is worth a shot. Can you believe the platinum they are offering for her pretty little head?" She squinted, rotating her neck. "By the grace of Athenis, what a bounty!"

"Indeed," Darvin said with a slow nod.

Kasta reached into her pannier and pulled out the remnants of her whisky. "Would any of y'all care for a drink?" She took a sip herself before tossing the bottle to Darvin. "Always love sharing a drink with a fellow bandit of the tombs."

Darvin took a sip of the whisky before passing it to his sister. She swigged the spirits down and tossed the bottle to Larria.

"Very kind of you, Essi," Tessile said, leaning against the wall.

Larria went to return the bottle to Kasta. The hunter raised her hands in a surrendering manner. "Oh, no. Y'all can keep that. If my partner and I here drink any more, we'll be far too under the influence to conduct a proper hunt."

Larria nodded and placed the bottle in her jacket pocket.

Kasta sniffled, looking into the distance. Dust and dead pollen irritated her nose. "Well, I reckon we best be on our way. You only get one chance to strike a lottery like this, and we don't want to be wasting no time." She pointed to each of the three bandits, her eyebrows arched high. "Y'all should keep that in mind as well."

"Oh, we will, Essi." Larria crossed her arms. She looked to Dresco, her head tilting sideways. "I'm sorry, sir. I must have missed your name. What was it again?"

Dresco swallowed hard. The nervous tension leapt from his body to Kasta's, sending a slow shiver down her calves and into her boots. "Vallion Tarro." Dresco's voice trembled in a failed attempt to mask his Imperial accent. "Just a simple treasure hunter."

Kasta cringed.

"Please don't let us keep you any further," Darvin said. He stepped aside and stood next to his sister. "We know you wish to get on your way."

"Indeed, my friends," Kasta said with a bow of her head and another two-finger salute. "Happy hunting to y'all."

"Why, thank you." Tessile spoke through a tight smile, tipping her hat.

The hunter and the knight continued past the three bandits at a slow pace. Kasta's heartbeat accelerated. She waited for an inevitable sound: the click of an unfastening holster. "Be ready," she whispered.

"Understood."

Kasta awaited that sound, but it did not come. 'Whew,' she thought with a deep sigh of relief. 'Maybe they bought it.'

Click

"Dresco, ride hard, full speed. *Now!*" The hum of circuits under Kai's skin elevated in tone and speed. The beast roared. Crevallus' gears also powered up. Dresco was following behind. The companions reached the bottom of the slope and turned the bend before the bandits could take a shot. But they would follow.

These passageways were narrow and unsafe to ride at full speed on truganback. Kasta managed to navigate the trails on the previous night, but she was unsure whether Dresco would have the same success. The momentum of a sharp turn could thrust a rider from their saddle and into the rock wall. But Kasta looked back to see that Dresco was maneuvering the curls and curves of the path, calm and in control. Discarding the excess supplies proved beneficial. The lessened weight allowed Crevallus to reach higher speeds, despite his injuries.

"They did not believe our act, did they?" Dresco's voice crunched through Kasta's ear speaker.

"No, Dresco. They did not." She ducked under a low-hanging branch that had grown from the red rock wall.

"I tried as long as I could not to talk."

A stampeding gallop rumbled from the corners of the pathway behind. "Keep up that not-talking thing a little longer. They're on our heels."

The two trugan ravaged the slopes, leaving a funnel of gravel and red dust in their wake. Kaiar hissed. Her cyberized body vibrated and overtook her organic functions. They were close now. Close to the valley. The path widened and the hill leveled. Kasta glanced over her shoulder. The bandits were on their tail, though not yet in firing range.

As they entered the mouth of the valley, Kasta could see it in the distance—a small airship waiting to rescue them from this canyon of death.

"Ha!" she said, closing in on their escape vehicle. "Free at last." But she saw a group of five on truganback. They stood between the hunter and the airship. "Damn," she whispered. "Pincered in." She drew her pistol. Kaiar's claws tore apart the sand. The five figures took shape, coming into clear view. "I'm not going down without a fight." But as they neared the riders, she saw that they were not bandits, nor Moon Shadow Riders.

Kasta slowed. She approached the figures, all dressed in blue shirts with gold or silver badges. "Kasta Krane?" the man in the middle said with a nod.

"That's me," Kasta said. Kai inched forward.

"I'm Deputy Brallagan of Vulture. We're here to escort you out of here."

As Kasta looked on, confused, two other lawmen rode forward, their palms thrust outward. The bandits came to a halt.

"What the hell is going on here?" Tessile yelled, her hand slapping the back of her trugan's saddle.

Deputy Brallagan yelled over the chorus of roars and hisses arising from the congregated trugan. "We are escorting these two citizens away from the Valley of Tombs."

The younger law official next to Brallagan added, "They are emissaries of the law offices of Vulture."

"Law offices of Vulture?" Tessile said with a fake laugh. "Just a moment ago, they claimed to be bandits and raiders. Now they're emissaries of the law?"

Kasta shrugged. "I'm whatever I need to be at the time, fellas." Kaiar treaded backward, away from the bandits.

Darvin rode toward the airship. His face flushed purple. "Damn it, you idiots. That's probably Kasta Krane. There's a bounty on her head!"

Two law officials pointed their shock-cannons in his direction.

Tessile looked to Darvin, shaking her head. A fury ignited in her eyes, freezing her brother's tongue.

"Listen here, folks," Brallagan said. His hands rested on his saddle. "You should know that even if this woman *were* Kasta Krane, the bounty on her head is illegal in more than seventy-five percent of Vanden territories now."

"That's good to hear," Kasta said under her breath.

"Indeed," Dresco responded, overhearing her.

"Well, it sure as hell ain't illegal in the Valley of Tombs." Larria's finger stabbed toward the law officials.

"Maybe not," said one of the female deputies at the end of the row. "But this woman and her companion are under our protection now. You are not permitted to pursue them any longer. Ride off now."

"Very well," Tessile said to her fellow bandits. Her head jerked sideways, and the three riders dispersed.

Deputy Brallagan gestured toward the vessel. "My friends, the airship will depart upon your request." He wiped his blue-grey forehead with his handkerchief. His pigmentation favored grey to such an extent that he could have passed for an Imperial, had it not been for his wide gills.

Dresco clasped his hands together. "Oh, thank you so much for your gracious help, Deputy," he said with a boyish tone.

As they rode toward the airship with a host of law officials at their side, Kasta turned to take one last look at the bandits, who stared right back. She removed her goggles, and with a half smirk, revealed to them her distinctive cyan eyes.

The airship was sharklike, with a narrow nose and long triangular tail. Its jagged armor was of a grey-silver plated metal. Kasta and Dresco guided their trugan up the ramp and entered the vessel at its side, escorted by Brallagan. They stepped through the passenger cabin's wide hallway. A smell of mahogany drifted through the airship, propelled by its air-cooling system. She took a deep breath and slid her hand over a glossy wooden table in the middle of a seating section, feeling the chill of its copper edges through her gloves.

They led the trugan to the back room, which acted as a small stable. There were two troughs, one filled with water and the other with dried jerky and mixed vegetables. One of the female law officials also led her trugan to the stable.

Deputy Brallagan rubbed his salt-and-pepper goatee. "Deputy Delena will accompany you on your flight," he said, pointing to the female law official who had stepped aboard. "Her jurisdiction is out west anyway."

On looking closer, Kasta recognized Deputy Delena. They had spoken when she had arrived at the Barren Rock marshal's office to turn in Quintis Saveer. She was playing cards with another lawman that night. They had spoken several times in passing—nothing but banter and small talk. But it was strange to see her all the way in eastern Vanda, thousands of miles from Barren Rock. What was she doing here?

"Nice to see you, Deputy Delena," Kasta said with a limp wave. She was glad that Brallagan had said her name, for she did not remember it.

"Likewise, Krane." The deputy's belly jiggled with her nod.

Deputy Brallagan shook their hands before he stepped off the airship, bidding farewell.

"Give me that," Kasta said, snatching her hat from Dresco's head. She tossed it on the table and sank into the soft leather chair.

"My goodness, I forgot I was still wearing it." Dresco's fingers slid through his hair. He sat at the neighboring table across the hallway.

Kasta leaned back and looked out the window, rounded to fit the curvature of the wall. Framing the glass was the same copper that lay along the table's edge. The airship buzzed from tail to nose. Rumbles below the floor climbed up her feet, rattling her knees. An electric blast surged from the side of the ship. The buzz turned into a supersonic barrage. Lightning streamed from the fuselage and tail. Dresco smiled, looking out the window. Electrical power streams flashed over his shimmering grey eyes.

Kasta bit her lip. Her fingers tapped against the table. The airship lifted off flat from the ground, powered by the electric fusillade. She looked out the window and saw two riders on truganback. They held their place in the distance, watching the takeoff—a pair of Dast's Moon Shadow Riders. One was Jarrus, Dast's top trigger man. Kasta recognized his stance. The other, she could not make out. It was either Lynara, his demolitions expert, or Giavi, his combat medic.

The ship soared into the sky and drifted away from the Valley of Tombs. Kasta let out a shuddering breath. The terrain fell farther away, and the lightning-propelled vehicle elevated toward the violet sheen of the atmosphere.

"Oh, I just love the feeling of flight. It is so exhilarating." Dresco leaned over the oval window. His right foot tapped against his left thigh. Delena sat two tables away on the opposite side of the hallway. The data system on her lap commanded her attention.

There was a small cabinet where the floor met the bottom of the wall. Kasta leaned over and flung the cupboard open. To her delight, she found a light malted whisky. She seized the bottle by the neck and popped off the cork. Her shaking hand brought the whisky to her lips. While not one of her favorite vintages, the light flavor mixed well with the wooden smell of the airship.

"You are afraid of flying, aren't you?" Dresco eyed her hands.

"No!" Kasta said with an abrupt and defensive shake of her head. She then realized how much her hand was trembling.

"It would explain why you have been so reluctant regarding any form of air travel."

A sip of whisky burned her lips as she pulled the bottle away from her mouth. "It's not flying, necessarily," she said, clutching the table's edge. "I don't like putting my life in someone else's hands."

Dresco leaned back. A stream of voltage flashed against the hull outside. The electrical glow highlighted the grey streak in his hair. "I can understand that," he said with a slight smile. "But I am sure the pilot is well mannered and highly skilled."

"Well in that case, I feel completely at ease." Kasta took a gulp of whisky. "Thanks for your words of comfort, Dresco." A sudden belch followed her words. "Next thing you'll tell me is that you said some prayer to the Guardians for our trip—so our safety is guaranteed."

The knight's arms crossed. "Despite your sarcasm, Miss Krane, you are not wrong."

"Please don't call me that, right now." Kasta moaned, pressing her fingers into her forehead.

The door at the front of the hallway opened. In strode a Draekalagon with a blue jacket, red leather slacks and a full-visor optical system draped over his eyes. "Welcome aboard the *Skyward Covenant*," the man said.

His yellow eyes widened. "I will be your copilot on this journey. Please use the ship's intercom if you have any questions or requests." He closed the door and reentered the cockpit.

Dresco sighed with a bitter sneer. "Forget what I said about well mannered."

"Oh look, more xenophobia," Kasta said through her teeth. "Just what I needed to hear right now." She flung her feet on the table. "Also, one other thing I wanted to talk to you about, Norte." Her eyes skimmed over Deputy Delana on their way to Dresco. "How did we get a bluecoat escort and passage on a vessel designed specifically for transporting lawmen? Was this your doing somehow?"

Dresco shook his head. "No. Absolutely not. I was relieved to see them, yes. But I did not call them in."

"I did." A familiar female voice came over the airship's intercom. All three passengers looked about the cabin in confusion.

"Well, hello there, Madame," Kasta grumbled.

"I was not eavesdropping, mates. I just asked the pilots to patch me through and overheard ye talking," the Madame was quick to announce.

Dresco sat up straight with a wide grin etched into his cheeks. "Madame Vaeliz, what an absolute pleasure it is to hear from you."

"Likewise, Sir Dresco." The Madame's voice came through crackled and distorted due to the poor transmission signal. "I trust that you and my favorite treasure hunter are getting along well."

Kasta caught Dresco sneak a glance in her direction. "Considering our circumstances, I cannot complain," the knight said.

"He's lying. He complains every chance he gets." Kasta buried her forehead in her palm. "Every. Single. Chance."

"Still not too keen on flight, are ye, lass?" The Madame's glowing smile was audible in her words.

Kasta swallowed two large gulps of whisky. "I asked for the ship, didn't I? What I don't get is why I'm in a law enforcement vessel and why I got a greeting from a bunch of good ol' boys down in the valley."

"And ladies!" Delena called out.

Kasta waved in the deputy's direction. "Yes, Delena. And ladies."

"You said you were being chased down by one of the most dangerous gangs in Vanda, the leader of which wishes to personally end your life." The Madame's voice faded away for a moment in a sharp crackle, then returned. "... Just wanted to make sure ye would make it out alive and... fastest ship available."

The whisky sloshed and rippled around the bottle, susurrant under the growl of the ship's electric turbine. Kasta squinted at the intercom speaker. "I didn't ask for a law enforcement airship, and definitely not for a host of blueshirts to walk me in."

Dresco leaned toward her. "Kasta, are you seriously berating the Madame for going the extra distance to aid in our escape? Stop being ungrateful."

Kasta rested back with a half smirk. "Oh yeah. Madame, which marshal's office sent out the airship?"

Vaeliz did not respond. Delena did. "Marshal Bovien," she said, looking up from her data system. "She had me and a couple of other lawmen following some leads on Breylu Dast in Ash Valley. We couldn't find no sign of him, but the marshal gave me a call. Told me she had arranged for this airship to come get y'all out of trouble."

Kasta slammed the bottle of whisky against the table as a judge would swing a gavel. "And what about the other lawmen outside?" Her hand wrung the bottle's neck.

Vaeliz's voice filtered through the intercom. "Those men were courtesy of Marshal Jos. Deputies and lawmen of Vulture. For the most part, I believe."

Turbulence interrupted Kasta's response. Her body tensed. "And how much is this all going to cost?" she asked, clearing her throat.

"Well…" The Madame hesitated. "Marshal Jos volunteered his men."

"Mhmm." Kasta's lips curled with a fake grin. Dresco watched her with a stoic, analytical glare. She continued, "And what about this here airship? I know Marshal Raelyn Bovien. There is no way she volunteered this voltage guzzler on Barren Rock taxpayer coin. Especially not if she was renting it from Ash Valley."

After a long moment of static, the Madame said, "No. The airship will have to be paid for."

"By who?" Kasta said with feigned innocence. Thick clouds drowned the airship. The vessel dove lower. As her body trembled, the hunter squeezed the side of her seat.

"I covered it for now." Vaeliz spoke with cautious deliberation. "When your mission is over, we'll deduct the charge from your pay."

"Oh, hell no." Kasta's voice was more thunderous than the electric bolts that fueled the airship's flight. "Involving the badges was your idea. You're paying for this."

The Madame's inflection turned somber. Angry, even. "No, Kasta. I'm not paying for every expense on your job. You know how this works."

Kasta pointed to the speaker, as if Madame Vaeliz was inside it and could see her. "Usually, I don't have a bunch of people trying to kill me when you give me a job. So, you owe me some extra."

"Oh, one hundred thousand platinum in hazard pay isn't extra enough for ye?"

"Must you two really do this now?" Dresco asked with a tilted head and twisted mouth.

"Shut up, choirboy," Kasta snapped. She flashed Dresco a grim smile and a wink. "It's called a negotiation," she whispered with her hand cuffed over the side of her mouth.

The leather on his seat squeaked as he scooted forward. He turned to look out the window. "It's frivolous quibbling."

The Madame's tone lightened. "I'll split it with ye, mate. Fifty-fifty. Because I value the work ye do for me."

"Seventy-five–twenty-five," Kasta said through a squint and groan. A shot of whisky burned her vocal cords.

"Sixty-forty," the Madame rebutted.

"Seventy-thirty or I walk."

After a short silence, a crackling sigh came through the speaker. "Deal," the Madame said.

"That's why I like to work for you, Madame. You always end up seeing reason." A half smirk fell on Kasta's face. She rested her legs on the table and clasped her hands behind her head.

"You know how important this is to me, Kasta." The Madame sighed. "I'll pay any price I can manage for you and Dresco to see this through."

Kasta's eyes widened. "By the way, I met a statue who seems to think that you are a rightful wielder of Vellon's Blade."

"You met what?" Vaeliz's voice elevated and turned to sharp static.

"Yeah," Kasta said with a chuckle. "A living statue. With a personality and everything. Seemed to think you were of some significant bloodline. Dresco says that *you* may actually believe that too!"

Dresco's eyes darted. He fidgeted in his seat.

"I see," Vaeliz said with a nervous inflection, followed by a short sigh. "That is of interest."

A loud clear of the throat came from Dresco. "This seems like a conversation best had in person!" He was close to shouting.

"Yes, perhaps," the Madame said. She was taken aback by the topic of her heritage. Defensive about it. Much more than Kasta expected her to be.

Or was it the part where she mentioned a talking statue?

"I am just glad that the two of ye are safe," Vaeliz said through a muffled breath. "The airship you are on is exceptionally fast. Unlike the big passenger floaters, it will outrun any land mounts. And you will not have to worry about being attacked while in flight. Imperial military aircraft tend to avoid Vandeni law vessels." She had a laugh at her own words.

Dresco leaned over his armrest. "Thank you so much for your assistance, Madame. It is a blessing from the Guardians to have you as an ally. I bid you benediction."

The Madame's merry chuckle carried into her words. "Just find us our blade and get back in one piece, mates. I'm counting on ye both."

Kasta raised her bottle. "And I'm counting on your coins."

XVI
INTO THE DEPTHS

Madame Vaeliz was right about the *Skyward Covenant*'s speed. 'She's resourceful, I'll give her that,' Kasta thought, leaning over the passenger window. She caught a view of the curving mist and layered cliffs that surrounded the Southern Falls. She had never seen them from the sky before. 'She got us a high-speed airship on short notice,' her thoughts continued. 'A big passenger aircraft and we may have been up here for three days. Plenty of time for the Shadow Riders to catch us. Or worse yet, for an Imperial craft to intercept us.' Kasta nodded, drifting to sleep. 'The Madame made the right call.'

After a little less than a day, the *Skyward Covenant* reached the western side of Vanda. The journey would have taken two days on truganback pushing maximum speed, without stopping for rest.

The copilot stepped through the cockpit door and entered the hallway. "We're coming up on the western coast," he said. "Are we all landing in Barren Rock today?"

"No," Kasta responded as she awoke. "We're heading south. Drop us off a few miles outside some desolate little town where we can resupply and go unnoticed. Somewhere that makes Barren Rock look like an urban hub of modern activity." She yawned. "Somewhere like River Point. Or better yet, Skull Valley!"

"Alright." The copilot's long lizard snout snarled as he bowed his head. "Next stop, Old Skull Valley."

"But not too close!" Kasta called out as he stepped back into the cockpit. "Don't wanna attract any attention we don't need." She shut her eyes again.

"You sure you don't want to stop in Barren Rock?" Deputy Delena asked. "I'm sure Marshal Bovien would be happy to provide you with an escort."

"Nah," Kasta said, placing her hat atop her head. "We're trying to stay covert here. A host of law officials doesn't exactly help us in that regard."

"Yes, but at least they could protect us from another ambush," Dresco said.

Kasta did not know he was awake. "Yes," she said, looking at him through a tight squint. The light of Athenis reflected off his armor and into her eyes. "But I'd prefer to avoid an ambush altogether this time."

Dresco's foot tapped the wooden floor. "Of course, the offer still stands for a few of my fellow knights to join us. Knights who left the Order—who are loyal to the Guardians."

"Oh, yes. That's very discreet," Kasta said with a long roll of her eyes.

"I am just stating"—Dresco paused, choked by his own words—"that the stakes are very high here. For both of us."

Kasta's black hair whipped backward, her head turning toward the knight.

He held his hands up. "For separate reasons, of course," he added. "But I think we need some extra help."

"We'll be fine, Dresco."

The ship was silent for a moment, other than the roaring electrical currents outside and the rumbling gears below. "Kasta, sometimes we all need help," Dresco said with a delicate tone.

"Not me." Her lips pursed.

"I know you usually do not." His hand extended, as if he were offering it to the hunter. "I have seen you handle quite a bit on your own that would have killed nearly anyone else." He smiled. His hand fell. "But Kasta, I don't know that the two of us can handle this on our own. We have allies! We should accept their assistance!"

Kasta crossed her arms. "No."

Dresco buried his head and groaned. "Krane, I am trying to appeal to the logical side of you."

Kasta's eyes widened. She leaned across the hallway. "Believe me, you don't."

Dresco began to respond, but instead took a deep breath and leaned back. "Fair enough."

The airship landed in the afternoon. Despite the time zone difference, the companions and their trugan were well rested. Under the bright violet sky, they rode into Old Skull Valley. It was a country town with a population of a little fewer than one hundred. Their main source of revenue was grain farming. In other words, it was one of the last places that Breylu Dast or any other bounty hunter would search for Kasta Krane.

An old yellow stone made up the buildings. Decades had passed since the town had seen any form of renovation. Their dirt roads sat rough and unkempt, graced by the stench of trugan droppings.

Kasta was, however, fond of the town's weaponsmith. She paid him well for routine maintenance on her pistol. The town had no biomechanical engineer, so any medical attention for the trugan would have to wait. They filled their stomachs with locally grown produce and purchased some light, filling food for the journey: bread and seeds. Twilight approached. After refilling on water, they set out again, toward the coast.

The amethyst night sky granted the sand a purple eminence of its own. Traversing the terrain was arduous. The trugan scaled sequences of steep dunes with little flatland in between.

As Kasta and Dresco rode on, the sands became fine, and the landscape leveled. A lush thicket of blue ferns brushed against the trugan's knees. "We're getting close to the water," Kasta called out.

About an hour later, the taste of salt crept into the air. Gentle drafts carried an aroma of algae. And a whispering roar echoed from the distance—the roar of crashing waves. The blue ferns lay scattered throughout the ground, spread out in clusters. Between the ferns grew tall, twisted trees. Succulent leaves sprouted from their branches. Through these trees, the ocean sparkled in the moonlight.

A small town sat at the coastline: their next destination. Kasta could not remember the name of the town. She had never been there before.

The hunter and the knight rode past an old ruined structure. Only framework remained standing. There were no urban buildings or modern houses. Circular, though asymmetrical huts dominated the townscape, made from some sort of clay.

The trugan's claws crunched the seaweed dispersed throughout the beach. Kasta wished to ask one of the villagers to look at the map, for the locals would know the waters well. But the streets were empty. The companions decided to stay in the inn for the night, if you could even call it that. It was a hut with two beds. But for two platinum a night, there was no call for complaint.

She smiled, awoken by the salty smells and calm rumble of waves. The sky arrayed in grey-mauve, its natural violet hue hidden behind a thick overcast layer. Town locals moved about. While some dressed in casual slacks and baggy shirts, swimwear tailored from coral or dried seaweed was the most popular attire.

Kasta and Dresco navigated the town. They came to a building with a handwritten sign at its front. It read "Shellborn Government Office." They stepped within the hut. Large seashells and stuffed fish of the sea graced the interior. A man with slicked-back hair and a thin body sat at the desk near the back of the room. His skin was a dark shade of blue, a trait more common in Islander Vandeni than mainlanders.

Kasta showed him the map, though he was not sure what to make of it. He informed the companions that most of Shellborn was underwater. "Your best bet in finding someone to read that map is to ask one of the aquatic residents," he said.

They left the trugan at the local stable. To their delight, the stable manager was also a veterinarian. He offered to treat Crevallus' wounds. Kasta tipped him well. "You better give your best care to these two," she demanded, stepping out.

A lightweight skiff would be necessary to navigate the waters. Along the beach, a bikini-clad townswoman sold and rented boats. Kasta asked to rent her fastest skiff for the day. The local pointed to a scanty metal boat floating in the shallow waters of the maroon-hued ocean. The resident named the price of one hundred platinum a day. Kasta talked her down to sixty.

With a cool wind passing over, they pushed the boat out to sea and jumped aboard. Kasta operated the helm, while Dresco sat at the bow of the craft and brought up the anchor. The hunter was not a skilled sailor, but she had no desire to admit that. 'I hope Dresco knows what he is doing,' she thought.

The skiff zipped through the choppy waves of the coastline. Kasta felt the salty spray on her face. Foaming swells rippled in fitful sets. "Okay." She slowed the boat's electro-motor. "I guess I'm going down."

"You're just going to jump down into the water and ask for directions?" Dresco asked. "No dive gear or anything?"

Kasta removed her leather jacket and tossed it to the middle of the skiff. "Yes," she said with a smile. "That's the advantage of being a Posaedian Vandeni. I can breathe underwater, remember?" Her gills flared with her words.

The skiff rocked back and forth, its underside wailing with a metallic creak. Dresco looked down and shook his head. "Yes, but when was the last time you breathed in salt water? Is that not quite different?"

With one hand, she gave him a dismissive wave. With the other, she flung her vest against the deck. "If you want to go down there, be my guest." Her fingers began to unbutton her shirt. "Oh, that's right. You can't! Because your ancestors decided that living in the snow was better than having gills." She picked up the map, studying it once more.

Dresco grabbed hold of the gunwale, staring down at the water. "I just wish you would have bought some dive gear, that is all."

"I'll be fine," Kasta said with a grin, taking off her shirt. "Wait up here. I'll go ask some of these ocean bohemians for directions, and then we'll go find us an ancient sword!"

Dresco could not help but giggle. "If you think that is best, Miss Krane," he said.

"I know it is," responded Kasta. Two waves hit the skiff from opposite directions. With a slow exhale, she removed her boots. The motions of the sea were nauseating. "And call me—"

"Kasta, I know. Forgive me."

Kasta took off her slacks. She was wearing nothing but her green one-piece unitard.

"Oh, goodness," Dresco said, turning away.

"What?" Kasta said with a shrug. "Stop being such a child. Some of the villagers back on shore were wearing far less than this."

Dresco frowned. "Yes, but it is you."

Kasta's eyes sank. She pulled her hair behind her head. "I don't know whether to be insulted or flattered." As she leaned over the boat, the tides called to her. "Sit tight. I'll be right back." With the conclusion of her words, Kasta Krane jumped off the skiff and into the sea.

The water shocked her body, like needles had pierced the backs of her thighs. The sharp, cold feeling crept to her neck. The hunter's teeth clenched; her eyes shut. She opened her mouth and tasted the salt water. Her gills had yet to open. The blue light of Athenis and irritating brine seeped through her peeling eyelids.

As she descended from the skiff, her oxygen levels declined. But she felt a sudden sense of relief. The muscles in her chest relaxed. The three gills on each side of her neck opened, absorbing the water's oxygen.

'That feels nice,' Kasta thought, glancing toward the surface. 'Let's see if I can get back in the swing of this.' She aimed her head toward the ocean floor and descended several fathoms farther. Small, delicate fish scattered and scurried as she sank through their school. "Wow," she said, bubbles escaping her mouth. She had to slow herself. The increase in pressure was hurting her ears and compressing her temples.

Infrastructure came into sight. There were no coarse clay structures or run-down beach shacks on the seafloor. In fact, the subaquatic section of Shellborn appeared to be the lavish part of town. A massive seashell had been repurposed and reconstructed as a building, spiraling upward in swirls of coral-pink and white.

Neighboring the seashell was a coral reef, chiseled with circular entry points: a modest house. Fish swam throughout this dwelling, undisturbed by its Vandeni inhabitants. 'Clever little bohemians, I'll give them that,' Kasta thought, sinking past the marine rooftops.

The villagers swam with a natural saunter, which gave Kasta away as an outsider. Along with the fact that she was dressed in a one-piece undergarment, while the villagers wore either seaweed swimwear or seashell bikinis. Some of the villagers wore nothing. 'Oh, I wish Dresco could see this,' she thought with a smile. A mouthful of seawater passed into her gills.

Kasta's feet hit the ocean floor. She looked up and could see the skiff floating on the surface. "Good," she whispered through the water. "Don't want to wander too deep." The blue rays from Athenis above were enough to brighten the town. But bioluminescent corals and urchins hung from long poles on each side of the pathway, adding extra light. Kasta took a step forward. While walking on the ocean floor was no easy feat, it was the best way to get her bearings.

A young man and woman, both draped in seaweed attire, stood in conversation with one another in front of a small kelp forest. Kasta flung her arms downward and to the left, creating a splashing sound, which in Posaedian sign language meant "Hello."

The man looked to Kasta and returned the same gesture.

Kasta's underwater communication skills were rusty. In truth, they were never all that strong to begin with, though she did her best to sign, "I heard there is someone here who can help me read a map."

The woman looked confused for a moment. But one of her fingers shot up, a wide smile on her face. Her hands and lips began to move. "You wish to see Carina. Go to the..."

Kasta could not follow the young woman's directions. "Can you repeat that?" she signed with a tilt of her head. The hunter rolled her eyes.

She pointed to the surface with her opposing hand clasped over her wrist, the sign for "land walker."

The man and woman both smiled. The woman, rather than try to sign the directions again, pointed a finger westward.

Kasta could not remember how to say thank you in Posaedian sign language, so she bowed. 'Universal enough,' she thought.

As Kasta swam over the sandy trail of the ocean floor, she found a moment of peace. She had neglected her gills for too long; it felt as though she were taking her first breaths in ages. 'What if I just stay down here?' she thought, passing another seashell structure, this one black and serrated. 'I doubt any bounty hunters would look for me at the bottom of the ocean. Not even Breylu Dast.'

Kasta turned left at a fork in the path. 'Who am I kidding?' she thought with a shake of her head. The hunter kicked a clam shell in front of her. 'I'd be bored within a week.' She passed a mother teaching her son how to wield a spearfishing blade, communicating only with visual cues and splashes of the water. 'Not to mention, I like talking too much.'

A small, sunken submersible lay on the left side of the pathway. "This must be it," Kasta said. She halted her stroke and dug her toes in the sand. The porthole was open, though the inside was dark. She stepped before the entrance and knocked on the side of the doorframe. A wet, metallic sound echoed through the submersible.

A waving stream of long blonde hair floated in from the adjoining room. The woman looked to Kasta, motioning for her to come in.

"Carina?" Kasta signed.

The woman nodded.

Kasta floated into the underwater craft. She followed Carina into the next room. The space held an assortment of gems and rare stones. Kasta's jaw dropped as she beheld the collection. The platinum in Carina's triangular mirror alone had to be worth at least one thousand in coin at melt value.

"What is your name?" Carina signed with a wide smile.

"Kasta Krane," Kasta signed back.

Carina put her hand over her mouth. "The treasure hunter!"

"That's me."

Carina's arm stretched out, presenting the valuable objects dispersed throughout the sunken vehicle.

Kasta drifted forward with a half smirk. "These are the treasures you've hunted, you're saying?"

Carina smiled and nodded, her dirty-blonde hair flowing over the top of her seashell bikini. "How can I help you today?" she signed. At least that's what Kasta thought she signed.

"I have a map," Kasta said. "It was on paper, so I couldn't bring it down here. But—"

Carina was confused.

'Must be signing wrong,' Kasta thought. "Let me show you," she said aloud, leading Carina outside. She drew the map in the sand to the best of her ability.

Carina recognized it right away. "Those are the forgotten caves. Some say there's treasure there, but too many big fish. Lots of predators. Old legends say the caves are protected by magic."

'Just what I need, more magic caves,' Kasta thought. She signed to Carina, "Any idea how I can get there by skiff?"

Carina leaned over the finger-drawn map and sketched a sequence of six numbers in the sand.

"Coordinates," Kasta signed. "And how can I remember that?"

Carina snapped her finger, though it made no sound. She swam back into her submersible.

Moments later, she returned with a small object in hand: a clear bottle containing a piece of paper. The paper held the coordinates. Carina had written them in tar.

Kasta smiled, accepting the bottle. "You are of help, Carina. I wish I brought platinum to pay you. Or at least remembered the sign for—"

Carina pressed her middle and ring fingers to her purple lips and slid them downward.

'*That* is the sign for thank you!' Kasta thought, laying her hand on her forehead. She returned the sign to the Vandeni collector.

Carina's eyes glowed. She signed, "If I am ever on the land and I am looking for a good treasure, you help me!"

Kasta did not know what to sign back, but she nodded and shook Carina's hand. "Deal," she mumbled aloud through the water.

<hr>

Dresco piloted the boat through the choppy waters. Kasta sat at the bow wrapped in a towel. "You're actually a pretty good mariner!" she shouted over the roar of the motor.

"Was that a compliment from Kasta Krane?" Dresco yelled back. The skiff rode up a set of waves at a diagonal angle. "Are you actually starting to—dare I say—like me?"

"Don't push your luck," she said with a tight-lipped smile. As they moved farther out to sea, the maroon waters shifted to a deep shade of purple. The beach fell out of sight and the grey fog thickened. Kasta took a sip of water. A fish leapt near the side of the boat, stirring the hunter's hunger.

The motor quieted. The boat slowed. Dresco glanced at the compass next to the steering wheel. "These are the coordinates."

The shrilling wind sent a chill down Kasta's spine. She shivered, dropping the towel onto the deck. Her one-piece garment was still damp from her prior underwater journey. When the boat slowed to a crawl, she tied a small knife around her waist and jumped into the ocean. As her body submerged, her muscles tensed. The coastal waters in Shellborn felt like a hot spring compared to the open sea.

It was dark. Kasta could not see the ocean floor. But a stream of Athenis' light revealed a cliff with a curved peak, sloping downward through a great channel within the continental shelf. She surfaced and pulled herself to the side of the boat. "This is it," she said, dragging her wet black hair from her face. "This is the cliff from the map."

"Okay," Dresco said, turning toward her. "I presume that you are going to go under and look. What should I do?"

Kasta leaned forward, her feet dangling in the water. "Keep the skiff hot and keep watch." Her grip on the gunwale loosened. "If I am not back within an hour or so, I am probably dead. You'll be free of me."

Dresco's distasteful expression somehow bled through his helm.

"Hopefully by the next time you see me, I'll have the key." A bitter wind brushed her skin. Her teeth shuddered together. "Or at least something useful."

"Be careful, Krane," Dresco cautioned.

She released the boat's edge, submerging beneath the ocean surface once more. She sank into the cold darkness, and the goosebumps on her blue-grey skin enlarged. 'Only one cure for being this cold.' Even her thoughts shuddered. Aiming her head downward, she kicked with all the might that her legs could muster. The water temperature fell colder as she descended. But if she kept her body moving, her internal temperature would remain regulated, even as her blood cooled. As she absorbed the ocean's oxygen, the water numbed Kasta's gills—a jolting, though rejuvenating sensation.

While darkness enclosed her, the high rising cliffs revealed their form. Kasta looked above. The belly of the skiff was a shadow drifting along the surface, fading from visibility. The currents took hold of the hunter and pulled her down, her body like an anchor plummeting toward the depths. As she passed between the cliffs, her gills took a deep pull of water. She swam along the nearest wall and placed her hand on the surface. To the hunter's surprise, the stone that made up the cliff was not coarse but smooth and glassy. 'It almost feels like someone polished it,' she thought.

The towering cliffs leaned forward, staring down into their own chasm. Kasta looked to the other side. An opening near the top of the peak yawned wide. She gasped, engaging the wrong respiratory system. "There it is," she said aloud with an effervescent cough. "A cave."

The hunter kicked, propelling herself forward. She felt a rush of cold move down her spine as she crossed the subaquatic ravine. On reaching the other side, she placed her hands on the wall and pulled herself inside the cave. The pressure clamped each side of Kasta's skull with the sensation of a constricting bruise. She held still for a moment, letting a mouthful of oceanic oxygen pass through her gills.

Murky clouds rose from the bottom of the cave as her hands brushed against the surface. She sought a clue. Anything that could lead to what she was looking for. That was when a question dawned on her: 'What am I looking for, exactly?' Her feet slid over the top of a moss-infested stone. 'A key, yes. But what does it look like?' She reached the back of the cave and ran her fingers across the wall. 'I really should learn to think these things through.'

'Then again, where's the fun in that?' Kasta reached below. She felt a hard, narrow object on the tip of her finger. 'And what is this?' She brought the yellow-white find before her eyes and her question was answered: a bone. Vandeni remains by the looks of it. And it was not as old as she would have liked to believe. Kasta's trembling hand released the bone, allowing it to drift back to its watery grave.

Her legs kicked, sparing no strength. She had to leave this cave. Someone was watching. Maybe even following. There was no logic in this intuition, but Kasta could not shake the feeling.

She swam out of the cave. Her gills released a breath. Kasta's eyes followed the bubbles of carbon dioxide. She could no longer see the surface above—only darkness. Every instinct in her body told her to drift upward, to leave this chasm behind. A slithering nausea in the pit of Kasta's stomach told her that if she continued, she too would find eternal rest in an aquatic cave, a pile of bones in the darkness. A shadow grew in her mind, warning her of the dangers awaiting in the depths.

Kasta closed her eyes. She allowed the ocean's oxygen to flow into her mouth and out of her gills—an amphibious deep breath. 'Clear your head,' she told herself. 'If it were easy, everyone would do it.' Her eyes crept open. She looked into the fathoms below. In lightless solitude, a group of caves rested on the other side of the canyon. The foreboding feeling was gone. With a salt-flavored grin, Kasta kicked downward and torpedoed into the darkness. 'You can do this, Krane,' she thought as she descended. 'You can do this.'

A high-pitched squeak rang from behind. Kasta smiled and turned. She did not have to worry about this creature. A barreling cetacean and her calf glided across the water with a graceful arch. Their glossy beige skin glistened in the darkness. Kasta had never seen one below water before.

The creatures swam past. The mother floated to her side, bobbing her head toward Kasta. The hunter could not hold back a smile and waved to the dolphins.

The mother raised a fin and waved back. Her calf mirrored the gesture. They drifted still for a moment before swimming away with a spirited flutter.

The dolphins faded into the shadows. Another call echoed across the sea, matching the high pitch of the dolphins' squeak, but hollow—and far more powerful. What Kasta heard from miles away was the call of a raven whale: massive creatures of the ocean depths, though harmless by nature. Unless threatened.

Kelp and purple gorgonians grew around the cave's entrance. The oceanic plant life wrapped around with symmetrical intent, inviting Kasta through the corridor. The hunter accepted the offer from the purple and turquoise organisms, gliding into the cave.

Blackness surrounded her. Her fingers slid over the ground. She drifted upward and felt the ceiling's surface. The stone was smooth and glossy, as were the walls of the canyon. Her eyes adjusted, recognizing a pathway.

She floated through the aqueduct, keeping a watchful eye for clues that could lead to the key. On the other side of a corridor, the passage wound to the left. Blue rays seeped from the intersecting cavern; perhaps an opening in the cliffs allowed Athenis' light to reach the depths.

But it was not starlight that coruscated in the cave. Clusters of light lay scattered throughout the walls, emitting brilliant beams of electric-blue. Kasta came to a halt, able to see across the entire cavern. After drifting close to the specks of radiant blue, she said to herself aloud, "Glowing algae." She was unsure whether the placement of the bioluminescent organisms was a serendipitous coincidence or a well-designed mechanism.

The hunter swam through the tunnel, her arms sweeping outward. Ice-cold water passed through her gills, rattling her teeth. She slowed and glided her pruned fingers along the surface of the illuminated cave. If the light revealed one thing, it was that this cavern held no treasure for this hunter.

She floated to the end of the tunnel. A lone stream of blue shone through the corridor. But when Kasta passed through the ingress, she did not enter another tubular cavern. Instead, she found herself in a convergence point of caves, a grid of subaqueous pathways.

Kasta's eyes widened. There were dozens of cave entrances as deep as forty feet below. She glanced upward to see a half-dozen more pathways. The area was resplendent with the blue light of glowing algae. Kasta ran her fingers through her silky, sodden hair, her eyes circling the room. 'Where do I begin?'

'Where *do* you?'

Kasta jolted back, a tide of bubbles following her. Someone had spoken, but she did not hear it. She *thought* it. The words resounded only in her mind. Perhaps the salt water was getting to her and her own introspection had turned to a hollow-voiced man? With an accent she had never heard before...

'Do you even know what it is you are looking for?'

'This is fantastic,' Kasta thought. She leaned forward, probing the cavern for the source of the man's voice. 'I am literally hearing voices in my head.'

'That you are,' the voice said. 'But don't worry. You have not gone insane. At least, I don't think you have.'

She jumped again. This time she floated toward the center of the wide area. 'What *is* this?' she thought. Her eyes darted between the mouths of the caves. 'Why is this happening?'

'This is the Sanctum of Truth,' the voice echoed through her mind again. 'And what you are currently experiencing is happening for the simple reason that you are here.'

'Are you—?' Kasta swallowed before she finished her mental query. 'Are you a statue?'

'A statue?' The voice chuckled in her mind. 'What a peculiar thing to say. Perhaps insanity would be a proper diagnosis for you.' The voice paused for a moment. 'I am living and breathing just as you are, Kasta Krane.'

A shimmer passed by the corner of Kasta's eye. In one of the lowest caverns, she saw the outline of a figure. Though she could not see the details of its face, she saw scales gleaming in glaucous iridescence. 'It knows my name,' Kasta thought. Her heart accelerated.

'I know many things,' the voice said. 'Your mind is unsheltered to my perception.' Kasta sank into the sanctum, low enough to see the creature's limbless, fishlike form. 'And I perceive that you are lost.'

'Lost, what do you—? Hey, wait!' Kasta reached toward the creature as its long, lithesome body turned and lurched into the cave. She kicked downward, plunging into the cavern. Her teeth ground together. The water pressure closed in. She was low in the depths, even for a Vandeni who spent a great deal of time in the sea. For Kasta, who seldom swam in the fathoms below, it was almost too much to bear—as if the weight of the ocean was flattening her bones. However, she released a slow breath from her gills and entered the lip of the corridor.

A blue-lit tubular tunnel lay before her. She pulled her arms forward, her stroke slow and cautious. She saw him, the creature at the end of the cave. Its tail flittered with the delicate flow of the undercurrent. Though its body remained outlined in shadow, its fins curled in the light.

'You're a Syrenia, aren't you?' Kasta asked in her mind, approaching the creature.

'That is one of the least-offensive labels for my people, yes,' the voice responded.

'What would a Syrenia want with me?'

'You have entered this sanctum seeking something. Something of great value. I am the keeper of this sanctum. The question is, Kasta Krane, what do *you* want from *me*?'

The creature's body fluttered and sped to the right, farther into the caves.

"Wait," Kasta called aloud. 'Where are you going?' There was no response. Kicking through the tunnel, she felt weighted down and winded. She stopped and floated still for a moment. Resting her hand on a nearby stone, she felt a sharp, stabbing pain. An urchin had made this cave its home. With a wince and shake of her hand, she moved toward the end of the tunnel. Another crossing lay ahead.

Kasta looked to the left and looked to the right, picking at the fresh wound. 'Damn it, where did he go?' she thought.

'To the right,' the Syrenia's voice said in her mind. 'And stop picking at that urchin stem that you managed to get embedded into your hand. You will only push it deeper into your skin.'

'Noted,' Kasta thought with a nod. She drifted to the right-hand path.

'That's a rather uncharacteristic injury for someone so adamant about minding their surroundings.'

Kasta flinched at the Syrenia's quip.

'Sorry,' he said with a sincere tone. 'I don't mean to expose your deep thoughts. Sometimes it just happens. I've noticed that many land walkers find it quite rude.'

'No apology necessary,' she thought, rounding a circle. Her lungs begged for a deep breath. Her head grew heavy and spun with the bend. 'So, are you here to help me or hurt me?'

'That depends.' The Syrenia floated stagnant while Kasta drifted away from the roundabout. 'Well, no, I won't hurt you. I just may not help you. But I mean you no harm. Not unless you bring harm to me.'

'No, sir,' she thought with a slow nod.

'Good.' The fishlike creature turned around and swam away. 'So, tell me, Kasta Krane, why do you seek the Relic which you seek? Why do you seek Vellon's Blade, the Defender of Liberty?'

Kasta answered with her actual first thought. 'Profit.'

'Then you are wasting my time.' The Syrenia sped off through the water and turned a corner. 'Enjoy your trip to the surface. Mind the changes in water pressure on the way up.'

"Wait, wait!" Kasta called aloud, reaching toward him. "That is not the only reason. Truly."

A wide fish head veered from around the corner. 'Oh, no?'

'There is a strong, powerful, wise woman. Madame Sariya Vaeliz. I believe she may be the rightful wielder of this ancient Relic.'

'Ah, yes.' The Syrenia's words echoed, sinking into Kasta's mind. 'I see this Sariya Vaeliz clearly in your thoughts. Indeed, she seems a worthy and dutiful soul. But do you genuinely believe her to be a descendant of Vellon?'

Kasta hesitated. Her stroke slowed. 'I... have reason to believe she may be.'

'And what do you believe will happen if she wields this Relic?'

At first, Kasta thought up a lie about Vaeliz obtaining some transcendent, divine power. But against this creature, a lie would get her nowhere.

'Nothing,' Kasta thought with a damning mental tone. 'At least, not what she thinks will happen.'

'I see.' The Syrenia's telepathic voice dripped of disappointment. 'Then why do you and your companion go to such great lengths to obtain this weapon? And don't say profit.'

Kasta's lips parted to the flooding taste of salt water. 'Well, Dresco believes all the stories. But me, I just want the Madame to have it. Especially if it belongs to her family. If it gives her any sense of hope—or hell, if it puts the Imperium in its place, I'm all for it.'

The Syrenia added, 'If it helps in any way to *defend liberty*?' The cave's blue light brightened at the path's end.

"Yes, exactly," Kasta thought and mouthed at the same time. To her own surprise, she was not lying.

The Syrenia swayed into the next chamber. 'Now this Dresco Norte that you travel with. He believes in the power of Vellon's Blade, does he not?'

Kasta followed the scaled creature and nodded. 'Oh, you have no idea. You have to be there to believe the extent of his blind faith.'

'Why do you not hold these beliefs?'

'Because I don't believe in magic.'

'Have you not seen enough magic already on your journey? Did you not mention something about a talking statue?'

'I don't know what that was. But it certainly wasn't magic.'

The Syrenia's voice turned firm. 'One who does not believe in a Relic's power has no right to seek it. The sword of Vellon has cut the chains of slavery, sharpened the daggers of rebellion, united warring cultures in a universal yearning for freedom.' He floated in the high shadow of a circular chamber. Blue algae surrounded him with blazing effulgence. 'It is the most important object to ever grace our world.'

Kasta stopped in the entryway. She looked up. A blue aura silhouetted the Syrenia. 'But those are just stories,' she thought, her hand cutting across the water.

'All stories reveal at least a bit of truth, Kasta Krane.'

The alcove drifted into an oval-shaped dead end. Kasta's feet floated a foot from the floor. The Syrenia looked down at her; his focused eyes sparkled in the algae's glow. He was reading her. She had to conceive a topic that he would approve of, fast. Before her mind drifted to objectionable thoughts. 'What's your name?' Kasta thought with an inviting smile.

The Syrenia swam lower. 'My name?'

'Yes,' Kasta thought, laughing aloud. 'What shall I call you?'

'Vaktarae.' His voice rumbled in her consciousness. 'At least that would be the simplest way to conjure my title in a land walker's mind.'

Kasta's back brushed against the smooth, muculent wall. 'Why do you protect this sanctum?'

'It is the caste I am sworn to. I am a keeper of truth, a steward of ancient wisdom, both abstract and tangible.'

She extended her hand. 'Do you choose your caste?'

Vaktarae's tail left a splashing trail of bubbles as he swam closer to Kasta. 'Why are you so interested in me all of the sudden?'

The hunter shrugged. 'I don't know. How many Vandeni have an opportunity to talk with a Syrenia? I'm a curious woman.'

The Syrenia's thin lips fell to a slight frown. 'Evidently.' He swam back toward the top of the alcove. 'But if we may return to settling *my* curiosity?'

'Absolutely.' Kasta mouthed the word she thought.

'While I do take satisfaction in your curiosity of my people, that is not why you are here. And I dare not say too much, for risk of upsetting the balance of our world.'

'Upsetting the balance?'

'Yes,' Vaktarae responded, though Kasta did not mean to pose the question to him. 'Our world is held in fragile equilibrium. The Syrenia have determined that equilibrium is well-served if we keep to our own waters.'

'But what if the world falls to imbalance by other means?'

'Why should you be the one to remove Vellon's Blade from its domain?' Vaktarae asked. His corneas narrowed in vivid luster. He was ignoring her query this time.

Kasta's mind shifted to her quest. She released a slow breath from her gills—an underwater sigh. 'Well, as of right now, the two frontrunners to find it are myself and Breylu Dast. And Dast is a murderous psychopath.'

Vaktarae bared his needled teeth. 'And what about you? You are not a killer?'

Kasta shrugged, raising her upper lip. 'You can read my mind, can't you? You know that I am not!'

'I know that you don't think you're a killer, yes.' The fishlike creature glided to the middle of the chamber. 'But what about what you did to this Breylu Dast?' Kasta froze. She did not hear the flowing ocean, nor her gills absorbing its oxygen. Only Vaktarae's voice. 'Twelve years ago. You gave him a reason to hate you as he does. You bred his mind of vengeance; you set him on a path of automation.'

'Breathe, Krane,' Kasta thought to herself as a shivering, shallow breath escaped her gills. 'Just breathe.' She felt nauseous. A lump grew in her throat. 'Just breathe.'

The Syrenia drifted upward. 'But I don't wish to reprimand you, Kasta Krane. And I do not wish to keep you in this sanctum until the sheer water pressure causes your Vandeni body to faint.' His tail plashed through the water as he circled the alcove. 'However, if you are going to try to convince me that you should wield Vellon's Blade due to some sense of moral superiority, you are indeed wasting our time.' Vaktarae swam toward the exit with a delicate oscillation.

'I don't want to wield it,' Kasta's inner voice whined.

Vaktarae's body coiled around, veering toward her. 'You mean that even if the sword *did* have mystical abilities, capable of giving you power enough to live in glory, to rule the world, to make you rich, you would not wield this power? You would pass it to another?' His circular eyes popped out and grew wide.

Her mind fell blank.

The Syrenia's ethereal voice fell to a whisper. 'You have not even thought of this, have you? No wonder I could not gauge an answer.'

Kasta bit her lip, shaking her head. 'No. I would not want this power. Not at all. I'm a treasure hunter. Not a hero, nor an interloper.' She hesitated, unable to believe her own thoughts. 'I just want to bring the sword to Madame Vaeliz. If the legends behind its power are true, she may be worthy of it.' Her protruding hand rippled the water. 'I do not want to use Vellon's Blade for a strange sense of glory or dominion over others. I only desire to be a keeper, a steward.' Kasta's teeth gritted. Her nerves shook. 'Like you, Vaktarae.'

Vaktarae's eyes angled downward. 'Very well,' his voice said with a placid reverberation.

"Very well?" Kasta said aloud. She looked down, following Vaktarae's gaze. A small section of algae, surrounded by the ever-present blue, was glowing green. Kasta's eyes widened. She drifted to the bottom of the concave, her hand stretching toward the green algae.

In her grip, she held a triangular stone, gleaming a vibrant neon over her skin.

'You have borne no false witness in the Sanctum of Truth. And you have no desire to use an ancient power for your own gain.' Kasta's head turned toward Vaktarae, who looked to the green stone in her hand. 'Bring this key to the Eldritch Forest. From there it will show you the way to a forgotten temple. A temple built for ancient beings, older than any structure that you ever imagined you would enter—even in your line of work.'

'And there I will find the sword?'

'You may,' Vaktarae said. He drifted toward the chamber's exit. 'But do not underestimate the temple.' His body slithered back and forth, slipping out of sight. 'Farewell, Kasta Krane,' he said, his voice still clear. 'Find the sword. Keep the balance.'

A tingle swirled through her fingertips. She felt as light as a jellyfish. 'I will. And Vaktarae, thank you. Thank you for entrusting me.'

'Thank you for giving me reason to.'

The Syrenia's voice fell on her mind once more. Holding tight to the glowing green key, she swam back into the tubular cave, exiting the chamber.

XVII

THE PLATINUM DRAGON

The water penetrated Kasta's skin and froze the blood in her veins. As she moved up the cave, the pressure was alleviated, and her skull eased its grip on her brain. The blue algae lit the way. 'A steward,' she thought. 'I'm a steward, now, apparently.'

Kasta drifted through the darkened area near the cave's exit. An aura of green radiated from the stone in her hand. The hunter held tight to the key stone, her body curling upward. Water streamed under her one-piece garment while her legs kicked. She ascended, slow and controlled. The pressure decreased, and the water warmed. As she passed above the twin cliffs, whitecaps and daylight came into sight.

The skiff's underside, however, was nowhere in sight. Had she pinpointed the correct area? She must have! Close enough, at least. She slowed her ascent, nearing the surface.

She espied it. The shadow of the skiff—forty meters away from its prior position. 'Oh, good,' she thought. 'Dresco must have had to move for some reason.'

Her head breached the surface. She took a deep, sharp breath, paddling toward the boat. Oh, how it felt good to breathe air through her lungs again. "Dresco, you're not going to believe this!" She reached for the sides of the skiff and pulled herself aboard. Her body collapsed over the nearest bench. While she drew a series of short breaths, her limbs sprawled limply.

Her damp garment stuck to her skin. Her drenched hair lay over her face. She reached for a towel and dried the roots of her hair, using her free hand to brush the sopping locks of black behind her ear. "Why are you so"—Kasta's query stopped short when she realized that the man she intended to address was not aboard the skiff—"quiet?"

With a curl of her upper lip, she turned around. Approaching from the skiff's rear was another vessel. A ship, treading the choppy purple waters with careless authority, its pointed bow on an impinging path. A body of navy-blue armor bulged outward in the middle of the hull and upward at the ship's stern, forming a triangular tail. From the top of a tower, an exhaust of electricity erupted astern. The fulminating fury formed a droning harmony with the crashing tides below.

The ship veered to the side of the skiff. Kasta caught a glimpse of the flag that waved atop the lookout tower: a crimson banner etched with two shock-cannons crossed behind a skull. "Oh, hell," she whispered.

She tucked the key stone into her towel and wrapped it up. Over the deck leaned several dozen men and women, some with their shock-cannons drawn.

One short man wore a black tricorn hat trimmed in silver silk. "Kasta Krane?" he said with a snort.

Kasta shrugged. "Would you believe me if I said no?"

The short man spit over the side of the deck. "Probably not, no. Considering we already found your friend here."

Two sailors pushed a struggling man in shimmering armor to the taffrail. It was Dresco. His hands were bound behind his back. "Kasta, get back in the water!"

One of the sailors used the butt of his sword hilt to knock Dresco on the side of his helmet. The knight groaned and struggled, leaning over the edge of the ship.

A swinging metal ladder unrolled and dropped between the ship and the skiff. "Captain Enkallio, at your service," the short man said with an elongated nod. "Why don't you come aboard and join us for a little chat?" He pointed to Kasta's sprawled-out clothes on the floor of the skiff. "If you're wondering, we did search your little boat. All weapons, data systems and other utilities have been removed."

"Sure," Kasta said with a crooked smirk. "Mind if I change?"

"Of course not," the captain said. "We may be pirates, but we have a sense of decency." He looked toward one of his sailors. "Terrin, watch Miss Krane closely."

The sailor nodded in return.

"But in a... modest manner," the captain added with a wag of his finger.

Kasta reached for her slacks. "Call me Kasta," she said, allowing the key stone to slip from the towel into the back pocket of her legwear. Terrin's sideways glare rested on the hunter. Kasta winked at the sailor as she wrapped herself in the towel and removed her wet undergarment. "How are we getting out of this one?" she uttered to herself.

The hunter stepped aboard the ship to an ardent array of laughs and cheers. Her hair hung damp under her hat.

"Welcome aboard the *Platinum Dragon*," Captain Enkallio said with a wide grin.

Kasta squinted at the captain. A pair of hands forced her forearms to her backside. "Your teeth are a bit white for a pirate," she said with an upward nod.

The captain spread his arms wide. His boots squeaked against the polished steel floor. "Appearances are everything, wouldn't you say?"

"No," Kasta was quick to respond. Electro-chains hummed behind her back, binding her hands. She looked to Dresco, who stared back. No doubt, an expression of panic hid behind his helm. Near the stairs that led to the upper deck, their gear lay spread across a table: Dresco's sword, Kasta's pistol, her utility tools, data system, anything useful.

The captain let out a snorting chuckle and looked to Terrin. "I guess elegance is lost on a body snatcher." The crew laughed, stomped their feet and yelled in approval.

"Body snatcher?" Kasta sprang toward the captain, though the tight grip of a nearby pirate held her back. "Body snatcher?!" she yelled over the rising roar of the tides; her eyes reddened. "I'm a treasure hunter, you sea slug!"

Captain Enkallio looked to his men on the upper deck. "She's a fiery one, ain't she, chaps?" His knees bent in an impish curtsey. The crew roared in the affirmative. "Just like they said she'd be."

"I'll show you fiery," Kasta snarled.

Terrin's red-and-black blouse flapped in the wind. She pointed at Dresco. "And look at the Imperial," she said with a chortle. "Dressed like he's ready to defend his lord's castle." The golden compass around her neck dangled as she leaned toward the knight. "No elegance lost on this one, huh, Captain?" She peeked at Enkallio.

"Not at all," Captain Enkallio said, staring up at Dresco. "Let's see his face, matey."

Terrin ripped the knight's helmet off. He grunted, thrusting his head sideways.

The captain stepped before him. "Hm," he said. His boots tapped against the metal deck. "He looks kind of soft for a bigger lad, doesn't he?"

"Imperials. All size. No strength," a voice hissed from the lookout tower above.

Dresco's eye twitched. He glanced up to see that the words came from a female Draekalagon. "How about you come down from there, and I will show you true strength? Lizard vermin!"

Terrin marched back toward the knight with her shoulders high. She raised her hand and unleashed a backhanded slap across the bottom of Dresco's jaw. A quiet resonation of oohs and aahs circled around the ship, including from Kasta. "Never speak that way about any of this ship's crew, are we clear?" Terrin said. Her fist tightened in her leather glove.

Enkallio placed his hand on her shoulder. "That's enough, Terrin," he said with a hardened whisper. Terrin groaned, taking a step back. "Please forgive my first mate," Enkallio said, grinning at Dresco. "She's a bit of a fiery one, much like your body-snatching friend there." He pointed to Kasta, who in turn responded with a fang-filled, sarcastic smile.

For a moment, the deck was silent save for the vigorous crush of waves striking the ship's keel. "Why would a knight be riding around with a body-snatching bounty hunter, anyway?" the captain said in a strained tone, his hands clasped around his hips. "Seems like an odd pairing."

Dresco spit a stream of blood onto the deck, which made Kasta chuckle. "You have no idea," the knight uttered.

"What do you want, Captain?" Kasta said, drawing the attention of everyone aboard. "Here we are, minding our own business at sea, and you intercept our humble little skiff." She shook her head. "Not very elegant of you, is it?"

Enkallio's eyes narrowed as he stepped toward her. "I think you know what we want."

Kasta looked down at the short man. "Weapons, platinum, some utility tools, our humble skiff?" She motioned toward Dresco. "An Imperial suit of armor? Worth a lot to the right buyer, I'm sure."

Dresco flinched and gasped.

"There's a price on your head, Krane. All of Vanda knows about it. Grow up now." Enkallio stood as straight and tall as he could.

"Let's kill her, Captain!" one of the men shouted from the upper level.

"Yeah!" another responded from the main deck. "Let's give her to the Imperials and drown ourselves in platinum!" Cheers erupted around the ship. Terrin and Captain Enkallio smiled at one another.

A young Vandeni woman began to scrub Dresco's blood from the floor. The knight fidgeted. "Wait," he said with a hesitant stammer. "If you let us go, we can pay you every piece of platinum that the Imperium is offering." The crew fell silent. "Plus—interest!" Dresco added.

The captain removed his hat. Grains of sand fell from his greasy black hair and onto the deck below. "That's quite a kind and noble offer, my good sire." He shook the hat out. "But word is that the Imperium is offering Breylu Dast twice what they are offering to anyone else."

Kasta shook her head; the captain's words spun around her mind, leaving her dizzy. "Really?"

The captain nodded. "I'm willing to bet he'd pay more for you than the Imperium at this point," he said, placing his hat back on his head.

"Dast is just as likely to kill you all as he is to strike a deal with you if you hold us for ransom," Dresco said, glaring down at the captain through his eyelashes. "We are much more reasonable negotiating options, Captain Enkallio."

"Maybe so." The captain placed his thumbs inside his black leather belt, which angled across his right leg and connected to his holster. "But our greatest chance of high profit is turning the two of you over to Dast. Grim as it may be, business is business."

"They don't even need to be alive, Captain." Terrin raised her fist in the air. "Let's make 'em walk the plank and send 'em to Dast in pieces!"

"Yeah!" was the belligerent consensus of dozens of screaming pirates.

The captain raised his limp hand, signaling his sailors to quiet down. They complied. "I'm a curious fellow," Enkallio said. The blue skin under his forehead tightened. "I want to know why the High Imperium is spending so much of their time and resources to kill a lowly body snatcher."

He stepped closer to Kasta. She swallowed as Captain Enkallio continued to speak. "And why she was going for a swim in the middle of the Western Sea, when all logic dictates that she should be in hiding." Kasta looked down, but the captain loomed before her face. Their eyes met beneath the brim of her hat. "These are the mysteries that just *ever* so slightly bother me. You understand, Miss Krane?"

Kasta winced. The captain's breath smelled of rotten fish and onions. "Of course," she said. "We were looking for a treasure chest. It is said that a crashed banking ship lay at rest in these waters. Looks like we were wrong." Though she smiled, Kasta swallowed hard, feeling the key stone in her back pocket. She hoped they would not notice it, that the blue daylight would hide the stone's green glow.

The captain's scruffy face dropped to a frown. "Miss Krane, I'm afraid you are lying to me. There's no way that you would put yourself in such danger for a treasure chest."

Dresco chimed in. "Then you do not know her!"

Kasta smiled widely and flashed a wink to her knightly companion. "He's got a point."

With a demented glare, Terrin stomped toward Kasta. "Then what were you doing in the Valley of Tombs?"

"Yes," the captain said with a snap of his fingers. "My first mate makes a valid point. We heard news that you had flown west from the Valley of Tombs." He chuckled. "Can you imagine my glee when it turned out to be you and your friend over here just floating into view of my spyglass?" He motioned to Dresco. "But my question is, Miss Krane—"

"Kasta!" she growled.

"It doesn't matter," he said as he closed his eyes and shook his head. "Why would a low-life body snatcher—"

"Treasure hunter!"

He stood on the tips of his toes and grabbed the hunter by the collar of her shirt. "Why would you call in a law official airship to take you all the way across Vanda when you are currently at risk of being shot on sight anywhere you show your face? What are you after?"

The captain's right hand wrapped over the handle of his pistol. Kasta stood over him with a tight-lipped smile. Her eyes sparkled. An idea came to her. "It's a pirate's quest!"

Murmurs circled the ship. Dresco's grey eyes narrowed in confusion. The captain's deep purple lips smacked together. "Explain," he said.

Kasta looked around the ship, making eye contact with as many of the pirates as she could. "Wayfarers of the great sea, my ally and I are on a mission for Madame Sariya Vaeliz!"

The pirates gasped. Some even recoiled. Kasta singled out a young girl with her hand over her mouth, the one who had cleaned up Dresco's blood. "We seek a great treasure," she said, her eyes piercing the young sailor's. "And the Madame has entrusted us with the task of bringing it to her." She looked to the pirates on the upper deck, shoulders high and chest out. "What do you say? Will you honor a fellow pirate? If you do, you will free us." She yelled into the shrill wind, "Hell, aid us in our quest!"

Kasta did not expect a rallying cry from the men and women aboard the vessel. But the dead silence that followed her speech left her staggered. She caught a glimpse of Dresco gawking at her. His jaw dropped.

"Vaeliz, you say?" Enkallio grumbled, a strain in his voice.

"Mmm... Yes," Kasta said with a stammer, her eyes falling aslant on the captain.

Enkallio stared up at her, unblinking. His plump cheek spasmed. "Sariya Vaeliz. That sea witch sank my favorite ship."

'Damn it,' Kasta thought with a sigh.

"You mean to tell me that you're searching these waters on an errand for her?" Kasta did not respond as Enkallio's fingerless gloves rose. An overgrown fingernail jutted into her face. "What is she having you look for?" he yelled.

The crew circled around their captain. "He's gunna kill her. Cap's gunna kill her!" one of them whispered.

Captain Enkallio's hands fell low. He began to pat Kasta's legs down, then moved to her torso.

"Whoa, whoa." Kasta's brow furrowed as she cringed. "So much for decency."

The captain's hand fell on Kasta's backside. He reached into her rear pocket and pulled out the key stone. He held the triangular object in her face, his lips tucked in. "What is this?" he asked with a snarl.

'Damn,' Kasta thought. She fought off her nerves, resisting the urge to tense up. "Ummm," she said with a squint. "A rock, my good captain. Don't even know how it got in there." She lifted her chin and shrugged.

"We'll see about that, won't we?" The captain tossed the stone to one of the pirates near the table. "Inspect this, along with the rest of their gear." Kasta was grateful that the key stone did not glimmer with such radiance in the daylight, though its peculiar shape had caught the captain's interest—as had Kasta's attempt to hide it.

Enkallio's face rose to hers again. A breath whistled through his nostrils. He glared up at the hunter through his sandy eyelashes. "You know you have beautiful eyes, lassie?"

Kasta's nose crinkled. "Ew, what?" She flinched and turned away. "Why are you making this weird? This was a perfectly fine kidnapping till you said that."

The captain's pupils dilated. He placed his hand under Kasta's chin, pulling her face back into view. "Your eyes. They have that same entrancing glow as the Northern Sea. That blue-green that you only find around the ice caps."

She groaned, struggling to free her chin from the captain's grip.

"Come on, Miss Krane. I'm trying to pay you a compliment here. Don't be rude, now." His voice shook with a hoarse snicker. "I have never seen eyes like yours before. They have captured my heart."

Kasta shook her head free. "Oh, how flattering," she said with a quiver. "Are you single?"

Dresco giggled. A nearby pirate rammed the hilt of his sword into the knight's ear. "Ow," he whispered.

"And my name is Kasta," the hunter added.

Captain Enkallio sighed. His upper lip curled. "Unfortunately, the rest of you is unimpressive. Unappealing, even." He sized her up with a grimace. His hand reached behind. With an effortless motion, he brought a serrated knife between him and Kasta. "Perhaps I will just keep your eyes, a collector's item in a display case on my shelf for jealous eyes to behold when they enter my cabin."

Kasta recoiled against the side of the ship but refused to look away.

"Or perhaps not," the captain said. The sky shifted to grey, for a cluster of dark clouds formed overhead. "Put them in the holding cells," he ordered. "Then we'll decide what to do with them." Turning away, he raised his hands toward his onlooking crew in a flamboyant manner. "Won't we, lads?"

The crew responded with merriment and cheer.

XVIII

To Negotiate with a Pirate

A group of four pirates grabbed hold of Kasta and Dresco, leading them across the deck. The circle of onlookers dispersed as they passed through. Dresco looked down and cleared his throat. "Nice name-drop of Madame Vaeliz there, Krane," he said with a bite in his voice. "You made them want to kill us even more."

Kasta flashed him a sideways glance and a nod. "I agree. Not my best moment." Her lips tightened, still bearing a salty taste. "But Dresco, would you mind telling me why we are in this situation in the first place?"

As they passed a Draekalagon pirate, he spit on Dresco's armor. Dresco took a step toward the sailor, but the electro-chains tightened, constraining his body. The pirates pulled the knight away and continued to escort the companions across the deck.

Kasta continued, "You couldn't escape? Fight your way out?"

Dresco scoffed. "Kasta, an armored battleship was pointing its heavy artillery at me. Cooperation seemed like the best option; would you not say?"

Kasta rolled her eyes. "Whatever, we're here now. Let's find a way out of this."

An out-of-tune fiddle whined under the rhythmic clapping of multiple sailors. "And just how are we going to do that?" Dresco asked, shaking one of the pirate's hands from his elbow.

The seafarers escorted the captives to the narrow section of the gang-way, toward the back of the ship. "That's the fun part," Kasta said with a wink. "Figuring that out."

"You actually are insane," Dresco said. His metal footsteps clanked against the deck. "I am going to be murdered at sea with an insane woman." A chirping flock of shadow gulls melded with the roaring ocean and wailing fiddle.

'Kasta.' A familiar voice echoed in the hunter's mind, removing any focus she had allocated to her captors, the vessel and the rest of the world. She stopped in her tracks.

"Move it, grave robber," said the gravelly female voice of one of the pirates.

'Kasta,' the voice said again, this time clearer.

"Vaktarae?" Kasta said out loud.

'Of course it is. Do you have any other telepathic acquaintances?'

"Fair point," Kasta uttered.

Dresco's eyelids fluttered. "Are you—? Who are you speaking to? Have you *actually* gone mad?"

'Find a way to set yourself and your companion free.' Vaktarae's voice rang hollower than it did beneath the sea, though just as sternly. 'I believe the sailor to your left has a key. Can you achieve this?'

'I can,' Kasta thought. 'But as soon as I get out of these chains, they'll just shoot me.'

'Just do as I say.' Vaktarae's voice thundered through the hunter's thoughts. 'And trust me.'

"Krane!" The sailor that Vaktarae had singled out tugged Kasta's arm, dragging her down the gangway.

"Ouch!" Kasta yelled, the electro-chains constricting her wrists.

"Follow my directions or those chains will keep squeezin' ya, lassie," the pirate said, raising a fist. "Now come on, this way." The pirate pointed down a set of stairs leading to the subdeck.

With a sharp sigh, Kasta leaned toward the knight. "Dresco, if I get you out of those chains, how many can you take?"

Dresco shook his head. His eyes narrowed on his companion in dismayed confusion.

Kasta spoke again, this time slower and with more emphasis in her words. "If I *set you free*, how many of them *can you take*?"

The knight stood tall. His armor reflected the maroon-purple hue of the ocean. "All of them."

"That should be just enough," Kasta said with a smirk. She thrust a shoulder into the body of the sailor to her left. The sailor dropped to the deck like a dead tree in a hurricane. Before the others could react, she headbutted the next pirate to cross her path.

Dresco followed her example and kicked one of the pirates overboard. He stomped on the face of the first sailor Kasta had attacked, holding his boot over the pirate's mouth. The fourth captor drew her pistol, though the hunter was quick to kick it from her hand. The pirate Kasta had headbutted pulled himself to his feet.

Leaning low, Kasta reached across the deck for the dropped pistol. Her bound hands wrapped around the handle. She set the weapon to incapacitate and fired a shot, her back turned to her target. The electrical beam struck the pirate, rendering him unconscious.

'The others must have heard the shot,' Kasta thought. 'The fiddle stopped.' The female sailor retreated toward the back of the ship. Kasta turned, fired a second backward shot, and the pirate tumbled to the deck.

The lookout sounded a high-pitched, beeping alarm. "The prisoners are loose!" she shouted. "The prisoners are loose!"

Dresco struggled to dig his bound hands into the sailor's jacket; the pirate still lay restrained by the knight's armored boot. "I can't find anything," Dresco yelled. "There's no key!"

Kasta grunted, raising her hands over her head. The chains tightened and compressed her wrists. She managed to bring her hands to her front, though the cuffs rumpled her skin white. She could not struggle anymore. If the chains tightened further, they could break her wrists. As Kasta leaned over the pirate, a group of his comrades charged from the front of the ship.

"Hurry!" Dresco barked.

"Okay. Okay. I found it!" she said, pulling a crooked metal key from the pirate's lapel. Kasta first attempted to slide, then to force the object through the keyhole on Dresco's chains. "That's not what this is for!" she yelled. "It doesn't unlock these damn chains."

Captain Enkallio and his subordinates approached. "Krane, stop this pathetic display!" he yelled with both fists clenched.

"The utility tool!" Dresco called out. "Cut the chains with the utility tool!"

"Right!" Kasta said. She grabbed the tool in the pirate's jacket and activated the saw setting. The machine buzzed, igniting sparks from the electro-chains that constrained her Imperial companion. "It's cutting," she said. "Just need a few seconds."

The aim of shock-cannons fell on the hunter and the knight from both directions. "We don't have a few seconds!" Dresco proclaimed. He pulled his hands apart, trying to help Kasta break the electrically tightened metal.

"Put the tool down, or we will all fire," Enkallio said. His shooting hand extended.

"Okay, okay," Kasta said. She dropped the utility tool. She had cut a section of the chain's steel to thin threads. 'That metal is strong,' she thought. 'But not strong enough to hold Dresco when it's cut down and red hot.'

"On your knees," Enkallio yelled. Terrin's index finger twitched over her pistol's trigger.

The hunter and the knight obeyed the captain's command. 'Okay, Dresco's pretty much free. Now what, Vaktarae?' Kasta thought.

The telepathic ocean dweller spoke with urgency. 'Kasta, brace for impact.'

"Impact?" she replied aloud.

Vaktarae's voice entered her mind again. 'Brace for impact and prepare to defend yourself.'

"Dresco, hold on to something," Kasta said, reaching for the side railing.

Though confused, he complied. As he grasped the taffrail, something rammed the bottom of the ship. Something enormous. An eruption from the depths, burning with enough rage to melt the floor. Metal creaked, rang and moaned throughout the deck as several men fell overboard.

"What was that?" a pirate shouted from the upper deck.

Another on the main deck yelled, "Something hit us!" As he spoke, the ship quaked again. With greater impact. The vessel rocked back and forth, tipping sailors into the sea from both port and starboard. The hunter and the knight held on to the railing with all their will.

In the disarray, the captain went to check on his men. Dresco stood up and pulled his hands apart, roaring from the bottom of his chest. Kasta was right. The knight was able to break apart the weakened chains with his sheer strength. He reached downward, seizing two short, curved swords from the incapacitated pirates. Panicking sailors fired on the knight. He swayed to the left, avoiding their volley.

And in a trice, his armor faded into the same dull grey hue as the deck. He was visible, though difficult to target, as though his shape was translucent. The knight charged the pirates, cutting through their shock-cannons and drawing their attention. Most of them.

The captain's eyes glazed over, fixating on Kasta. She scanned the deck for the shock-cannon she had used moments earlier, though she could not find it. The pirate captain drew his sword and rushed the hunter. "Oh, holy hell," Kasta said. She came to her feet and sprinted toward the stern.

Kasta's boots screeched against the floor on entering a room furnished with a tall bookshelf and a fine wooden desk. A curved golden sword hung mounted on the wall. "Captain's quarters," she said to herself, flinging her body over the desk. She searched the drawers, careful not to put any tension on the electro-chains.

"What have you done to my ship?" the captain yelled, tottering into his cabin. "What have you done, sea witch?"

"It's not me." Kasta's head poked out from behind the long, bean-shaped desk. "Looks like you have some enemies in unknown places, Cap." She dug through the drawers, looking for a key or anything she could use to break the chains.

"Today, you die, Krane!" He leapt atop the desk and swung his sword at her.

"Whoa!" she hollered, rolling backward. As she stood awaiting the captain's next move, another violent collision rocked the ship. The captain and Kasta fell to the floor.

She rose to her feet and rushed to the bookshelf. Something had fallen on the floor: a black velvet box. She kicked it open. "Mist Valley Single

Malt," Kasta proclaimed with a snicker. "Captain, you've been holding out on me."

The captain sprang forward with a downward thrust of his electro-blade. Kasta dodged the attack. The captain sliced through his bookshelf, shattering plates and tearing apart old hardcover books.

An object lay next to the captain's foot: something that had fallen out of his wardrobe in the commotion. Kasta dived down and picked up the thin piece of metal that lay on the floor: a black key with a skull engraved on the handle. "A *skeleton* key, Captain?" she said. "Not very original, you can do better than—"

A wild slash nearly caught Kasta's hat, but she evaded the captain's strike. Hearing the screams of his sailors, he stole a glance through the double doors. She seized the moment, sticking the key inside the keyhole of the electro-chains. The constraints did not loosen.

The captain turned and looked to Kasta with a twisted grin. "Oh, lassie. Did you really think the skeleton key would open your chains?" Enkallio trudged toward the hunter, his eyes bloodshot. "I don't even keep a key for 'em. They're controlled via data system. I'm not an idiot." The captain yowled, leaping toward her like a fencing frog.

She stumbled back. Enkallio's blade, wrapped in deadly electrical streams, fell toward her body. Her only defense was the chains that bound her. The hunter raised her hands high and turned her face sideways, closing her eyes. With a sizzling clang, Kasta felt the enormous tension between her wrists release. She opened one eye. Captain Enkallio had cut her chains in half.

Enkallio's grip tightened around the hilt of his sword. Kasta got off a wink before she rolled under the captain's desk, avoiding his next swing.

"Sir," a young Draekalagon pirate called out to the captain as he stumbled into the office. He was out of breath, his hands clasped around his knees. "Something is ramming our ship!"

The captain took another swipe under the desk before answering the sailor. "Is that right?" he screamed.

"Ye-yes, sir. There's a substantial breach in our hull. We're going down fast!"

Taking advantage of the distraction, Kasta climbed atop the desk. She reached for the golden sword displayed on the wall.

"Sailor, is that a shock-cannon I see there?" the captain asked, pointing to the Draekalagon's waistline.

"Ye-yes."

The captain trembled with rage. "Then stop giving me status reports and shoot the damn prisoner!"

The Draekalagon pirate's hand shook as he reached for the pistol on his belt. Kasta ignited the curved blade and jumped over the captain's desk. She thrust the sword down, knocking the pistol out of the pirate's hand. After landing on her back, she unleashed a sweep kick on the Draekalagon's ankle. He tumbled to the floor.

Kasta picked up the pistol and aimed it at the captain. She pulled the trigger, but the pistol fizzled with a declining purr. It would not fire; she had cut off a large piece of the barrel. "Damn," she said. The hunter backed out of the office and tossed the shock-cannon overboard.

The waves grew more ferocious as the ship sank. Each wall of water threatened to engulf those who stepped in their way. The captain strode forward with a stabbing thrust of his blade. Kasta sidestepped the attack. Enkallio's blade met the golden sword she had stolen from his cabin. The weapons hissed, their electrical currents crossing paths.

"Put down that sword," the captain ordered. Veins throbbed in his neck.

"No."

Kasta set her feet, grounding herself. Footsteps approached from behind. Vaktarae's voice spoke to her, 'Run, Kasta. To the upper deck.'

The hunter unleashed a left-handed haymaker into the captain's jaw. She turned and sprinted toward the staircase. The aim of a group of pirates fell on Kasta, though the volley of shock-cannon fire would not come until she rounded the corner.

A strong wind circulated around the ship. Kasta planted her back against the wall adjacent to the staircase. She looked to the front side of the lower deck. The pirates below moved in disarray and panic.

She saw her companion, Dresco Norte. The knight spun around with both short swords drawn, in a constant flow of natural, unpredictable motion, drawing the envy of the ocean itself.

Kasta rubbed her eyes. Dresco was not fighting with his pure strength but with speed. The pirates tried to shoot him, but every attempt either thundered to the skies or struck one of their comrades. Any sailor who challenged the noble knight in close combat ended up incapacitated or with an amputation. Even if Dresco did not camouflage himself with the violet-grey skies, the silver of the deck and the maroon of the sea, the pirates would not have stood a chance against the knight.

Two pirates scurried up the staircase. Kasta's eyes shot wide open. She turned from the wall with a slanted, downward slash of the golden sword. She cut one of the sailors across the chest and the other down his thighs. They fell to the ground. Kasta fled. 'They'll survive,' she thought.

The captain called out from the bottom of the staircase, "Body snatcher, turn and face me!"

'Brace yourself again, Kasta Krane,' Vaktarae said in her mind. Kasta had reached the circular platform that lay below the watchtower.

She had no choice but to enter a fetal position. "Dresco, hold on!" she shrieked. From the depths came another impact. The vessel shook from top to bottom in a violent aftershock.

The floor vibrated. Kasta peered toward the lower deck. Dresco still fought. His opponents quailed, their numbers thinning. Many fell to his onslaught. Others scurried to the orlop deck, desperate to repair the *Platinum Dragon*. Several had jumped or fallen overboard.

'Damn it, if I had a shock-cannon, I could help the poor fool out,' she thought. Dresco leapt over an electrical blast. The woman who fired the shot heaved in agony, beholding the short blade that he had thrust through her torso. 'On the other hand, it looks like he's doing just fine!'

Before Kasta could pull herself up, a trembling shadow appeared behind her. She turned her head. Captain Enkallio was preparing to strike. With a heavy groan, she kicked her heel into the shin of the pirate captain.

She sprang to her feet. Her fingertips tingled as they wrapped around the bars of the swinging tin ladder that led to the top of the lookout tower. The last collision had taken its toll on the ship, for it was sinking at a visible rate.

As Captain Enkallio crawled behind, a sharp object sped by. The lookout at the top of the tower was flinging small electro-knives. Kasta tucked her body flat against the ladder. A blade spiraled down, pinpointed to land between her eyes. She let go of the ladder, hanging to the side with one hand. The knife almost struck the captain.

"Hit her, not me, you bloody idiot," Enkallio screamed to the Draekalagon lookout.

The captain caught up to Kasta. He reached forward with his sword hand and swung at her. The hunter lowered the golden blade and defended herself.

"You're gunna pay for what you've done to my ship, Miss Krane," he screamed over the harsh winds.

A knife descended past Kasta again, this time an inaccurate throw. She and the captain exchanged sword strikes. Kasta's hand began to slip from the ladder's thin metal. Her other hand defended against the captain's assault. "You're gunna pay for trying to take me as your plunder," she said with a grimace.

A utility tool set to its knife function fell from above. 'The lookout must have run out of throwing knives,' Kasta thought. She swung the captain's decorative blade downward as he pursued her up the ladder, each strike a mix of attack and defense. The tin ropes dangled and swung.

Screams came from the men and women below. Water overflowed from the subdeck and onto the higher levels of the ship.

Kasta neared the top of the tower. The sentry leaned over the railing to push her off, but the hunter overpowered the Draekalagon woman and pulled her downward. Kasta did not check to see whether the lookout survived. She hoped she had fallen close enough to the swinging ladder to grab it.

The hunter set foot on the small circular platform atop the lookout tower. Captain Enkallio hurled himself over the rail. The opponents' eyes locked. Their blades met in a swift exchange of circling, stabbing and overcutting strikes. The captain backed Kasta against the paling. An unsteady flicker disrupted the circulation of her sword's electrical stream. The charge crystal was not supplying the sword with adequate power. If the crystal gave out, the electrical current would cease. The captain's sword would cut through the golden blade in an instant.

"Kasta, look out!" Dresco screamed over the croaking ship, the screeching wind and the thunderous fulmination of electric streams that powered the vessel. Kasta gasped. A pinstripe-clad pirate on the upper deck had a sniper rifle aimed on her.

"Agh!" she yelped, hitting the deck. The electrical stream soared overhead. Captain Enkallio also ducked. Kasta lifted her head, breathless.

Dresco rushed to the upper deck like a trugan on two legs, pounced on the sniper and cut him down.

The captain hopped to his feet. He slashed at Kasta, who still lay on the floor. She raised the golden blade above and blocked the oncoming attack.

Vaktarae spoke to Kasta. 'Kasta Krane, you and your companion need to get off that ship. It will be fully submerged in minutes!'

'Got it,' Kasta thought. She kicked the captain in the knee and leapt to her feet.

The voltaic swords met in a series of furious clashes. With one hand on the hilt, she unleashed a rapid combination of stabbing and sweeping strikes, backing the captain off. With a spinning slash, she singed a piece of his arm. He screamed in pain and slashed back in rage. Their blades crossed again.

"Face it, Cap, I got you beat." A crooked smirk crawled high on the hunter's face. "Should I give your body a proper sailor's burial or just... snatch it?"

That crooked smile dropped into a scowl when the electrical beam that ignited the decorative blade began to flutter. After emitting one last withering bolt, it deactivated altogether. "Damn it," she whispered.

An overexcited grin grew on Enkallio's face. "You were saying?" He swung his sword across the golden blade and cut it in half.

Kasta stepped back. Dresco called out from below. "Kasta, get down here, that watchtower is going down! It's going to crash into the electro-sail! Get off now!"

She looked behind. Dresco was right! The tower was leaning backward, falling toward the electrical streams that powered the entire ship. Vaktarae's attacks had crippled the lookout tower's foundation. She had another minute, maybe two, before she would fall into a lake of electric hell.

The captain treaded toward Kasta, his sword pointed at her. "You owe me a new decoration, Krane," he said. His pupils dilated as they focused on Kasta's eyes. The tower moaned with a guttural scrape. Gravity pulled her toward the back of the ship. She planted her feet to keep her balance.

The captain hopped forward. Kasta leapt aside and released a ferocious left jab, which connected with Enkallio's face. He lost his balance and fell back against the rail, the electric tower surging behind him. While his hand covered his face, Kasta unleashed an uppercut into Enkallio's gut. He grabbed his torso and dropped his sword. A swollen circle of red surrounded the captain's eye where her left jab had landed.

"Now who's got pretty eyes?" She grabbed the railing and hopped off the platform, back onto the swinging ladder.

The ladder swayed more than it was meant to as Kasta fled down its rungs. She hopped down rather than climbed. While more dangerous, it was faster.

The hunter's heart stopped. Then fluttered. Then raced, pounding her rib cage. The tower above began to topple. The flimsy tin ratline folded and collapsed along with it. Kasta looked down, and without hesitation, she jumped for the nearest deck. She would have screamed, but the hand of gravity and the salty winds stole her voice.

The hunter hit the floor, shoulder first. The shock coursed throughout her body. She groaned, turning to her back and placing a hand over her shoulder. "Must everything, *everything* break while I am on it?" she said to herself.

The hunter pulled herself up. She caught a glimpse of Dresco fighting below. He had reduced the amount of his enemies to about a half dozen. Bodies, some squirming and some motionless, lay scattered around his spinning, dual-wielded fury. The knight was the eye of a hurricane, though not the calm before the storm.

'Kasta,' Vaktarae's said. 'The first officer is in possession of the key stone. Obtain it from her before you leave that ship!'

'Understood.' She rushed down the stairs and saw Terrin. The stern-faced woman sought to set her sights on Dresco, but she had no success. Kasta leapt toward the first mate, tackling her to the deck. The hunter pressed her fists into Terrin's collar bone. "The stone, where is it?" Kasta said.

"I don't have it!" Terrin claimed.

Kasta noticed a triangular shape bulging beneath the pirate's blouse. "Seriously?" Her lips twisted as she reached under Terrin's shirt. She pulled the key stone from an inner pocket.

Kasta felt a dampness at the toe of her boots. The deck was flooding. "Dresco, we gotta go!" she called out. "Grab everything of ours that you can!"

Dresco and Kasta gathered any confiscated supplies that were within reach. "To the skiff!" Dresco said, thrusting a short sword through the shoulder of an onrushing pirate.

The pirate ship ruptured and cried out in a series of scraping moans. Its foundation was failing on itself. The companions dashed across the wet deck toward their boat, which the pirates had commandeered. Most of the crew had fled overboard. Dresco had incapacitated or dismembered the rest, save for one stubborn sailor.

"Stop!" Captain Enkallio yelled, leaning over the deck of his sinking ship. "You will go no farther." He held a wet pistol in his throbbing arm.

"I beg to differ," Kasta said with a chuckle.

"Miss Krane, you will feel my—"

"Her name is Kasta!" Dresco leapt forward and kicked the short captain overboard. The hunter and the knight looked at each other for a moment before they too jumped overboard, into the skiff they had rented from Shellborn earlier that day.

"Go, now!" Kasta yelled. She grabbed one of the short swords that Dresco had used to fend off the pirates and cut the steel wire that was towing the skiff along. Dresco fired up the boat's motor. Though the electrical power struggled to ignite on the first pull of the lever, it did so on the second. They blistered through the water away from the sinking pirate ship.

Each companion took a deep breath. The wailing of the pirate vessel carried across the sea as the mast collapsed. Kasta's cyan eyes crawled to Dresco. His grey eyes connected with hers. The hunter and the knight found themselves unable to do anything other than share a chuckle.

Which fast accelerated into roaring laughter.

"That was..." Kasta had to catch her breath, though she could not stop laughing. "That was incredible!"

Dresco's high-pitched giggle impeded his speech as well. "Incredible? Kasta, the display you just put on." He took a moment to find the words. "I stated that your sword-fighting style was wild and disorganized. And while I was entirely correct about that, I was wrong to believe you would never last in a duel. The way you swayed back and forth, evading attacks. Your speed, balance, creativity! The poor captain never stood a chance."

"Me?!" Kasta smiled. Her eyes sparkled brighter than a pair of cyan stars. "You just took on more than a dozen pirates, with two swords you had never even wielded before. You took on the whole ship! I only fought one man, really."

"Yes," Dresco said over a gleeful sigh. "On a swinging ladder, on top of a tower."

"Stop it," she said with a playful tone. "This was all you. You just took on a whole hive of sea rats. Your modesty is useless right now, Norte." She leaned back, pointing at the knight. "I give you credit on this one. We survived because of you."

"We survived because of us," Dresco said, steering the skiff to the east. The pirate ship was more than half-sunken. The sailors' screams fell in line with the current of the ocean and the crumbling ship.

"What supplies did you save?" Kasta asked, searching for fresh water.

Dresco looked down at the pile of items he'd tossed aboard. "My sword. A tiny Rogue Islander pirate tried to attack me with it. He could not even lift it over his head."

Kasta gave off a dry laugh. She leaned over and tossed her hat onto the floor.

Dresco continued, "Also, some water and your pistol."

"Both, now!"

Dresco smiled and tossed the pistol and canteen to his companion. "What about you?" he asked.

Kasta gulped down half the bottle of water. With a wipe of her chin, she said, "I got your helmet, my supply pack, my data system—" She smiled as she reached into her pocket and pulled out the key stone. "And this." She tendered the triangular object to Dresco.

"What's this?" he asked.

"It's the key," Kasta said. "That'll get us to Vellon's Blade."

Dresco fell into boisterous laughter. "How did you get it? What happened?" His shoulders shimmied. "Oh yes, and how did you destroy their ship? I was meaning to ask that. I just could not get around to it when I was fighting off the crew."

Kasta looked down. "Long story. All related."

"Kasta, I must know!"

The hunter smiled and kicked one boot over the other. "Dresco," she said, leaning back. "I met a Syrenia down there."

"No!" he said, slumping atop the skiff's helm.

"Yes!"

Dresco exhaled. "An angel of the deep. Is that who you were speaking to aboard the pirate vessel?"

Kasta nodded. "Yeah, and he helped us take down the ship. I don't know how, but he did." She tossed a cluster of debris that had fallen from the ship into the water. Among the wreckage, Kasta caught a glimpse of a glass bottle: the captain's fine whisky. "Ooh," she said, licking her lips. "That's what the little creep gets for holding out on me." She clasped the bottle by the neck.

"This is further proof then," Dresco said, looking off into the blue-and-violet horizon. "Our quest is a divine one."

For a moment, she thought Dresco was referring to the captain's bottle of whisky. But she was quick to realize that he was speaking of her encounter with the Syrenia. Looking to the knight, she shrugged.

Kasta's mind felt an extrasensory presence. Once more, Vaktarae's voice entered her thoughts. 'Are you both well?' he said.

Kasta's face glowed. 'Yes, Vaktarae. How about you?'

'I am well. I appreciate your concern. Just trying to make sure that these sea thieves find their way to the escape boats.'

'Most of them can breathe underwater anyway, right?' Kasta thought with a soft chuckle. Dresco's gaze narrowed on her.

'Yes, but not all of them,' Vaktarae replied. 'Draekalagons, despite their reputation as skillful seafarers, last about as long down here as I would up there.'

A grin fell on Kasta's face. 'Hey, Vaktarae,' she thought, staring off into the distance, toward the pirate ship. The vessel tilted back, its bow pointing upward. 'Thanks for getting us out back there. We'd have been dead by nightfall if it weren't for you.'

'No need to thank me, Kasta Krane.' His voice sparked in her mind. 'Just remember your place in all of this.'

In the distance, a colossal tail breached the ocean surface. It was a whale. The creature's tail stretched vertically; the two ridged, triangular flukes swayed back and forth. It paused against the horizon before plummeting into the sea, followed by a trail of rainbow mist.

And a high-pitched, hollow call.

XIX

ADVENT

Kasta was unsure whether the pirates had transmitted a message to Breylu Dast or to the Imperium. She was not going to take any chances. If Dast found out that she was taken captive off the coast of Shellborn, he would already be on the way. 'In fact, in all likelihood, he would already be near.' With that thought in mind, Kasta made sure not to linger in Shellborn long. They paid the stable fee for the trugan, refilled their canteens with water and embarked north, toward the Eldritch Forest.

They traveled cross-country and through canopied forest passages, not stopping for food or rest. Athenis set and the skies darkened. The trugan galloped under swelling shades of amethyst and sapphire, pushing the limits of their endurance. Kasta turned and smiled; Crevallus was keeping up and responding well to his rider.

She led Dresco to the top of a hill. Kaiar and Crevallus treaded across the narrow ridge. Their claws scraped against the coarse stone, and the steep terrain halved their speed. The night sky fell on Kasta and Dresco with a cold stare, as though the companions were tears caught in the blink of an amethyst eye. The trugan were panting and hunched over. They had sprinted thousands of miles, exhausting their cybernetic organs.

It was time to stop for the night. While Kasta knew that the shadows would give them cover, so too would it cloak their enemies. Any bounty hunter, assassin, Imperial Knight or Moon Shadow Rider could be lurking in the darkness.

The companions found shelter in a cave along the mountain ridge. They did not make a fire, despite the brisk temperature. They ate only the dried meat and canned foods that remained in their supply packs. The trugan had fallen asleep, Crevallus' head atop Kaiar's hip.

"You have to tell me everything about the Syrenia!" Dresco demanded with a boyish pitch in his voice, leaning toward Kasta.

She cleaned a piece of jerky from her teeth with her tongue. "Dresco, I already have."

"No!" The knight bounced as he sat. "You say they communicated with you using telepathy. What was that like? Why did they give you the stone? Are they as beautiful as the stories say?"

"Calm down." Kasta raised her hand toward him with a chuckle. "We're being hunted by half the bounty hunters on the planet, remember?"

"Oh, yes," Dresco whispered with an apologetic frown. "But can you please tell me?"

"It wasn't just his voice. He could read my deep thoughts, my memories, my fears."

"And in his wisdom, he decided you were worthy of taking the key?"

Kasta shrugged. "Either him or the sanctum itself? I don't really get how it works." She reached forward and grabbed Captain Enkallio's bottle of malted whisky. "And they look like big, shining fish for all I saw. It was dark down there."

Dresco yelped with excitement. "Magnificent! So, what made him decide that we—that *you* were worthy of taking the key stone? Did he say?"

"That's the strangest part." She bit her lip. "He allowed me to pursue the sword because I told him I didn't want it for myself. That I wanted someone else to have it."

Dresco uncrossed his legs, shifting his weight to his knees, and cleared his throat. "But he was disenchanted when you told him that you sought to profit from Vellon's Blade."

"Yeah. I told him that I wanted to bring the blade to the Madame, for she may be its rightful wielder. And that I had no desire to wield such power for myself."

Dresco's expression turned awkward. "Is that true?"

Kasta's nose crinkled. Her purple lips creased as she struggled to pop off the bottle's cork. "It must be," she said, a strain in her voice. The cork plopped loose. "If there's one legend about the Syrenia that proved to be true to me today, it's that you cannot lie to those fish people. They see right through you."

"Interesting," Dresco uttered, more to himself than to his companion. He looked toward the mouth of the cave, his eyes catching a glint of starlight. "We are close. So close to finally finding what we have sought for... how long now?"

"Feels like years," Kasta said. Her head fell against the stone wall while she took a sip of whisky. She grinned as the icy burn sank into her tongue.

Dresco chuckled. "Am I truly *that* intolerable of company, Kasta?"

Her lips twisted with a crooked smile. "No! That's not what I meant. Come on! It's just been wild is all. Riding back and forth across the continent, getting stuck in temple traps, Imperial prices on my head, bounty hunters trying to kill us, talking statues, talking fish, dueling a ship full of pirates." With a raspy chuckle, she took another sip of dark, smoky whisky. "Yet, somehow, we are still here." She looked to the knight and winked. "For a little longer anyway."

Dresco stood. He lumbered across the cave and sat against the wall next to her. "Can I get a sip of that?"

The bottle spilled as Kasta pulled it away from her lips. "Come again?" she said with a cough.

Dresco reached toward her. "Let me have a little of your malted spirits, there."

Kasta's eyes widened. Her head tilted sideways. "You don't drink, Sir Norte."

"Like you said, we're still here. When you list all that we have lived through thus far, the question 'how much longer?' does pose itself, would you not say?"

Kasta looked at the knight with a slow nod. "Fair enough." She handed him the bottle.

"Besides," Dresco said, raising the bottle to his lips. "I am on a divine quest. The Guardians will understand."

Kasta covered her mouth, bursting into laughter. She did not want to make too much noise. While it was unlikely that anyone would track them on such a remote route, she remained cautious.

However, she laughed even louder when Dresco coughed after swallowing a sip of whisky. "It's good," he croaked, his eyes bloodshot. "Flavorful, decadent."

"Have you ever had a drink?" she asked, still giggling.

"Only ale and wine, when I was much younger," he said with a clearing of his throat. "Never this... pirate nectar." He handed the whisky back to Kasta.

She took hold of the bottle by the neck. Her eyes sparkled with an enigmatic glow, though she maintained a flippant smile. "So, how many of them did you kill?" she asked, her voice high in pitch.

"Of whom?"

"The pirates. I was just curious. You were quite outnumbered. I can't imagine that the survival of our captors was a top priority of yours."

"I cannot be certain how many I slew," Dresco said, leaning back and looking up. "I was not making it my priority to end their lives, but I did deliver several strikes which may have proven fatal." His hand extended toward his companion. "Sorry, I know that violates your code."

She shook her head. "Don't apologize. You did what you had to do."

Dresco came back with a swift response. "Would you have?"

"What?" Kasta asked with a squint.

"Would you have killed those sailors if you had to?"

A heavy breath vented out the side of her mouth. "I can't say. I suppose if our positions were reversed, I would find out. But like I said, you do what you have to do."

"Why?" Dresco asked.

"Why what?" she replied, kicking her feet out.

"Why do you hold that code so strictly? The real reason. I must know."

"Ugh." Kasta removed her hat. "I used to be in a gang, Norte. A bad one. The Red River Gang."

Dresco nodded. "I know. The Madame told me."

"No." She bit her tongue. "I was one of their triggerwomen. I collected bounties for 'em. I hunted their enemies. And a lot of the time, they didn't give me the option to take my targets alive."

The knight swallowed, at a loss for words.

Kasta's head bowed low. "I hated it. Every minute of it. But the gang took me in as a kid; you could say they raised me in a twisted way. I hated killing, but I was weak. I felt loyal to them." She stuttered for a moment. "And to Breylu."

Dresco's jaw dropped. "Dast?"

"Yep," she said under a sigh.

His head shook back and forth. "Wait, you were in a gang with Breylu Dast, the man who is now obsessed with killing you?"

"Yeah. We were partners. My first treasure hunts were with Breylu. We were a good team for a couple of kids, too."

"So that is why he hates you?" Dresco said with a downward point of his finger. "Because you left that life behind? He felt betrayed by you—abandoned, even?"

Kasta flinched, pouring another gulp of whisky down her throat. "You could say that," she said with a raspy whisper.

She handed the bottle back to Dresco. "I knew there was more to the story than jealousy and competition," he said.

Kasta's face sank. "Anyway, I couldn't do it anymore. I decided I was going to play it straight. Made a vow never to kill again. But I had gotten quite good at hunting people. So, I figured 'get paid for my talents' and joined up with a marshal's department."

"Hold on," Dresco said, one eye twitching. "You were a law official?"

"Yep." Kasta smirked. "Crazy, right?"

He took another sip of whisky, this time much slighter. "I can't even begin to imagine that."

"Neither could they." She shook her head. "I moved from town to town, looking for a city that fit me. Most lawmen didn't like my more… rough-and-tumble approach. And I didn't like being told what to do. Eventually, I found a decent fit with the Vulture department."

"Is that how you met Marshal Jos?"

"Sure is." Kasta looked toward the stones and dust on the ground, coated with fresh beams of moonlight. Her eyes sailed back to her companion. "But it was still just not for me. I needed to be able to move freely. Most of all, I missed treasure hunting. Life in the law was just too slow. So, Kasta Krane, the Merciful Hunter was born. Decided to go after bounties and treasure alike." She flashed a crooked smile. "And here we are."

Dresco blinked in rapid succession. "And it is an exciting life indeed," he said. "But don't you ever get lonely?" His hand dragged against the coarse ground. "Working alone, traveling from town to town, job to job?"

"Do you?" Kasta asked. She crossed her arms.

"Of course." He placed the bottle down and moved his hands over his knees. "I miss my friends from the Order, though I doubt many of them miss me. I miss my family: my mother, my sister. My titan wolf, Maigavara. By Athenis, she is beautiful. Have I ever told you about her?"

Kasta rubbed her forehead, covering her rolling eyes. "*Yes*, Dresco. What about your family?" She reached for the whisky bottle. "Your sister. Tell me about her."

"Veth," Dresco said with a deep sigh. "She is an arcane soul." A smile came over the knight's face. He gazed into Entaega's moonlight, creeping through the lips of the cave. The white rays framed the knight in an aura of cosmic radiance. "She's valiant and willful. Much like you."

"Alright," Kasta said as she raised the bottle. "Cheers to Veth Norte."

Dresco chuckled. "I remember when we were children, we used to run around our hometown, pretending we were knights, fighting off dragons and enemies of the Imperium." His hand dragged across his face, from forehead to chin. "Those are some of my happiest memories: playing in the snowfall with my elder sister. Armed with nothing but a couple of sticks and our imaginations."

Kasta winced, forcing down a gulp of whisky. "That sounds nice. I don't recall ever playing as a child. I didn't run around with a stick either. They gave me a shock-cannon, set to kill."

"Oh my," Dresco said with an expression halfway between a smile and a frown. "Anyway," he said, stammering. "That feels like it was all a dream now. Veth and I no longer speak."

Kasta squinted. Her head cocked forward. "Why not?"

"Well," he said, lying across the floor on his side. "Our childhood dreams came true. We both became knights of the Imperium. She earned respect from the Clerisy and the military, displayed divine devotion to the Order and achieved the rank of High Paladin."

Kasta cleared her throat. "Is that a high rank?" she asked softly.

Dresco chortled. "Very high. The second highest in our Order."

"Were you a paladin?" Kasta asked.

"No," he replied. "A captain."

"Is that a high rank?"

"No. It is a... fairly high rank. Somewhere in the middle. It's not important." He let her finish a gruff chuckle before continuing. "The Order began to change. The scriptures were reinterpreted, the prayers were rewritten, ancient art was replaced. The Etsinnae were no longer spoken of as our eternal enemy, but as a myth, an archaic metaphor."

"Sounds like modernization."

"That is what the Order called it." Dresco snatched the bottle of whisky from Kasta's hand. "That is what Veth called it. We argued at the dinner table, we argued in meetings. She stood by the Order's alterations. To me, it was blasphemous. She was so high in rank, so dedicated to the Clerisy that she could not see any form of corruption or error, no matter how prevalent."

He took a large swig of whisky. Some escaped his lips and dripped down his chin. "Then it happened. The Testament's Rebirth. Ancient scriptures that were once recounted as truth are now painted as allegories. The stories of the Etsinnae faded further into fable. The Clerisy itself was dismantled. The balance of power and structure which held High Imperial theocracy together for almost three thousand years was eradicated. Absolute power now belongs to the Cleric-Eternal.”

Dresco hesitated. His eyes shut for a long moment. “So, I left the Order of the Guardians, the institution which I had pledged my life and soul to. Because to me, it was unrecognizable.” The knight took yet another sip of whisky. “To Veth, my resignation was betrayal. She attempted to convince me that I was abandoning our creed, our country—hell, the Guardians themselves.” He nodded once. “But in the end, I knew what was right. And what was right was to leave the Order behind. Many other knights felt the same.”

Kasta rested her hands on her knees. A cool gust circled the cave. “Have you thought of trying to work it out with her?”

“Of course,” he said. “It has been a grim time for our relationship. It has been even harder on our mother.” He handed the bottle back to Kasta. “If we make it out of this alive, I am going to make everything right with Veth. I will sit down with her and we will work out our differences.” He looked skyward. “Guardians, give me the strength.” Kasta placed a cigarillo in her mouth. He ogled her with an enigmatic scrutiny. “What about you? What are you going to do when we complete our quest?”

She shrugged. “Take a few weeks off. Enjoy my platinum. Play some cards. Do some hunting.”

Dresco responded with a refined slur, “No family you want to spend time with?”

Kasta sneered, shaking her head. “My entire family is dead, Norte.”

“You have a family, Kasta.” His grey eyes grew wide and warm.

“No. They are dead. Raiders killed my parents when I was a little kid. I have no living family that—”

"That's not what I mean!" Dresco said, his voice rising in pitch. "You have Marshal Jos, Madame Vaeliz. They care about you, deeply."

Kasta waved him off. "Pff. They care about the business I bring them. That's about it."

The knight's body wobbled as he reached across his companion for the bottle of whisky. "Kasta, you and I both know that is not true!"

"It is, though."

"No! Marshal Jos asked me to keep tabs on you."

Her eyebrows rose. "Did he really?"

"Yes," Dresco replied. "In Vulture. He was incredibly worried about you. That was why I felt bad when I thought I had lost my data system. I would not be able to message him."

Kasta laughed and shook her head. "That old square."

"And the other Marshal. Bovien. She has gone to great lengths to help you as well: sending her men across the region, supplying you with an airship." He took a small sip of whisky and dragged his hair behind his ears. "She obviously cares for you as well. You may not have blood relatives, but you have a family."

Kasta seized the bottle. "They are protecting their investment." She took a swig, followed by a puff from her cigarillo. "And future investments."

There was no reply. Instead, the companions just passed the bottle back and forth for several minutes.

Dresco finally broke the silence. "So, do you think we'll find it?" he mumbled with a belch.

"Find what?"

"Vellon's Blade, Krane." His voice fizzled like a popped bubble. "You know that I believe we will find it. But do *you* think we will? Or is it still just a wild-goose chase?"

"Yeah." She locked her fingers behind her head. "I think we'll find it." Her mind went blank. She began to fall weary. "After all we have been through, I'd be pretty damn furious if we didn't find it."

They locked eyes in silence, then broke out into laughter. She put her finger over her lips, signifying a need for quiet, though she struggled to follow her own direction.

"To our divine quest," Dresco said. He raised the captain's whisky taking a sip.

Kasta snatched the bottle and took a swig of her own. "To treasure hunting."

Kasta's eyes crept open as the warm blue light of Athenis streamed into the cave. The trugan still lay in slumber, as did Dresco. He had fallen asleep on Kasta's shoulder. The hunter grunted, then chuckled at the knight's gaping mouth and soft snore. She nudged his head with a delicate shrug. "Time to get up," she whispered.

The knight groaned, his forehead creasing. His head lifted from her shoulder. "What time is it?" he asked, his eyes still shut.

"I just said. Time to get up." Kasta stood and walked to the trugan. Both beasts leapt up, eyes wide and mouths salivating.

"I feel awful." Dresco moaned.

The hunter laughed through her nose. "Drink some water. Eat something. You'll feel better." She gathered a dried piece of meat from her supply pack. She split it in two and tossed a half to each trugan.

She looked to Dresco. A tuft of frizzy hair covered his bloodshot eyes. 'Lucky he can't see himself,' she thought. "Come on." She tossed him a canteen of water. "Fix yourself up. If we can ride at the pace we did yesterday, we should reach the Eldritch Forest by nightfall."

"I am never drinking again," the knight said, massaging his temples.

"You're a treasure hunter now, Norte. Spirits are all that'll lift your spirits!"

The knight groaned in response.

The companions gathered their belongings and exited the cave. They made their way down the slope back to the desert plains. In the distance, Kasta spotted a group of riders moving toward them. The hunter was quick to alter their path. It was unlikely that they were any threat, but she refused to take the chance. Showing her face to strangers was dangerous enough. Anyone who had heard of the price on her head could take a shot at her, bounty hunter or not. 'The chance to make a chunk of money makes people do some crazy things. Case in point: me. Right now.'

A moderate windstorm sent funnels of sand over the hardpan. Kasta covered her eyes with her goggles. She turned to check on Dresco, who seemed to be handling the storm and his steed without much difficulty. She did not like riding in such an open space, though they moved at a high speed. There was no cover, no vegetation other than indigo cacti and dry shrubs. Even at the pace they moved, a skilled sniper such as Vinai of Oglund could hit them.

Great relief came when they arrived at the Copper Desert Pass. The pathway was narrow, greeted by an assortment of vibrant flora: spiraling spiked vines hung from the indigo cacti. Lush stems of ovate-leafed plants reached for the tops of the ridges, their arms dancing in the wind like golden-green flames. Though narrow, the pass was straight enough for the companions to maintain their speed. The lack of areas to take cover lessened the chance of an ambush.

They rode through the pass for several hours. The late afternoon heat of Athenis sweltered in merciless dominion. Every bit of shade, from a moribund tree or overarching cliff, felt like a gift.

Reptilian hawks glided overhead, squawking and hissing. Their shadows whisked across the amber dirt. Dresco spoke to Crevallus. The trugan grunted in turn, sometimes in agreement, sometimes in rebuttal. The beast's turquoise eyes shut in contentment as his rider ran an armored hand down the back of his neck and told him tales of the Guardians. Kasta decided against taking a break. They were near their destination, and potential adversaries could be close behind. 'Or in front.' The hunter shook off that morose thought.

The companions exited the path and found themselves on flat desert again. To their right, a cliff descended to a layer of barren terrain; to their left, a vast expanse of sandy plains separated by a creek. In the distance to the front, there rested a group of white trees, dead, hollow and twisted. Athenis did not seem to touch the territory. It was lost in its own shadow, unaware of the flowing creek or the surrounding desert climate.

'The Eldritch Forest.'

Kasta and Dresco passed the perimeter of the wood as Athenis retreated below the horizon. The ashen bark of the trees overlapped, spiraling upward and spreading wide at their crowns. The trees avoided one another, each alone in standing death. There was no chirping of birds, save for the infrequent hoot of an owl. The hum of the creek faded. Crevallus hissed as he stepped through the dark, hollow dirt. The hunter and the knight did not speak to each other. Kasta wanted to but could not find the words. She could not speak at all.

She swallowed. For some odd reason, she was no longer afraid of Imperial assassins or an ambush from Dast. She dreaded what this forest may hold: malevolent spirits who patrolled under the moonlight, witches who took refuge in the dead trees, monstrous creatures that the world had left in the darkness of this wood.

But Kasta's fear passed like a wave breaking on the shore when she reached into her jacket pocket and removed the key stone. It was glowing—a brighter green than before. And as she and Dresco rode farther into the forest, it gleamed brighter. "Not gunna quit now," she said with a smile. "Definitely not."

A perimeter of trees circled an empty area. Nothing but hollow-brown dirt lay on the ground. Kasta stopped. She looked to the sky. Entaega looked down, its half-moon light absorbed by the ring of trees. Vharris loomed close by in the form of a crescent, resting against the ardent sapphire and amethyst shades of the atmosphere.

Kasta looked to the key stone. Its green glow flickered and pulsated. "This is it," she said under her breath. "It has to be." She walked across the empty territory. As she stepped toward the center of the circle, the green of the rock pulsated faster. Kasta stopped when it turned solid. Streams of light flowed from the key stone, bending and vibrating along her glove and through the air. She knelt low and placed the rock on the ground.

Under the surface, something growled. A rolling tremor erupted from beneath the companions' feet. "Seismic quake!" Dresco yelled.

"No," Kasta said, planting her hand on the ground to keep her balance. "We've found the keyhole. The door is unlocking."

The rumble grew louder, and the ground shook harder. A rounded tip emerged from the topsoil. Rotating like a globe, it burst through the terrain. Stone scraped and gears ground as the phenomenon revealed itself. A black sphere stared down with an eye of shadow—awakening. Spinning armillary rings twisted around the structure. The hunter and the knight stepped back. Dirt erupted from the ground in bombarding clusters. The glossy orbital edifice arose in the middle of the treeless circle, invading the empty land.

With a clash, the sphere halted. One of the rings stopped spinning and supported the orb's weight. Pipes and pillars extruded from the bottom, burrowing into the soil. An opening formed at the structure's center. Out of the opening slid a set of black stairs.

The companions looked at each other. "Have you ever seen a structure like this, Kasta?" Dresco asked with a gulp.

"Never," she said, her breath held. "Never in all my days of treasure hunting have I even *heard* of this kind of structure. How would they even build something like this? How would—anyone?"

Dresco shook his head. After standing in awe, sizing up the sphere, they hid the trugan in the forest. Kasta retrieved a baldric with an adjustable strap from her pannier, fashioned to hold a sword.

As they treaded back toward the massive orb, it almost looked natural—like a black meteor, buried and forgotten since the time of its impact. But its perfect shape told a tale of architecture. The armillary rings would have required complex, sophisticated engineering.

They approached the staircase. Kasta looked to Dresco and nodded. "You ready?"

"Yes," he replied. "Let us enter."

Kasta stepped on the first stair. "This structure has assuredly sat dormant for thousands of years. It was likely very sacred to the most paranoid and devout of the ancient Vandeni." She took a shallow breath. "There could be traps at every corner, unpredictable contraptions, anything. So, Dresco, it is important that we—"

"Mind our surroundings," he said, finishing the sentence for her.

"Yes," she said with a slight smile and a nod. She adjusted her hat, taking a final glimpse of the surrounding forest. "And watch your step."

The companions treaded up the staircase. Vertigo kicked in as they climbed higher. There was no handrail. 'Don't fall off and die before you even get in, Krane.' She kept her hand on the handle of her pistol. It would likely be useless against whatever dangers lay in the foundation of the spherical structure, but it gave her comfort, nonetheless.

As they stepped closer to the top of the stairs, Kasta saw dull script engraved in the scraped marble above the entrance. The writing system was so ancient that she could not read any of the words, save for one character, the largest character written above the doorway. A character with a meaning that had remained unchanged and inscribed the same throughout temples, sanctums and tombs, regardless of when in history the Vandeni built them. The symbol was of three leaves on top of a flaming triangle, and its meaning was "Vellon."

XX

THE TEMPLE OF VELLON

Kasta lowered her optical system when she set foot inside the temple. Her boot hit the surface with a cold echo. She set her optical system to scan for any threats: traps, faulty architecture, corroded foundation. She went to activate the night-vision setting as well, but it proved unnecessary. Flames burst from torches laid along the hallway, across from one another, two by two. Kasta's eyes widened as she stared on the erupting flames, not orange in color but bright green.

"Is this caused by geothermal power of some kind?" Dresco asked, standing stiffly.

"No," Kasta said. Her eyes were dry. "Definitely not."

"Well, I assume you have a rational explanation for this?"

The hunter's eyes remained unblinking. "No." She took a careful step forward. The black stone floor was smooth, yet her boots had no problem gripping the surface. Seeing that her optical system detected no threat, Kasta grabbed the nearest torch and yanked it off the wall.

She turned to Dresco. His armor mirrored the green glint of the surrounding flames. Kasta used her mouth to remove one of her gloves and ran her hand through the fire. "It's cool," she said with a gasp. "I could keep my hand in there for several seconds without burning it."

Dresco raised a finger. "But it is bright!"

"True," she said as she put her glove back on. "Let's go."

The companions stepped with care. The black hallway offered no sound but the rapping of their footsteps and the crackle of the flames. As they approached the middle of the hall, she noticed a piece of art to the left: a depiction of several men gathered around a large sphere, the very temple through which Kasta and Dresco were walking. It was not a carving but a three-dimensional engraving. The sculptures appeared to sway and dance in the flicker of green flame.

'This artistry is beyond when I estimate this temple was constructed,' Kasta thought. 'Based on the script and architecture, I date this temple at about eight thousand years old. Maybe even a little older.' Above the engraving sat the same symbol she had recognized outside: Vellon. "This type of art should not have been invented at the time this temple was built," she whispered to herself.

Dresco overheard. "It has the hand of the Guardians," he said.

Kasta did not attempt a rebuttal.

The hallway rounded and curved to the left. The hunter and the knight crept around the bend. Kasta's optical system zoomed in on several spots and marked them red. "Careful," she said. The next hall burst into a green fiery luminescence. "My optical system is picking up a few hot spots along the hallway. Could just be old foundation or loose stones, something screwing with the sensors. But it could also be a death trap."

Dresco cleared his throat. "Keep an eye out for death traps. Noted."

Kasta nodded. They carried on down the hallway. The air felt colder—almost wet as they moved along. They approached an area that the optical system had marked red. "Step around here," Kasta said, pointing the torch to the left side of the hall. "My system doesn't like that." Both companions approached the area and steered clear.

The hunter looked closer. "Looks like it's just a damaged stone," she said, adjusting her hat. Her data system was picking up interference. Its readings were unclear.

"Can't be too careful," Dresco said.

They continued forward, caution in their steps. Kasta halted again. "Hold it!" she whispered with a growl. "My threat indicator is going crazy on that wall up ahead." She pointed to the left wall, about halfway to the end of the hallway.

Dresco's head tilted. "Do you hear that?" He put his hand to his helmet as if he were cuffing his ear.

"Hear what?" Kasta asked, one eye squinted.

He took a step to the right. "Water. Flowing water."

She tiptoed toward the wall and pressed her ear to the surface. "You're right! Could it be possible that their irrigation system is still functioning? How?"

"They have green fire. And it is their irrigation system that puzzles you?"

Kasta's head rocked back and forth. "Good point," she said with a slight smile. She directed Dresco to the other side of the hallway. The cold of the stone wall penetrated Kasta's glove and tingled her skin. Near the area that her data system had marked as dangerous, there was another engraving, as detailed and intricate as the last. The art depicted a group of Vandeni gathered around. Below, there was a single Vandeni, swimming in a pool of water, threatened by a swaying blade. His face was desperate. He was struggling.

Next to the piece of art was a narrow pipe. On the other side of the pipe was another engraving. It portrayed the same swimmer from the other piece. He floated through a river, his face etched in relief.

"I get it." Kasta raised a finger.

"Get what?"

"The sculpting," she said with a thin smile. "It depicts a test. The subject enters the pipe and falls below to the pool." She pointed to the pipe on the wall. "If they are worthy of...whatever they are testing—entering the temple, guarding its contents—they swim to the riverbank. If they are not, they drown."

"A Vandeni? Drown?" Dresco asked, his chainmail rattling.

"Yeah," Kasta said with a nod. "Notice how he is struggling here, as if he can't breathe." She raised the green-flame torch over the wall. "The early-ancient Vandeni's amphibious traits were not highly evolved. They had to train their gills for extended periods of time. This test was one of adaptation and survival instinct." She shrugged. "Just my interpretation."

"So, the Vandeni had yet to evolve to their full aquatic potential when this structure was built..." The knight looked to the ceiling, then across the hall and down at the floor. "Just how *ancient* is this temple?"

The air escaped Kasta as he posed the question. "Very, very old." Her sidling steps met the floor with a dreary pulsation. "I would have estimated about eight thousand years at first. But it may be even older." She bit her lip. "It may be much older."

The hallway curved at a sharp angle, almost completing a hundred-and-eighty-degree turn. When the path straightened, it slanted upward. The black hallway burst in the light of green flames with Kasta's first step on the slope. There were no intricate sculptures or inscriptions. Only one familiar symbol etched into each wall: Vellon.

A shiver ran down her neck as she beheld the symbol basking in the green of the flames. She felt a tingle in her stomach and a weightlessness in her knees. 'Pull it together, Krane,' she thought. 'We're almost there.'

A faint wind drifted down the hall. Her optical system began to flash red. Kasta slowed her step. The sloping footpath came to a stop; a piece of the floor was missing. When she reached the edge and leaned over, she could not see the bottom. Only blackness. On the other side of the opening stood a tall oval doorway. A towering platform stood halfway across the gap.

"Look out!" Dresco shouted.

Kasta jumped backward. An assemblage of rusted blades swung from the ceiling, back and forth across the opening, which fell into a black abyss. "Holy hell!" She cuffed her palm over her forehead. "Now that is a trap."

"I picked up on that."

Kasta frowned. The jagged blades shrilled across the gap. They veered from their path and clanged against one another, moving with no consistent trajectory.

"We have to get across," she said, looking past the chasm. "That has to be it." She pointed to the doorway on the other side. "Whatever this temple is protecting, it's in there." After setting the green-flamed torch on the floor, the hunter crossed her arms. "We can jump it."

"We can do what now?" Dresco's voice shook.

"We can jump it," Kasta said with an upward nod and a snap. "It's all in the timing. First, we'll jump to the little platform in the middle. From there, we'll jump to the end. It's not even that far."

"Yes," Dresco said, feigning laughter. "You make it sound quite easy—but did you consider the half-dozen blades swinging from just about every direction?"

"You just have to time it right!" Kasta said with a wry smile. "Watch this." She hunched low and shook out her fingertips.

"Wait." Dresco blocked her path, reaching for his sword. "Watch *this*." He stepped to the edge of the walkway and swung his electric-charged weapon across the opening. Dresco's sword clashed with three of the swinging blades, sending them into the blackness below. The knight sheathed his sword and turned toward his companion with a cocksure nod.

She nodded in turn. "That does make it a bit easier, I suppose."

The remnants of the slicing death traps that Dresco had cut still dangled from the ceiling. In their fragmented state, they could not reach low enough to bring harm. "There is no way I can cut the blades on the other side." The knight bent down with a shake of his head. "They are too far."

"Just toss me your blade when I get to the middle," Kasta said. "I'll cut them from there."

"Perhaps."

Kasta hunched over again. Her arms swung out as she released a sharp breath. She lunged forward and sprinted toward the chasm. On reaching the edge, she leapt for the platform. She darted through the air over the deep blackness below. Had she put too much power into her jump? 'Did I overshoot the platform?' The abyss beyond stretched wide, eager to swallow her.

But her boots hit the ground. She pivoted, digging her palm into the floor. "Hah!" she yelled out, sliding to a stop.

However, her palm felt a vibration; the surface on which she had landed began to tremble. "Ahhhh!" she shouted. The small platform careened back and forth.

"Kasta, move! It's coming down!"

As Dresco bellowed his warning, she sprung to her feet and leapt for the other side. She did not have time to gauge the timing of the intact swinging blades. A crumbling crash resounded behind. The blades shrieked by her head as she flew past them.

Somehow, Kasta hit the surface on the other side. Her torso slid against the black floor. She took a series of deep breaths, thinking, 'Everything just *has* to break while I'm on it.'

"Kasta, you made it!" Dresco called out. "I can't believe you made it."

"Of course I did," she said with a chuckle, pulling herself to her feet. "I'm Kasta Kra—aww!" As Kasta brushed the dust from her jacket, she noticed a cut under her left shoulder. "I got nicked, Norte." A drop of blood smeared across her finger as she pressured the wound.

Dresco reached across the chasm toward his companion. "My goodness. Are you hurt?"

"Nah," she said with a shake of her head. "I'm alright." Her face turned to a frowning sneer. "I really liked this jacket, though." She pulled on the dark-grey leather.

Dresco slouched and shook his head. His scoff slipped through his helm. "How do I get across now?" The knight sighed. "Most of the central pillar has collapsed."

She half turned toward the doorway. "Just wait for me. I'll get in there and get what we came for."

"No," Dresco barked with a downward thrust of his finger. "Madame Vaeliz sent me to aid and protect you. That's what I am going to do. I shall not stray from your side."

"Dresco, if you jump across and knock down the rest of that platform, we may never get out of this giant ball."

"Do not disrespect this sacred place, Kasta Krane!"

Kasta winced. "Okay, shut up. Let's just figure out how to get you across." She placed her hand on her chin. "If you time it right, you may be able to jump to the center platform and then immediately jump the rest of the way."

"Okay," Dresco said, vacillation in his voice.

"But don't linger there. You're going to have to land with one foot, then use your momentum to fling yourself across the other half of the fissure. That massive body and heavy armor of yours will bring down that old stone in less than a second."

"I can do it," he said. Before Kasta could instruct Dresco to wait for her signal, the knight lunged forward with a roaring battle cry. He leapt toward the center scaffold. As instructed, he used his momentum to leap from the platform to the other side of the gap.

However, his timing was off. Several of the swinging blades sliced into the knight's armor. He wailed, descending into the darkness.

Kasta charged forward and leaned over the edge, extending her hand. She grasped the knight's forearm. While her grip was tight enough to catch his fall, he was slipping away. Her teeth ground as she struggled to pull him up. Dresco grabbed the ledge with his free hand, pulling his own weight. Together, they lifted his body to the surface.

"Holy hell, Norte, that was terrible timing," Kasta said, panting.

"I agree." Dresco lay on his back, checking his armor.

The hunter's left eye squinted. "You got hit by those blades pretty hard. Did you get cut?"

"Just a few scratches." He smirked as he spoke. "I do not wear this armor for nothing, you know?"

"Fair enough." Kasta hopped to her feet. The double doorway stood before her. She strode forward. With a hollow crack, both glossy black doors swung outward and began to creep open. She looked to Dresco, who had stepped next to her. "I know that I asked outside. But are you ready for this?" She angled her hat downward.

"I think so." His voice shook.

A twisted smile fell on the hunter's face. "Let's do it." She stood straight and walked toward the room, her hand on top of her holster. The oval doors were still sliding open. Above the room, there was a familiar ancient symbol: Vellon.

Kasta's breath quivered as she entered the room. It was cold. A sage-like aroma fell on the air. She stepped with caution. As she lowered her optical system, the chamber illuminated in green flame, though it did not ignite from torches. The fire streamed around the walls, creating a rectangular line of light.

The floor was the same black stone as the rest of the temple, though of a finer cut. Angling inward, the ceiling formed a diamond shape.

At the opposite end of the room, a silhouette flickered in the green firelight. A short stairway ascended to a statue of a cloaked figure, kneeling with its head angled downward, its hands wrapped around a cut of gleaming silver. Above its grasp was a black hilt, which led to a golden-bronze cross guard. The golden-bronze metal was topped with a grated crystalline material, out of which extended a blade.

"By the Guardians," Dresco uttered as if he were holding back a whimper. "The Defender of Liberty." The knight dropped to his knees and began a prayer.

Kasta lowered her optical system and scanned for threats. Everything came up clear. "This is it? No elaborate traps? No swinging blades? No falling sand that's going to bury us?" She looked to her Imperial companion. "The statue is going to come to life when I take the sword, isn't it?"

Dresco ended his prayer and stood. "You are going to have to go up there and find out."

Kasta's lips twisted. "You don't want to get it?"

He stood tall, his arms crossed to his front. "No. It should be you."

The crackle of the green flame echoed around the small chamber. "Fine with me." The hunter chuckled. "What? Are you afraid the sword is going to infect you or something? Because you're not a rightful Relic wielder?" Her voice turned mocking. "That it will corrupt your soul?"

Dresco did not respond. He remained stiff and unflinching, as if standing at attention.

Kasta laughed, looking up the staircase. "Come on, lighten up. We did it! We found the blade!" She shrugged. "Or a blade."

"I know." His tone was neutral.

"Okay," Kasta said with a sharp sigh. "Watch my back." She stepped on the first stair, restraint in her stride. 'Mind your step,' she tried to tell herself. 'Mind your environment.' But the statue had beguiled her gaze. The cloaked figure knelt with a guarded presence, though it was luring her closer, welcoming her. She looked to the long blade that sat in the statue's hand—and her thoughts turned to the platinum she would receive for turning it over to Vaeliz unscathed.

By the time she was halfway up the stairs, Kasta's mind turned to the significance of the item she was about to grasp. Whether or not any of the stories surrounding Vellon's Blade were true, it was one of the greatest archeological finds in history. 'Greatest treasure hunter in Vanda,' she thought. 'Hell, in the world. And now, everyone will know it.'

Kasta Krane reached the top of the stairway. To her relief, the statue of the cloaked figure did not come to life. She reached forward. Her fingers grasped the bottom of the hilt. Her palm pressed tight against the trident-shaped pommel. She only gave the blade a light tug, but it budged from the statue's grip with a chiming metallic slide.

A smile crept onto the hunter's face as she held the long, shimmering sword.

But before she could take a moment to celebrate, Dresco's voice called to her. "Kasta…" His voice tremored. Was it with fear? Or awe? "Kasta. L-look."

Her eyes flitted to the sword. It gave off a faint green glow. At first, she assumed that this was from the reflection of the flames above. But it was not. The aura was emanating from the sword itself. "What the—?" Kasta's jaw dropped. She froze in place. She felt a tingle, a surge beneath her skin.

"Kasta…" Dresco uttered. He was unable to speak another word.

She pulled back her sleeve and removed her left glove. Her vein, which ran down her arm and into her wrist, was glowing a bright green, the same shade that beamed from the sword. "Dresco," Kasta said as her eyes scanned the flowing luminescence of her blood. Even the cut she had sustained on her triceps bled green. She swallowed and grasped the sword tightly. Her hands shook. "Dresco!" she screamed, looking down on the knight. "Dresco, what is happening to me?"

Dresco reached toward her. "Kasta, do not be afraid!"

"Afraid?" Her eyes widened. "My veins are turning green. This damned ancient sword is corrupting my soul, like Veros said it would!"

Dresco marched forward and stopped before the bottom stair. "Kasta, you must calm yourself. Let me help—"

"Take it, Dresco!" She scurried down the stairs with the sword held in front, her body emitting a green aura. "You have to take it!"

"I cannot do that," Dresco said with a shake of his head. He raised his hands and backed away.

"Yes, you can, Dresco. The Guardians, the Relics, you are devoted to this stuff. I'm not. Please, take it from me. It won't corrupt you as fast."

Dresco crossed his arms. His hands turned to fists. "I cannot do that."

"Why not?" Kasta pleaded. Her peripherals caught a bright stream of light bursting from her neck. The green glow was prevalent in any vein that passed near the surface of her blue-grey skin. "It's going to kill me!"

"Kasta, no. It will not. Listen to me..."

Her attention was stolen. There was movement—behind Dresco's shoulder. Across the gap, at the end of the hallway, someone approached. A group approached. She reached for her pistol and fired a series of shots across the hallway, pushing Dresco aside. "Take cover, Norte! Now!" she ordered. She herself found protection behind one of the oval doors.

The knight leapt behind the other door. He rolled to safety as a series of electrical blasts streamed into the ancient room from across the hall.

The shots stopped. The black floor lay in smoke. Kasta held her breath. Dresco looked to her, his shoulders hunched. He crouched as low as possible. Her eyes lay fixed on him—silence threatened to become an endless fate.

And then, the silence broke. "Hello, Kasta," a crackly voice called out from across the hall.

Kasta responded behind clenched teeth, "Breylu."

XXI

AMBUSH

"How do you get yourself into these situations, Kasta?" Dast spoke with an amused darkness. "Here you are in the middle of nowhere, in an uncharted temple. You've got an ancient sword in there with ya. And all that stands between me and you is this hole in the floor." A few of the other Moon Shadow Riders chuckled. "And a couple of head-hunting blades."

"I don't have Vellon's Blade," Kasta said as she slid the sword into the baldric and fastened the weapon to her back. "It's all a sham. It doesn't exist."

"You're a liar, Kasta," Dast said with a cold growl.

"And *you're* a psychopath, Dast." Kasta peeked around the corner. She looked for a way out, or anything that she could use to her advantage. But she saw nothing. "How the hell did you find me, anyway?" she asked; she had to buy some time.

The knight leaned toward her. "What do we do?" he whispered.

"I tracked you, of course," Dast shouted from across the hall. "Come on, Kasta. You know me." He let out a coughing chuckle. "We've been picking up on your trail here and there for a couple weeks." He paused a moment. "We thought we had you in the Valley of Tombs. That was a clever little escape you pulled; I'll give ya that. But, my dear friend, you led us right where we need to be. You led us to the sword." Dast moaned in gratification. "And to think my gang and I had our weapons set on incapacitate in the Valley of Tombs."

Kasta's brow lowered. "I thought you might have."

"Oh, yes," Dast said, his crackly voice falling flat. "We were going to interrogate you and then go find the blade ourselves. But you ended up doing the work for us." His rate of speech quickened, bearing an eager tone. "Also, when you sink a pirate ship offshore, the news spreads quite rapidly. Picking your trail up again wasn't much of a challenge."

"So why don't you just hand the sword over?" the voice of one of the other Moon Shadow Riders called out. "We won't hurt you."

"I already told you crooks, I ain't got no sword," Kasta said. Her finger twitched over the trigger of her pistol. "And if I did have it, I sure wouldn't give it to you."

"I know you wouldn't," Dast said. "But Jarrus here doesn't know you like I do. And his sense of wrath has been growing since you shot him in the Valley of Tombs."

"Broke my arm when I fell off my trugan, Krane," Jarrus professed.

"Poor baby," Kasta said. She signaled to Dresco, asking him to look for a way out.

"You see, Kasta," Dast said, pacing back and forth. His boots clacked against the solid floor. "If you had set your shock-cannon to kill, you'd have one less of my gang to worry about. And now look what you have done. You've knocked out my medic." He waved his hand toward the motionless body of the outlaw whom Kasta had shot before taking cover.

"I can take you all on," Kasta said with a grin as she twirled her pistol. Her smile evaporated when she looked down. Glowing blood seeped from the wound beneath her shoulder.

"Then come out here. Do it," a female voice shouted.

'Lynara, the demolitions expert. Is she going to try to throw an explosive?' Kasta wondered. 'No. They would have done it by now. They wouldn't risk damaging the merchandise... Would they?'

She gripped the hilt of Vellon's Blade tightly in her fingertips as it rested on her back. Dresco peered around the door. "Watch for the sniper," Kasta hissed. "I don't see her over there. She's probably set up and stationed at the end of the hallway."

Dresco nodded.

"Sir, I'm having trouble locking onto their heat signatures," a different female voice said, faint under the striding clanks of the swinging blades. "This structure is interfering with my equipment."

Dresco's armored fingers wrapped around the door. "Is that—?" He gasped. "Is that an Imperial accent I heard?"

"Your ears do not deceive you, Sir Norte," she replied with bold vibrato.

Dast stood with both pistols drawn, his bionic corneas glowing red behind circular specs, beaming through the darkness. "Crow has been instrumental in tracking you down. Hacking satellites, obtaining privileged information, things I didn't even know were possible."

Dresco ogled his fellow Imperial through the crack between the door and the wall. "You are a daughter of the High Imperium, of the Order of the Guardians. Why would you ride with a man like him? He is a murderer. If you honor our lineage, our religion and our culture, you will aid us. Not impede us."

"I do not," Crow said with a cold taciturnity.

Kasta stole a glance around the door. Nellik of Grathank and Jarrus were unwinding a chain. 'They are going to try to make it across,' she realized. She crawled back to the corner and looked through the crack.

Dast put up hand signals, directing the members of his gang into various strategic positions. "Why don't you come with us, Sir Norte?" he asked, his eyes aimed above the brim of his tall forest-green hat.

Kasta and Dresco looked to each other. The knight's helmeted head tilted to the side. "Come with you?" he asked. "Do you not want me just as dead as Kasta?"

"You can bet I do, Imperial parasite," a male voice hissed.

"Easy, Nellik," Dast said. He gave the Draekalagon a pat on the back. Nellik's long fingernail tapped against the trigger of his heavy carbine. "You've put your cultural bias aside for Crow, perhaps you can for Sir Norte, here."

Nellik of Grathank fired a series of rapid-fire shots at the door Dresco hid behind. Dresco entered the fetal position. Dast placed his hand on the barrel of the shock-cannon to stop Nellik from firing.

"Stop this!" Dast ordered.

"He's a *knight*," Nellik growled. "He's a glorified conqueror of my homeland."

Dast chuckled, his lips shaking through his snakeskin mask. "Please forgive my colleague, Sir Norte. But I do have a proposition for you."

"I will not turn myself over to you, Breylu Dast." Dresco spoke with a low roar. He looked to Kasta, who nodded to him. "And you need to keep your lizard on a leash!"

Crow and Dast put their hands on Nellik's chest as his long snout flared. "I guess the cultural bias goes both ways," Dast said with a shake of his head. "Hear this though, my good Imperial Knight. If you lay down your sword and come to us in peace—if you agree to let us kill Kasta, we will share the reward money that the Imperium is offering for her." He extended an arm and crossed another behind his back, leaning forward. "How would that make you feel, Sir Norte, to return to the Imperium as a hero who helped bring an end to one of their enemies, to have returned a Relic to its rightful place in the holy domain of the Guardians?"

Dresco slammed his armored fist into the doorway. "I will never betray Kasta. And I will dedicate every breath in my body, until I can draw breath no more, to preventing you from obtaining this Relic!"

The Moon Shadow Riders looked to each another, exchanging sharp whispers. "So, you do have the sword," Dast said with a slow nod.

"Knew it." Lynara's face sprouted a soft smile.

Kasta looked across to Dresco and rolled her eyes. "Seriously?"

"Sorry," Dresco said with a sigh. "I forgot."

Dast reached across the chasm. "Stop apologizing for her lies, Sir Norte. I have a new offer for you. Walk across that chamber and strike down that evil woman you ride with. End her pathetic existence. Then bring me that sword." Dast's fist clenched. "I'll give you twenty percent of what the Imperium owes me for bringing in the sword and her head." He stood straight. His forest-green poncho fluttered. "That will net you two hundred thousand platinum, my good knight."

Every bit of air escaped Kasta's lungs. "Wait," she said as her insides began to crawl. "The Imperium is offering you a million platinum for my head?"

Nellik grunted. "Four hundred thousand for you. Six hundred thousand for the sword."

"Holy hell!" She looked to Dresco, wide-eyed. "They want me dead that bad just for looking for a damn Relic? What in the name of the moons is this world coming to?"

Dresco's voice and body faltered at Kasta's words. But his attention diverted back to the Moon Shadow Riders. The knight's voice rumbled as he spoke once again. "My honor cannot be purchased. I am beyond any of your so-called bargaining *tactics*. The only way that this shall end is with my sword through your bodies: a warrior's death. More than any of you deserve."

Kasta used her shirt to wipe the sweat from her brow. "Dresco, we need a plan," she whispered. "They are going to come across."

"Strange that someone so honorable and beyond financial gain would ride with one as selfish and narcissistic as Kasta Krane." Dast's words crawled up Kasta's spine like a coiling snake. She clutched her pistol.

Dresco looked to her with a self-assured nod. "At least she isn't a murderer. She has more honor than you ever will."

"Oh, my good sir." Dast holstered both his weapons, shaking his head. "That is where you are wrong. I have taken life, yes. I'm not proud of it, but at least I'm honest about it." He pointed to the door that Kasta hid behind. "Unlike the hellion that you ride with."

Kasta's fist clenched "Quiet, Dast!" Every nerve in her body flared and told her to jump out from behind that door, firing her weapon. She would not live, but she could take Dast down. And some of his goons with him.

"Kasta does not kill," Dresco said with a swipe of his hand. "I already know that she has in the past. When she was in a gang with the likes of you, bred to be malicious and malevolent. But she has moved beyond that. She has a code now. She is merciful."

"Oh," Dast said as he crossed his arms. "So, has she told you that she tried to kill me?"

Kasta stood up. Her shoulders arched forward. "Breylu. This is all between you and me. So, let's just settle it. Stop talking!"

However, Dast continued, "When she decided to leave the gang, I tried to stop her. Not to hurt her, but to talk. I wanted to know where she was going, why she was leaving. Instead, she drew her blade. I drew mine as well to defend myself. But she did not hesitate when she had a chance to strike. She cut off my leg and rode into the night."

Kasta's eyes shut. She felt as if an undertow had pulled her into a bottomless sea.

Dast's voice trembled. "She left me there, bleeding, lying in the dirt. My partner, my greatest ally, my friend. She maimed me and rode off. She never called for help, she never checked on my condition. She left me to rot and die."

Dresco looked to his companion, his shoulders slumped and breath shallow. "Kasta, is that true?"

Dast's crackly voice rolled on. "She'll do the same thing to you, Sir Norte. It's what she does. She bleeds you for all she finds you are worth and then leaves you behind."

The knight's hands scraped against the door. "Kasta, he is lying, right? Please tell me he is lying."

"No, it's true." Kasta shut her eyes and turned away. "It is true."

She peeked again through the crack in the door, her stomach still spinning with nausea. Lynara had unpacked one of her explosives: a high-capacity voltage grenade. The explosive was laser guided, controlled via data system. The outlaws were going to try to flush them out, and this intricate weapon would minimize potential damage to Vellon's Blade. Then they would shoot the hunter and the knight dead when they fled from cover. Or climb across to confirm the kill.

"Dresco," Kasta said with a sharp whisper. "I'll—" She lost the words. "I'll explain all that later. But for now, we need to get out of here."

"Understood," Dresco said, a bite behind his words. "What do we do?"

Kasta squinted through the crack. "Okay, you go out there and draw their attention. Use your sword to absorb their shock-cannon fire. I'll do the shooting."

"But the sniper," Dresco said, cocking his head toward the hallway. "I cannot draw her fire or absorb it with my blade. Sniper rifles are too accurate."

"We have to try," Kasta said with a shrug.

"Yes." Dresco spoke under his breath. "But we have to try something else." He stood tall and reached for his waist. "I'm going to go after the lizard sniper." His armor turned to the same black as the stone that made up the interior of the temple. "You take as many of the others out as you need to and get out of this temple."

Kasta's lips pursed as she shook her head. "Dresco, they have infrared tech in their optical systems. Hell, Dast has optical tech built into his eyes!" The voltage explosive glowed in a blue light and hovered over the ground. They were preparing to send it across the chasm.

Dresco's armor darkened further, turning as black as the shadows. "Just cover me."

The swinging blades on the nearest side split into two pieces, and their lower halves fell into the hole below. Dresco had cut them.

"Oh hell," Kasta whispered. The Moon Shadow Riders looked across, confused.

"What's going on?" Dast yelled. "Crow, what cut those blades?"

"Working on it, sir." Crow looked around the room, adjusting her two-eyed optical system.

A snarled scream reverberated through the hallway. "That was Vinai!" Nellik proclaimed. "Something must have happened to her!"

"It's the knight," Crow yelled. "He's camouflaged. He went after Vinai!"

"Go get him!" Dast ordered.

That was Kasta's cue. She made sure Vellon's Blade remained secure against her back, then sprinted around the door and jumped across the chasm. Her foot hopped from the remaining middle platform to the other side, where three of the Moon Shadow Riders stood. She thrust her shoulder forward, burrowing herself into Jarrus' broken arm. The outlaw screamed as Kasta landed on top of him. Pinning him down, she glanced upward. Dast stared down at her, his luminous eyes burning in a mix of bewilderment and anger.

"Her—her neck," Lynara uttered, referring to the fiery-green of the hunter's veins. "Why is it—why is it glowing like that?"

Dast raised both of his pistols. He hesitated, studying Kasta. "Who cares?" He fired.

"Oh, hell!" Kasta screamed as she rolled away, avoiding the electrical streams. She turned and fired back.

Dast ducked for cover.

Kasta sprinted up the hallway, zigzagging to avoid oncoming fire. Dast and Lynara chased behind. A voltage grenade launched over Kasta's head. The hunter stopped, falling prone as the grenade exploded in a web of high-powered electricity. She rushed to gain her feet and turned her head. Dast and Lynara closed in, pistols drawn. Kasta aimed for the two Vandeni outlaws and fired several shots.

Lynara prepared to throw another grenade. After drawing her one-handed sword, Kasta lunged toward the grenadier. She kicked the explosive out of Lynara's hand and grabbed her by the back of the neck, her sword hovering over the outlaw's throat. Kasta backed down the hallway with her hostage. "I'll kill her, Dast. Back off."

"We both know you won't," Dast grumbled, both of his pistols aimed at her. "You are far too weak to take someone's life face-to-face."

"Wrong," she said, backing down the hallway. "*You're* just not *smart* enough to kill *me*." Kasta kicked Lynara in the back and sprinted away. Dast fired an electrical stream, but Kasta had already rounded the bend. She raced along the inside of the sharp curve.

"Kasta, look out!" Dresco's voice called from down the hall.

Rushing toward Kasta was Nellik of Grathank. His green-scaled snout narrowed. He went to fire his carbine, but Kasta was faster on the draw. Nellik ducked down and avoided her fire. The Draekalagon rushed her, pulling his thick curved electro-blade. Kasta lifted her own blade and blocked his strike. Each combatant raised their shock-cannons, taking aim. The weapons discharged—but they twisted away from each other's line of fire. Neither had a clear shot.

Their swords clashed again. Kasta swung at Nellik's feet, but he jumped. Nellik swung for Kasta's head; she twirled away. The blades crossed with an electric hiss.

'My agility will eventually tire him out,' Kasta thought. 'He's bigger and stronger, but if I keep him swinging, my endurance will outlast his.' She sidestepped and turned sideways, dodging his strikes. 'But I don't have time for that...'

Around the corner came Dast and Lynara. Kasta pivoted, ensuring Nellik's back would fall under their aim rather than her own. 'If Breylu is gunna kill me, it's not gunna be with a shot to the spine.'

Dast jumped into the fray with his sword drawn. He lunged at Kasta, trying to stab her. She bent backward and avoided his assault.

Lynara entered the battle. Her pistol drawn, she aimed for Kasta, who reached for her own shock-cannon. The hunter fired on Lynara, incapacitating the demolitions expert.

However, Kasta's sword locked with Nellik's. Her pistol dropped to the ground; she needed two hands to stay the towering Draekalagon's strength. His sharp reptilian teeth slid over his snarling lips. As Kasta lifted her short sword over her head, holding off Nellik's killing blow, the barrels of Dast's pistols stared her down. Sweat dripped from his furrowed brow. His cybernetic green eyes narrowed, melding with the flames that lit the hallway.

The hunter held her breath and waited for the end.

But Dresco emerged from the shadows. His camouflaged, blackened armor slammed into Dast as the knight tackled him to the ground. Dresco flipped to his feet, raising his sword. With a lunging step, he unleashed a ferocious slash on Nellik, who deflected his blow. "Kasta, run. Now!"

Kasta gasped and heeded her companion. She sprinted down the hall. Though around the upcoming bend, Crow and Vinai advanced. Vinai knelt and aimed her rifle at Kasta.

The sniper fired a high-powered bolt of lightning at Kasta's face.

Kasta ducked to the ground, rolled forward and hopped back to her feet.

Vinai aimed for her torso.

Kasta spun to the side.

The outlaw markswoman fired three shots at Kasta's feet.

The hunter leapt over the high-powered electrical streams, holding on to her hat. A rush of adrenaline flowed through her blood. Her instincts and augmented reflexes were a step ahead of the sniper. But one direct hit would stop her heart.

"Into the pipe!" Dresco yelled.

'What is he talking about?' She reached for her pistol. 'Damn it, I forgot. I dropped it!'

"Now, Kasta!" the knight hollered. "The pipe on the wall."

The pipe by the art piece! The entrance to an ancient chamber—to a test of adaptation. At least, that was her interpretation.

Kasta did not question Dresco's thinking. She made a break for the pipe. She looked over her shoulder. The knight used his longsword to attract and absorb oncoming shock-cannon blasts. Dast pointed one of his pistols at Dresco's face. The knight swung at it. The pistol did not break; it shattered. The impact sent Dast plummeting to the ground.

From around the opposite bend, Jarrus approached. He fired several shots in rapid succession from his pistol. He did not hit the knight. But it did distract him.

From the top of the path, Vinai of Oglund fired her sniper rifle. Kasta ducked low, but Vinai was not aiming for her this time. The shot hit Dresco, who screamed as the electricity circled and penetrated his armor.

"Dresco!" Kasta yelled.

"Run!" Dresco croaked with all the power that his voice could summon. His armor was smoking. He stood and again engaged in sword combat with the Moon Shadow Riders; the gang surrounded him. Dresco reached toward Lynara's incapacitated body with a free hand. He picked something up from the grenadier's utility belt.

'What is he doing?' Kasta thought. But Crow rushed toward her, freezing her body and stealing her focus. The pipe was near, but the Imperial outlaw's sights were on the hunter.

The clanking steps of Dresco Norte advanced. He hurled his sword as if it were a spear into the leg of Crow. "Go, Kasta!"

She sprinted the remaining distance and dove into the pipe. As she crawled through the horizontal section of the channel, the surface dampened her clothing. The pipeline led to a downward slope. 'I hope this actually leads to a pool of water,' she thought. 'If this leads to a pile of spikes, I am not going to be happy.'

Dresco stuck his head inside the pipe. He had retrieved his sword, now dripping with scarlet-red blood. He held it high, defending against a volley of oncoming shock-cannon fire. "Let go, Kasta!" he demanded. He was hyperventilating.

Kasta grabbed the wall to prevent herself from falling down the vertical part of the pipe. "Get in here!" she shouted.

"No!" Dresco's blade absorbed another volley. "That is not my destiny." Another sniper blast struck his armor. The knight yelped. Then gasped. "It is yours. Bring the sword to Madame Vaeliz." His voice trembled. "The future of our world lies with you, Kasta Krane."

The knight held his sword high above his head. "Dresco, no!" Kasta called to him. But the knight did not show a shard of hesitation. He displayed what he had stolen from Lynara's belt: a high-powered grenade. After activating the weapon, he dropped it into the pipe. The imminent explosion left Kasta with no choice. She released her grip as Dast encroached on Dresco.

She began to fall, her hands held high. The explosion erupted above. A pile of rubble followed Kasta's plummet. She heard a series of thunderous shock-cannon blasts—and a sonorous scream on top of the fusillade. A scream of anguish.

As Kasta fell into darkness, Dresco's voice fell silent.

XXII
THE RETURN

A loud splash intercepted Kasta's scream. Liquid and the taste of moss filled her gaping mouth. A powerful stream forced her along a tubular duct. The water thrashed and twirled the hunter, her limbs flailing with the violent flow of the current.

After barreling through a narrow opening, she flipped and slowed. No longer constrained by the channel, Kasta's body floated through calm water. Her boots touched the hard bottom. Blackness was all her unadjusted eyes could perceive.

She kicked off the floor and reached for the surface. Kasta looked up, churning aside debris and shrapnel—remnants of the explosion. 'Why didn't he just jump in here too?' she thought as she grabbed hold of her hat, which drifted above. 'Damn fool didn't have to die.'

She let out a murky breath from her gills. Her hand reached upward and felt the ceiling. She then realized that there was no surface to ascend to. Water filled the chamber from top to bottom. 'He would not have been able to breathe,' she thought. Her limbs floated limply. 'But he didn't know that. Damn it, he didn't have to die!'

Her lip quivered. Debris swished around the airless chamber. 'Well, no point in me dying too.' She swam along the wall, looking for an exit. The walls resembled the black stone in the temple above. But Kasta could see nothing else in the darkness. 'Even if Dresco did manage to reduce the pipeline entrance to a pile of rubble, it won't be long before Dast and his goons figure out a way down here.' She grasped the hilt of Vellon's Blade. 'They didn't come this far to let me get away with this damn sword.'

As Kasta clutched the blade, an idea came to her. She caught a glimpse of the green light seeping from her neck. After unfastening the sword from her back, she removed her gloves. The green emanated from her veins and the sword itself, creating an orb of light around the hunter.

'This stupid old sword may be infecting my body and corrupting my soul or whatever,' she thought. 'But at least it's a good lantern.' She looked to the bottom of the chamber. Her body bobbled when she saw an opening: a rhomboid crevasse on the opposite wall of the duct that had jettisoned her into the flooded enclosure. 'Time to get out of here.' She held Vellon's glowing blade to her front.

'The Imperium offered Dast six hundred thousand platinum for the sword.' Her eyebrows rose. 'The market price just went up, Madame.' A thick, slanted smirk fell on her face. 'Especially considering that it is probably shaving years off my life as I wield it.' The hunter looked up at the tip of the blade. Despite its great length, it was light, a featherweight heavier than her one-handed sword.

Kasta drifted inside the thin rhomboid opening. She turned back, looking to the pipe from which she had entered the chamber. 'But was it worth it? Was it worth his life?' she wondered as Dresco's sepulchral final scream echoed across her mind.

She twisted away from the chamber and began to swim through the small channel. "Now I get his share. Of course it was," she said out loud through a stream of bubbles. 'Besides, it was his choice.'

The current flowed stronger as she drifted through the channel. It was narrow. 'How far will this carry me?' She remembered the purpose of this chamber: to test the worth of ancient Vandeni. If they were able to navigate the channel, if their undeveloped gills could adapt, they were deemed worthy of... something.

But of what? Guarding the temple? Entering the temple? Wielding the sword? Either way, Kasta's gills kept her body oxygenated, an evolutionary advantage that she appreciated more than ever.

The stream quickened. She no longer had to paddle her feet; the current alone was enough to carry her. "Oh, by the Guardians," she said aloud with a roll of her eyes. 'Please don't tell me *this* is where they put the blades of death.' Kasta caught herself. '*By the Guardians*? Why would I say—?'

A shallow breath fizzled from her gills. 'Dresco. You really didn't have to die.'

The waterflow turned rough and rapid. 'Okay, blades of death. Here we come.' As the current roared and whitened, the channel took a sharp turn and flowed into a wide river. 'No blades of death. This day just keeps getting better.' She floated to the surface and took a deep breath. Though she could respire while submerged, something about the thick, murky water made her feel as though she could *not* breathe.

Kasta looked behind. No one had followed, at least not yet. She swam a long-armed freestyle stroke against the current and was able to pull herself to shore. She took several heavy breaths as her fingers dug into the mud, her left hand still grasping the hilt of Vellon's Blade. Her teeth rattled. Her wet clothes hugged her skin. Icy water seeped through her undergarments and inside her socks. Her hat had drifted into the nearby shallows, trapped between a pair of jagged rocks. After freeing it from the clutches of the stones, she shook the water from the brim. She placed the hat on her head, put her gloves back on and strapped the blade to her back.

The forest looked unfamiliar. It was dark. Kasta attempted to turn on her optical system, but it was water-damaged beyond repair. She tossed it into the river.

The hunter hid behind a tree, still shivering. "The river was flowing from north to south when we rode beside it outside the forest," she muttered, looking to the current. "It is flowing west here, which means it forks through the forest at some point." She looked to the moons in the sky. "Which would mean that we left the trugan up about a half mile…" She paused, then pointed to the east. "That way."

A half mile was not a long walk. But in drenched clothing, it felt like hours. Kasta traipsed on like a thick cloud in a faint wind. While her steps were slow, they were heavy. Too heavy. The Shadow Riders would already be searching for her. Cold, wet and disarmed, she was an easy target. However, after navigating the forest, she found Kaiar and Crevallus.

Both trugan hissed as Kasta approached. "Shhh," the hunter said with her finger over her lips. "You have to keep it down, guys. They'll be after us." Her shivering hand brushed against Kaiar's snout. "We have to go. Now."

Crevallus' claws crushed the dirt beneath. He trotted toward Kasta and brushed his horn into her shoulder.

"What is it, boy?" Kasta took a step back, wrapping her arms around her own torso as her teeth chattered.

Crevallus raised his neck and unveiled a gnashing snarl.

"Shhh!" Kasta said, ducking low. Her eyes darted left and right, scanning dark forest. "What's wrong with you, Crev?"

Kaiar looked to Crevallus, her forked tongue flickering.

Crevallus grumbled, his head jerking backward, toward his saddle.

A twig snapped under the forceful pressure of Kasta's boot. She looked to the dirt, her shoulders drooping low. "Dresco," she uttered. "Crev, I'm sorry. He didn't make it."

The male trugan's vertical pupils stretched wide. His long face sank. A whining groan escaped his scaly lips. Even Kaiar looked deflated.

The trees loomed with creeping curiosity; their pallor intensified in the moonlight. Kasta took off her jacket, for its dampness only made her colder. "Crev, I really am sorry. There was nothing I could do. They snuck up on us." She took a blanket from Kai's pannier and wrapped it around her torso as though it were a cloak. "But we *have* to go. They'll tear down this forest to find us, and I got what we came for." She climbed on top of Kai's saddle, stuffing her jacket into the pannier. "So, let's go."

Kaiar let out a soft yet scathing hiss. Crevallus raised his front claws and unleashed a growl.

"Crev, stop it!" Kasta demanded, thrusting her finger toward the male trugan. "Either follow behind or stay behind. Up to you. But you have to shut up." She squeezed one hand tightly around the reins and one around the hilt of Vellon's Blade. "Let's go, Kaiar. Swift, but quiet. Now!"

Kaiar at first hesitated. But after a kick in the torso from Kasta's boots, the trugan pressed on with a soft gallop. Kai hissed. She glanced back to see if Crevallus followed. He trailed behind, but not fast enough to keep up.

"Don't worry about him," Kasta said, patting Kaiar on the neck. She shivered as a bitter draft penetrated her skin. "If he wants to mope around and die because his rider died, that's his choice. But you and me, girl, we're gunna live through this."

A thought circled Kasta's mind like fire on dry brush. 'How do you know he's really dead?'

She shook her head. "Of course he's dead," she whispered. "He must have taken at least five bolts of shock-cannon fire. No one could survive that."

'He survived the first two, didn't he?' The words sank into her thoughts as Vaktarae's had in the Sanctum of Truth. Though this was not a foreign voice. 'Who's to say he couldn't have taken a few more?' It was her own.

Kasta ignored her mind as Kaiar galloped through the forest. Crevallus fell farther behind. None of the Moon Shadow Riders were on her tail, which was a relief. "Even if he *was* alive," she uttered, so soft that she could not hear herself, "there is nothing I could do now. Who knows what Dast and his gang would do with him? They'd take him far away—back to the Imperium, probably."

Kaiar's eyes crawled up toward Kasta. She hissed, responding to her rider's words.

'They'd question him. They'd torture him. Eventually, they *would* kill him.'

Kasta's eyes rolled. "That's not my problem anymore. I have the damn sword. I have what I came for. He knew what he was getting into when he signed on to ride with me. And the idiot knew what he was doing when he blew up our only escape route and stayed behind to take on all seven Moon Shadow Riders." The hunter sneered.

'He saved your life.'

"He didn't die for me," Kasta grumbled. She saw the edge of the forest in the distance. "He died for the sword. Going back would be a disservice to him." She took a deep breath and shook her head. "He sacrificed himself so that Vellon's Blade would make it to Madame Vaeliz safely, not so that I would live."

The same thought returned. 'He *saved* your *life*.'

The hunter sighed. Her limbs fell limp. The green aura emanating from her skin shined against the blanket in which she had wrapped herself. 'Damn it, Dresco,' she thought, giving Kai's reins a slight tug to the right. The beast was confused—until Kasta kicked her in the torso and pulled harder.

Kaiar's claws tore through the terrain as she turned around. Kasta whipped the reins against Kai's neck. The trugan's cybernetics hummed with the acceleration of her gallop.

"Damn it, Dresco!"

The hunter rode back toward the heart of the forest. Back toward the temple and back toward the Moon Shadow Riders.

Kasta pulled on Kaiar's reins, and the beast slowed. She hopped off the saddle, springing toward a wide tree. Crevallus hissed from behind.

"Easy, boy," Kasta whispered. She adjusted her hat and retrieved her sniper rifle from Kai's back. She also grabbed her backup pistol. It was not as elegant or upgraded as the pistol she lost in the temple, but it would get the job done.

As she wrapped Vellon's Blade in a cloth to hide its striking green, Kasta pointed in the trugan's faces. "You two, scout the woods and watch my back," she said. "And watch each other's. Take down any of those Moon Shadow goons if you can." Her fingers slid down Kaiar's snout, between her pale-silver eyes. "But don't get hurt."

A shudder came down Kasta's neck, though she no longer felt cold. Her blood was boiling. "Go," she ordered, holding her rifle across her breast. The two trugan dispersed in different directions, snarling as they faded into the shadows.

Kasta took a deep breath and lunged forward. With her back against a tree, she clutched her rifle and opened the weapon's chamber. The charge crystal was supplying adequate power. The electrical current was stable.

She dashed to the next tree.

Each tree felt slighter, as if it offered less cover than the last. She knelt and brought the stock of the rifle to her shoulder. Her eye strained, looking through the scope. Without her optical system, she saw only magnified darkness.

Kasta's teeth ground together as she ran across the hollow dirt. Her wet socks scrunched under her boots and made her feet tender. Her knees were weak.

A spherical image rested in the moonlight: the temple. Its silhouette overshadowed the trees, a great void in the wood. Kasta entered a prone position. She looked to the temple through her scope, though she saw no signs of life or movement. She saw nothing. 'I really wish I had my optical system.' The hunter shook her head.

She heard something. Footsteps. Approaching from the rear. 'Damn it,' she thought as her eyes shut. 'They got the drop on me.' The footsteps drew nearer. Kasta's only defense was to hold still. Entirely still.

With a casual stride, Jarrus, Dast's triggerman, passed by, a cigar dangling from his mouth. He sighed, standing tall with his hands clasped around his hips. Kasta leapt to her feet and charged the man, her electro-blade drawn. The outlaw was swift to pull his pistol, but Kasta tackled him down, landing on top of his broken arm once again.

One of her hands covered Jarrus' whimpering mouth. Her other held the blade to his neck. Kasta's face tensed as she pinned the struggling man. He writhed and resisted, but soon gave up. His forest green eyes moistened. He tried to speak, though Kasta's glove muffled his voice.

"You call for help, you die. Are we clear?" she said, her blade tight to his throat. The man took two quick breaths as her gloved hand released his mouth. "Hello, Jarrus," she whispered.

"Nice to see you again, Kasta," he croaked. "I see the boss has driven you to start killing again."

Kasta sneered. "Don't flatter Dast behind his back, Jarrus. That doesn't score you any points."

"So, you won't kill me?"

The hunter's eyes narrowed. "You seriously want to find out?"

Jarrus coughed and shook his head. "No. Not in particular."

"Good," Kasta said. Her hair fell into her eyes from beneath her hat. "So, answer me a few questions, pistol boy. And don't lie to me. I'll know if you are lying." Her voice turned raspy and vicious. "Where are the rest of the Moonshiners?"

"I think Crow and Nellik are on a separate patrol, looking for you. The boss, Vin and Giavi are at camp. Just southeast of here." Kasta snarled and pressed the unignited sword deep into his neck. "Northwest. It's to the northwest!" he said, shrinking into the ground.

"I told you not to lie, Jarrus." She pulled the sword back and ignited its electro-current. "My partner. Is he alive?"

"Wait!" Jarrus called out. "You're really still going to kill me?"

"Is Dresco alive?"

"Your boyfriend is a melting corpse in a metal coffin," Jarrus said with a slack-jawed smile.

Kasta held the ignited blade less than an inch from his neck. "Stop lying!" she said through her teeth.

"Nellik! Crow! Help! I found Kas—!"

"No." Her fist slammed into Jarrus' forehead, interrupting his cry and knocking him unconscious. "I don't believe you." She searched the outlaw's pockets. "I don't... believe you."

She had to hurry. One of the other gang members may have heard Jarrus' call. While he did not have much that would be useful, she did take his pistol from his hand and a cigar from his jacket pocket. "*Of course* he doesn't have an optical system," she said, a sigh escaping the side of her mouth. The electrical stream on her sword fizzled and sputtered. Expensive electro-blades were built to resist exposure to water, but not as much as Kasta's had. The circuitry was drowning.

Kasta lunged from tree to tree until she found a clear view to the northwest. Her skin still glowed green. She pulled up her shirt's collar to hide her luminous neck. In the distance, she saw the camp—a faint outline in the darkness.

Her scope was outfitted with a basic night-vision setting. Through a dark-green haze, Kasta saw Dast preparing his saddle. Giavi stood lopsided, dazed by the cannon blast he had taken in the temple. Lynara lay on the soil, still unconscious. Vinai sat with one hand on her rifle, surveying the woods.

Propped against a tree was Dresco Norte. Kasta closed her off eye, setting her rifle's sights on her companion. She could not tell if he was moving. Or even breathing. "Come on, Norte. Please don't be dead," she whispered. "Give me a sign here." But his body remained motionless. She saw no trace of Crow or Nellik. Perhaps they *were* patrolling the surrounding area, looking for Kasta.

She needed a plan, and she needed one fast. She could try to pick off the outlaws at the campsite, but she could only take out one before the rest made for cover. Maybe two. The others would follow the direction of the shot. If Dast released their trugan, they would sniff her out.

An idea knocked on the walls of Kasta's mind. "Snipe the sniper," she said out loud. Her sights moved over Vinai. The crosshairs drifted up and down the Draekalagon woman's snout. The hunter held her breath. With a light squeeze, she fired her rifle. The stock kicked back, slamming her shoulder. A stream of white and blue cut through the forest. Thunder resounded throughout the wood, following the spiral of lightning. Vinai of Oglund fell to the ground, unconscious.

Kasta's prediction proved correct. Dast and Giavi made for cover. She did not have a clear shot at them. She would have to advance to a different location. But at least she had taken out the gang's only sharpshooter. Or so she thought.

A bolt of lightning burst across the wood. Every reflex in Kasta's body, biological and bionic, sent her sprawling backward, though the shot was inaccurate. The hunter groaned as she crawled behind a tree. Another shot blazed through the woods, striking her cover. Kasta's heart fluttered, irregular and rapid. "Holy hell," she said, gripping her rifle.

She peeked around the corner, her scope to her eye. Aiming a rifle at Kasta was Crow. Another shot came her way. Kasta sprang back behind the tree. "Give it up, Krane," the Imperial girl called out. "If you don't surrender, Mister Dast will kill Sir Norte. He just instructed me to tell you so."

"So, he is alive," Kasta whispered. "Or is *she* lying?" The hunter put the question aside. Crow knew her position. In a matter of moments, the other Shadow Riders would close in. "How do you know how to use that anyway, kid?" Kasta asked, a snarl in her voice. "Aren't you a tech guru or something?"

"I'm an outlaw, Miss Krane," Crow said with an arrogant chuckle. "Did you really question my ability to fire a shock-cannon?"

"No," Kasta said as she removed her hat. She tossed it into a flat spin beside the tree. A series of shots sped by. Kasta leapt out, her aim following the trail of sniper fire. Crow's astonished face rested in her sights. Kasta fired, sending the Imperial to the ground. "I *do* question that impatient trigger finger, though." She stepped away. "And call me Kasta," she uttered.

The hunter picked up her hat and sprinted toward the temple. She looked behind, aiming her rifle toward the camp. Giavi and Dast were not in sight, nor were their trugan. Dast had let them free. She needed to conjure a plan, a distraction.

Yet another idea happened on Kasta as she approached the spherical structure. She darted across the open space, keeping an eye out for Nellik. 'He could be anywhere,' she thought.

A grin slid up her face. The key stone that she had retrieved from the sea lay on the ground, pulsating in vibrant green. She seized it.

"Yes!" she whispered with a pump of her fist. The temple sank back into the soil, loud and quaking.

Kasta lit the cigar she had stolen from Jarrus and tossed it near the burrowing temple. "That'll throw them off," she whispered, scurrying for cover.

She crept from tree to tree once more. Several trugan growled and stampeded through the woods, following the scent of the cigar and sound of the tunneling temple. Kasta nodded as she tiptoed away, approaching Dast's camp at a wide angle. She looked through the sights of her rifle. Dast was not visible, but Giavi was. For the third time in a week and second today, she fired on the young outlaw. He fell, incapacitated.

Cold sweat trickled down Kasta's forehead from her damp hair. Two remained. She continued to approach the camp, wiping her brow with her sleeve. 'Where the hell is Dast?'

"Kasta!" her enemy called out, his voice cracking on the last syllable of her name. "Step over to our encampment now, hands up, all weapons on the ground."

She swallowed.

"Kasta!" Dast called again. "If you don't give yourself up now, the knight dies. Helmet off, set to kill. Point-blank shock-cannon blast to the head."

"Jarrus told me he was already dead!" Kasta shouted.

"He ain't. He's still breathing."

She looked through her scope. Dast hid behind Dresco's motionless body, using it as cover. "Okay," Kasta cried out. "I'm coming over now. But you can't shoot me when you see me."

"That is a risk you are going to have to take, Kasta," Dast said. "You ain't holdin' no cards at this table."

She sighed. 'How are we getting out of *this* one?' Her fingers stretched across her rifle. 'Think, Krane. Think.'

"Okay, okay," Kasta yelled. "I'm keeping my pistol on you till I get over there, though."

"No!" Dast barked.

"If I come over there unarmed, you can just shoot us both." A grimace fell on Kasta's face. "If I have my pistol on you, at least I can kill you if you hurt the Imperial." She checked the sights on her rifle one last time. "At least I'd see the literal light in your eyes go out before your big, scaly goon takes me down." She assessed the forest for a moment. "Where is Nellik, anyway? I know he's hiding around somewhere."

Dast's voice fell icy and stern. "Then at least we'll both die happy."

A shooting star flashed across the purple sky. Kasta approached the encampment, laboring through the dirt. Her knees grew weak. "You don't know the kind of people you're dealing with in the Imperium,

Breylu. These aren't crime bosses or corrupt local government officials. They're authoritarian religious freaks, hell-bent on spreading their influence."

Dast paused. "Maybe," he said, his chin held high. "But they serve my interests, so who am I to complain? I'm doing one high-class job for them. I'm not marrying the Cleric-Eternal." Dast chuckled, holding up Dresco's limp body.

"These are bad people you're in with, Dast. Even for you."

"Maybe so," he said with a slow nod. "But they are paying me a lot of platinum to kill *you*. How bad could they really be?"

Kasta's face fell to an indifferent frown. "At least you have standards." She paused. A pair of wrathful eyes glowered from the trees. Her feet dug into the soft soil. The hunter fired her sniper rifle, aim guided by instinct. The electrical blast did not strike Nellik. But it flushed him from the branches. Kasta's shot swayed his aim. His rapid-fire carbine discharged, but he missed his target.

Kasta floundered to the dirt and rolled behind a tree. "Nellik, are you serious? Your boss and I had an agreement, here!"

A snarling voice responded, "You should not have come back, Krane."

Kasta swallowed, glancing around the tree. "But I barely even got a chance to catch up to you two!" She put her rifle down, reaching for the two pistols holstered to her belt. Nellik faded into the shadows. Silent as the dead forest, the Draekalagon was stalking her. "Dast, what the hell?!" she yelled, crossing her pistols over her torso. "Get your lackey to stop shooting at me."

Dast laughed as he spoke. "Kasta, I told you. You don't hold any of the cards. Hand over the sword and surrender. And we let your friend go. If you don't, he dies. I'm gunna give you thirty seconds."

Kasta grunted. "You really are a snake, Dast!"

"Twenty-seven... twenty-six... twenty-five..."

"Okay, fine!" Kasta said with a sigh. "All my weapons are on the ground." She placed her pistols by her feet. "Now let him go!"

Her peripherals caught a slinking shadow; a draconic outline crawled down the tree. His sights were on her. Kasta bent her knees and leapt, looking upward. The fiery eyes of Nellik burned in the moonlight. She clutched his carbine, pulling the weapon and Nellik down with the aid of gravity.

The shock-cannon discharged as Kasta snatched it from the Draekalagon outlaw's hands, though the electrical stream did not strike her. She was alive and conscious when her body hit the ground.

Kasta groaned, lifting her back from the dirt. 'Where is he?' she thought. She heard a snarl. Nellik revealed himself with a thrust of his sword. Kasta rolled sideways, evading the stab. She drew her own sword and blocked Nellik's next attack.

Propelled by nerves and adrenaline, she hopped to her feet and swung at the Draekalagon's shoulder with a feinting sidestep. He blocked the strike. Kasta's electro-sword sputtered and fizzled out again. Nellik was swift to recognize this deficiency and slashed her weapon with his long, curved saber.

Nellik's strike split the unpowered blade in two pieces. The impact forced Kasta off-balance; Nellik was again swift to react. He twirled around, tripping her with his tail. Breathless, eyes frozen wide, she backed away on all fours. Nellik reached for his carbine. Her rifle was out of reach. She went for her pistol—but it was too late. Nellik's aim rested on Kasta.

The Draekalagon hesitated, catching sight of the black hilt over her back.

Dast called out to his cohort, "Nellik, did she tell you where the sword is?"

"She has it," Nellik hissed back. A serpentine smile slid up his thin green lips.

"Damn right I do." Kasta's hand glided toward the hilt of Vellon's Blade. 'Artifact or not, I'm out of options,' she thought as pulled the sword from behind her back, cutting through the concealing cloth. He would fire before she could strike. She could toss it at him like a javelin, though a miss would leave her unarmed. Her only hope was that her sudden movement would catch the Draekalagon off guard, that it would disrupt his aim or allow Kasta to dodge his assault.

He did not dither. He did not miss. Nellik's aim was perfect. Though the blast of lightning soared at the speed of light, to Kasta the beam approached in slow motion. She blinked and awaited her end.

But that end did not come. She held the glistening green sword over her head. The electrical stream curved away from her body, magnetized by the blade. Kasta's jaw dropped. Her heart stopped—or was it moving so fast that she could not feel it? 'That is not possible.'

Nellik fired again, a rapid barrage of shots. Each bolt of weaponized lightning deviated, arcing toward the blade. Unlike Dresco's sword, Vellon's Blade did not absorb the electric streams. The shots disappeared when they grazed its green aura; they evaporated.

Nellik froze, stepping back. "What sort of devilry is this?" he said with a raucous gasp.

Kasta hopped to her feet. Another blast discharged from his carbine. The hunter held the long blade in front; the electrical streams dissipated before touching the metal.

Her opponent reached to his back for another weapon: his scatter-cannon. He fired. A funnel of electricity propelled from the long weapon. The beams clustered when they closed in on Kasta, fluxing toward Vellon's Blade. He unleashed a cannonade of scattered shots. The sword tamed and swallowed the bolts.

Nellik drew his own blade. His scaled skin tightened around his eyes as he took a cautious step toward her.

From the darkness came a reptilian hiss. And it was not the hiss of a Draekalagon. Behind Nellik, Kaiar approached, her claws treading through the dirt with predatory intent. Nellik halted. With a lurch, he spun around, pointing his scatter-cannon at the trugan.

"No!" Kasta called out.

She dove forward, grappling the Draekalagon's long torso. Kaiar pounced. Her front claws pressed into Nellik as she tackled him to the ground. Kai bumped Kasta, knocking the hunter down as well. Nellik squirmed and panicked in a futile attempt to escape the trugan's grip. The hunter stood and kicked Nellik in the side of the head, rendering him unconscious.

"That's my girl," Kasta said.

She gasped and lunged for cover. Several shock-cannon blasts surged through the woods. Kaiar followed her rider's example and crouched low. Dast was firing at them. "He must have realized he's lost contact with Nellik," Kasta said, cocking her neck toward the Draekalagon's unconscious body. "Thanks for watching my back there, girl."

The trugan released a soft grunt.

In the forest ahead, Crevallus galloped through the woods, fleeing from the Moon Shadow Riders' trugan. "Go help Crev," Kasta said, pointing toward the pack of adversarial creatures. "I'll take care of pon-cho-man back there."

Kaiar hissed and charged into the woods.

"Where are you, Kasta?" Dast called out. She saw the outlaw leader. He still took cover behind Dresco, a pistol pressed to the knight's head. "Your time is up!"

Kasta grabbed the first shock-cannon she saw—her backup pistol—and sprinted toward the encampment. "I'm here, Dast!"

"Don't come any closer!" he ordered. He did not have his circular specs equipped; his bare, glowing eyes cycled from green to blue. "What did you do with Nellik?"

"Do with him?" Kasta leaned against a tree for partial cover, appearing casual. "We had a couple cups of coffee. Caught up on small talk. Ya know, 'How are the ladies treatin' ya? How's business? What's your favorite brand of Draelek liquor?' Quite the charmer, that Nellik." She chuckled. "He says hi, by the way!"

"Hold your tongue, Kasta," Dast said with a shallow sigh. "I know you didn't kill him, so tell me where he is."

She squinted. "Why do you care so much?"

Dast's finger crept up, pointing toward her. "Is it that difficult for you to imagine caring for someone else? Like I cared for you?"

Kasta shook her head and rolled her eyes. "Go to hell, Dast."

"I've already been there. *You* put me there." His voice crackled as his hand wrapped around the back of Dresco's neck. "How naïve I was to think you ever cared for me. Though, you must really care about this one. I honestly can't believe you came back. You, Kasta Krane, putting your life on the line for someone else. Captivating... mystifying. I must know. Why?"

Dast grabbed Dresco by the hair, holding up his head. The knight groaned. He *was* alive. He looked to be in great pain despite being unconscious.

'Hang in there, Dresco,' Kasta thought. "Put you in hell? Breylu, I cut off your leg, but I didn't cyberize you." Her lips pursed. "You've spent your life blaming me for something *you* did to yourself!"

"You did this to me!" Dast said, his stance widening. "I have lived with the stain of *your* sin. Cybernetics brought me salvation. Without them, I would have just been a man with a metal leg—forever broken. Have you ever considered what it is like to lie on an operating table, hoping just one more cybernetic implant, one more mechanized organ will make you feel alive again?"

Kasta sighed. "That's not *my* fault."

"Predictable." Dast jammed the pistol to Dresco's head. He spoke through a snarl. "Kasta Krane. Afraid of nothing but herself. Numbed to compassion. Unable to admit wrongdoing."

His words withered her. Following a shallow gasp, the hunter screamed, "You think I don't feel responsibility, Breylu? Every day. Every damn day of my life, I remember the look on your face when I left you bleeding in the desert. I remember the whimper of your voice when you cried for my help." She tried to swallow, but the lump in her throat would not allow it. "I'm sorry, Breylu."

Her body trembled, and her eyes dried, pierced by his glowing gaze. "Whether you believe me or not, *I am* sorry. Not for your cybernetics. You chose that path, pal. I was first to draw my blade. I maimed you. I left you for dead. But I was leaving no matter what and you were in my way. I'm sorry. But not for that. No, not for any of that."

The outlaw leader's face contorted. "You despicable—"

"I'm sorry I didn't ask you to leave with me." Though her body felt weak, her voice projected with strength. "I *couldn't* take you after I cut off your leg. The gang would have caught up, tortured me and put me back on the hit squad. But I should have told you I was leaving. I should have... I should have asked you to come along, to escape. You were my only friend in a dark time, and I left you in that darkness. I'm sorry for the pain you have endured. I'm sorry that I didn't trust you."

Breylu's face sank. He relaxed his grip on Dresco. His eyes softened, drowned by pain. "Twelve years." That pain swelled to wrath. "Twelve years to seek reconciliation. And you choose to ask for forgiveness now?"

"If I'd have tried, you would have killed me."

"And that is your weakness. You do not have the *strength* to trust, to trust I would bury my thirst for retribution if you sought me out, to trust that the consequences of your actions would be just." Dast clasped the handle of his pistol, his hand shaking, his jaw clenched. "You chose to run. And the consequences of your cowardice have caught up to you."

"Enough of this!" Kasta said, stomping her foot. "You have my guy and I have yours. You no longer hold all the cards. It's just you and me." She paused and took a breath. Gripping the hilt of the sword, she crept farther from the tree. "Let's walk toward each other. No weapons, no tricks. I'll tell you where Nellik is if you give me Dresco." Her teeth slid over the side of her lip. "And I'll give you the sword."

Dast's eyes narrowed. His face scrunched beneath his mask. "I don't believe you," he said with a callous strain.

"Of course you don't," Kasta replied. "Do you think I trust you?" She stepped away from the cover of the white tree. "But it's the situation we are left with. Put the shock-cannon down. I'll give you the sword; I'll give you Nellik. Give me Dresco and let me walk out of here. You will still have a substantial reward to collect. The Imperium won't care about killing me once they have the Relic in their possession, anyway. They'll probably pay you for part of my bounty if you bring them Vellon's Blade."

"I hate your very soul, Kasta Krane," Dast said. "But you make a valid point," he added with an abrupt, cheerful tone.

"Okay," she said, stepping forward. "On three, we drop our pistols. And you have to drop both of them, Dast."

Dast slid away from Dresco and crept toward the center of the encampment. "Of course," he said, a grin outlined beneath his mask. "On three—" Dast counted to three and dropped both of his pistols. Kasta dropped hers, treading toward the camp. She lumbered through the woods, feeling the eyes of the Moon Shadow trugan on her.

She stopped. Kasta Krane and Breylu Dast stood across from each other, five feet apart, face-to-face.

"You look nice," Dast said with a nod. "When was the last time you took a shower, though?"

Kasta's eyes widened. "Just before you started chasing me across the Vanden desert, trying to murder me."

"You confuse murder and justice." His fingers brushed against his thumb. "Just give me the sword."

She shook her head. "Not until you unchain Dresco."

Dast stood tall, crossing his arms. "Not until you tell me where Nellik is, and the rest of my gang that you have left scattered throughout the forest."

"Nellik first," she said, her index finger aimed at Dast's face. "He's a few trees over from where you were shooting at Kai and me. Knocked out cold."

"Okay," Dast said. His bushy eyebrows arched high on his forehead. "Let's set your Imperial pet over here free." He turned and stepped toward the tree to which they had chained Dresco. Kasta followed behind, never taking her eyes off Dast. And she was right not to.

Dast turned with a dagger drawn. He thrust the blade forward, aiming at her stomach.

She jumped back. Her hand reached behind, drawing Vellon's sword.

Dast flinched, beholding the blade's green aura. "What on Eramaa?"

Kasta lifted the blade above her head. She slammed the Relic downward, aiming nowhere in particular. Dast evaded her swing. But a tremor shook the terrain beneath. A wall of soil arose and curled across the campsite, crashing over the outlaw like a breaking wave. Kasta froze; sweat swamped her brow. She squeezed the hilt of the ancient Relic.

Dast crawled through the dirt, his hand reaching for his pistol. Kasta sprinted toward her enemy and stomped on his chest. "Hold still, snake!" she said, baring her teeth.

Dast's cybernetic eyes reddened as he struggled under Kasta's boot. He focused on the glowing blade, and the veins emitting the same bright green on her neck. "What the hell is this?" he uttered. "The sword! So, it is true—" He let out a croaking laugh. "Kasta, don't you know that the use of ancient Relics corrupts the soul?" With a groan, he clasped her foot. "I guess that wouldn't matter much to you, would it?"

"That's enough philosophy regarding good and evil from you for one night," Kasta said. She raised the sword high and prepared to swing, not for a killing blow, but a wounding one.

"Stop!" a hoarse voice called out. Kasta looked up. Nellik stood with his carbine pressed into Dresco's neck. His vertical pupils narrowed as teal blood dripped from his head. "Let the boss go or the knight dies, Krane."

Dast let out a grim cackle, clutching her calf. She cringed and quivered. "A fitting end for an isolated soul. Tell me—was it all worth it? The greed and alienation? Do you regret leading a life devoid of allies and companions?" His fingers constricted her leg, sinking venomous hatred into her veins—choking her soul. "Do you regret letting your enemies live?"

From the darkness of the woods, a hiss came. "I have allies, Breylu," Kasta said with a smirk. "Just not the most conventional kind." Out from the shadows, a horn appeared, followed by a growling beast. Crevallus approached Nellik, fangs bared and claws pointed inward. Nellik turned his aim, but the creature pounced; his massive jaw clamped down on the outlaw's arm. The Draekalagon screamed as Crevallus dragged him into the woods.

Dast shook Kasta loose. The hunter rolled sideways and leapt to her feet. Nellik had dropped his carbine when Crevallus attacked him. Kasta rushed toward the fallen weapon, and Dast reached for his pistol. Her fingers wrapped around the shock-cannon—Dast grabbed hold of his own. She took aim, unloading a barrage of rapid-fire shots.

Dast groaned as the streams of lightning struck his skin. His body convulsed and he dropped to his knees. With a shuddering scream, his augmented eyes lost their glow and turned to their natural indigo shade. The convulsions continued as he fell to the ground, still gazing at Kasta while powerful streams of electricity washed over his eyes.

As the electrical fury subsided and faded away, Dast's squirming stopped. His body lay sprawled on its side—motionless, smoking and limp. Kasta's lip quivered. She glanced at the lethality toggle on the side of Nellik's shock-cannon. It was set to kill.

The hunter's teeth rattled. Her trembling hand dropped the shock-cannon to the dirt as if it were a diseased rat. She buried her shame. Only one thing mattered now. Kasta held the sword tightly. She dashed to the tree where her companion stood restrained. With little effort, Vellon's Blade broke his chains. "Dresco," she said, flinging her hands over his shoulders. "Dresco, talk to me!"

Kasta placed her fingers on the knight's neck. His pulse was irregular. His breathing was slow. "Dresco, come on!" She bit her lower lip. "Kaiar, Crevallus!" Her voice cracked, her mind heavy and her stomach twisting. "We need to go, now!"

The two trugan galloped toward the camp. Some of the Moon Shadow Rider mounts still chased them. "Dresco!" Kasta called out again, strapping the sword to her back.

The knight cawed and mumbled.

"Stay with me, Dresco." She placed his forearm around her neck and wrapped her arm around his torso. She screamed, lifting the knight's massive frame. "Don't you die on me now, damn it."

XXIII
SACRIFICE

A soft, low tone repeated in slow triplets from a brass life support system. A glass encasing fed an electrical stream into four tubes, powering the device. Hushed chatter echoed up and down the hallway. From outside the window, sparrows sang over the collection of gentle noise. And Athenis' blue beams reached through the window. They stretched over the bed and brushed the grey face of Dresco Norte. He opened his mouth for a breath. His left eye twitched, sliding open.

Kasta gasped as she turned away from Marshal Jos, who sat adjacent to her. "Dresco!" She slid out of the cold metal chair and leapt to her feet. Reaching forward, she placed her arms on the bed.

Marshal Jos chuckled, his mustache shadowing his smile. "Well, well, look who's finally awake."

"Where—" Dresco coughed and cleared his throat. "Where am I?"

Sterile and sanitized scents flooded Kasta's nose as she leaned over the wooden bed frame. "Barren Rock, Dresco." Her eyes gleamed with her smile. "You're in the medical center."

"You've been out for two days, Mister Norte." Jos' lip jutted forward. He adjusted his vest. "Kas hasn't left your side for more than about fifteen minutes the whole time."

Dresco's glazed eyes burst open. "Kasta," he croaked. He clambered back, propping himself against the pillow. "The blade? Where is the blade?"

"Hey, hey," Kasta said, her fingers wrapping around his shoulder. "It's perfectly safe. Locked up. Under the protection of four lawmen."

Dresco sighed in relief.

"You're in no condition to be chasing swords anyway, Mister Norte," the marshal said. "You were barely clinging to life when we found you."

Dresco's head tilted, his gaze fixed on Jos. "You found me?"

"Yep." The marshal crossed his hands and nodded. "Me and some other marshals assembled a hunting party to go after Breylu Dast and the Moon Shadow Riders. He's been a target of the law for a while, but this time, he went too far. I knew Kas wouldn't like it, but it had to be done."

The marshal slapped his knee, letting out a gravelly chuckle. "Little did I know that Kasta had already taken care of Dast and his gang. Probably shouldn't have been surprised. What did surprise me was when one of our party tracked movement a couple miles away. We caught up, and lo and behold, Kasta riding across the desert at full gallop with you on the back of her saddle."

Kasta smiled as she looked at Dresco. The dark circles around her eyes sank and twitched.

Jos continued, "Luckily we had some medical supplies. But if Kasta wasn't such a skilled rider, and if she hadn't resuscitated you, you might not be here, Mister Norte."

Dresco's eyelids narrowed. "Resuscitated me?"

Jos stumbled out of his chair and adjusted his jacket. "I'm going to call the doctor in," he said, clearing throat. "She wanted to be alerted when you awoke." He stepped out of the cubical room and into the hallway.

Dresco looked to Kasta, his lip curled. "You did not give me the kiss of life, did you?"

"I didn't know what else to do," she said. Her eyes fell to the rectangular copper floor panels. "You were barely breathing."

Dresco turned away, his nose crinkling. "I was wondering why my breath tasted like whisky."

"Shut up!" she said with a snarling smirk and roll of her eyes.

Raising his eyebrows, Dresco smiled with pride.

She leaned over the knight. "Oh what, you're a funny guy now? Get shot with a few electrical beams and you're a funny guy?"

A loud laugh began to burst from Dresco's chest, but it instead erupted as a violent cough.

"Hey," Kasta whispered as her hand grasped his shoulder. "Lie back down. You have to stay relaxed." She pulled the blanket over his brown hospital tunic.

The knight rested his head on the pillow. "Did you really fight them all? All of Dast's gang?"

"Yeah." Kasta's boots squeaked against the metal floor. "Crazy, right?"

"Unbelievable," Dresco said. "They were surprisingly skilled warriors. Did you..." he paused. "Did you uphold your code?"

Kasta shook her head. "I tried to. But it came down to Breylu or me. I didn't have much time to think about it."

"I'm sorry, Kasta." Dresco reached from under the blanket, grasping the hunter's hand. A thin smile found her lips. "But thank you," he said. He squeezed her hand. She felt the warmth through her glove. "Thank you for coming back for me. I owe you a debt that only the grace of the Guardians could pay."

A beeping machine passed through the hallway. "You don't owe me anything," Kasta said with a limp wave. "You saved my life first, remember?"

"Ah, yes," Dresco whispered. "That was only my duty. Plus, I knew you would come back for me if I survived the assault."

"You *knew* I would come back?"

"Yes," he said with a cocksure nod. "Of course I did. I figured it would be several days later with a group of lawmen and bounty hunters—and a well-devised plan. Maybe one that didn't involve bringing Vellon's Blade back into the clutches of the people trying to sell it to the Imperium." The companions chuckled. Dresco added with a smile, "But I knew you would come back."

"Hey," Kasta said. "I didn't know how long you could make it. You took four or five full-power shock-cannon blasts. One is supposed to be enough to kill you."

"Well," he said with a shrug. "I told you that the armor was not just for show."

Kasta nodded. "Evidently." She knelt low, her elbows resting on the bed, her chin atop her forearms. The floor felt cool on her knees. "Speaking of your heroic and knightly act in the temple. How did you know for sure that I was right about that pipe? That it didn't lead to a deathtrap or a dead end?"

Dresco's eyes hid behind a slow blink. "I didn't."

"Uh-huh," she said through a half smirk. "And how did you know that the grenade that you tossed in there wouldn't hit me too? Or send shrapnel through my body?"

"I could not be completely sure of that."

"And how did you know I would actually be able to make it out of the chamber once I slid down there?"

Dresco looked to the ceiling. His response was swift. "You're Kasta Krane. You can get out of anything."

The companions stared into each other's eyes for a moment, then shared a loud, boisterous laugh. Again, a violent cough interrupted Dresco's amusement. Kasta put her hand over his shoulder.

She heard the voice of Dresco's doctor down the hallway. "By the way," Kasta whispered. "Should I tell the doctor about the Relic turning my blood green?" She peeled off her glove, displaying her surface veins. "I've returned to normal since I left the sword in the marshal's office."

"No," Dresco whispered as he reached out, grabbing her forearm. "They will not have anything that can help with that here. The Madame is an expert on such things."

Kasta put her glove back on. "You're right. They'd probably just lock me up if I showed them something like that."

A woman wearing a brown trench coat atop a darker brown dress shirt entered the room. "Good afternoon," she said with a wide smile. Marshal Jos followed her in. "I'm so glad to see that you're up."

"Hello, Doctor," Dresco said. He lifted his head from the pillow, sitting up as straight as he could.

"Relax," she said, extending both hands, one holding a data system. "You've had a rough couple of days. You're lucky to still be here. I know it's customary to your people, but please don't worry about presenting yourself right now."

Kasta crossed her arms, eying the floor with a crooked smile.

"I'm Doctor Alaeva. First of all, welcome to Barren Rock Medical Center." The doctor looked at her data system and scrolled down. "I know you may feel a bit woozy and weak right now, but considering that you were shot five times, you are actually in excellent shape."

"He looks ready to enter a jousting tournament already, doesn't he?" Kasta gave Dresco's bicep a soft, fake punch.

"There *are* going to be a few complications," the doctor said. "So, bear with me here." She took a deep breath, then exhaled with a sharp whistle. "The electrical blasts that entered your body were very powerful. Almost no living being can withstand that kind of voltage." She stepped next to the bed and displayed a digital scan of Dresco's body. "Your armor and implants protected you, absorbing most of the shock. But"—she zoomed in on a diagram of Dresco's nervous system—"your nervous system did take some damage."

The room drowned in silence, save for the hum of the life support system. "Now," she continued. "You will experience some side effects from this. Hearing loss, memory impairment, blurred vision. But these symptoms are temporary." She sighed and zoomed in on the diagram. "You will also notice here that many of your nerve endings were severely damaged. Certain sensations, be they pain or pleasure, you will no longer be able to experience."

Dresco's fingers curled into a fist. "B-but... just temporarily?"

Doctor Alaeva held unwavering eye contact with Dresco. "Some of them may return over time." Her voice sank. "But, sir, many physical sensations may never return to you."

Marshal Bovien entered the room. She stopped and rested her shoulder against the wall. Kasta flashed her an upward nod.

The doctor continued, "But the good news is that you are recovering quickly. You should be able to go home before you know it. As I said, Sir Norte, you're lucky to be with us at all."

Dresco stared toward the foot of the bed, his mouth stuck at a slight gape. "I know," he uttered. "It's just a lot to take in."

"Of course," Alaeva said, her hands crossed in front. "Take your time and process this."

Dresco looked up and forced a smile. "Marshal Bovien!" he said. "How wonderful to see you."

"Glad to see you awake," Marshal Bovien said with a tight-lipped smile and a bow of her head. "How do you feel?"

"I've felt better," Dresco replied. "Though I just found that I am in fabled fortune to feel anything at all."

"I'll come back in a bit," the doctor said. She stepped toward the room's exit. "Call one of the nurses if you need anything."

Bovien stepped into the room, her thumbs in her pockets and chin held high. "I've got some good news. I just got done speaking with a few marshals throughout the region." She looked to Kasta, a sparkle in her narrow beige eyes. "The bounty on your head has been deemed illegal in every town and city in Vanda."

Kasta pumped her fist in the air. "Hell yeah!"

Bovien nodded. "Yep. Several arrests have already been made of bounty hunters looking to take a shot at you. It wasn't easy, but it looks like we've got every law office in the region watching your back."

"This means more than you know," Dresco said in a soft voice. "Thank you, Marshal Bovien, for taking care of this."

Bovien looked to Dresco with a bow of her head.

Marshal Jos scratched the side of his neck, just below his gills. "Now, Kas, you still have to be careful. The bounty on you may be illegal. But that's not gunna stop no one desperate enough to make a fistful of platinum."

"The way I hear it, Marshal Jos," Bovien said as she leaned forward, "it was about *fifty* fistfuls." Her eyes turned to the hunter. "Only you could piss off a whole government this bad, Kasta. And all over a little tomb-raidin' spree."

"Treasure hunting," Dresco interjected with a cough. Kasta simpered.

Bovien's shoulders sank. "Oh, great. I see you have a sidekick now." She walked toward the door. "Kasta," she said, looking over her shoulder. "Mind if I have a word with you?"

"Not at all," Kasta replied. "Just give me a minute here."

"Of course," the marshal said with a slow nod. "I'll be outside."

Kasta nodded back. She crossed her arms, looking down at Dresco. "You look good. Mind if I go visit Marshal Bovien for a second?"

"Of course not!" the knight said with a wave of his hand. "You have been by my side for too long. Get some fresh air."

"I'll stick with Dresco here," Jos said, his smile reassuring. "We have some stuff to catch up on, I'm sure."

"You got it," Kasta said.

As she turned to exit the room, a nurse walked in with a thin data system in hand. "Okay," he said. "Looks like everything is fine here. I just wanted to quickly go over the cost with you."

Kasta stopped in her tracks and stepped backward. The nurse stammered as the hunter gawked at him with a predatory frown. "It's um—" He let out a fake cough. "It's going to be a thousand platinum—"

"A thousand platinum?" Kasta's shoulders hunched forward. "Are you serious?"

Marshal Jos fell into grumbling laughter.

Dresco reached out. "Kasta, it's fine," the knight said.

Kasta stretched her hand toward Dresco, her fingers spread wide. "No!" she said. "It is not fine." She crossed her arms, staring down the nurse. "What kind of scam op are you running in this med center? This is the second time you've tried to cheat us here."

"I'm sorry," the nurse said, twisting the ring that rested on his finger. "It's just our standard charge for these services."

Kasta thrust her index finger in the face of the nurse. "Your standard charge is a rip-off, you filthy little—"

"Kasta, it's fine!" Dresco leaned forward. "I do not mind paying. Their service seems to have been excellent."

Kasta took a deep breath. Her finger intruded on the nurse's personal space again. "We aren't done," she muttered through clenched teeth.

The light of Athenis caressed Kasta's skin. The desert aromas freed her senses; she felt as though she could float. Marshal Raelyn Bovien was leaning against a pillar that connected the building to the wooden sidewalk. She held a cigarillo in her hand. Kasta walked up behind the marshal and tapped her on the shoulder before reaching across her body and snatching the cigarillo.

"Would you like one of your own?" said Bovien, looking up through her chestnut-brown hat.

"Yes, please," Kasta said as she took a long drag.

Bovien traded Kasta a fresh cigarillo for the lit one. "You look tired," she said, looking into the hunter's eyes. "Why don't you get some rest?"

"Believe me, I will, Marshal," she said through a thick cloud of smoke. "When this job is officially over, I'm going to take a few weeks off. Hot springs, whisky, hunting, play some cards." Kasta's darkened eyelids shut for a long moment. "Hell, maybe I'll just sleep."

"Sounds nice."

The marshal stepped down the stairs, off the sidewalk and into the street. An old man and petite young girl passed by, each on an appropriately sized trugan. They both waved at Marshal Bovien as they passed. The marshal returned the gesture and tipped her hat.

"Oh, it will be," Kasta said. She blew out a smoke ring and followed behind. "I'd invite you along. But I know you don't like to stop working for more than, say, eight hours at a time?"

Bovien flashed a wink as they crossed the street. "Next time? How about that?"

Kasta pointed her cigarillo at the marshal. "I'm gunna hold you to that," she said with a half grin. They crossed the street and set foot on the wooden sidewalk. Kasta tilted her head back, welcoming the smell of wood, smoke and brewing coffee from the nearest general store. "So," she said, letting out a sigh. "Any sign of the Shadow Riders?"

Bovien shook her head. "None. My department and three others have swept the Eldritch Forest and surrounding area numerous times. Those bastards are nowhere to be found."

"Damn," Kasta said. "Not even Dast's body?"

The marshal shook her head again as they rounded the corner.

"The others must have moved him." Kasta tried to stop her voice from trembling. She turned away from the marshal. Her eyes fell to the street.

"Hey!" Bovien's calloused fingertips clasped Kasta's shoulder. "You did what you had to do."

"I know," the hunter said with a sharp, trembling sigh.

The clear skies of day fell on the main street of Barren Rock. The electrical beams on each side of the road flowed across, the violet atmosphere a calming background behind the encasing glass cylinders that powered the city.

"But the other Shadow Riders, they aren't going to just forgive you for this, Kasta." The marshal flashed the hunter a sideways glance. "They are going to come after you. Even stronger than the last time."

"I'll be ready," Kasta said with a smirk.

Bovien's chin tucked in. "But will you have a magical sword to help you out next time?"

Kasta put her arm over the marshal's shoulder, stopping their stride. "Quiet. Imperial spies could still be lurking around here."

The marshal raised an eyebrow and let out a single chortle. "Not in my city, Krane. They know not to mess with me or my deputies. Toughest in the region."

"Maybe so," Kasta said, her eyes staring deep into the marshal's. "But until I get that sword to my employer, I can't be sure."

Bovien stuck her thumb in her belt, eying the hunter beneath the brim of her hat. "May I see it?"

She paused and gave the marshal a crooked stare. "Vellon's Blade?"

"Yeah." She tapped Kasta's shoulder with the back of her hand. "How often does anyone get a chance to get a good look at a Relic? I barely saw it when you brought it in the office."

"Screw it," Kasta said with a shrug. "Why the hell not?"

Marshal Bovien ordered her deputies to open the office vault. The large lock was unbolted. Inside sat several bars of platinum, gold, electrum and other metal alloys. The two women stepped within and closed the vault door. At the back of the room sat a solid black crate.

"Go ahead and open it," Kasta said, motioning toward the crate. "Just do not, under any circumstance, touch it."

"Okay," Bovien said. Her purple lips tightened. She approached the case and unlocked the three buckles on its side. She flung the top open. The long ancient weapon lay within, resting tranquilly.

Until a vibrant green aura engulfed the blade.

"Damn it," Kasta said as she removed her gloves. "It's still happening. And I'm not even touching it. I'm only near it."

"What the—?" Bovien covered her mouth with both hands. "You said holding this thing affected you. But this—Kasta! Your skin is turning green."

Kasta pursed her lips, displaying her glowing forearm. "Anywhere my veins show." She sighed.

The marshal's fingertips dug into her forehead. She opened her mouth to speak, though no words followed.

"Yeah," Kasta said. "I had that reaction at first. Now I'm kind of..." She shrugged. "Hell, I don't want to say used to it, but—"

"Used to it?" The marshal removed her hat and shook out her short red hair. "Used to it? Kasta, I'm no believer in the whole 'corruption of the soul' or 'offending the Guardians' nonsense. And I know you're not either, but—" Her gapped teeth emerged as her jaw dropped. She looked to the glowing green sword, and Kasta's neck, wrist and arms, all matching the Relic's hue. "But you should really get that checked out. At the very least, you have contracted a rare blood infection. Or worse, a symbiotic parasite."

"Maybe." Kasta beheld the crossing bloodlines at her wrist, so bright they left an imprint on her retinas. "But Dresco told me to wait to talk with Madame Vaeliz. Said she'd know what to do about it."

"Vaeliz? Come on, Kasta," the marshal said, her eyes rolling to the floor. "Barren Rock has some of the best doctors in Vanda. Maybe better than anywhere but Mist, Edge Cliff and Onyx Canyon."

The hunter's upper lip rose. "And some of the most extortionate."

Bovien walked toward her. "They're pricey but you get what you pay for. I know Vaeliz and the knight are supposed to be experts on this kind of thing. But this is a medical issue, Krane. Are you going to take medical advice from some old pirate?" She shook her head.

"It may seem absurd, but I think the problem will go away once I hand the sword over to Madame Vaeliz."

Bovien's lips twisted, her beige eyes looking through the cyan windows of Kasta's soul. "You can do what you want, but I don't think that's a promising solution. What does Jos think?"

"No!" Kasta's eyes widened and her brow rose. She placed her hands on Bovien's shoulders. "Marshal, you cannot tell Jos. Please, do not under any circumstances tell Marshal Jos about this."

Bovien looked down at Kasta's glowing wrists, then over her shoulder at the sword. "He crossed your path in the desert and escorted you all the way here. How exactly does he not already know?"

Kasta's head rocked from side to side. "He knows that the sword glows," she said, motioning to the blade. "But not that *I* do. I covered up any green veins for the ride home."

"Why don't you want him to know?"

"You know how he gets. He worries, he gets all inquisitive. I don't have the energy for that right now."

Bovien grasped the back of the hunter's hand, which still rested on her shoulder. "It's just because he cares."

"I know," she said with a groan.

The marshal released a deep breath. "Don't worry. Your secret is safe with me."

"I appreciate that, Marshal," Kasta said, patting Bovien on the shoulder before letting her hands rest at her side. "I better get back into the hospital. Gotta see when we can get Dresco out of there and put this damn vision quest behind us."

The marshal nodded and stood tall. "I'll open up the vault for you."

Kasta stepped forward. "Hey, Raelyn. What you did for us, interrogating Imperial spies, getting us an escort and an airship out of the Valley. You didn't have to do all that."

Marshal Bovien looked over her shoulder. "I know," she said, maintaining a slight smile and steady eye contact. "You've been of immense help to Barren Rock over the years. You've done a lot to keep this city safe, and as this town's chief protector, I was happy to return the favor."

She gripped the hunter's hand and forearm with a firm embrace. "And I'm always obliged to help out a friend."

Kasta leaned forward, returning the double handshake. "Well, thanks for watching my back, Marshal."

"Always, Kasta."

Two days later, Kasta Krane and Dresco Norte set out from Barren Rock. Madame Vaeliz allowed them to use one of her cargo airships. Despite the slow travel time, the companions were glad to take a few days off from traversing Vanda on truganback. Dresco was not well enough to ride a great distance.

The cargo ship landed near the Vaeliz estate. Kasta and Dresco rode toward the residence. Kaiar and Crevallus were washed, groomed and repaired while in Barren Rock. They left the trugan in the stable and entered the Vaeliz residence. Juxel greeted them, offering carbonated beverages and chocolates. Dresco accepted. Kasta refused.

After much impatient bemoaning from Kasta, Juxel led the duo up the spiral staircase and down the hallway to the conference room. On their entry, Madame Vaeliz turned around. She wore a black silken dress with pointed shoulders and an open cut over the sternum; maroon embroidery accented the cuffed sleeves and stitching.

"My friends," Vaeliz said with a warm smile. "How delightful it is to have ye back."

"Madame," Kasta said with a tip of her hat. The hunter held a solid black case in her other hand.

"Good to see you, Madame Vaeliz." Dresco stepped forward and placed his helmet on the table. He bowed low.

"Please do not strain yourself for me, Sir Norte." The Madame's lanky face remained welcoming. She stepped around the table and placed her hand under Dresco's chin. "Are you feeling any better?"

"I think so," Dresco said as he tapped his foot. "It is hard to tell sometimes."

"He's fine," Kasta said with a smirk. "A few minutes ago, he was laughing it up with your servants, eating chocolates in the lobby. He just likes your attention."

Dresco looked to Kasta with an exaggerated frown. "There you have it. She's outed me."

The Madame crossed her hands in front of her waist, her gaze shifting between the companions. "I see you two are getting along better."

Kasta shrugged. "We have our good days."

Vaeliz turned. Her dress flowed behind. "I heard you saved each other's lives. That's what I had in mind when I put ye together, mates. A true team, able to combine your strengths and cover for each other's weaknesses."

Dresco smiled and nodded. "You were right, Madame. I could not see it at first. But Kasta Krane..." He looked to the treasure hunter with his head held high and a proud smile. "She may have the temperament of an outlaw. But she has the honor of a knight."

Kasta's heart skipped a beat. She did not know how to show it, but Dresco's words meant a great deal to her. "Thank you," was all she could conjure in response. "Thanks, Dresco."

The knight nodded, his smile remaining.

Kasta looked to her employer. "And thanks for the field support, Madame. Hell, we sure needed it."

Vaeliz extended an outward palm. "It was my pleasure, mate. And do not forget, it was in my best interest to see you succeed as well."

"Yeah," Kasta said, her eyes dropping to the case. "About that." She stepped forward and placed the black protective shell on the table. "Here it is. I hope it's worth all the money you owe me." She let out a grating chuckle.

Vaeliz's hands clasped together. Her fingers tapped her knuckles. "Would you please show it to me, Kasta?"

"Sure," Kasta said. "Maybe it's been long enough. Maybe it won't affect me anymore."

The Madame nodded. "Let's have a look."

Kasta opened the case. Vellon's Blade lay inside, proud under the dim light of the chandelier. Then, it began to glow in an intense and bright green. Kasta's veins echoed the luster of the sword. "Damn it," she said, slamming her hand on the table. "It's still trying to mess with my blood."

Vaeliz gasped in awe, though she was smiling. Her viridian eyes turned glossy beholding the ancient sword. Dresco cleared his throat. He looked to the Madame with an unblinking stare.

Kasta removed her glove. "I don't know, Madame." She exhaled out the side of her mouth and displayed the green veins of her wrist. "This can't be good. That sword was doing some weird stuff when I was swinging it around in the wild, too: absorbing shock-cannon fire, moving the terrain. It must have bonded with me, formed some kind of—symbiosis."

"Indeed, it has," Vaeliz said. She stood tall, her chest jutting forward.

"Well, can you fix it?" Kasta asked. "What do I need to do? Just get away from it? Give it to you since you are its rightful wielder or whatever? You do realize that if I have to go to doctors for the rest of my life because of this damn sword, you are paying my medical bills, right, Madame?"

"Kasta." The Madame hunched over, bringing herself to the hunter's eye level. "I can help you. But I am not the rightful wielder of this Relic."

Dresco's footsteps clanked against the floor as he approached.

"What do you mean?" Kasta asked, one eyebrow lowered. "Dresco said that you were a descendant of the House of Vellon."

She motioned to Dresco, who looked to her with a slow shake of his head. "I said we had considered the possibility," he said.

Kasta put on a fake smile, letting out a series of shallow breaths. "But I don't get it. Veros referenced you. If it's not you, then—?"

"It's you, Kasta." The Madame's eyes glistened as her pointed chin rose high.

Kasta blinked rapidly. She shrank back, shaking her head and clearing her throat. "Come again?"

The Madame repeated, this time with a slight smile. "It's *you*, Kasta. You are the rightful wielder of the Defender of Liberty, that blade you have brought before us. You are of divine blood, the last descendant of the House of Vellon." She stepped across the marble floor and grabbed Kasta's wrist. "And Kasta, the blade has accepted you." She spoke with a gentle softness as her finger traced the glowing line of Kasta's veins.

Kasta glanced sideways at Dresco. "Hey, Norte. Want to give me some insight as to what the hell is going on here?"

"Of course," Dresco said, leaning on the table. "You, Kasta, have proven capable of wielding the most sacred of the Seven Relics, the Relic which centers the power of the other six."

Kasta sighed and leered at the floor. "Oh no, not you too."

He carried on. "At first I was skeptical. I thought you were too arrogant, reckless and self-important to wield such a hallowed and divine weapon. But, Kasta, I was wrong."

"Hold on." Kasta stepped back, her arms out and palms forward. "You both knew about this the whole time? And you didn't tell me?" Her stomach turned. She did not know whether to feel betrayed or angry. Instead, she felt sick.

Vaeliz stepped forward with open arms. "Kasta, this isn't how we wanted to do this. Trust me. We deemed it was our only option. I know you. We had to make this seem like any other job. You would not have gone after the blade if you knew why we wanted you to do so."

Kasta's head snapped forward. "Damn right, I wouldn't."

"And there was no way to know if the Relic would accept you," Dresco said. "Blood is no guarantee."

They spoke with patience and grace. But their words punctured Kasta's mind like disparaging screams. "Dresco," she said with a slow bitterness. "You couldn't tell me at any point during our journey? Maybe when it turned out the Imperium was trying to kill me or when my rival was hunting us down?"

Dresco offered his hand, but she backed away. "I wanted to tell you. So badly, I did. But I could not risk you giving up on our quest. On *your* quest." He clenched his armored fists together. "Kasta, this is a time to rejoice. We now have a weapon to defend Eramaa against the oncoming threat of the Etsinnae. You will lead our world to victory."

Kasta bit her lip and shook her head. "Lead the world to victory? What? Come on, I can't be the last descendant of the House of Vellon. That's absurd." She looked to Vaeliz out of the corner of her eye.

"You are, Kasta," the Madame said with a long blink and a bow of her head. "Both Sir Norte and I have done countless hours of research on the matter. It's conclusive."

"At first, I was appalled by the idea of you wielding the blade." Dresco crossed his hands behind his back. "I thought you were a recluse, motivated only by pride and self-interest. But you are not. Everything about you, from your line of work to your conduct, makes sense to me now,

Kasta. You did not become a bounty hunter to stoke your bank accounts with platinum. You wanted to protect people, to keep your country safe from those who would harm it. And you refused to bring fatal harm even to the worst of them. Your merciful code is one of sanctity."

Kasta took off her hat and buried her face in her palm. "What are you talking about?"

"You did not seek ancient treasures for profit or a sign of status." The knight's eyebrows rose. He leaned forward, his shining armor mirroring the green of her veins. "You care about these trinkets which you have found. You want to keep them safe and preserve that part of your world. I have seen this. You fit the profile of a Relic wielder, Kasta. I was simply too distracted by your exterior to see it at first."

Madame Vaeliz stood over Kasta, glaring down with pride. "The Etsinnae, the oldest enemy of Eramaa have already returned. They have returned in the guise of the High Imperium. Only those who bare the blood of the Guardians can stand against this evil. The blood of the Guardians flows through your veins; it informs your actions. With Vellon's Blade, you will defend the peace and equilibrium of our world and—"

"No."

Vaeliz's eyes narrowed. "Pardon me, las?"

Kasta shook her head and crossed her arms. "No, no, no. Absolutely not."

Vaeliz's pointed chin protruded. "If you would just allow me to explain, Kasta. The fate of Eramaa depends on you—"

Kasta sighed. "Unbelievable. I come all this way to bring you this ancient overgrown butter knife. And you make up a story about me being magical to try to duck out of paying me. I respected you, Madame

Vaeliz. I didn't think this was your style, but you better pay me my money."

Vaeliz looked to the floor. She let out a nervous chuckle. "Kasta, I was never not going to pay ye! Don't be irrational. I know this is a lot to—"

"Pay me," Kasta interrupted.

Dresco reached for his companion's shoulder, but she shrugged him off with a furious thrust. "Kasta, please." He pointed toward her forearms and neck. "Can you not see the glow of the Guardians' grace in your veins?"

"Pay me now."

XXIV
UNDER BLUE TWILIGHT

"Why are you still here?" Kasta asked, taking a small sip of whisky. "We're done. Go bother someone else."

Dresco sat stiffly on the opposite side of the campsite as he unfastened his armor. "Because I've picked up a taste for treasure hunting." He looked to Kasta with a firm nod. "Where are we off to next?"

Her eyes rolled. "Oh please. Dresco, I'm sick of your deceit. You're just trying to get me to go back and use that stupid sword. I'm not going to do it. I will never do it."

Dresco added a log to the fire in front of him. "Kasta, Relics are mystical objects. Even if you are a rightful wielder of their power, I understand why it would be intimidating to harness such strength." He looked to her with a reassuring grin. "It's okay to be afraid."

"I'm not afraid!" Kasta let the bottle seep through her fingers and into the dirt below. A dusk wolf howled in the distance. "I just don't believe in any of that crap. You know that. Why would you do that to me?"

"How can you still say that?" Dresco asked, his hands falling atop his knees. "After all we have been through, all we have seen?"

Kasta sighed as she lit a cigarillo. "Yes, we have seen some crazy stuff, Norte. I won't deny that. We've seen some stuff I'll never be able to explain. Does that mean that I am ready to believe that I carry the blood of a Guardian? Or that I am somehow meant to save the world from a cosmic threat? No. And I never will be."

Dresco looked to the stars. The grey in his hair danced with the soft breeze. "Well, I have faith that you will."

"Faith," Kasta said with a scoff. "Look how far that has gotten you."

Dresco shrugged. "It got me to you." He reached behind and grabbed a bowl of wheat, which he proceeded to hold over the campfire. "And it got you to Vellon's Blade."

"And look how that turned out." She pulled her leather jacket tight over her midsection. "You should have told me, Norte. You and the Madame should have told me."

"Maybe," Dresco said with a nod. "But perhaps, all is as it should be."

Kasta sighed. She grabbed a piece of jerky that sat next to her and split it in half. She threw the two halves to Kai and Crevallus, both of whom accepted the offering. "If you insist on sticking around, I won't stop you," she said, peering up at Dresco through her hat. "But if you mention that damn sword again, I will leave you behind in this desert faster than you can say a morning prayer."

"No," Dresco said as he held out his hand. "I know better than to try to persuade you in any such manner, Kasta Krane." The knight looked on the hunter with a gleaming smile. "I just have to believe that you will make the decision on your own."

Kasta awoke with a gasp. Cold sweat dripped from her scalp to her brow. She looked around the campsite. Dresco lay sound asleep. The trugan lay close, each using the other's body heat to maintain warmth. Kasta looked to the night sky. Vharris and Entaega faced off as mirroring crescents among the fields of white, red, blue and green stars. Then, a warm, tingling sensation furled up Kasta's arm. She winced, though the feeling was not painful, nor uncomfortable. The crescent moons stared down, offering a window to the heavens and illumination of the empty desert. The sensation on Kasta's arm would not subside. She could no longer resist the urge to look. She peeled back the blanket and turned her bare arm. Though faint, her veins still glowed a distinct shade of green.

Continue Reading for a Preview of
Endless Frontier Book 2

ENDLESS FRONTIER
BLOOD AND SOUL

FIRST, THEY SURVEIL. THEN THEY INTIMIDATE. AND AT LAST, THEY ANNIHILATE...

Two years have passed since Kasta Krane left the ancient Relic in the hands of Madame Vaeliz. She has returned to what she does best - hunting treasures in forgotten temples for the highest bidder.

But the world falls into shadow. The High Imperium crosses the Vanden border, hunting militant terrorists. Imperial spies monitor Vanden citizens with digital surveillance programs. Imperial knights patrol the streets while the Clerisy rewrites local laws.

Deep in an ancient tomb, searching for a lost treasure, Kasta finds no reason to consider the state of the world. But the reach of the Clerisy is long, and she will soon find that once you are in the grasp of the High Imperium, it never lets you go.

Endless Frontier Book 2 Preview
Blood and Soul

I.

Sleep is for the Dead

At the end of an ancient hall sat a statue of a man on a robust throne of marble. A woman stood under its flickering shadow; blue-grey was her skin and purple was her snarl. Old maps and ancient records had beckoned her to this tomb, promising great riches. Her search had yielded nothing but bones and dust. She eyed the statue's resting grimace, wishing he would come to life and challenge her to a game. If she won, the treasure would be hers. If she lost, her misery could end. 'Oh, how I long for simpler times.'

Her mood soured further when hushed chatter echoed through the great hall.

"Have you heard?"

"Heard what?"

She cracked her neck and followed the sound.

"The Imperials took over another satellite."

"I'll be damned. Mapping satellite again?"

"Communications."

"I'll be damned! Before we know it, they'll be able to find us at a moment's notice and listen to all our conversations."

"And know everything there is to know about us."

"Tell me about it. As soon as they get access to our data systems, there's no stopping the snow bastards from watching our every move."

"Privacy is a thing of the past."

The woman's boots stomped against the floor as she stood before the two men. She squeezed her lapels and exhaled a steady stream of smoke. "I'm hearing a whole lot of political yammering from the two of you." She pointed toward the chatting miners, a cigarillo resting in her gloved fingers. "You're getting paid to dig, not talk."

One of them returned to brushing the sand below his feet. "Sorry, boss."

The other tapped his hammer against the wall, rolling his eyes.

The woman rubbed her forehead and pushed up her black hat from beneath its leather brim. "Hey, choirboy!" she yelled, looking down the hallway. "Keep these greenhorns in line. They're gossiping about the exploits of your fellow Imperials again."

The tall, grey-skinned Imperial straddled the shadows and the light. Dust streamed from his black tunic. "Can you blame them, Kasta? They have been stuck in this crypt for over two months. And their country is being occupied."

Kasta Krane's cyan eyes sparkled upon seeing the approaching Imperial. "All that matters while we are down here is finding that chalice. The more we dig, the faster we'll find it." She smiled. The tip of her cigarillo crackled with a burning glow. "The faster we find it, the faster we can get out of here. The faster we get out, the faster we can all get paid."

The Imperial man stopped and looked down on her, his arms crossed behind his back. "True," he said with a long blink. "But perhaps you can cut the excavators some slack? There is surely a lot on their minds."

Hammers clanged over the miners' chatter. Brushes met stone with a coarse rustle. "I don't cut anyone slack, Dresco," Kasta said, thrusting her cigarillo toward his face.

Dresco's eyes narrowed on the flaming ember. "That... is the truth."

"Stop the chatter!" Kasta yelled. And the chatter did stop. "Passing time won't speed up time."

The treasure hunter's hands rested behind her back. She heard their scoffs, and she felt their scowls. A crooked smirk found a home on her face as she marched down the center of the hall. The rhythm of digging and hammering quickened in the circumference of her steps.

Behind her, Dresco checked in with a group of miners. "Any luck on breaking through to that hollow section?"

"Nah, boss," a female miner answered. "We keep breaking new ground only to find more titanium behind the wall—about the furthest thing from hollow I could think of."

"Hmm." Dresco's deep voice reverberated through the hall. "That is quite frustrating."

"You sure the readings were correct?"

"Kasta has scanned the area several times. There's an opening. We just need to keep breaking ground until we find a way around the barrier."

"Understood, sir."

"Good work, Dithany."

Kasta looked again to the statue at the end of the hall. She whispered, "I have survived a murderous gargoyle with wits as sharp as his blades." She mimicked the figure's permanent scowl. "Yet it will be your lifeless eyes that witness the death of me."

A man to the right stood waist deep in a hole. He was drenched in sweat and drew heavy breaths. "You okay?" Kasta asked, squatting nearby.

"Oh yeah," he said, leaning on his drill. "I'm making progress, boss."

"Why don't you take a break?" Kasta nodded upward and crossed her hands.

"Oh no. I'm fine—"

"Take a break. Get some water. Get a few hours of rest." She trapped the bearded man in an unblinking stare. "Understood?"

"Yes, boss." His arms shook as he pushed himself out of the hole. The Vandeni gills on his neck widened with his croaked breath.

"Seriously, drink some water."

Kasta eyed the hole with a sneer. Dresco stepped behind her. "Want me to have someone else take over this section?" he asked.

"No." Kasta lowered her optical system over her eye. "In fact, get someone to cover it up. He was digging a hole to nowhere." She plodded down the hall in the direction she had just come from, a soft grunt deflating her posture. "You know what, maybe we should cover up everything. I'm starting to think that the Chalice of Kronwell isn't even here. We should terminate this contract."

"Kasta, we will find it. It's here! You found letters speaking of this very chalice being buried in this very tomb—notes written by Kothius Kronwell himself!"

Kasta turned and walked backward, looking into the grey eyes of her companion. "Whoever wrote the letters said they were Kothius Kronwell. Could have easily been fake. General Galent's advisors were known for their deception."

When Dresco caught up with her, the duo walked side by side. "Months of good treasure-hunting work has led us here. The minute you found the letters in the wreckage of Galent's fortress, I knew it. I knew we would find the chalice, and I still feel the same."

Kasta's boots thumped against the stone floor. "Do you ever think about how annoying your optimism is to other people?"

"Umm." Dresco squinted in contemplation. "No?"

"I assure you. It's very exhausting." Her stride grew longer. "There's a ceiling on how high my spirits can be lifted, Norte."

Dresco stopped to allow himself an ebullient bit of laughter, then trotted in front of Kasta with a heavy gait. A smaller miner struggled to lift a boulder from the ground, even with the aid of an electro-leverage tool. Dresco placed one hand on the stone and pushed it aside, giving the excavator access to the site he wished to dig.

Kasta looked down the hall at the group of miners around the metal barrier. "They still haven't made any progress?"

"No, no. They just keep uncovering more titanium. Perhaps we should try reaching the hollow section from underneath?"

"Maybe." Kasta stroked her chin. "But what if the metal plate isn't shielding anything at all?"

"What do you mean?" Dresco crossed his arms, looking down on the Vandeni woman.

The chamber resonated with clangs, clatters and coughs. Dust flooded Kasta's crinkling nose, and she let out a sniffle. "I don't know. It's just a dumb idea. Probably nothing."

The grey-skinned Imperial leaned her way with a slight smile. "I'm listening."

"Well, I was just thinking." Kasta pointed toward the metal plate. "The wall came down in that section so easily." She motioned to the long hallway and the many excavators rummaging among its confines. "Every other surface in this damn tomb took days, even weeks, to bust through. But that part of the wall came down in a few minutes."

Dresco raised a finger. "Almost as if it were meant to come down."

"Exactly!" She stepped toward him. "Why construct a thin, weak wall of stone with a thick, reinforced layer of titanium behind it?"

"And why leave a hollow chamber carved behind the metal?"

"What if—?" Kasta's gloved fingers snapped. "What if it isn't a chamber at all? What if it's a cleft?"

"What for?" His eyes widened. "The metal wall—the metal wall slides into the cleft!" he shouted, answering his own question.

Kasta's long black hair flipped over her shoulder as she turned. "Stop! Stop digging," she said, running toward the group of miners. She and Dresco stopped before the imposing barrier of titanium.

"What is it, boss?" A thin cigarillo dangled from Dithany's lips. Her welder bled sparks as she rested it on her shoulder. "Got something?"

Kasta nodded. "I think so. This may not be a protective seal of a secret room, but some type of device that pushes in—a gliding contraption of sorts."

"Boss is talking crazy again, isn't she?" a worker murmured.

"What is she rambling about this time?"

"If you are lucky, my crazy rambling is gunna make us a lot of money." She looked to her towering Imperial companion. "Dresco, get me a brush. And ten miners with soft hands and a delicate touch."

Dresco nodded once and stepped away.

"It's not what's hiding behind this thing. It's what's hiding on it."

Kasta and the crew spent hours brushing thick layers of sand from the sheet of metal. Kasta's heart raced as clumps of dirt fell to the ground, revealing fine grooves in the titanium. Her body tingled with joy when the grooves took shape as script and artwork.

"The Chalice of Kothius Kronwell!" a tall Imperial miner said. He and his coworkers crowded the dim shimmer of the wall. Three engravings of goblets stood ten feet apart from one another, each with different text above.

"Can you read it, boss?" Dithany asked, stepping close, her jaw dropping.

"Of course I can," Kasta answered. "Look close, Dith. This is a two-thousand-year-old tomb. Vandeni languages of this era aren't all that different from our own." She looked down on the miner with a wink. "It's really just an extravagant font." The treasure hunter's cyan eyes looked to the inscription above the first chalice and read aloud. "A toast to the living." She moved to the second chalice. "A toast to the dead." And the third. "A toast to life after death."

Gasps and murmurs circled the tomb with a cold echo. "So, it would seem that the chalice is here," said the reptilian voice of Oltheck. He spoke through sharp clenched teeth. "Or it was. But how do these stupid little art pieces help us find it?"

Kasta crossed her arms and looked down, an assured grin on her face. "It ain't just art."

"Look to the lines," Dresco said, his fingers tracing the thin circular indentations around one of the engraved chalices. Kasta nodded as he spoke. "They aren't just lines. They are panels."

"So, what are we waiting for?" Dithany shrugged. "Let's press them."

"Not so fast!" Kasta held out a finger. "We don't know what will happen when we press those."

"We haven't sprung a trap yet!" a voice said in the crowd.

"Yeah! Even the sarcophaguses didn't have any."

Dresco turned toward the crowd. "This is one of the last tombs built in this valley. If it does house any traps, they will be sophisticated and elaborate."

"In this case," Kasta said with a sigh , "we may have to consider the dangers of both the modern and the mystical."

"The mystical," a miner said with a scowl. "Do you really think General Galent and his army of dead soldiers will rise from the grave if we press those buttons, boss?" He earned some laughs from his workmates. "You're the last person I'd expect to believe in those old Valley of Tombs superstitions."

Kasta turned and caught the miner in a cold stare. "I've seen far stranger things."

"And in this very valley," Dresco added.

The heckling stopped. And the hall fell to deathly silence.

Kasta stroked her chin, studying each of the three panels. Dresco approached. "What do you think?" he asked with a tight-lipped whisper.

"I think—" Her breath stopped with her words. "I think we should press that one." She pointed to the left panel. "That one." She pointed to the center panel. "Then that one." She pointed to the right.

"Why?"

"Because life, death and life after death seems most logical."

"You don't think there's more to it than that?"

With a slight frown, her skewed glance landed on Dresco. "You have any ideas?"

"No."

"Then I'm going to press the buttons." She treaded toward the first chalice. "Everyone stand back. We don't know what the hell is going to happen when I mess with these."

"What about you, boss?" the soft voice of a female digger said from the onlooking crowd.

"You don't want me to stand by?" Oltheck asked, raising his pistol. "I'll shoot anything that comes out: living, dead or malevolent fiends from the grave." His clawed finger tapped the side of his weapon. The dig team joined him in a laugh.

"Appreciate the offer, Oltheck," Kasta said with a tip of her hat. "But you don't gotta worry about me. I'm Kasta Krane. And despite the efforts of the aristocratic dead, I still walk their halls and hunt their treasure." Her chest jutted forward, and her stance widened. The workers chuckled. "So y'all can just stay back and keep an eye out for traps and whatnot. But Oltheck," she pointed toward the tall, scaled man. "Keep that pistol close—just in case."

He nodded and grunted, his nostrils flaring at the end of his long snout.

"Okay." She gave a loud clap. "Let's do this." With a step forward, she shook out her hand before pressing on the first panel. The heavy metal circle pushed in with little effort. Behind the walls, there was a metallic click, softer than expected. Kasta's eyes darted around the room—to the floor, from side to side, to the cracked ceiling. Her heart raced. Her fingers shook. She stepped sideways. The floor felt as sturdy as before; no traps yet.

She came to the second panel. With persistent caution, she pressed the depicted chalice, to the same deadened metal click. She froze and swallowed. Something rumbled beneath the floor—or was it behind the walls? The excavation team took a step back, Dresco shielding them with his outstretched arms. Kasta prepared to jump, roll or shoot.

After a few seconds, the rumbling stopped and she relaxed her stance. "This is good," she said with a smirk. "It's doing something." She looked to a member of the team, his face stricken with panic and anxiety. She offered the young man an assured wink, and the tension on his face washed away.

"Okay," Kasta whispered, pulling down the black lapels on her leather jacket. "One more." She took long steps to the third depicted chalice, the "life after death" chalice. Swallowing a stubborn knot of tension, she pressed the button. The panel sank into the wall, requiring a stronger push than the other two. That same weak click came in response to her touch.

But nothing happened. "It didn't work!" said one of the workers.

Kasta stood hunched over with her knees bent, looking around the ancient corridor. "Wait," she ordered, holding up her fist.

But still yet, nothing happened.

"It's busted!" said another digger. "After all that, it doesn't even work."

"I think it does." Her stance relaxed. "I think I just didn't press the chalices fast enough. Something was rumbling back there after I pressed the first two. But it went away."

An Imperial miner looked down on her, nervous skepticism etched on his grey face. "That abysmal quaking noise?"

"The noise will not hurt us, Anson." Dresco smiled upon his slighter fellow countryman.

"But whatever is making it might."

Kasta turned with a stern glare. "I do not by any means guarantee your safety on this expedition."

"We know," Oltheck said with a nod.

"It's in our contracts!" Dithany added with an odd enthusiasm.

"Just a friendly reminder," Kasta said with a smirk, which flattened in an instant. "If I run from panel to panel, I can probably hit them all in time."

"Umm, Kasta," Dresco said, stepping forward. "Why not just have one person standing at each station? The next person in line can press the circular pane in after the last person."

"That's..." Kasta tapped her finger against her holstered pistol. "That's not a bad idea." She turned to her subordinates with a roguish grin. "But who is going to volunteer to press the 'toast to the dead' button?" She bit her lip as the hall fell silent.

"Well, I guarantee one thing," Oltheck said in a snarling yet playful tone. "It won't be one of the Imperials."

The entire crew fell into laughter, all except Dresco and Anson. "Your primitive notions regarding the valor of our people are misguided and repulsive!" Dresco's thunderous voice put an end to the excavation team's laughter. His brown hair fell in his face as he turned toward Kasta, his stomping steps ignited with fury. "I'll do it!" His grey forehead furrowed as he stood stiff at attention before the second panel. The slighter Imperial stared upon Dresco with gleaming pride.

"Look at that," Oltheck whispered out the side of his thin mouth. "I got him to do it." The group surrounding him laughed, especially one of his fellow Draekalagons.

Dresco's lip twitched as he stared upon the deathly inscription.

"And the third panel?" Kasta asked with indifference.

"I'll do it!" Dithany said, chin high.

"You sure?" Kasta asked. "That could be the dangerous one."

"I know the risks, boss." Dithany adjusted her vest and approached the panel. "I've been digging up this damn metal wall for over a week. I wanna see what it's hiding."

"Okay then," Kasta said with a nod. "I'll go first. After it clicks, Dresco, push yours in right away." She looked over Dresco to Dithany. "Dith, yours is the toughest to push in for some reason. Channel all that Islander grit into your elbows."

"Swift as the wind. Strong as the sea," Dithany said, her Rogue Haven accent thicker than usual.

Kasta pointed at the two volunteers, her finger in the shape of a pistol. She cracked her neck and leaned forward, then pushed her "toast to the living," panel in. Metal slid against metal, then stopped and clicked. "Go, Dresco!" Kasta barked.

Dresco had started pushing his "toast to the dead" panel in already. With little effort, he pressed the circle as far as it would go until it clicked.

The roaring within the walls returned. Dithany hesitated, her eyes following the noise.

"Dithany, now!" Kasta ordered.

The slender Rogue Haven woman's teeth gritted as she pressed her shoulder into the panel. The large rendering of the chalice sank back and clicked in place.

The rumble in the walls quaked harder and roared louder. Kasta stumbled; the whole tomb shook. "Step back, step back!" Kasta yelled.

She did not need to warn them. The miners, diggers, cannonslingers and archeologists all scrambled.

"Don't panic. Don't panic." The treasure hunter's tone was stern, though calm. "You're going to kill us all if you set off a trap right now." The structural tremors made her nauseous and dizzy, though she refused to show it. "Hold your position and watch your head."

Dresco had some soft, calming words for a group of diggers. The panicked screams of the crew died after the quaking stopped. The metal plate rolled back, sinking into the wall. "You were right!" Dresco yelled with a euphoric laugh. "It retracts into the cleft!"

"Damn straight," Kasta said with a passive wave, though she remained alert. "I'm Kasta Krane, greatest treasure hunter in the world." Her crooked smirk landed on Dresco. "And we were right."

The crew clapped and cheered. Dresco motioned for them to settle down. "Ladies, gentlemen, please! Mind your surroundings. The tomb is still in motion. Watch for signs of a collapse." He pointed to the ceiling.

The metal wall slid and scraped. Dithany had fallen while the tomb shook. She stood and stepped closer to the wall. With a sonorous slam, the titanium surface stilled. The tomb fell to rest after a final undulating tremor. Slowly, the third circular panel opened as an aperture from center to border. Dithany stepped closer.

"Stay back, Dith," Kasta ordered. But Dithany moved closer yet.

The aperture opened in full. Within a small compartment was a golden-red chalice. Oval gems of green and purple circled the cup, sparkling in the shadows. Black arches adorned the rim, inlaid with spherical rubies.

"By the good of the Guardians, we finally found it!" Before Kasta could find the words to stop her, Dithany reached forward.

"Dithany, wait. No!" Dresco's warning came as Dithany's hand clasped the chalice by the stem. The floor splintered.

"Run!" Kasta yelled.

The sundering ruptures spiraled outward like a weaving web. The surface beneath Dithany's feet split, then collapsed. Kasta leapt forward. Dithany reached for her hand, and Kasta reached past it. Soaring over the chasm, she ensnared the Chalice of Kothius Kronwell.

Endless Frontier: Blood and Soul Available August 29, 2025. Pre-Order Today!

Author's Note

Hello! I hope that you have enjoyed this journey with Kasta and Dresco. I have dreamed of publishing this book from the time I first began worldbuilding in 2016 until the first copy went to print. I cannot thank you enough for giving this work a chance. I love writing and readers give me the opportunity to write for a living. Another important piece of an independent author's lifeblood: reviews. Reviews are what allow a book to be seen by other readers. If you could find the time to leave an honest written review on Amazon, Goodreads, Barnes & Noble and/or any other book review platform, you would be doing a great service for *Endless Frontier* as a series and for me as an author in my young career. Please go to brettlurie.com and sign up for my mailing list for a free prequel novella featuring a daring heist by the Moon Shadow Riders. I will also share tidbits on my writing process, and announce events such as signings, interviews and convention appearances.

The illustrations within this novel were crafted by the talented hand of Violet Bast. Check out her *Endless Frontier* art prints and follow her projects at https://linktr.ee/violetbastart. Contact her if you are interested in commissioning her work.

If you enjoyed this tale, check out *Folktales from the Endless Frontier*, a collection of short stories and novellas that provide exciting origin stories for characters like Kasta Krane, Marshal Bovien, Sariya Vaeliz, Marshal

Jos and the Moon Shadow Riders. Airship heists, escapes across the desert and duels to the death await!

Our story is only beginning. When Athenis rises again, a threat from the north shall be revealed, and the hunter and the knight shall return. I hope that you enjoyed your preview of Book 2 of the *Endless Frontier* series. *Endless Frontier: Blood and Soul* will release on August 29, 2025. Pre-Order today!

About the Author

Brett grew up splitting his adventure appetite between fantasy quests through Tolkien's vistas and Eastwood standoffs in Sergio Leone westerns. His debut weird western saga, *Endless Frontier* pulses with reverence for flawed protagonists, supernatural showdowns, and mystical science magic. A scholar of political theory during his academic studies, Brett chose to apply his knowledge of statecraft to his woldbuilding.

An avid RPG gamer and comic book collector, Brett brings captivating women leads, amphibious races, and a magic system based on wireless electricity powered by charge crystals. With an endless frontier to explore, Brett looks to expand tales of high-voltage rivalry and unlikely alliances. His happy place is in the mountains with a cup of coffee on the table and his cat, Raven, on his lap.

www.ingramcontent.com/pod-product-compliance
Lightning Source LLC
Chambersburg PA
CBHW030106310726
48970CB00004B/1170